My Daughter's Keeper

Adiva Geffen

Producer & International Distributor
eBookPro Publishing
www.ebook-pro.com

My Daughter's Keeper
Adiva Geffen

Translation from the Hebrew by Zoe Jordan
Edited: Arlyn Roffman

Contact: adivageffen@gmail.com
ISBN

MY
DAUGHTER'S
KEEPER

ADIVA GEFFEN

ReadMore Press

DISCOVERING THE NEXT BESTSELLER

Sign up for Readmore Press' monthly newsletter and get a FREE audiobook!

For instant access, scan the QR code

Where you will be able to register and receive your sign-up gift, a free audiobook of

Beneath the Winds of War
by **Pola Wawer,**

which you can listen to right away

Our newsletter will let you know about new releases of our World War II historical fiction books, as well as discount deals and exclusive freebies for subscribed members.

And Ruth said: 'Entreat me not to leave thee, and to return from following after thee; for whither thou goest, I will go; and where thou lodgest, I will lodge; thy people shall be my people, and thy God my God; where thou diest, I will die, and there will I be buried; the LORD do so to me, and more also, if aught but death part thee and me.

— **Book of Ruth Chapter 1, 16-17**

"Remember the past, live in the present, believe in the future."
— **Abba Kovner**

Israel, Moshav Pa'amonei Shir

When I was five years old, I was punished for the first time in my life. For seven days, I was forbidden from leaving the house or having friends over. It was a heavy punishment.

"This is how you learn not to pry into other people's things," said my mother.

"But…"

"I said a week," her face was red. "No argument."

"Fine, Mom," I said, tears streaming down my cheeks.

Uncle Brock, Mom's brother, patted my head and promised to come every day to play Monopoly with me. Brock was my smartest, best uncle. Actually, he's my only uncle.

In the evening, Dad tried to reason with Mom to forgive me. My dad is a pilot for El Al and he has a heart of gold. I was certain that he would convince Mom to let it go.

I heard them arguing.

"She's still a child, forgive her."

"When you were ten you were already looking after your brother and bringing…"

"I didn't have a choice. Those were different times, Illy. You don't have to go through what we went through to become a good person. Let's be thankful that she gets to live in a different world."

"She's got to learn the hard way. That's how I had to learn."

I didn't hear what Dad said, but it made her laugh. Dad always managed to appease her. In the morning, Mom told me that I needed to go to visit Granny Tulla and Grandma Irena to apologize but not to bother them too much.

My brother Gadi, who is four years older than me, jokingly called the grandmas 'Tullerina.' Grandmas "Tullerina" were both over ninety. Irena was plump and had lung disease, a souvenir from the millions of cheap cigarettes that she loved to smoke. Sometimes, when it was hard for her to breathe, they hooked her up to a ventilator. Unlike Irena, Tulla was thin and full of energy but had problems with her vision. Dad claimed that she was half-blind but just didn't want to acknowledge it because she was proud.

Tullerina's house was behind ours. When Mom hung the laundry, it was right beside their window. When they came out to warm themselves in the sun, they would sit on the grass in the shared yard while Chekhov, their cat, chased lizards. When Irena made her famous cutlets, the smell would fill the whole yard and waft into our house.

"Who's there?" the two asked in unison, as always.

"It's me."

"Who are you?" the two of them asked together, as always.

"I'm your granddaughter, Noga," I replied, as always.

"Come in, Noga," said Granny Tulla. "Noga who loves yoga."

"And don't forget to wipe your feet," said Grandma Irena.

I entered.

In the large room, two big armchairs sat beside one another along with a little armchair for the cat. There was a big radio and the walls were filled with black and white photos of people dressed like in old movies.

Most of all I loved the food they made. Dad would say that those delicacies, such as the krupnik barley soup, the onion pie, or the krantz cakes belonged on the tables of the righteous. I loved their chicken soup most of all. Uncle Brock would always say that their soup could cure any illness, even heartbreak. Grannies Tullerina would sit on their armchairs and listen to the radio. Tulla sat on the blue one and Irina on the green. Chekhov sat on the little one.

The two of them looked up at me. I looked at the cat.

"Yes, Noga?" they said.

They always talked in unison. My dad says that they were Siamese twins in a previous life.

"I came to... to... to say... sorry," I said in a voice so quiet they could barely hear me.

"What did you say?" the two asked together.

"Sorry that I took those things that were under the mattress."

"What things?" asked Granny Tulla.

"The things that Grandma Irena keeps... sorry," and I began to cry.

"Come on, now," said Tulla, *"Tell her that you forgive her."*

"Irena looked at me and then spread her arms wide. I put my head on her big belly and smelled the fried onion and dough and it comforted me. She hugged me tight, which was even better than just forgiveness.

"And Grandma Irena," I said, *my head still on her belly.* *"I won't go through your things again, ever, for the rest of my life!"*

The two grandmothers burst out laughing. I didn't understand why.

"Okay, that's over with. Now: soup," Tulla said and served me a bowl of soup that could also cure a bad mood.

"What were those things I took from you, Grandma Irena?"

Granny Tulla looked at Irena and said, *"It's not important. It was something like Moses in a box."*

"But... it wasn't Moses in a box, is it something for praying?"

"We'll tell you when you're older."

"It's something Christian, isn't it?"

"Who told you that?" Grandma Irena turned red and her leg began shaking.

"Ariel, who's in the class above me and knows a lot of things, he said that it's not a Jewish thing."

"Jews, Christians, Muslims, we're all people, Noga – everyone has the same God. You'll learn that, too."

"We'll tell you when you're older," Irena repeated.

"Why? Because it's a secret?"

"Exactly," the two said in unison. *"Now it's our secret and when you're ready, you'll know."*

When that would be, they did not say.

Most of the kids in my class had big families. They had grandmas and grandpas and many uncles and aunts and cousins. At their Passover Seders, there were twenty or thirty relatives present.

Our family was tiny: one uncle and two grandmothers, my brother and me. Uncle Brock wasn't even married. Dad would say that his brain was too full of math.

On Holocaust Remembrance Day, my grandmothers would light a special candle, the memorial candle, and they would sit for an entire day and look at old photos that they kept in a shoebox. They would talk in their funny language, Polish, and sometimes they cried. Quietly though. The people in our village called them the grannies from the Holocaust.

The grannies from the Holocaust were inseparable. They did everything togeth-er. Laundry. Cooking. Traveling. Laughing. Thinking — sometimes they suddenly said the same sentence. When one felt bad, the other immediately felt bad too. When Tulla was sad, Irena would cry. The two loved spaghetti with mayonnaise, burnt schnitzel, and Chopin.

I had to know why Grandma Irena had Christian things under her bed. And why did Mom get so angry that I took them and showed my friends? When my Bat Mitzvah came, I asked Grandma Irena if I was ready yet. She wrinkled her forehead, patted my head, and said, "Not yet. When you're older."

And Granny Tulla said, "When you're older."

They said the same thing when I finished high school, when I was drafted into the army, when I went on a trip to South America, and even when I'd already kissed Amir Barnes, my first boyfriend.

It was only when I was writing a paper for a history course at the University of Tel Aviv that they decided I was ready.

"Come during Passover and we'll talk," the two said, laughing.

"Let it go," said Mom. "Why do you need to know everything?"

I knocked on the door.

"Who's there?"

"Noga."

"Noga who does yoga?" I heard Irena coughing and Tulla laughing. Her laugh, even though she was over ninety, was a rolling laughter that filled the house. Irena no longer laughed. She coughed.

"Noga in a toga," I answered them like I used to. Like always.

"Come in and don't forget to wipe your feet," like they used to. Like always.

When I entered, I found the two of them, as always, sitting in their armchairs. A plaid blanket covered Tulla and a duvet was laid over Irena. Chekhov the cat's armchair stood empty. He had died of old age. When we had suggested getting them another cat, they had refused. God forbid he should feel lonely after the two of them passed on.

Grandmas Tullerina looked festive, smiling as if they had been waiting for me.

"So?" They asked together. "Are you ready?"

"Very much so."

"Stubborn just like her grandmother," they said and laughed.

I was so excited. Finally, I would learn all the secrets of the Christian crosses they were hiding, the black and white photos, the place that they came from, and where Mom and Dad had met because they had never, ever told me or my brother.

"Why don't you tell me?" I would ask my dad, who would send me to ask Mom, who would say, "Come on now, leave it alone, go ask your father."

At home, our parents talked about everything. They talked about the mulberry tree that needed pruning, about the insect that was eating the grass, about the elections, about health, about the president of the United States — just not about themselves.

Why? Why was everything a secret?

It was time to open that big box where the secrets had been tucked away. Grandma Irena asked me to help her move her armchair as close as possible to Granny Tulla's. They clasped each other's hands. Then Tulla said, "Where were we?"

"The secret," I whispered.

"Now, we will tell you the story from the very beginning," said Irena and closed her eyes. She was already weak.

"If you have the time and patience," said Tulla. I did.

CHAPTER 1

Warsaw 1938

"I met my beloved Johann at university in Warsaw. I remember the very second, the precise moment. I stood beside the second-story window of the Faculty of Medicine building which looked out over the garden and I noticed a young officer walking in his full-dress uniform…"

"Wait, Granny," I stopped her, "what do you mean 'my Johann'…?"

"Don't interrupt," Mom fumed.

"Granny Tulla, who is Johann?"

"My husband."

"You had a husband who was a Polish officer? I don't remember you ever mentioning him."

"Tell her," Granny Tulla said to my mother.

"Noga," said Grandma Irena, "you must learn this basic rule: when you are listening to secrets, you don't interrupt."

"But a Polish officer?"

"Noga! We said we would start from the very beginning, did we not? So, let me tell you in my own way."

"As I said, I met my Johann at university. I was studying for my final year in medicine. He was walking, dressed in his impressive uniform, in the big university plaza. I thought that he was the most handsome man I had ever seen in my life. He looked striking in his clean pressed uniform, which stretched across his solid frame, his pants tucked into his polished boots. His shoulders were decorated with the insignia indicating his stature as a cavalry officer and with awards for excellence, all glittering in the sunlight. He looked like a prince out of a fairy tale that morning. I stood gazing at him, and my heart… my heart skipped a beat. It danced and sang as it had never done before. I panicked.

"A battle of inner voices immediately broke out within me: stop this at once! What are you doing, ogling a Polish officer? How can you get so worked up over a gentile? An attractive goy, maybe, but he's not for you. You are the daughter of Rabbi Eisler. A daughter of the Jewish people. But he… he's a Polish Catholic. You're allowed to look, but nothing more.

"My heart did not listen to the arguments. My heart did not care. My heart raced like crazy and radiated waves of heat in every direction. I had never been so excited. I took a few steps away from the window. That's it, I thought, he will go his own way and that will be that. But fate plays by its own rules. The officer stopped, took off his hat, raised his head and eyes, and stared at me. Deeply, as though examining me. He put his hand to his forehead like a salute then burst into the building. Only the pounding of his boots clomping up the stairs could be heard. What was happening?

I stood frozen on the spot. I was unable to move.

And my heart, my heart beat hard. So hard, I worried that all of Warsaw could hear it.

"Here you are," he said suddenly standing before me, holding his officer's hat under his arm, his red hair burning and his eyes fixed on mine. "I worried that you would disappear from me. Captain Johann Yezhnev at your service," he said and saluted.

"Rachel," I said. "Rachel Eisler, fourth-year student at the medical school."

"If you permit, I will call you Rachelle." I nodded. Poles had a hard time pronouncing my name.

"Would you be so kind, Rachelle?" He held his arm out to me. I surprised myself, placing my arm on his without hesitation, and let him lead me to the university's great garden.

There, on a white granite bench, we sat and talked. We talked and talked. He was funny and smart, and I laughed as I had never laughed before.

He told me of his life in the regiment, of his childhood, entertaining me with stories of his clean-freak mother, his father Bronek the watchmaker. And I told him about my father who was a rabbi and educator, about our customs and the Hebrew language, which fascinated him. He also asked to know the meaning of the name Rachel. Rachelle, as he called me. I told him the story of Jacob who worked seven years for Rachel and seven more until he could have her.

"Amazing," he laughed. "And she waited for him?"

"Of course, she loved him."

"Now that's love," he said. "For true love, I would be willing to work for twenty years."

We went on chatting and laughing until we heard the voices of his friends who had come looking for him. They had to hurry back to the regiment. It was time to go our separate ways.

"Promise me..." he gazed at me.

"What?"

"That you will wait for me as Rachel waited for Jacob."

"But Jacob also had Leah in the meantime," I reminded him.

"There will be no Leah. I will be back in a week, and you will stand here by the window and smile, and we will go for a walk in Wozienki park, the most beautiful spot in all of Warsaw."

"I don't know."

"Promise me," he said and knelt down before me.

It was so romantic that I felt like I was in a movie. But still, I hesitated.

"Please, Rachelle," he said. "It's me, your Jacob asking."

I promised. How could I refuse him? He got up quickly, gave a little bow as if I were a queen, and went on his way. I was filled with joy and felt as though butterflies were fluttering all around me until suddenly, dark clouds arose and a voice inside cried: No, not even for a moment! After all, he's a goy. He's not of your people. I was tempted, but why did I agree? Why did I promise to wait for him? What business do I, the daughter of Rabbi Eliezer Eisler, granddaughter of Abraham Eisler, scion of four generations of rabbis, have with this Polish officer?

That night I couldn't sleep. I heard voices arguing. It's unsuitable, forget him, shouted one voice.

But he conquered my heart, replied another.

He's Catholic!

There were some voices that encouraged me and others that warned me, those that pacified and those that reprimanded. A week later he returned, formal and serious. And all of the voices went quiet, just butterflies fluttering over us.

We went for a walk in Wozienki Park that morning, as he had promised, and my doubts melted away.

He whistled a nocturne for me before the statue of Chopin and I taught him the names of the plants in the greenhouses of the great palace. And so it went, week after week.

The fifth time we met, he took me in his arms and kissed me gently as though afraid I would break, and the expression 'floating on air' suddenly made sense to me. A month later, beside the same bench, he knelt down on one knee and offered me a diamond ring.

"My beautiful Rachelle, will you do me the honor of being my wife?"

I burst into tears. Yes, yes, yes, yes! I wanted it so badly. I had been waiting for it. Dreaming of it. I had hoped he would propose and yet, I couldn't promise him anything. First, I had to speak with my father, Eliezer Eisler.

I knew that I was about to break my father's heart, that it would be excruciating for him to see his only daughter in the arms of a Polish gentile. Usually, when a Jewish girl married a gentile man, her family sat 'shiva'[1] as if she were dead, to symbolize that she had been erased from the community, that she no longer existed. And now, when I should have been bringing him comfort, making him happy in his old age, and giving him grandchildren, I was instead bringing him heart-breaking news.

My father, Rabbi Eliezer Eisler, was born in Pruszkow.[2] He had lived there all his life and was head of the yeshiva and the community court. He was a revered Jew. Though steeped in traditional values, he did not hesitate to allow me, his only daughter, to study medicine at the University of Warsaw and was proud of the fact that I would be a doctor.

The moment I entered, he glanced at me and immediately asked what happened. I told him that everything was fine, but he knew that something was amiss.

I was amazed to see how old he had become over the months that we had not met. It has been two years since my mother passed away, and my father was still

---

1   To observe the Jewish mourning period

2   A city close to the Polish capital of Warsaw, Pruszkow was a commercial center for the surrounding villages. When the Second World War broke out, there were some 1500 Jews in the city. In November of 1940, all of them were forced into the newly established ghetto in a small fenced area and made to do forced labor. The ghetto was liquidated in January 1941.

in mourning. The longing and the sorrow made him a sad and gloomy man. Life without her was difficult for him.

We sat in his little yard and talked about everything. We talked about his health, his aging community, and the young people who had new and different dreams and wanted to rebuild the land of Israel. He asked about the university, about my studies, and about his sister in whose home I lived. He wanted to know what was happening, with whom I spent my time, what I did in the evenings. "Tell me everything and don't hold back."

So, we spoke in a general way about my life and my studies, even about Germany and Hitler. We spoke about every subject apart from the essential one, until he raised his eyes to me and said, "Yes, my daughter, I am listening."

The words stuck in my throat, refusing to come out. I knew that I was about to break his heart.

"Tell me, my daughter, God is with you, what happened that you are so frightened before me?"

I told him everything, of the laughter and the joy. Of the happiness that Johann brought into my life. I told him everything and he listened. His eyes, the color of honey, turned grey and sank inward, a green color coming over his handsome face. He breathed so heavily that I worried about his health. When I finished speaking, he cast his eyes downward and was quiet. He didn't say a word, but his lips moved as though he was speaking with God.

"Father..." he did not answer. He just looked at a distant point somewhere in the kitchen.

"You are hurting me," he whispered, his voice broken into pieces.

"Beloved Father, forgive me," I kissed his hands.

Still, he did not look at me.

"Please understand, Johann is the love of my life, I cannot have it any other way."

He dropped his head and said, "You are making a mistake, Daughter."

"But you taught me..."

"To be loyal to your God, to your people."

"This is a great love, true love like you and Mom had."

And my father, the beloved rabbi, the revered teacher, the educator whose insight was sought by all, slammed the table with his fist.

"Don't you dare, don't you ever take her name in vain. Reconsider," his voice softened. "You must understand, Daughter, this is a tough choice. You will be an outsider for the rest of your life, both among us here and among them there. The Jews will denounce you and the Gentiles will hate you for taking one of their men."

"We will be together, Father, the two of us, him and I, and if God wills it..."

"And the loneliness, the distance from your family, your friends... please, Daughter, reconsider this choice."

"When you get to know him, you will see how handsome, how gentle he is and you will like him."

"I have no intention of meeting him," he said in a cold, distant voice. "I should have listened to my Sarah. She didn't want you going to Warsaw. She always said that to send a pretty young woman such as yourself to university would only bring trouble."

"Father, please, our future son will be your first grandson, our daughter your granddaughter, please!"

I was so afraid he would tear me from his life, that he would give up on me.

He placed a hand on my head and prayed. His lips moved in a murmur. Who was he praying to? His wife Sarah? His God? On whose behalf? For me? For us? For the grandchild that would come? I did not dare ask. It was enough that he didn't sit shiva for me or remove me from his life, as others had done.

I left the house quietly that night while he sat staring out the window. I hurried to tell my beloved of my decision. Yes, I would be his wife. I had no way of knowing that that was the last time I would see my father. Who could have guessed that just a few months later the Germans would enter his village, burn his synagogue, load the Jewish youth, elderly, women, and children to a clearing in the forest, and there would shoot and annihilate an entire community? And why? Simply because they were Jews. Because the Germans did not like them.

In his last letter to me, my father wrote, "Life is about to change, Daughter. We see the German soldiers, hear the planes overhead and the tanks on the ground. Who knows where all of this will lead? There are several families who were frightened and escaped over the Russian border, but I am not among them. I am not afraid. After all, the Germans are a cultured people, and we have already endured a war... I hope for you that your officer knows how to look after himself and will return safely from battle..." The letter was written in November 1939 but in the meantime, I was enraptured in a beautiful world, enamored with my great love.

Johann waited for me at the Warsaw train station and greeted me with a bouquet of red roses.

"Did you speak with your parents?" I asked when he picked me up in his arms.

"What does it matter? You're here, that's what's important."

"What did Bronek and Marta say? Did you invite them? Will they celebrate with us?"

"Enough, my love," he said and his tone changed. "Not now."

"Johann, please, what did they say?"

"First we will dine. I reserved a table for us."

My heart suspected the worst.

"They... they... but what does it matter, what's important is that we are here together. I am yours, and you are mine."

"Nonetheless, what did they say?"

"You must know? My mother got hysterical, she screamed like a madwoman, and then threatened to kill herself."

"That's terrible!"

"She always threatens it, and Father too. They said that if I marry you, they will declare that they have just one son, that I will be as though dead to them. Yes, dead. And they wouldn't even mourn me. Terrible things."

"And you?"

"I am happy with you, and I don't want to talk about this any further," he held me about my waist. "Tell me, where does your intoxicating scent come from?"

His parents kept on sending him disdainful letters, threatening to disinherit him, to erase his name from the family book, to declare him dead, as a traitor to Poland, and so forth. They sent the priest, the bishop, and his twin brother Andre to reason with him, but Johann remained firm. In love and determined, he was unwilling to give in.

When his brother Andre came to his regiment's encampment to attempt to change his mind, I was engrossed in my fifth-year final examinations. While Johann had chosen a military career, Andre had gone to study history and literature.

"We are different," Johann answered me when I asked about him. "Perhaps we look alike, but we are different in character."

"How so?"

"He does whatever Mother asks. He wants to be a secondary school teacher, perhaps even to teach at a university, but I have bigger dreams. I am the ambitious one in the family. You'll see, one day I will be the commander of the Polish army and you, my beautiful wife, the entire army will cheer for you."

I do not know what they talked about, but when we met afterward, he told me with great pain that Andre spoke like their mother Marta and would not even attend our wedding.

The wedding ceremony took place in City Hall. We waited in the ugly grey corridor until a clerk with a limp called our names. It was not quite the setting I dreamed of for the big day we had been looking forward to. Johann turned up in his full-dress uniform and looked like a prince, and I wore a blue wool suit that I had borrowed from another student. I held a bouquet of pink lilies in my hands and a wreath of daffodils on my head with a white tulle veil that reached my waist. A bored clerk wrote down our names and asked too many questions. In the evening, we celebrated at the Sweet Heart Coffee House, where Johann drank vodka - a lot of vodka - glass after glass until his eyes turned glassy and he mumbled incoherently. It scared me. In the middle of the party, he disappeared. I found him lying in the coffee house kitchen beside the bottle he had polished off. Snoring. My new husband.

I stroked his head, wondering, do you have regrets? Are you angry at yourself for the choice you made?

His friends helped me lead him to the room we had rented in The Four Angels Hotel downtown.

I spent the whole night looking out at the beautiful, sleeping city as he lay before me full of wine, dreaming his dreams. I paced the room, back and forth, restless. Had I made a mistake? What business did I have marrying this gentile? Had I betrayed my people? Maybe I should escape, fast, before we consummated our marriage.

He woke with the dawn, reached out his hand to me, and stroked my hair. "Rachelle, my love," he murmured and immediately all my doubts disappeared as though they had never been. "My darling." I rolled over to his side and let him lead me in the paths of love as I floated above the clouds, I was happier than I had ever been.

And so, we were married, my Johann and I, with no relatives, no family. Just a handful of loud Polish officers. I sent my father a photograph of the wedding. In the letter back, he wrote to me: Rachel, my beloved daughter, I pray for you from afar, may God be with you. If you choose to visit your aging father, please do so unaccompanied.

Just like that, without blessings or congratulations.

I knew that his heart was broken, but love is a powerful thing and I could not help but follow my heart.

We were so preoccupied with our happiness that we did not know that somewhere, fate had begun to scheme an end of the world as we knew it, that soon everything that seemed so safe to us would crash.

"And now, Noga my dear," said Granny Tulla, "I have to rest…"

"Wait, your father called you Rachel, Johann called you Rachelle, so why does everyone call you Tulla?"

"Patience. Everything in its own time. For now, give me a kiss and we will resume in a day or two." Chuckling, she pointed at Grandma Irena who was asleep on the armchair opposite. Her head slumped and her hands were folded across her big belly and I heard little grunts.

"What happened to her?"

"Jenny!" Tulla shouted and Jenny, their caretaker, ran into the room and began to lightly slap Irena's arms and back. She told me to leave.

"Not good so much speaking, they too much excited," she said and led me out of the room.

When I came back to my room in the evening, my mother was waiting for me.

"See what you did?"

"And you? You knew that Granny Tulla married a Polish officer?"

Her face turned red instantly.

Just as Granny Tulla had always said, fate has its own rules, and the following day we took Grandma Irena to the hospital, then home, then back to admit her again. Every time I asked Tulla to continue with the story she would say, 'just wait for her to get better', or 'not right now', or 'not yet' or 'It's Irena's story now, anyway.'

CHAPTER 2
Israel, Blue Bell Village

When we celebrated Grandma Irena's 90th birthday, it did not occur to us that it would be her farewell party.

All week, as we planned for the celebration, she had been lively and happy. On the night of the party, she wore a spring dress and an orange silk scarf that Dad had bought her. Her eyes sparkled as she listened to all the compliments that Mom and Dad gave her and the blessings from the friends who gathered together from all over the country. She shamelessly devoured the pink cream cake, danced a waltz with Uncle Brock with style, drank vodka (more than she should have), and then stood in the middle of the room singing the most idiotic song which the grandmothers loved to sing at every opportunity for some reason: the song of little Maier climbing the big Himalayas, 'Was macht der Maier am Himalaya.'

Brock, Dad, and Tulla joined her and the three of them screeched the idiotic song in German while Mom laughed and laughed and finally gave in and joined them.

What is little Maier doing in the big Himalaya mountains?

How is Maier, little Maier, in the big Himalayas?

"She was overexcited," Tulla confided to us the following day. "I could hardly get her into bed."

Grandma Irena was so happy that evening. One month later, she passed away.

She died in her sleep. She went to bed at ten o'clock after drinking a little glass of vodka, as she had done nearly all her life, put on the Nivea face cream whose virtues she believed in wholeheartedly, blessed the world for its goodness and God for his mercy as she did every night, and fell asleep forever.

"Like the righteous do," said the rabbi and, without asking too many questions, took her to the double plot at the cemetery that Tullerina had acquired for themselves.

"When we are angels, we will still be together," they explained.

Dad thought that was funny. He said that she was too heavy for any cloud to hold her up and certainly not both of them. My father loved the two of them very much and called them my mamas, and from time to time, Mama Tullerina, the nickname my brother made up, that made Irena blush and Tulla chuckle happily.

Maybe it was only me that noticed, but at the last moment, before the coffin disappeared, Tulla placed the baggie with the packet of crosses beneath Irena's white shrouds and then began to whistle. The weirdest part was that Mom went over to her, hugged her, and began to whistle too. When I asked what they were doing, Granny Tulla told me that one day I would understand.

"Irena went to a place that suits her," said Tulla. "Straight to the Garden of Eden."

"I miss her already," said Mom. Uncle Brock hugged Mom and they went out. From the window of my room, I could see them, his hand on her shoulder and the two of them talking and talking. Mom and Brock had a lot of conversations just the two of them.

Her gravestone was engraved, "For wherever you go, I will go," from the Book of Ruth, Chapter 1, verse 17.

"What's that?" I asked Mama, and she said that it was not the time for such questions.

Tulla, on the other hand, told me, "You will understand everything in time," and added, "and good thing I managed to make her happy and hang the curtain that she knitted."

In the days following Grandma Irena's parting, we looked after Granny Tulla. We were worried that she would be lonely, that she would wish to join Irena, her eternal companion.

Granny Tulla was two years younger than Irena. My parents were concerned that the separation from her soulmate of over seventy years would shorten her life, but Tulla had much to arrange.

She explained, "I've been keeping busy with the business of living for many years now." She was as vital as ever.

"Who will tell me the whole story?" I asked her on one of my visits.

"Me," Mama surprised me. "That's what Irena decided."

"When?"

"You don't need to know everything," Tulla laughed and Mama pulled a blanket tight around her legs.

"From now on, just listen, and please don't interrupt. That was also Irena's instruction. Can you handle that? Or..."

"Of course," I promised.

CHAPTER 3

Nuzewo, 1938

In the small, peaceful village of Nuzewo, lived the Zbigniew family. Some of the family's men made their living working in the nearby city of Ciechanow. The city had a monastery and a large fortress at its center, and the Lydynia River crossed through it. Ignatz Zbigniew looked after his small farm, which he had inherited from his parents, and hoped that one day his son Oleg would inherit it from him and work the fields and care for the cows.

On Sundays, the whole family wore their Sunday best and rode the carriage to the central Ciechanow church that all of their relatives attended. Among them were the childless Uncle Solly and his wife, who always pampered their favorite little girl.

"Who has such a cute nose and eyes like big diamonds?" her aunt would boast of her. "Look, she is the most beautiful girl in the world," while her uncle Solly would say that it was more important for her to be brave, smart, and independent. Only her mother would say that a girl needs luck, not beauty and intelligence.

When she finished high school and her parents found that she had turned into a pretty and strong-willed young woman, views regarding Irena's future were divided. Her brother Oleg studied at the preparatory college in Ciechanow and the tuition was already a burden on the family. The question was whether the daughter should continue with her education or, as was the custom of the young women in the village, join her mother at home to help with the house-work and learn to sew until a husband came along.

"Who wouldn't want our daughter?" boasted her father. The girl cast her eyes down. She knew that the young men of the village were already looking at her and that her father preferred she help her mother manage the home. But she wanted to study and not be ignorant like the other village girls. She was determined to get her way.

"A girl needs a profession, not to rely on a husband," she proclaimed.

"Look at her," Uncle Solly said proudly. "She is better than five boys, and we can find her a husband when the time comes. Not just anybody, either, but the finest young man."

Since Uncle Solly was the rich brother, everyone listened to his opinion that it would be good for the girl to continue learning.

"You can stay in our home," he added. "Aunt Olga will be very pleased for you to live with us, and when the time comes, you can work for me."

So, it was decided. For two days of the week she would sleep at her aunt and uncle's home, and the rest of the week she would take the train back to the village.

The accounting school was in the center of Ciechanow. Some twenty girls were studying there, all of whom dreamed of finding work in their chosen profession along with a reputable husband and not just some shepherd or cloth merchant.

"I don't understand... how is this family related to us?"

"When God was handing out patience, where were you?" Mama laughed.

"Tell me, Noga," Tulla turned to me, "You haven't figured out who that stubborn girl is?"

"Maybe..." The truth is, I already suspected but I wanted Mama to say it.

"Her name was Irena," said Mama.

"Irena. Irena, who would one day be Grandma Irena?"

"Precisely."

Now things were starting to make sense. The secrets were coming out.

CHAPTER 4

Ciechanow[3] 1938

"In Ciechanow," my mother went on, telling Irena's story as she knew it, "Irena met the handsome Andre who would one day offer her a diamond ring and ask her to marry him. Later she would also hear the stories about his twin brother Johann, who rebelled against his mother, and Rachelle – Rachel, the terrible Jew who had stolen him from his parents. But let's not get ahead of ourselves.

Irena was as happy as could be, earning honors in her studies, helping Aunt Olga, and listening to Uncle Solly's stories.

Andre's father, Bronek Yezhnev, was a watchmaker and the only one in the city. His little watch shop stood on the main street beside Uncle Solly's general store, which was the biggest retailer in Ciechanow. There you could find tools, furniture, electric appliances, children's bicycles, cameras, and even slippers and nightgowns. Solly felt blessed in his work: the register was constantly ringing, the customers were happy, and he was planning to open another location across town.Every now and then, Solly would bring his friend Bronek his gold watch to be cleaned, adjusted, and repaired.

"My girl," he addressed Irena one day, "Could you bring Bronek my watch? It's a little off."

"What do you want from the girl," the aunt protested, "Better she should finish her homework."

---

3   Ciechanow is a city in the Mozovia region of northern Poland, on the banks of the Lydynia river, about 100 kilometers north of Warsaw. Until the Second World War, the city had a large Jewish population. Like Poland's other Jewish communities, the Ciechanow community was destroyed and most of its people killed in the Holocaust.

"Why are you interfering, old lady?" Irena noticed that her uncle winked at his wife as he said this and that Olga nodded her head in understanding.

Irena knew the watch shop and loved to visit. Its walls were covered with clocks. Each of them showed a different hour, made a unique tick-tock sound, and rang in its own way. To Irena, entering Bronek's shop felt like being in a fairy tale.

On one visit she asked, "Bronek? Why does each clock show a different time?"

"To keep it interesting for me," he laughed.

"And why does each have a different ring?"

"I find it pleasing; they are just like people. Each has its own sound."

"Why?"

"Otherwise the world would be boring," he replied as he pulled a monocle from his pocket, pressing it to one eye, focusing intently, and gently prodding the innards of the afflicted watch.

On this particular day, Irena happily did as her uncle asked and took the watch to the clock shop. Snow had begun to fall. Soft flakes fell on her hair, wet her face, and covered the trees, the bushes, and the sidewalk with a pure white blanket. The world looked so beautiful and festive, as though preparing for a holiday. The fresh smell of snow filled the air, hinting that something good was about to happen.

And so, on that morning at Bronek's watch shop, Irena met Andre and her life changed forever. She was a student at the school for bookkeeping, and he was a student of History and German at the university.

"Here comes the young woman," Bronek smiled and offered her a cup of hot tea.

She refused politely. She wanted to go out into the snow to enjoy the beauty of the world outside.

"Wait," he said. "Where are you rushing off to?" He laughed. "Tell me, Miss, did you happen to see the student..." he raised his voice. "Here he is! Good morning Andreush, my boy." She turned and encountering him, immediately understood why she had felt that something good was coming.

"Do you know Irena?"

He nodded and blushed.

"Irena is learning bookkeeping," he said with pride. Andre looked deep into her eyes until she felt a kind of heat filling her belly, rising to her chest and throat...

"Join us for a cup of tea?" asked Bronek.

Irena pulled back her hand. "No thank you," she mumbled, "I have to get going."

"You have an offer of the best tea in town, made by my wife Marta," said Bronek, and removed the monocle from his eye. "Here, Uncle Solly's watch is fixed. Sit here and I'll be right back."

She remained standing, wondering how she was supposed to behave without cheapening herself. Truthfully, she desperately wanted to stay, to look deep into his blue eyes, but she was embarrassed.

Andre kept looking at her.

They did not speak. They remained silent. Irena was afraid to say anything lest she come off as stupid.

Meanwhile, he was perfectly happy to stare at her.

"Do you live here? In Ciechanow?"

"No, I live in the village Nuzewo. Do you know it?"

"Yes. How nice, and where is your school?"

"Behind the cinema. What exactly are you studying?"

"I'm taking history and German and in a few more months I will teach at the preparatory college, and maybe after that at the university," he said and blushed.

When Bronek returned to his shop, he found them quiet. Irena's eyes were fixed on the cuckoo clock while Andre watched her with a smile.

She came back the next day.

Bronek grinned when she explained that Uncle Solly claimed that the watch still wasn't working properly. Only later did she realize that it was all part of the plan. She waited one, two, three moments, scanned the shop, and was disappointed to find that Andre was not there.

"Did... did your son return to Warsaw?"

"He's shoveling the snow at the house. Sit and I'll fix your watch."

When Andre came in, his face was red. "I waited for you by your school," he said quietly.

"There was no school today." Her heart beat so intensely that she was afraid Bronek and Andre and everyone on the street could hear it.

"If I understand what I'm seeing, Andre," Bronek interrupted, "it seems as though you like Irena."

"Dad, stop," Andre blushed.

"Great, I'm pleased, and it seems as though you like my son back," he pinched Andre's cheek. "Go to the coffee shop. They have divine hot chocolate and sandwiches," he quickly slipped some coins into Andre's hand and urged them out the door.

"It's all good, trust Bronek. After all, I understand time better than anyone, and when I look at the two of you, I think of all the time that's slipping away."

Andre took her arm and opened the door for her as though she were a princess.

"Just one thing, don't hurry to decide," laughed Bronek. "Our Andreush has a twin brother, no less handsome, no less smart. First meet Johann, and then you might choose him?"

"Dad, stop!"

She did not want to meet Johann or any other young man in the world.

"Is your brother Johann also studying in Warsaw?" She asked when they sat in the coffee shop, sipping hot chocolate.

Andre simply said, "No."

"What is he studying?" she asked again, and he said that he was no longer studying and they hardly saw one another.

"But you're twins!"

"We aren't alike at all, he and I… I would rather not talk about him," his voice hardened for a moment, then he smiled. She did not ask again.

Yet the mystery of what had happened between the two brothers continued to plague her. A few weeks later, when they were planning the engagement party, she could hold back no longer and asked her beloved, "But… what did your brother do to you?"

And Andre, the soft and sweet guy who would sing to her under the cherry tree, who would bring her fragrant wildflowers, stared at her hard and brusquely replied, "We said we would not talk about that," and immediately added, "I insist, do not talk about it with my mother or ask her anything about him. Ever."

When she tried to get some answers from Uncle Solly, he only revealed, "It's because of Johann's bride,"

"What did she do?"

"She? Didn't do anything… believe me, buttercup, if you want to be liked in that family, you'd better let it go,"

Only later, when her mother-in-law came to treat her as a daughter, did she dare to ask.

"What does that mean an unsuitable wife?" Irena asked.

"She's not one of us," said Marta, the mother-in-law. "She's Jewish, like the people who murdered Jesus our savior. That woman bewitched my Johann, the outstanding officer who has been awarded medallions, sucking the blood of a good Polish man just like all the Yids."

"I know Jews, they're not all like that."

"Everyone knows that they drink the blood of Christian babies."

"That's not actually true, those are just stories. My father has Jewish friends and he…"

"They're friends of Ignatz? I hope you didn't catch anything from them," she smirked. "You aren't going to educate me," Marta fumed. "They are inferior, dangerous, blood-sucking creatures."

"Marta, enough!" Bronek tried to calm her down. "The doctor said you must not get worked up."

"Ratfink!" spat Marta. "Rusalka[4] did it."

"Who's Rusalka?" Irena asked.

"A witch, and anyone who looks at her gets trapped in her net. His brain becomes porridge. My poor Johann."

"Maybe best you go lie down," Andre held out his arm to his mother to help her go up to her room.

"At least you brought us a real Polish girl who believes in Jesus, even though her father is just a simple farmer."

"Mom, stop," Andre's voice was hard. God forbid anyone should speak of his fiancé like that.

"You know," Marta whispered to Irena on a different occasion, "that their marriage isn't valid."

"Why?"

"They were married at City Hall. It doesn't count," Marta spat with disdain.

"That's valid," Irena dared to reply.

"Nonsense," screeched Marta. "Reasonable people get married at church. You wait and see, one day he will see the light and return to us." Irena did not respond.

---

4   Rusalka is a mythical, supernatural figure who appears as a water nymph in Slavic mythology and uses her rare beauty to tempt passing men, luring them to their deaths in deep waters.

"Is it so much to ask?" Marta crossed herself. "That we get rid of that witch and have my good Johann return to us."

That was how Irena first heard of Johann's wife Rachelle, the mysterious Jewish woman that both Marta and Bronek cursed ceaselessly. The more they cursed, the more Irena's curiosity grew. Sometimes she felt lonely in Andre's parents' home, especially when winter came and snow covered her window.

I wish I could meet her, she thought. We could be sisters. Each a bride to a twin. She was a romantic. She hoped that maybe she could change Marta's mind, to make their bond stronger and bring the family back together. Irena was a romantic.

CHAPTER 5
Ciechanow 1938

By May, the snow had melted and gardens were blooming and colorful, and Irena and Andre's wedding took place. Everything seemed so certain then.

When the heavy clouds of evil advanced towards Poland, everyone thought it was only temporary. But soon, the grass and flowers would be covered with the blood of Poland's heroes. Nobody took Hitler seriously, although the German masses were marching and saluting him. That madman, as the Poles referred to him, who shouted and threatened and swore that he would conquer the world, claimed he had plans to wipe out everyone who was not pure Aryan. It never occurred to anyone that in less than a year, with the September invasion of Poland, all of their dreams, all of their hopes, and all of their plans would come apart.

Even when convoys of refugees marched east toward the Russian border, their wagons loaded with blankets and pillows, their faces expressionless… still they did not believe it. Where were the refugees from? From Germany. And why were they fleeing? Didn't they see? A terrible storm was coming. Everyone should watch out. You should run too before the long hand of war touches you. Leave everything? After all, I just planted my fields, fixed the roof, had a baby. In Ciechanow, everything was as usual.

People prefer to ignore the uncomfortable; what does not meet the eye does not exist. The young people planned to build houses and fill them with babies, the elderly dozed like lizards in the sun, and the women filled the air with the delicious aromas from their cooking, the world behaved as usual, not knowing that to the west, Satan was taking steps and that once he decided to strike, nothing would stop him.

Andre and Irena were preoccupied with their own happiness. All of their attention was focused on making wedding preparations: guest lists, bridesmaids' dresses, and plans for the food and drink they would serve.

The ceremony took place in the old church in which Marta and Bronek had been married and where Andre and Johann had been baptized. Afterward, according to plan, the guests would go on to the wedding party in the luxurious venue: the Victoria Hotel.

When Irena left the doorstep of her home the afternoon of that very day and stepped into the carriage that waited to take her to the ceremony, she felt more beautiful than she ever had before. She knew that everything around her was perfect. Life was good, she smiled to herself.

There was just one thing that cast a shadow over her happiness: the absence of Rachelle and Johann. She had hoped that Bronek and Marta would change their minds and that the family would be reunited.

"Are you inviting your brother Johann?" She asked Andre, and he, ashen-faced, told her not to interfere. She insisted and asked again.

"Maybe ask him to come alone, without his Jewish wife?"

"You were asked to leave it alone," he raised his voice. "You worry about the dress, the flowers, that you comb your pretty hair, and the rest will work out. Why does it even matter to you?"

"Family is important to me."

"They aren't your family. This is all because Mokosh put the evil eye on him."

"Who is that?" she wondered aloud.

"Mokosh is the leader of the witches. She sent Rusalka to him and she bewitched and confused him," he said and spat twice. She looked at him, stunned.

"Andre, you are a historian. Since when do we believe in demons and spirits?"

"Don't interfere," he glowered. "He's no longer part of the family. That's it."

"He's your only brother!"

"I said enough!" He shouted and swatted with his hand as though to hit her, regretted it, and left the house. She saw him leaning against the front door rolling a cigarette and smoking angrily. Andre? What happened? Where had the nice young man who had courted her gone, who spun her so elegantly when they danced the waltz, who brought her a bouquet of snowdrops and promised his love to her?

She did not ask again.

She was lonely in Ciechanow. All of her family and friends had stayed in the little village. She loved to walk, to dance, to paint, and sing, but Andre's household was strict. If only Rachelle were here, she thought. We could be friends, spend time together, go for walks, and enjoy ourselves. Together we would stand up to Marta, who demands that everything be done her way.

She was curious to know who this Rachelle was that Johann, the beloved, high-ranking Polish officer was willing to abandon his parents and follow her. Irena was a romantic and the great love between the officer and the Jewish girl excited her.

She rejected what Marta said about the Jews and about Rachelle especially. There had been several Jewish families in the little village where she grew up. Their houses stood crowded densely together, one practically touching the next. As though connected, as though protecting one another. They spoke amongst themselves in a strange language and the men looked unusual in their dress and customs. Strange white threads hung from their shirts and they would kiss the little boxes hanging in their doorways.

The Jews did not attend church. They did not work on Saturday, but they did work on Sunday. On Christmas, they did not put lights on fir trees and they even conducted their weddings differently.

Her bookkeeping teacher was Jewish, as were the milkman and the clerk at the post office, which was why each wore a black skullcap on his head, her mother explained to her.

Her parents had Jewish friends. Sometimes they came to visit Irena's house. At harvest time, or winter sowing, her father would invite Lazar the Jew to help him on the farm. Why him? she asked.

"I trust him, The Jew never shows up to work drunk, he is content with less pay than the others, and most of all, he is pleasant to talk to."

Once when she was a child, she had asked her brother Oleg what he knew about Jews.

"Steer clear of them," he had warned her. "They aren't even human. Everyone knows that they are dangerous demons, and they have tails and sharp teeth like bloodsucking vampires."

"Why?"

"That's how they are, and at night by the light of the moon they kidnap little Polish children and drink their blood."

"Why?" she burst out crying. "Why would they do that to us?"

"Because they're Yids. That's why you always have to beat them."

During evening prayers, Oleg would scare Irena and say that if she was a bad girl the Jews would come and kidnap her.

"Give me the coin that Uncle Solly gave you."

"Why?"

"Because that way I can protect you from them when they come to drink your blood."

"Why would they take me? Don't they have children of their own?"

"They only want the blood of Christians. Give it to me, quick!"

Irena would run away from him and her mother would hug her and tell her that there was nothing to worry about because Jews were just like everyone else. Humans.

"And do they really have tails?"

"Stop listening to your brother's nonsense," her mother scolded.

"But he says…"

"Enough," said her father. "Better go put food out for the chickens."

When she got older, her father told her that the Jews had settled in the Ciechanow region more than four hundred years ago. They did not have a homeland as the Poles did. They had a different religion and their messiah was Moses, and they prayed in a synagogue, not in a church.

When Yaakov Aharonovich, the Jewish cloth merchant, came to visit them, Irina hid under the table.

"Get out of there, you silly girl," Mom laughed.

"But I'm scared of them! He will drink my blood!"

Yaakov bent down to her and said, "We are human beings like you and we all believe in the same God."

She looked at him, "But my brother said…»

"I like to drink milk and your mother's secret tea, the best in all Poland. Come, look, I brought you some silk for a holiday dress," Yaakov smiled at her. He seemed nice.

"But you …" she burst into tears.

"Do not listen to your brother's nonsense," said Mother and hugged her, "Yaakov is our friend. Come sit with us."

When she was a little older, Irena accompanied her parents when they were invited to observe the holidays with the Jews in their homes. She loved going to the Bar-Mitzvah celebrations because of the candies that they would throw to the children.

When Marta cursed the "vile" Jewish girl that had bewitched her beloved son, Irena would slip outside. There was no point in arguing with her. Marta was not willing to listen to anybody. She only cared about her own opinions.

The morning of her wedding, Irena looked like a princess in her white dress sewn flawlessly by her mother. She held a bouquet of white orchids in her hands and on her head, she wore a magnificent beaded crown that Uncle Solly had brought from Warsaw.

In honor of the occasion, her father wore his officer uniform from the First World War while Bronek stood neat and tall as a proud soldier with Marta, who could barely hold back her tears.

"Do you, Andre, wish to…" said the priest.

And Andre, pale and excited, replied "yes."

And then he turned and asked Irena. "Yes, yes, I do, I do!"

Everyone cheered.

They exchanged rings and the priest placed her hand in his and told them the importance of their union, of a man and woman joining together. Irena did not hear a word. She just gazed at her handsome husband and thought how wonderful it would be when, in a few hours, Andre could remove her dress and they would embrace and kiss until they were one, as her mother had explained to her.

When they left the church under a shower of rice, laughing, hugging, and happy on their way to a carriage drawn by four white horses, Andre suddenly stopped and his face went white, as though he had suddenly come down with something.

"Andre! Andre, what happened?"

He began coughing and breathing heavily, his face ashen. God, she thought, what if it's a heart attack, or worse.

"Andre, my Andre! Let's go," she whispered to him but he did not respond.

What should she do? She looked for her mother, for Marta, for Uncle Solly, but everyone had already rushed to the party and she didn't see anyone she knew nearby.

"Come, Andre," she tried to drag him. "The carriage is here." But he did not respond. His gaze was peculiar, as though he were transfixed.

"Keep walking," he finally said to her. "Go. Get in the carriage and go." Irena remained standing where she was.

"I said go!" He pushed her with a brutishness that she had not seen from him before.

"Andre, my love, what happened?" She put her hand to his heart. He recoiled.

Good God! How could he be so insensitive to her? Maybe an attack of insanity, some illness that they hadn't told her about? What had he seen that had shocked him so badly?

Suddenly Andre dropped her arm and crossed the road. She followed right behind him.

"Wait," she shouted, trying to make it over the cobblestones, struggling to hold up the train of her dress.

There, in the tree-lined boulevard, she found him standing facing an officer in uniform. Could this be Johann? She remained standing a few steps away. Johann looked like the mirror image of her new husband, apart from his reddish hair.

"What are you doing here...? Who let you...?" she heard Andre shout.

"Andreush, my brother," Johann spread his arms wide, trying to hug his brother. "You thought I wouldn't come to celebrate with you? That I would not come to give my blessing to my twin?"

"Leave me alone," Andre recoiled.

"Congratulations little brother." He always called him that, since Andre had been born ten minutes after him.

"You're crazy," she heard Andre shout. "On what authority... why? You know that you are not wanted here."

"We came to make you happy, to get to know your lovely wife."

"We?" Andre took a step back. "You're telling me you brought... her?"

"She is a part of me. I'm here now so give me a hug. It's a big day, Andreush, I am so eager to meet your wife."

"You have to go before you start a scandal."

"Our mother is still controlling... wait, little brother, over there... who is that gorgeous woman staring at us – is that your wife?" Andre turned and glowered at Irena.

Irena knew that he would be angry but she was so curious.

"Irena," she introduced herself as she came closer and shook his hand. "Irena Yezhnev, as of this morning." She loved the spark in his eyes, the big smile, and the warm hand that enveloped hers.

"I'm the brother they've been hiding from you," he gave her a bow. "Johann, the black sheep. Now tell me, what is a gorgeous woman like yourself sees in my ugly brother?"

"I love him."

"Brother, you're a lucky man," he laughed, then added, "You found yourself the perfect husband — almost as good as me, only I am already madly in love with my wife.

Before she managed to reply, to tell him that she would love to meet her sister-in-law, Andre punched him and Johann pushed his brother back.

"Stop that, Andre, what's gotten into you?"

"Get away from here! Why did you follow me?" Andre pushed Johann again and tried to hold him. Another moment and the two would begin fighting in earnest.

"Stop!" Irena pleaded. "Stop it!" She pulled Andre towards her, trying to separate the two.

"Come, we have to get going," he pulled his wife after him.

"Just a moment," Johann stopped them. "You are hurrying to your party. We are staying at the hotel next door. When Mother and Father get tired and leave, and when all of the relatives are as drunk as they get, call us and we will join you if you aren't too drunk already yourselves."

"That's out of the question."

"Just one dance. It's tradition."

"No! What don't you understand? You are not wanted here!" Johann turned red as though he had just been slapped.

"I'm sorry to hear that," he turned to Irena. "If you knew my Rachelle you would fall in love with her too. She's an amazing woman, generous, brave, almost as pretty as you."

"Stop it, Johann. You came, you saw, you even managed to meet Irena, don't turn my happy day into a day of battle."

"I would like it if they could come..." Irena whispered. "We will dance until the morning." She held the train of her dress as though dancing already.

"I told you not to get involved."

"It's my wedding, too."

"Goodbye," said Andre, and started walking.

"You're getting rid of us?"

"I don't recall inviting you."

"You disappoint me, little brother," said Johann. "You know where we are and if you change your mind... And you, young lady, I suggest you be strong in the face of my brother, and Marta who controls him, and that you be free of prejudice." He began to walk away, tall and upright, swallowing his pride.

"Johann, wait a moment!" Irena dropped Andre's hand and ran after Johann. He turned and smiled at her.

"Wait, just a moment, Johann, brother-in-law."

"There's no point, drop it."

"Where do you live? Maybe I can manage... I will try what I can, I so want to get to know her, both of you."

"Not far, less than twenty kilometers from here. Here," he pulled a piece of paper from his pocket which bore their address inscribed in gold letters and handed it to her. Irena folded it quickly and shoved it into her dress. "I pray you might manage. Good luck, sister-in-law. I am pleased with you." He bowed to her and disappeared.

Andre waited for her, frowning. "What did you say to one another?"

"I just bade him goodbye. Enough, Andreush, come let's celebrate our wedding day."

Only late at night did Irena request of her husband that perhaps they might invite the other couple to join after all.

"No," he ruled. "End of discussion."

And so, the days passed, and after spring came summer, autumn, winter, and spring again, and already it was getting warm once more and the days were long and bright.

August of 1939 — how could they have guessed what was to come?

The farmers harvested the wheat and prepared the fields for autumn. The women pickled vegetables in glass jars and planted flower bulbs that would bloom in the spring, and the storks began to plan their migration to warmer climates.

Somewhere in western Poland, the tanks were already being polished, the canons aimed, and the biggest, strongest military in the world planning to plant its big, iron fist in the land of Poland.

Who could have known that those happy days would change so fast? Too fast.On September 1st, 1939, just a month after Nazi Germany and the Soviet Union signed the Ribbentrop-Molotov[5] agreement, and without declaring war or giving any notice, German forces invaded Poland. A short while later, on the 17th of September, the Russians invaded from the east.

The invaders had a significant military advantage: fifty-six divisions, thousands of canons, tanks, planes, and over two million German, Russian, and Slovakian soldiers quickly eliminated any Polish resistance. The battle was lost before it began.

It was a preview of what was about to happen to all of Europe.

After five weeks of fighting, Poland surrendered.

Ciechanow was conquered almost without a fight on September 4th. The Germans entered the city, asked the residents to remain in their homes, and promised that nobody would be hurt if they obeyed the army's orders. The next day they took over the city hall, replaced the clerks with their own men, and made it their headquarters. Several days after the occupation, they began to turn their sights on the Jewish population, which now numbered fewer than three thousand, since many Jews had the foresight to escape eastward over the Bugg River to an area occupied by the Soviets.

Compared to Hitler, the Russians appeared merciful and the east looked like a safer place in those days. Just two days after the occupation, the city-dwellers awoke to the sounds of explosions and the strong smells of burning in the air. By evening, word had spread that the Germans had destroyed the Great Synagogue and had blown up a number of Jewish houses.

New laws were written, primarily against the Jewish population. Jews were forced to wear a yellow tag for identification, their belongings were looted, their homes confiscated. They were forbidden from taking public transportation. Teachers were removed from the schools, and the Germans established a Jewish police force, the 'Judenrat,' which was responsible for carrying out the German policies towards their own people and destroying the magnificent Jewish community of Ciechanow in the process.

---

5   The first part of this agreement was a financial contract of 200 million marks. The second part was a non-aggression pact between the two countries *stipulating* a period of ten years.

CHAPTER 6

When the Germans invaded Poland, Irena and Andre were a recently-married couple who had only just begun to build their lives together. While they knew what was happening in Europe, they believed, with the naivety of young lovers, that nothing could touch their happiness, that the soldiers marching in the streets were not a bad sign of things to come, that the tanks surrounding the city hall would not hurt anybody, and that the planes overhead did not threaten their country.

Even if they heard of property being looted here or a home being vandalized there, they believed that it was all just temporary. Andre, who studied German at the university and was well-versed in German culture, claimed repeatedly that they need not fear what was going on. After all, the Germans were a cultured people.

"There's nothing to worry about," Bronek argued. "The Germans came, the Germans will leave. Sit tight and it will all be fine."

At the beginning of the summer, a few months before the invasion, Irena discovered that she was pregnant.

She was weak in the mornings and felt her body changing, growing rounder, her breasts filling out. She still had not gone to the doctor to check but she felt certain...

Pregnancy. How wonderful! Soon they would have a baby. That's what everyone was waiting for. She was still embarrassed to tell her husband; perhaps she was afraid it was just a mistake and did not want to raise his expectations.

The family doctor confirmed her suspicions, but, in the same breath, cautioned her to be careful. He had known her since childhood and had always been concerned that she would not be able to give birth.

"You're too delicate, my dear," he once explained to her and her mother.

She asked, "What do you mean by that? Will I not be a grandmother?"

"She has narrow hips, but we will stay optimistic."

"This pregnancy is a miracle, but be extra cautious." He told her now.

"You think..."

"I recommend resting, lying down, and not making too great an effort if you want to keep this pregnancy. We shall see..."

Still, she did not tell Andre.

Marta, who kept an eye on her, began to suspect that something had changed and pestered her with questions.

"What was with you this morning?" she asked. "I thought I heard vomiting."

"Maybe it's something I ate, I'm fine."

"Are you sure? Maybe it's something else."

A few days later Marta told her that she looked like she had put on some weight. "It suits you. Is there some good reason for it?"

Irena denied it but realized she would not be able to keep her secret for long.

In the evening, when they retired to their room, she told Andre that maybe now was a good time to consider moving into a home of their own.

"Now? Why?"

"Because I don't think there will be room enough for three here."

"What three... wait... you... are you..." She nodded. "Are you sure?"

"Yes. The doctor said that..."

"You're saying I'll be a father!" He shouted and she clapped her hand over his mouth, so as not to wake his parents.

"The doctor said that..." she tried to stop him but he was drunk with happiness.

"Wait," she pleaded. "Wait another month," but he hurried off to tell his parents.

Marta sobbed happily and Bronek went to bring the vodka that he saved for special occasions. He and Andre finished a full bottle and the two women had to drag them to bed.

"Andre," Irena told him the following day. "Maybe we should talk to Uncle Solly about the land he has in the village. We can build our dream house on it."

"Leave those worries to me," he said. "Many Jewish houses are becoming available right now."

"Those houses belong to families."

"They were confiscated. The Jews abandoned them, no? They left the city, it's abandoned property."

But the celebration was premature and, as the doctor had warned, the baby was born before his time and was too weak to survive. When they told her the baby had died, she did not say a thing. She wept silently, a cloud of sadness over her beautiful face.

"Don't cry," said Uncle Solly. "I'm sure you will have at least ten more children."

"We also lost a baby," said her mother. "Why are you so worried? You are still young."

Andre did not say a word to her.

She saw him pacing the yard, smoking cigarette after cigarette, a sign of his inner turmoil, and she felt guilty. Had she disappointed him? Was he sorry that he had tied his life to hers, a woman who couldn't even bring him children?

"Next time we will look after you better," said Marta, whose greatest dream was to hold her own grandchild. Irena swallowed her tears. How could she tell them what the doctor had told her that she could not have children? That another pregnancy would be a risk to her. He had already suggested that they register to adopt a child. How could she tell Andre all that? She waited for the right moment, which never came. There was always something: he was busy with his exams, Marta was ill, then they were staying in the home of relatives, another time he was drunk.

One morning Irena woke up to the dog's loud barking. She looked at the clock. It was 6:10. What was the matter with Max? She wondered and curled up in her warm blanket. It was January and cold out. Everyone in the house was still asleep. Maybe he wanted attention. Maybe he was thirsty. She waited a while. But it seemed as though he was possessed, barking endlessly, only stopping now and then only to let out a heartbreaking yowl, as though he sensed some evil approaching.

At eight o'clock, Andre turned on the radio and listened to the news. Ten minutes later Bronek went to the clock shop and asked Irena and Andre to keep quiet because Marta was not feeling well. At 8:15, Irena heard the neighbors quarreling. A morning like any other.

At 8:30, the doorbell rang and the dog resumed barking like mad.

"Andre," Irena called, "Max is whining again." She heard the door creak and Andre calming the dog. She remained in bed, wondering if today should be the day for her to broach the difficult conversation with her husband…

Andre and Irena lived on the first floor of Andre's parents' home. Irena dreamed that one day they would build a house of their own on the plot of land that Uncle Solly had promised to give her. But meanwhile, Andre preferred that they live with his parents. "This way we can save lots of money," he argued. But Irena knew that he was worried about leaving them alone, that he was anxious about his mother. Ever since her beloved son Johann had converted and married that woman, whose name they were all forbidden to utter, Marta's health had been deteriorating.

Irena waited a few more minutes underneath her warm covers until she heard Andre enter the room.

"Irena… please get up, now, it's something awful."

Andre stood pale before her, holding a white envelope in his hand. It bore a stamp with the insignia of the Polish government.

"This just arrived," he said. "I sense something bad…" Irena took the envelope from him and opened it.

"The government of Poland regrets to inform you that your son Johann Yezhnev has been taken captive…"

Irena read the words again, and again, hoping that, eventually, the message would change. They had not said where he was or mentioned what condition he was in.

"Oh God, Irena, this will be the death of my mother."

"Your mother is stronger than you think," said Irena. "She will manage. We have to tell his wife…"

"Irena, please."

"Andre, my love, your brother has a family. Maybe they have even had a baby by now." She was shocked by him. His face turned red. "We have to tell his wife Rachelle."

"We don't know where they live."

"We do know," said Irena and waved the slip of paper that Johann had given her. "This is the village where they live. Johann gave me their address. He hoped that maybe…"

"Don't interfere with this."

"Have you forgotten Rachelle? Andre, she's his wife."

"Not in the eyes of the church. She isn't one of us, she is a Yid who bewitched my brother." He raised his voice. "For the last time, do not get involved!"

"We must speak to Marta."

"Dad will know what to do," he said, and took the envelope from her and crossed the road to his father's clock shop to tell him the terrible news.

Hard days loomed before them, thought Irena, who saw Andre through the window, walking through the snow. The family must come together, look out for one another. They must support and embrace each other. Surely this was not the right time to deliver her own bitter news.

She could not stop thinking of Rachelle. Somewhere out there was a woman who did not know the fate of her beloved. Meanwhile, from the moment she learned of his falling into enemy hands, Marta grew energized. She became a lioness, a warrior mother, and began to run from one government office to another to protest, to try to have him released, to get news of him. She sent letters and packages with the hope that they would reach her son. That wife of his is like a disease to our family, thought Marta, and surely, she hoped, when he is released, he will remember who his real family is, who really cares for him and will come back to us, to eat cookies and the pork sausage that I packed for him, and the Vishniak wine, and will forget about 'her.'

Irena tried, again and again, to talk Andre into traveling together to notify Johann's wife of his captivity.

"Irena, stop it! As far as I'm concerned that woman does not exist, and in the eyes of the church, too."

"But she…"

"Is dead."

She tried to reason with Bronek, to elicit his sympathy

"She's his legal wife," she said.

"No," he said. "Only the church validates marriage. They are not wed in the eyes of God."

"Stop making it so hard for them. You must listen to your husband," said Uncle Solly when she came by his office to ask for his advice.

"It's not right."

"Just be patient. German prison is no summer camp and who knows if he will even..." Solly stopped mid-sentence, afraid to predict the worst. A heavy silence descended upon the room.

"In that case, I have even more reason to go tell her."

"Better that you go to the specialist I found for you," he urged her. "A grandchild will bring joy to all of you and especially for poor Bronek and Marta. That's what you need to do right now."

She tossed and turned all night. If nobody was willing, would she have the courage to visit Rachelle alone and deliver the bad news? After all, she was Johann's wife and she deserved to know.

Irena decided. She knew exactly what she had to do. What she could not have guessed was that from this moment her life was about to change, along with the lives of those around her.

"What happened?" Solly hurried to her when she came into his office the next day.

"I have made a decision," she told Solly. "I will go to her even if Andre won't come with me."

"Think about it... something bad could come of this."

"I will approach it carefully and intelligently," she assured him. "Without hurting Marta. I have to – she is part of my family, that's the least I can do for the poor woman. Uncle Solly, will you help me? I need your assistance."

"What about Andre?"

"In the end, he will understand. Will you help?"

"Have I ever refused you?" he said. "Just be careful. God forbid that Marta should find out. She would never forgive you."

While Irena was planning her journey, finding the right day and a good excuse for traveling without arousing suspicion, dark days fell upon Ciechanow, and her trip was delayed.

It was a day like any other day. The dog dozed by the fireplace, Irena cleared the snow that had piled up on the path to the door, and an appetizing aroma from the pot of soup on the stove wafted through the house. The peaceful morning was interrupted all at once when Bronek returned from his clock shop earlier than usual. Irena was the one to open the door for him and noticed immediately that he looked pale as though he had just seen something terrible.

"What happened now?" cried Marta as soon as she saw him. Ever since the bad news of Johann, everything worried her.

"They took Izak's children."

"I don't understand. Who took them?"

"The Germans. Yesterday. All three of them."

"What will they do with them?"

"They have lists… They gave an order. Don't you see what's happening? They're getting rid of the Jews."

"All the Jews?"

"No, for now just the young, healthy ones, anyone able to work. They're sending them to a work camp, where they will do forced labor. They're prisoners there and the living conditions are terrible."

"Well," said Marta, "It's them, not us. Let them work a bit. Why are you so upset? Work never hurt anybody."

"Didn't you hear? The Germans are talking about a Final Solution for the Jews."

"And that's what you're all worked up about?" Marta let out a small laugh. "They're saying they will give them some new place to settle and live. Look at you, our son is a prisoner of war and you're worried about the Jews?"

"They're Poles, like us."

"Just so you know, lots of our friends think that we should get rid of the Jews, that maybe it's time to cleanse the city."

"Where will they take them?" asked Irena.

"To a work camp beside the village Oswiecim: 'Auschwitz.'"

"I know that place," said Andre. "It's actually nice there."

"Don't get so worked up." Marta brought him a glass of wine. "Better we worry about our son."

Since the occupation, many things had changed beyond recognition.

German soldiers marched in the streets, sometimes stopping the locals and checking their papers. There was a shortage of vegetables and eggs in the shops. It was said that the German army had confiscated everything in order to feed their soldiers. From time to time they declared a curfew and it was forbidden to walk around at night. Cinemas closed and firewood was rationed, but that was nothing compared to what was imposed on the Jews of Ciechanow. Like everyone else, Irena saw the great exodus of the Ciechanow Jews eastward towards the Russian border, the demolition of the beautiful synagogue by the Germans as soon as they took over the city, the local Jews moving to a different part of the city, to the ghetto, and living there in terrible overcrowding. On the radio, she heard Hitler's screaming threats that it was time to be rid of the Jews.

Some of Ciechanow's Jews escaped in time leaving behind their houses and all of their belongings. Those who did not were forced into the ghetto. Some Polish citizens took over these houses until the Germans issued a command that it was forbidden to invade the houses without permission and only a few were granted such a privilege. Meanwhile, many suddenly had glittering chandeliers, new dishes, and white tablecloths, and the cultured among them showed off their newly acquired paintings and tapestries.

One morning as Irena walked to the bakery, she heard wailing, cries, and the sounds of shattering glass. A crowd of local people was gathered around the furniture shop that had belonged to Menachem Levy, fighting. They watched as thugs smashed the large glass window, broke into the store, and began carrying away pieces of furniture. The onlookers watched, stunned.

"Quick, take what you can, it's free!" shouted one of them and ran inside.

"It belongs to the Jews," yelled a young man carrying a table on his back. "Free for the taking."

"Quick, quick!" Two women ran in front of her carrying wicker chairs. Some hurried away to avoid seeing what was happening or getting involved and only a few who dared raise their voices in protest.

Yes, the city had changed. Some said, "So much the better, finally we are rid of them, thank God those bloodsucking Yids will no longer mix with the Poles." On more than one occasion, Irena saw children throwing stones at an elderly man or a woman pushing a baby carriage with the yellow badge on their sleeves.

Meanwhile, the painful sight of young Jews standing close together beside the city hall, clad in their coats, each with fear in their eyes and a suitcase in their hands, waiting to be sent away, became so common that people stopped reacting. As if the displacement of human beings had become a routine matter.

"I have an idea," said Marta when Andre told her they were looking for a house. "Let me look into it." Marta believed in the connections she and Bronek had among the new rulers.

A few weeks after the occupation, a German officer by the name of Hans Albrecht visited Bronek's watch shop. For a moment Bronek feared that the Germans might confiscate his store too, but he soon found that Hans simply loved watches and clocks. He loved to hear them ticking, their ring, the staccato movement of the hands. Bronek's shop looked like a congenial place to amuse himself.

He told Bronek that before enlisting he had served as a watchmaker's apprentice in his village, and he missed it. Bronek and Hans Albrecht spoke about clocks, about the weather, about Polish schnapps and vodka, and afterward, they spoke of their children and their wives. And so it was no wonder that after several such visits, Hans was invited to their home.

It was Marta's idea. She believed that good relations with the Germans would help her discover the fate of her son, and might speed his release or at least open certain channels for her.

Irena, however, was disgusted by the German who, after a few glasses of schnapps, became rude and loud and tried to stroke her bottom. Marta demanded that Irena help her with preparations for the guest. She refused. As she saw it, bonding with the enemy was traitorous. Andre thought differently and implored her to be kind to him. He believed that the Germans knew how to be good to those who were good to them, and he had plans.

"Tell me, little one," he embraced her, "You want a house of your own, isn't that right? So, let him touch your bottom and sign the paper, that's all I ask of you."

After the first dinner, Hans became part of the household. Sometimes he would bring along friends and bottles of German schnapps, sometimes sausage or a fine cut of meat that could no longer be acquired in the market. After several such visits, he promised to find out what had become of Johann, of whom the family had heard nothing since the news of his falling into captivity.

Not everyone in town looked kindly upon these new social ties, especially in light of the mobilization of young people for the Polish underground that had begun to organize in the south of the country. There were those who avoided greeting them when they entered their favorite coffee shop. When she went shopping, Irena felt the bitter gaze of others boring into her back.

Marta claimed that they were just jealous. "Believe me, any of them would be happy to trade places with us. Only yesterday, dear Hans had brought them German sausage and schnapps."

It was no wonder that while indulging in their gluttony and joy, Heidrich, one of the officers who joined in the dinners, had an idea.

"What do you do, Andre?" he asked. Andre blushed and told him that he taught German and history, then muttered that lately his salary had been reduced since he had fewer students than before.

"He's a talented boy," Marta interrupted. "He speaks German like he was born German."

Hans looked at Heidrich, who said immediately, "If you want, you could work for us. The work is good and the pay is excellent."

"No!" screamed Irena, "He can't! He promised my father that…" Marta shot her a withering glance.

"Great," said Hans. "Come to our offices tomorrow and we will discuss it."

To Irena's chagrin, Andre was invited to be a translator for the German headquarters in occupied Warsaw: to be a liaison for the Polish population.

"It's an important job," his new friends told him.

Marta was proud of her son, but Irena continued to try to dissuade him.

"It's easy work," he explained to her. "Just translating the instructions, the commands, and in a few weeks, when I get settled, you can come and join me."

"But Andre…"

"I expect you to be supportive," he said. "Think of the future that awaits us – the Germans will stay here forever. For your information, some of my good friends have asked me to try to arrange some work for them too."

"It's called collaborating with our enemies."

"Enough," he rebuked.

"Be happy for your husband," said Marta. "He's building important connections for us." Marta, whose maternal grandfather was a German quarry engineer, with many relatives living in Germany, was proud of her German lineage.

"Please Andre, turn it down."

"Impossible! You want them to send me away to a work camp too?"

"You? Why?"

"They told me that they're recruiting Poles, too. Listen, my love: give me sons, maybe girls too, and everything will be fine."

"With the help of the Lord Jesus our Savior," she crossed herself.

"Hopefully soon we will be given a house of our own. Think of the goldfish that will swim in the small pond in the yard of our new home, with a white fence and daffodils."

She knew she had lost the argument.

"And who will look after Johann's wife?"

"We said that that matter is closed," he said angrily. "I don't want anything to do with her. Are you trying to ruin everything I'm working toward?"

"Why do you think it would ruin it?"

"God forbid they should find out that my brother married a Jew. Everything we are planning will be for nothing, do you understand?!" He raised his voice, saw that he had frightened her, and immediately changed his tone and embraced her. "I ask that you rest. Gather your strength. After all, we want at least two boys, and maybe a daughter who will be as beautiful as you."

She was silent. He was waiting for her to get pregnant and bring him children. Many children to fill the house they spoke of. And that was precisely what she feared. What would happen if he discovered the truth? After all, she would have to tell him eventually.

CHAPTER 7

1939 - 1940 Krasne

Johann had plenty of reasons for building our house in Krasne. He loved the serenity and calm, the beauty of the place, the beautiful lake that we could see from our bedroom window, and no less important, the village was close to Johann's regiment's base, on the way between Krasne and Bialystok. We were happy in that peaceful, little town.

Here come the long summer days
Days of happiness and laughter
The larks chirp in the sky,
Daffodils smile from their garden bed
The day is long, the sunset glowing
And my heart rejoices in true love

I sang the whole summer of 1939 from the moment we moved into our home in the village on the golden lake. I was so happy in our flower garden that I practically floated. I did not know how soon that happiness would end.

We had arrived in the village by carriage. Eventually, the carriage made a turn, Johann stopped, wrapped his arms around me, swung me around, and set me down, and said, "Look."

Before us, stood a beautiful house with ivy climbing up the walls, covering it in green leaves. I faced the greenish metal gate which opened onto a marble staircase. On both sides stood tall cypress trees that looked like they were waiting to welcome the new homeowners.

"The entire kingdom for my queen," my beloved said. "Look, my dear, this is our house."

I cried, "Why, Johann, really? It's amazing, my love..." and I leaped into his arms.

He froze for a moment and then burst out laughing. He laughed so hard that he stumbled and I fell on top of him. The carriage driver saw and hurried to help us up. Once we arrived at the door, Johann, according to tradition, picked me up in his arms and across the threshold of our home.

It stood empty except for one lonely table. I looked at it.

"Don't worry, my love," he laughed and spread out several blankets. "The furniture will arrive soon." Who cared? The floor was enough for our love.

The house in Krasne was the only house in which we lived together. It was a short-lived happiness. How could we have known that we only had a few months remaining? The dark clouds that would cover all of Europe were already darkening in the west, and a terrible storm would soon come and destroy everything, all of people's naive hopes and dreams. How could we know that on Polish land, millions of people would be murdered without resistance just because they were of the race that someone had decided was unwelcome? But in the meantime, we were still in our home in Krasne and I was floating like a happy butterfly.

There were barely sixty families living in the village. I eventually learned that seventeen of them were Jewish families. I could identify them immediately, especially the men who wore the black shtreimel hats on their heads and whose prayer shawl tassels emerged from their shirts.

What do lovers need? Just to look into the eyes of their beloved and believe that their bond will last an eternity. Three days after sleeping on the floor, embracing, and eating only bread and cheese, the crates with our belongings arrived.

The dogs barked like crazy, the cows awoke and lowed, and the village children ran happily ahead of the two wagons that brought our furniture and household items. Many curious eyes followed us as we began to organize the house. In the evening, two smiling neighbors knocked on the door and offered us an aromatic potato pie.

I invited them inside and they laughed, casting a quick glance around, giving us their blessings, and hurrying off to tell others of the beautiful house, of the red carpet, the velvet cushions, the sixteen-armed chandelier, the radio, and the telephone that the army had installed.

A new life began.

We were far away from Johann's parents, who were so opposed to our union, and far from my father, who carried his grief silently and would send me long letters full of love without acknowledging my status as a married woman.

Johann would come to the village on weekends and immediately go out to tend the big garden that surrounded the house and then, weather permitting, we would take our little paddleboat out on the lake and he would sing funny songs to me in his deep voice.

Sometimes his friends from the regiment would join us and find themselves rewarded with a good meal and fine wine. The villagers soon learned that I was a doctor, and I immediately became well-liked. I was called upon time and again to bandage a child who had fallen, to help a woman in labor, to treat an elderly woman who had tripped and broken her leg, or to treat eye infections. When I refused payment, they would give us what they could, and more than once I found fresh eggs by our door, bouquets of flowers, good cheeses, or homemade pies.

On our evening walks, people would wave to us from the windows of their homes, or come out to greet us warmly, inviting us in to taste the cabbage soup or the fresh honey cake they had made.

"They tell me that everyone here is in love with you," said Johann. "Don't be modest, that beautiful bouquet of daffodils on the stairs was certainly meant for you."

"You know what I think of neighborly relations."

"You're right. Next week I will teach the children to fish."

"Are you competing with me?"

"I'm learning from you," he said and took me in his arms.

My Johann.

There was only one thing that disrupted our happiness.

Church.

We had to be smart concerning the matter of church.

Going to the Sunday sermon is much more than a visit to the church. It is an important social gathering, a way to make friends and share in the joys and sorrows of others, to gossip, and whatever else.

Johann said that as far as he was concerned, I could stay home. And if I wished, he would stay home too. It seemed unimportant to him, even though he had grown up in a devout Catholic household.

Two weeks after we arrived, the village priest, Father Adam, came to visit us bearing barley bread and wine. Father Adam was beloved in the little village. He was seventy years old when he left his big church in Lodz and chose to manage the little community in his old age. He wanted to spend the end of his career closer to his community.

He was very friendly and asked that we try to come to the sermon since it was a nice way to be a part of the community. Before he left, he asked casually if I attended church regularly.

This matter of church had not yet come up between Johann and me. He claimed that he was an atheist and the matter was not at all important to him. But in the little village, a place where everyone knows everything about everybody else, I knew that they expected us to participate. The church was an important place. Until now, I had not had to explain that I was Jewish and the neighbors assumed that the Polish officer was married to a devout Polish Catholic woman.

Only this time, I was being asked directly. It was clear to me that the priest had come to clarify, that perhaps there were already rumors about me. About the high-quality cut of pork that I refused to buy, despite the butcher's insistence, the candlesticks on Friday nights or the menorah in our home. I didn't hide it, I just did not publicize the matter of religion.

Johann pulled Father Adam after him to see his garden and the matter was postponed. It was clear to me that it was just delayed and that I would have to speak with Father Adam sooner than later.

A week later, I went to the church alone.

When I entered, he said that he had waited for a visit and that he was sure I would come, which pleased him. He was happy to speak to me on the subject.

"You know..."

"That you are Jewish, yes, it was clear to me."

"Does that bother you?"

"Not here. It's a very tolerant community. I understand you were well-received and that people really took a liking to you."

"I feel like I am expected to attend church. What should I do so as not to offend or make anyone angry?"

"Be calm, my child," he said with a peaceful smile. "There are Jewish families in the village, only you...are a little different. I suggest..." He stopped speaking and got lost in his thoughts. For a moment I thought he had fallen asleep.

"We will take the main road," he said suddenly.

"What does this have to do with the main road?"

"The main road is always central, visible. I think it is better that you not hide the fact that you are Jewish. It will be harder for you and others if they find out that you were hiding. As if you were cheating."

He placed his hand on his chest and said, "I suggest that you come to church on Sundays after the service, and after the ceremonies, wait for Johann beside the church. If they ask, answer honestly that you are a daughter of the religion of Moses and that you pray in your own place of worship."

"But..."

"Trust me, my child," he said. "Everything will work out with the help of your Moses and our Jesus."

The following Sunday, I waited, as we had agreed upon, beside the entrance to the church. When Johann came out, Father Adam was by his side. He greeted me warmly and asked about my well-being. I felt eyes boring into my back, the questions prompted by this encounter.

"It's a shame you were not at the sermon," one of the neighbors said to us. "It was so interesting."

The priest held my arm and said, "Our Rachelle will serve her God in her own way."

"Because you are...?"

"Yes," I answered simply. I knew that shortly everyone would know.

I did not know that knowledge of my being Jewish would have dangerous consequences in the future. That the day would come when the neighbors would report me as a Jew.

Meanwhile, everyone loved everyone, regardless of their religion or beliefs.

People were as friendly with us as ever. The villagers grew accustomed to seeing me waiting for Johann at the end of prayers and the priest greeting me warmly. I would open the curtains when I lit the Shabbat candles without worry.

Sometimes I would send almond cookies or buns I had made to the priest via Johann, and he would accept my offerings and give his blessings. Sometimes he would come to visit us for Friday prayers and listen to the blessings. We knew that he was doing everything in his power to pave the way for us so that I would be accepted as part of the community, despite my religion. And indeed, after the rumors spread, after I was asked, again and again, after checking and whispering, the villagers got used to their Jewish villager Rachelle. That's what they called me, 'our Rachelle.' Sometimes they called me 'Doctor Rachelle.' It was still easier for them to say than Rachel.

We were so busy with the small joys of a new couple, so preoccupied with our love, that we ignored the rumors that came to us from Germany of the news of the race laws being imposed on my people and the threats of Hitler who promised to cleanse Europe of the Jews.

Even when we saw Jews moving east, toward the Russian border, we were still not worried.

In any case, what could we have done? My fate was tied up with that of Johann, a decorated Polish officer. Sometimes the refugees would stop beside my house and I would serve them fresh water or something sweet for the children. I would look at them and ask myself if they knew anything? Did they feel that it was time to move on from here? What were they afraid of?

I was not afraid. I believed that Hitler would be satisfied with the annexation of Sudetenland.

"He will get his fill and he will ease up," said Johann when I told him of the convoys of refugees moving east, people who had been uprooted from their homes. There were refugees who told of persecution of Jews all over Germany, of decrees and race laws, of Kristallnacht, in which synagogues all over Germany were burned down. They believed that this was just the beginning, that Hitler meant everything he said.

"Who, him? That little, screaming man?"

Johann refused to worry and I gave in to his complacency.

On September 1st, 1939, our lives and those of millions of Europeans changed. Our Poland had just been the first step in a series of occupations. This next step wasn't another annexation or fiddling with the borders. This time there was a declaration of war.

That same week, Johann was on a special vacation. He wanted to get our garden ready for autumn planting. The phone rang. Both of us froze.

Only the military headquarters could call us.

He looked at me, his face serious, as he listened to the instructions and afterward said, "War."

Johann was being called urgently to return to his battalion which was being transferred from eastern to western Poland, to the Poznan region. That was all I knew.

He went to perform his duty.

"I am going to save Poland," he said as he prepared to leave. "For you and for our six children."

"We agreed on two," I laughed.

"We'll discuss that later. Wait for me, my love?"

"I will wait, my love. Go and show them."

"You remember where the gun is, yes?"

"Surely I won't need it."

"But you remember?!" I nodded my head. Yes, I remembered.

We stood silently for a moment, as if in prayer, and I silently whispered words of King David that I remembered, 'I shall pursue my enemies and overtake them and I shall not return until I finish."[6]

"Wife, what did you whisper just now, speak Polish," he laughed.

"I just said you should be strong my love. Go, conquer our enemy."

"My love," he said and took off his medals of excellence and pinned them to my coat. "Now you are also a hero of Poland."

We laughed. I did not know that this medallion would have an important role in my story. He held me close, got on his horse, and passed his hand over my head again. He began to ride, his curls moving in the wind, his face growing blurry in the distance. A cry issued from my mouth, as though a sword had pierced my heart. I began to run after him, begging him to stop, not to go, to stay here with me, but he went on and disappeared until I could no longer hear the receding sound of his horse's hooves.

I was overcome with grief. Something within me told me that maybe this was the last time I would see him. Then the fear abated and I immediately wiped away those terrible thoughts. After all, my husband was a heroic soldier, a courageous warrior. He would come back and bring us victory.

That same night I prayed to the God of Abraham, Isaac, and Jacob to watch over him, and my father, and the beloved village, and our country, Poland.

---

6   Book of Psalms 18:37

CHAPTER 8

The battles were short, fast, and painful. Germany's iron fist landed a victorious blow to Poland's army. Rumors of war had reached our little village. We saw long convoys of refugees moving east, the tanks leaving deep grooves in the earth as they passed, and the Polish military trucks coming and going.

We could hear the thunder of the cannons from afar. Only a few households in the village had a radio and one of them was ours. It was our primary source of information. In the evening, the neighbors would gather in our small kitchen with a cup of hot tea and cookies that I had made, taking the opportunity to ask for medical advice and listening to news from the front.

We went on listening to the reports from the front, trying to understand what was really happening. There were moments when it seemed that we might be victorious, and we were happy, only to immediately realize we had been mistaken. Every now and then, someone would bring a newspaper, a few days old, full of promises and hopes that the army would stop the invasion, that our soldiers would beat back the intruders. After three weeks passed, we began to understand that all was lost. The convoys of refugees grew greater, and they told us what was happening in western Poland. I prayed to my God, in my heart, as they prayed to Jesus, son of God, and his mother, Mary.

The bitter news arrived on September 29th. Warsaw, our beautiful capital, had fallen to the Germans. That was a hard pill to swallow. People burst into tears and as they left, they took my hand and expressed their wish that Johann would return safe and sound. I hadn't heard from Johann in quite some time.

I had received two letters from him early on. One was written three days after the invasion and the second two days later. I missed him so much that it hurt. I wrote to him every day telling him of the daffodils and the joys and sorrows of life in the village. I would drop the letter in the mailbox in the village center and add a prayer for his safety.

Rumors of what was going on in the occupied capital were beginning to reach our peaceful village. Merchants who stopped in the village to sell their goods told us what they had heard of refugees fleeing the battle zone, and what the Germans were doing. That's how I learned that only two weeks after the fall of Warsaw, the Germans began to erect the ghetto. A few months later, an order was given for all Jews to move there. From that moment on, Jews were forbidden to live in the city apart from those streets that had been enclosed by the Germans with a wall. This was the first step in the horrific killing spree that would result in the murder of over six million people whose only sin was that they had been born Jewish. The Germans did not wait too long to prove that they stood behind their threats and that they were determined to wipe out my people.

The crowding in the ghetto was intolerable. Four families lived in one apartment. The hunger and density brought disease alongside exhaustion and severe mental distress. Corpses began to pile up in the streets, which only made the situation more dangerous. Ghettos were established in cities all over Poland along with forced labor camps. Jews were forced to work in arms factories, sewing uniforms, paving streets, and all under terrible conditions with scarce food supplies and insufficient nutrition. Mortality in the ghettos was high.

My people were left defenseless. They were outside the protection of the law. There was explicit instruction that it was forbidden to shelter a Jew or help in any way. In the Germans' eyes, we were subhuman and deserved extermination. Our lives were worthless.

My situation was different. On the one hand, I was a Jew, the daughter and granddaughter of a rabbi. But on the other hand, I was the wife of an officer, a Polish war hero, who was fighting the Germans. It was as though I had two identities. Two women: Rachelle, the doctor, the wife of Johann who had promised to wait for him to vanquish the Germans. And Rachel the Jew, whose people were being uprooted and shut away in the ghettos. Rachel, who seemed estranged from what was happening to them.

Month followed month, and something inside of me changed. I felt a greater closeness to my battered people. I reconnected with the roots from which I had moved away. I found a small, supportive community among the families that remained. I was actually prouder than ever of my Jewish identity, my Jewish faith. They took me in as part of their family. Now I spent Friday nights in the homes of my Jewish friends. Sometimes at the home of the teacher, or the welder, or the shoemaker, helping the women put the children to bed.

And Johann? And my father who was alone?

What would become of me?

Would they take me from here and place me in the ghetto too?

My mind said: Get up and run, save your life, follow the Jews that are getting out of here. Go east.

But my heart would not let me. I was afraid to leave the village in case Johann should return. I waited. I had to wait. I had promised him.

Other voices came on the radio. German voices. The new lords of Poland. They spat out commands and explained that it was important for regular life to carry on and that everyone must do as they normally would and pay attention to the instructions. Obey, obey, obey. That was the word repeated over and over again.

Now we had to obey the foreigners who controlled Poland. There was silence in the small, peaceful village. Every so often the quiet was shattered by a truck loaded with German soldiers sitting upright, their faces frozen, or by motorcycles, patrol planes circling above us, or by the sounds of the endless convoys of refugees heading east.

And I waited. I knew that the moment Johann could, he would come to get me, or at least send a telegram, message, letter. He would not forget me…

I also did not hear anything from my father. I wrote to him many times and received no response. Sometimes I would head out down the main road, offering sandwiches to the refugees and checking to see if any of them had heard what had happened to the people of Pruszkow,[7] the town where my father lived.

---

7   In November of 1940, the Pruszkow ghetto was established with 600-1000 Jews inside. The crowding was terrible. One-hundred and eighty workers remained in the town who were sent out to do forced labor. In 1942 the remaining workers were finally sent to the extermination camp, Treblinka; only a few dozen of Pruszkow's Jews survived.

CHAPTER 9

They would listen and sadly shake their heads.

"It's near Warsaw," I would explain. "My father was a rabbi." They had not heard anything. They were heading east, toward the Russian border; maybe the war would not reach them there.

"I know that they moved all the Jews from there to the ghetto," a woman holding a baby told me one day.

"Are you from there?"

"No, but my husband's parents..." she wiped away a tear. "They didn't make it."

"What will become of my father? He isn't well."

"Sorry," they said, their faces impassive, and continued on their way.

One day a letter came from Bialystok. One of my father's students had found my address among his belongings and he wrote to me the first chance he had. Evidently, the Germans had moved my father along with the rest of his community into the Pruzskow ghetto.

Your father was a righteous man. He did not complain about the terrible conditions. He continued to keep our spirits up until his illness overwhelmed him. Even in his final moments he spoke of you, his only daughter, with love and hoped with all his heart that at least you might be saved.

Along with the letter he included photographs that he had found in my father's room. One of them was of Johann and I on our wedding day. He had kept it though it must have been painful for him.

I mourned him for seven days. For seven days I prayed and asked for his forgiveness. I begged that he demand of God, in whom he so ardently believed, to help our people.

My Jewish neighbors kept me company for the duration of those seven days. They brought me food, stews, and baked goods, and came evening after evening to say the mourner's prayer and to bless his memory. Even Father Adam came to express his condolences.

Should I have gone to him, to be with him in his last moments? Could I have done anything to help? Would he have forgiven me? I felt great guilt bearing down on me.

My father's death undermined the hope I had maintained up until that point. At the same time, the once peaceful village was growing tense and unbearable.

I tried to carry on with my routine life. In the mornings, I tended to the flowers in our garden. I went on caring for the sick, visiting the elderly in their homes. I organized the village women and together we knitted woolen hats and mittens for the refugees who passed through.

Then I discovered that Johann's seed had been planted within me and new life was growing inside my body. Two months after the war began, I knew for certain: I was pregnant. But my happiness was clouded with sorrow.

We had so badly wanted a child, a baby of our own, but was this really the time to bring a child into the world? Who knew what awaited him in the future? Was this any time to raise children when all around us were tanks and planes and convoys of refugees filling the roads?

Father Adam, a dear friend, would make sure to pass by my house to check if I needed any help, or if there had been any news, but I had not heard from Johann. With my father gone, too, I had nothing left. He would whisper a prayer on our behalf, and for the village, then continue on his way. I was very busy in those days. Many people suffered great anxiety, growing sicker and sicker on account of the stress, and the local doctor was happy that I was lightening his load.

In mid-October, bitter news arrived in the village. The milkman's son had been killed in a battle defending Warsaw. For many days we heard his mother weeping and his father's angry cries. I made sure to visit them daily to look after the poor woman. Later came the grandson of the mayor, poor boy; the doctors had had to amputate his leg and he would come to me for treatment.

And Johann? It was as though he had simply been swallowed up by the earth.

When I called the telephone number that I had for him, nobody answered, as though it had been permanently disconnected. I called anyone who might be able to help, who might know what had become of his regiment, but I found nothing. I feared the worst.

There were clashes in the village. Our Poland, our beautiful homeland had been conquered, and there was a feeling of shared destiny among the villagers.

"How is Johann?" Neighbors would wave to me.

I would wave back, "I still have not heard from him, unfortunately."

"I pray for him," said one.

"I'm sure he is on his way back to you," said another.

"Maybe it's better like this — in times of war, no news is better than the news," said the elderly Masha, who made her living telling fortunes.

Shared destiny. That's what I believed. All of us in the same boat: Poles and Jews. Until one morning a shiny, black car crossed the main street of the village. The car stopped beside the council house.

The word 'Gestapo' was whispered and a no less terrible word: list. They were making a list.

I felt like I couldn't breathe. Ten minutes later, the mayor, Anton Ruslinksy, was ejected from the building with a grim expression.

"The poor man was shamefully let go," the rumor spread in the village, "and they put some clown in his place."

"What are they looking for here?" I asked Welda, his secretary.

"Just…" Welda began to speak and blushed red, "a list of the Jews who live in the village."

"For what?"

"They said they have a plan for you."

The Gestapo had arrived in my peaceful village and had demanded lists.

Johann, I prayed that night, come back here. I felt as though the floor was collapsing, as if there was no solid ground beneath my feet.

A few months after Johann left to fight for his country, the Jewish families who still remained in the village had received an order from the new head of council, Valdak Soviensky, that required us to wear yellow badges. Then the chickens and cows, the plows, and all of our tools were confiscated and handed over to the "trustees." Jews were prohibited from using public transportation, from leaving their homes after six in the evening, and other restrictions that the clown who sat in the municipal offices would announce with twisted pleasure. I was in a strange position.

On the one hand, I was the Jewish descendant of a long line of rabbis, and on the other hand, married to a Polish war hero. I lived between the two worlds. I received my yellow badge but when I got it, the head of the village council winked at me, "You don't have to. After all, you're one of us. How's our Johann?"

The situation for Jews grew worse and there were frequent rumors of thugs in the area stopping Jewish carriages and hauling out their wares, stopping Jews and shaving their beards, stealing their produce and fruits from their trees.

Valdak, the new mayor, was a drunken fool, a boor, and man of the people, whose primary job was to carry out the instructions of those who were really in charge. As a reward, he confiscated the fine house of Shlomo Lazar, the school principal, for himself.

"It is unsuitable that a Jew should live in such a splendid house, it belongs to the council," he announced, justifying his actions.

Shlomo Lazar gathered his family and disappeared into the dark of night.

The mayor enlisted several other town idlers to help as council members, giving them fancy new uniforms, money for vodka, and in particular, permission to abuse the Jewish families. While some Jews had left, others had decided to stay. They said they were not worried. After all, they'd been here for five, six generations. They wore their yellow badges that set them apart from the rest of the villagers and thought that that would be the extent of their hardships.

One dark night, Yosef, one of the village Jews who remained, came to me and requested my help. His wife Esther had fainted and the village doctor, apparently according to some new orders, refused to treat her. He claimed that he was busy, too tired. The excuses of a coward.

I hurried to their home. Esther smiled at me. "I'm fine, I'm sorry he disturbed you." But she was not fine. She could barely lift her arms.

I checked her. She was very weak.

"What happened Esther?"

"A lot of stress, unease."

"A good recipe for weakness and dizziness. When is the last time you ate?"

"I don't know," her eyes looked sad.

"You have to get stronger," I gave her some of the vitamins I had. "I recommend rest and drinking lots of fluids. Why are you stressed?"

"We were informed that they took my father and younger brother to the work camp, who knows if I will ever see them again."

"You must believe, with all your heart, that they will return."

"From what I have heard it sounds like people are dying there of hunger and diseases. My father is not a healthy man."

I stroked her face and waited for her to fall asleep.

Before I left the house, her husband pulled me into the kitchen.

"Tell me what is happening to her."

"She is very weak. We must look after her. Stress in her condition is a real threat."

"She has not slept for weeks. Since they took her father and brother, she won't stop crying. I hear her roaming the house all night."

"I gave her a sleeping pill just now – she will sleep tonight." I gave him the three more pills that I had. "I will try to get more vitamins."

"We have to get out of here. Every day it gets harder. Do you think we will manage?"

"In her condition, I am afraid not," I said. "Where would you go?"

"To the Russian border. At least there they aren't chasing Jews and there is work. Bad things are happening to our people. You should look out, too."

"I am not sure that she will manage the challenges of the road. It's too dangerous."

"I don't know where it's more dangerous, here or there. I hear about things happening here and in the nearby villages and worry for my family."

"Just wait a few more days until she recovers somewhat."

"We don't have a few days… Yesterday two village urchins came into my yard, stole three chickens, and uprooted a tree, then laughed, just like that, in the middle of the day."

"Police?"

"Police," he smiled bitterly. "You know as well as I do who the new police are: a gang of good-for-nothings chosen by that clown. Hitler opened the door and now all of us are as good as…"

"Not all of them are like that."

"But nobody will stop them. Yesterday a family stopped on their way east. They told stories of atrocities, of soldiers who entered their neighbors' house and shot the whole family, just like that. Then they laughed and as they came out, they shouted to anyone hiding in their houses, that that's what the Fuhrer will do to all the Jews, that this was only the beginning."

"I will come by tomorrow and check if she's gotten any better."

"What about you?"

"I am waiting for my husband. He knows that I will wait for him for as long as I have to."

"Run away, Rachel, this storm will sweep everyone away."

"My husband is a Polish officer."

"You think that matters to Hitler? You have to escape."

"I am waiting for my husband, for Johann, and if he comes back and doesn't find me... I promised him."

"If you change your mind... Listen, when my wife gets better, we will go to Bialystok. If you come after we go, look for us there."

"The Germans conquered Bialystok, too."

"According to the agreement they made, they gave it back to the Russians. We will go there and, hopefully, we can quietly wait out the war, or until the madman is removed. You can join us."

"Johann will come back and then I will decide," I told him and he hugged me warmly.

When I arrived at Yosef's house the following day to check up on Esther, I found it empty and saw some of the villagers collecting pieces of clothing and furniture left behind by the fugitives.

My village slowly emptied out of all its Jews.

Was I nervous? Was I afraid for my life?

I had many friends, I believed, and so I was not afraid that they would hurt me. Also, the fact that I was married to a Polish officer was significant – even that clown Valdak would tip his hat to me when he passed by my house. He would inquire how I was and ask that I pass on his greetings to my husband the hero.

Three months passed and I still had not received any signs of life from Johann. I waited for him. I had such good news to tell him.

CHAPTER 10

Krasne 1940

Two weeks after Andre left town, Irena traveled to Krasne, the village where, according to Johann's note, her in-laws lived. She was forced to hire a carriage as it was impossible to make the journey there by train. She explained to Andre's parents, who did not approve, that she was traveling to help her mother take care of her father, who had fallen down and injured himself. Marta protested, suggesting that maybe she should join her since maybe, just maybe, she might once again be in that special condition and God forbid something might happen to her.

"Don't worry, I will be back in two days."

"But maybe..." Marta warned her daughter-in-law. "Just be careful, the Germans are checking papers and identification."

"Everything is in place," she waved her papers, which she kept in her pocket. "It's just a two-hour trip, Marta, don't worry. I will arrive tonight or tomorrow morning at the latest."

Bronek placed pillows and blankets in the carriage so that she would not be shaken about too much, if at all. Marta packed her sausage sandwiches, fruit, and cheese. They remained standing in the street and waving goodbye to her until the carriage had traveled too far away to be seen.

The cold chilled the bones, the carriage bounced over the potholes that were left in the paths from the rain, the road was muddy and slippery and the cart driver, Yuzhik, stopped more than once to lay down wooden boards so that the horse's feet would not slip. A light snow fell and covered the slick mud. The journey took longer and longer as every so often they were passed by heavy tanks that plowed the trails and they were forced to move aside. Tarp-covered trucks and motorcycles passed them, spraying mud on them. More than once they were stopped by German soldiers who checked the carriage and underneath the blankets lest they be smuggling some weapons or hiding some Polish underground soldiers of the Krajowa army, which had already begun to harass the German army.

There were planes overhead. "That's a Messerschmitt," Yuzhik announced, proud of his knowledge of weapons and planes. But she barely listened. She was thinking of Andre. She felt pained that she had had to hide the truth from his parents. That was not how she had been raised. And what would Andre say when he heard what she was doing? It's all for the good, she calmed herself, maybe this visit will bring the family together and peace will come, at least to their home.

"Poor Poland," said Yuzhik, who was young and eager. "If I did not have to support my family, I would show the Germans."

"Don't worry," Irena said. "Our army will recover and strike them a hard blow."

"You think so?"

"Wait and see. Long live free Poland!"

"Amen," said Yuzhik. "From what I understand, the military has been smashed to smithereens."

"You'll see. It will rebuild itself."

He crossed himself twice.

When they reached the village, the sun was already high in the sky.

Not a living soul could be seen outdoors. Every so often she heard a cow which was instantly answered by dogs. Then crows in the treetops joined the chorus. The village looked as though it had been entirely abandoned. Yuzhik stopped and waited. On the paper that Johann had given her, there was no street name. All she had was the name of her brother and sister-in-law.

"Here," Yuzhik pointed to a figure approaching, followed by a group of geese.

"Do you know where the house of Rachelle and Johann is?" She asked the man as he approached. He shook his head and replied that he had not heard of them and did not know. Nor did the woman who they found hanging her laundry. Nor the two youths who were coming back from school.

To her amazement, nobody seemed to know. Nobody had heard of them and, even more troubling, even if they happened upon someone by chance, he refused to speak with them.

She examined the note again. No, she had not made a mistake, it clearly said: Krasne. This was definitely the right town.

"I think that they are afraid of us," Irena said, and Yuzhik nodded. It was wartime. Everyone was afraid of everyone else, certainly of a woman traveling alone. Who knew what kind of troubles she might be bringing along with her? Perhaps she was sent to spy on them? To find out if they were hiding, God forbid, a Polish soldier or worse, a Jew? They roamed around and around, asking again and again until Yuzhik suggested that they return home.

But Irena was not willing to give up. She had not come this far just to turn around empty-handed. They made another round of the village and then another but still nothing.

"People don't know who you are or why you came here," the shoemaker explained. He was the only one who responded and opened his door to them. "Everyone is afraid, they don't want to interfere. The best thing to do would be to go to our priest, Father Adam. He knows everyone in the community, I am sure he can help you."

CHAPTER 11

She smiled at him. That was a great idea.

In small places such as this, the priest knew everyone and everything. He would help her. They turned onto the path leading to the little church at the edge of the village.

They stopped at the entrance to the church yard.

Hearing the approaching horses, Adam Pozhinsky, the village's priest, came out to greet them. Irena came over to him, kissed his hand, and asked if he happened to know the whereabouts of the young couple Johann and Rachelle — or Rachel, as some called her. He listened impassively and invited her inside.

"Why are you looking for her?"

"I have to inform her of something, something important."

"My daughter," the priest stopped her. "I have to know why it is that you are looking for her."

Irena hesitated for a moment. "I must tell her that her husband, Johann, has been taken captive. She does not know yet." The priest closed his eyes, as though praying.

"Terrible news," he said finally.

"I felt that she deserves to know."

"I'm sure you're right," said the priest and then crossed himself. "And who are you to her?"

"I am her sister-in-law. I am married to Andre, Johann's brother. Could you take me to her?"

"I am sorry to disappoint you but she is no longer here. She left two weeks ago," said the priest. "She left without any note or forwarding address."

Irena felt that what she wanted most at that moment was to sit down on the ground and cry. Rachelle had left? Had her whole trip been in vain? Where had she gone?

Was he afraid of interfering, or could he possibly be hiding something from her?

"Please," she said. "Father, help me, I came all this way because I thought that she should know what has befallen her husband. I wanted to be with her for this hard moment. After all, we're family," she burst into tears.

"Listen," said the priest. "I am a little busy at the moment. Could you come back in three hours? In the evening. In the meantime, I will try to find out if anyone knows where she went."

"Thank you," she kissed his hand and turned to leave. Yuzhik hurried toward her.

"Please come by around five o'clock. Meanwhile, you can eat at the tavern. They have an excellent pork pie."

Yuzhik grimaced and complained. He begged her that they please set off before dark because there may be more snowfall and the road could be dangerous and the horse was tired. She promised him a few more zlotys and he calmed down.

At exactly five o'clock, Irena knocked on the door of the priest's house, beside the church.

Ludmilla, his elderly housekeeper, opened it and, after checking that there was nobody there besides Irena, led her into the dining room.

"Good evening, your holiness," she said and stopped.

Another man was seated beside the priest. When he saw her, he rose to his feet and bowed to her. He was short and round and sported a black mustache.

"Let me introduce Gregory Balantov," said the priest. "This is Rachelle's sister-in-law."

Irena remained standing and waiting. It was clear that Gregory was not there by coincidence.

"Come, sit," said the priest. "Taste the soup."

"Thank you," she went on standing. Waiting.

"You will never taste beet borscht as good as Ludmilla's in all of Poland."

"Thank you," replied Irena. "But all I can think about is what has become of my sister-in-law."

"I think it's best that you eat something."

She finally relented and sat. The old woman filled her bowl with hot soup.

"Now listen," said the priest. "You need not worry. She is in a safe place…"

"Where?"

"Patience, my daughter," he placed his hand on hers, signaling that she wait until Ludmilla leave the room with the plates. "Rachelle, Johann's wife, is in Gregory's cellar…"

"Why?" Gasped Irena. "What happened?"

"Shhh…" The priest placed a finger over his lips. "We must speak quietly. These days it is hard to know who is with you and who would sell his soul to the Germans to betray you."

Irena felt the blood rush to her face. If the priest knew what Andre was doing, maybe he would not have shared his meal with her.

"For her safety, we were forced to move her to a safe place."

"God," Irena was stunned. "What did she do?"

"Her? The opposite, she did only good. But she is of the wrong people."

"I don't understand, my sister-in-law is the wife of a war hero."

"Certainly, but the war hero's wife is Jewish. The Gestapo have already begun sniffing around here looking for Jews. The village thugs took this to mean that the Jews' time was up."

"But her husband is an officer in the Polish army."

"It doesn't help, and it might only make it worse. The Gestapo asked the mayor for a list of Jews. When the thugs started harassing people on the list, I suggested that she leave. The other families who lived in the village were already on their way to the Russian border. She refused to go, she said she had to wait for her husband, that God forbid should he return from battle and not know where she was, so she preferred to stay. Then what happened… happened, and for her safety, we decided to find her a hiding place."

"Jesus Maria, poor girl…"

"She is in good hands," said the priest. "Gregory is her lucky star."

"Thank you, holy father, please take me to her."

"We must wait until after dark, then we can go," the priest sighed. "We can't be too careful these days. You never know who might be spying or reporting or hunting Jews."

"Hunting? You hunt animals, not people!"

"We are in different times now, my child. My village has changed; Poland has changed. The Germans have let loose the demon of anti-Semitism, and people are being hunted and handed over to the Gestapo, sometimes in exchange for a bottle of vodka and some sausage."

She waited another hour and when the village grew silent and the lights went out, they set off. Gregory left before them, and she and the priest walked casually, quietly, speaking in a whisper, as though they were not in a hurry, as though they had just gone for an innocent evening walk in the fresh air.

"Gregory's wife does not know," the priest whispered. "She is sick and barely leaves her bed so there is not much chance that she will go down to the cellar."

Beside a stone house at the end of the path they saw Gregory holding a lantern, and he motioned to Irena to follow him. The priest went inside to visit Gregory's wife and distract her.

Gregory went around to the back of his house and there, hidden behind the yew trees, she noticed a grey door that could barely be seen from the path. He knocked three times on the door, waited a moment, then knocked one more time and once more, then opened the door and motioned for her to come in. He stayed standing guard.

She was met by the sharp smell of mold. She felt dizzy for a moment but covered her face with a handkerchief and went inside.

"Rachelle?"

Only the screeching sounds of frightened mice replied.

"Rachelle, it's me, Irena. I'm Andre's wife."

Slowly her eyes grew accustomed to the darkness and she saw a mattress in the corner of the cellar and on it a pile of blankets and pillows.

"Rachelle, answer me. I'm Irena, Andre's Irena. Rachelle, I'm your sister."

She groped her way forward, and several cockroaches scurried away.

"You know who Andre is, and I'm Irena, his wife."

Now she felt that someone was watching her. She knew that it was Rachelle. She went on speaking from the heart. Was that her face? Were those her eyes peering out from behind that shelf filled with jars of jam?

"Rachelle? Is that you?" She detected black eyes burning like a bonfire, and black hair woven into a braid.

"Don't be afraid of me," Irena took a step closer. "I came to ask how you were."

"Stop!" Rachelle shouted and leaped from her place with a jagged knife in her hands. Irena froze. "What are you doing here?"

"I'm Irena, your sister-in-law, Andre's Irena."

"What do you want?" The young woman gripped the knife in front of her.

"I am your friend, not your enemy."

Rachelle approached Irena and sniffed her like a cat, trying to find out if she had come in peace. Irena remained standing quietly, her arms folded, facing Rachelle.

"Who else is with you?"

"Just me, I promise."

"When did you arrive?"

"In the afternoon."

"Who did you speak with?"

"Nobody. Everybody I asked knew nothing about where you were, even who you were... until I asked the priest."

"Father Adam? You spoke with Father Adam?!"

"Don't panic, yes, Father Adam, he is the one who brought me here and he is upstairs now, at Gregory's."

"Well... in that case nice to meet you," she replied and reached out a hand to shake. "Sorry for the welcome."

She set down her knife and sat down on the mattress. Irena sat in front of her. She knew that suspicion had given way to curiosity.

"What happened? What are you doing here?"

"Everything is fine," Irena replied. "I wanted to meet you, and I had the chance..."

"Is it Johann?"

"He's fine, only..."

"Only?"

"We received a message that he... I'm sorry Rachelle."

"What happened? Speak!"

"We were informed that our Johann was captured and..." Irena heard Rachelle's strangled cry, like a wounded animal. Then she went silent.

After a few moments, she asked, "What kind of condition is he in?"

"We don't know. Marta, his mother, tried to find out... I'm sorry, I thought you needed to know."

Rachelle closed her eyes as though trying to digest the new information. Irena heard her ragged breathing. She did not cry or shout. Only her heart wept bitterly.

"I had a bad feeling when he left," she said.

"I am so sorry."

"And you made this whole trip to tell me."

"I thought you had to know what happened. The army informed his family in Ciechanow."

"And they… they don't see me as his wife, and you…" Irena nodded. A wave of affection came over Rachel. Through the agony, she smiled at the brave young woman.

"Did your husband send you?"

"I came on my own."

"Andre?"

"Nobody knows that I'm here."

"Do they know where Johann is?"

"Just that he is in a German prisoner of war camp. Marta is trying to find him."

"My God, look after him." In one motion she was on her feet, her face red and breathing heavily, as though she meant to escape. She stood that way for several seconds before crumpling to the mattress like a marionette as if the thread that held her had been cut.

Irena approached and sat down beside her, stroked her burning face, and murmured comforting words.

"He'll be back, you'll see."

Rachelle shook her head. "I feel a kind of emptiness. Something bad has happened to him."

"You must not lose hope, we will wait for him together." Rachel smiled through her tears. "You're not alone anymore, I am here with you."

"You are my angel. God sent you to me."

Irena felt her body fill up with new energy. She felt strong and brave. Suddenly she was not afraid of anyone. Nothing would stop her. At that moment she decided to help her sister-in-law as much as she was able. To support her, help her, pray for her.

How could the two women have known that a lifelong friendship would begin that day in Gregory's moldy cellar? That a great, rare love between two special women had been born at that moment. That they were forming a rare bond of generosity and devotion.

"Our days of happiness were numbered," bemoaned Rachel.

"Other days will come again," Irena reassured her.

"Are we being punished for our love?"

Rachel wept silently, her hands muffling any sounds that might arouse suspicion. God forbid the neighbors should hear and endanger Gregory's family, Irena, or herself.

"Forgive me," said Granny Tula, and went outside to the yard. Her face was wet. Mom looked at her quietly.

"What happened to her?" I asked.

"It's hard for her to revisit those days in the cellar, those moments when she realized that her whole life had been turned upside down, and all hope felt lost."

"Do you want us to stop?" I was glad when she shook her head no.

"Why did Gregory agree to risk his family and himself?"

"He was a believer and saw it as an act of Christian kindness."

"Were there many like him in Poland?"

"Very few. There were some who did it for money or jewelry. In exchange for some handsome sum, they would smuggle Jews east. There were monasteries that hid children and there were those who gave Jews refuge in their cellars, barns, yards, and groves without expecting anything in return. We call them 'The Righteous Among the Nations'. Unfortunately, there were not many of them."

"A little humanity in the face of horror."

"It's not so simple. What would you or your brother do? What would anyone have done? To hide Jews in your home and know that if you were caught, you and your children would be killed…"

"I don't know, that's an impossible dilemma."

We sat quietly for a few minutes until Granny Tulla began to speak again.

"Are you all right?"

"Listen, my dear Noga," Granny Tulla turned to me. "The Poles, like the Austrians and the Lithuanians, were happy to hand over Jews to the Germans. Their hatred of Jews ran deep, that antisemitism had been there forever, hidden, and when the Germans came in with their atrocities, it basically gave permission to the rest and it spread like a plague. But yes, there were others who helped us and were willing to take risks. There were people like good Gregory who did it because he believed it was what Jesus would have done."

"How do you know?"

"When we met after the war, he told me that he saw this as his own small war and believed that in that way he could restore some of Poland's honor."

"Shall we continue?" asked Mom.

"Please, let's."

"Remind me where we were?" Mom asked and winked at Granny Tulla.

"We were still in the cellar at Gregory's house. When Irena came and took care of Rachel."

"Good. Now, please no interruptions, no questions, no arguments. Just listen, please."

Irena pulled the crying woman to her into an embrace, whispered words of comfort to her, stroked her hair, rocked her like one would a baby, and then suddenly she realized. She sensed everything.

"Are you... expecting?" she asked and placed her hand on Rachel's belly.

Rachelle nodded. "Johann so wanted a child, a baby of our own, to have my black eyes and his red hair. I think in his heart he thought that maybe if we came to his mother with our baby, her grandchild, she would accept us, she would be happy and forgiving but... now..."

"Does he know?"

"No," she shook her head gravely. "He left for war before I knew myself. Now, he's a prisoner... and I, who knows? I had to leave the house. The Gestapo and their henchmen are looking for me. Even my friends and acquaintances from the village turned on me."

"This hiding place saved you."

"Look at my new palace: the mice are chewing on my leg, and the cockroaches and huge ants are after the little bit of food they give me. I am afraid to fall asleep lest they crawl on me... the smell... the mold... the dense air. My poor baby, what kind of world am I bringing him into?"

"You mustn't lose faith, Rachelle."

"Faith? Don't you see that all is lost? This world is no place for babies."

"When do you expect to give birth?"

"It won't be long now, another two months maybe."

"Two months is a long time. Everything could change."

"I've lost hope, Irena. Maybe it would be better if my baby were never born," her voice cracked.

"Don't talk like that. You will have a beautiful baby," Irena wiped her tears.

"I have no strength left… there's no point."

"Rachelle, you are not alone. You have me."

"I only stayed here because of the pregnancy. To wait for Johann, because maybe he will come back… After all, some came back… And I can't go east, to Russia, what if I were to give birth on the way when it is so cold outside, and snowy, but to have him here? You know that they're shooting Jews like dogs — a baby crying will alert all the Gestapo collaborators right to my door. I'm lost," Rachelle went on. "Don't you understand? I'm a terrible burden to anybody who would wish to help me."

"Stop, wait," said Irena. "Nothing is lost. Let me think."

"Blessed woman," whispered Rachelle. "Go back to your house, your family, your husband. Hurry before the snow covers the path, before Andre finds out."

"Not yet," Irena got up from where she sat and pulled a packet of tobacco out of her jacket pocket. She rolled herself a cigarette, something she occasionally did in private, and only when Andre was not around.

Rachelle remained sitting, rocking as though in prayer.

No, Irena decided. I can't leave Rachelle alone, it's too dangerous. Who knows how long she can hide in this musty cellar with the rats and mold, and the baby… an infant needs good food, fresh air, sunlight, and if he cries… it will surely bring the Jew-hunters. Of course, she said to herself, I have to get her out of here, but where?

"Rachelle," she turned to her. "Maybe I can get you to your parents' home?"

"My parents' house?" Rachelle laughed bitterly. "No such thing, it was destroyed. The Germans sent all of the Jews from my city to the ghetto. My father became ill and died."

"In that case," said Irena quickly, "come with me."

"With you where?"

"To Ciechanow."

"To his parents? Marta and Bronek will hand me over to the Germans the minute I arrive at their home."

"No, you're carrying Johann's child in your womb. When they hear that…"

"They won't want this baby. It's a Jewish woman's baby. They see me as an abominable Jew."

"Trust me. You and I will face them together, and my Andre will support me. You'll meet him, he's a good man, generous. It will all work out fine."

"You're amazing," Rachelle embraced her. "But I worry that you might be naive. It's not a good idea."

"And stay here? When someone could find you here at any moment and endanger Gregory and his family along with you and the baby? Listen, I decided, that's it. You're coming back with me. Let me consult with the priest to plan how we will leave the village without anyone noticing…"

"But Irena, you're not…"

"Don't worry. When Marta finds out you will give her a grandson, all will be forgiven. She's been dreaming of a grandchild, waiting for this moment." It was not the right time to tell her that Marta was disappointed with Irena for not showing any signs of new life herself.

"Wait a minute, let's think if…"

"It's the best option. Please trust me, Marta is a good woman inside. Perhaps angry about the match, but a baby will soften her."

"She's waiting for a grandchild from you, from Andre."

"False hope," Irena whispered.

"What did you say?"

"I said I have a lot to prepare." She went out, then poked her head back inside. "Trust me, sister."

Irena entered Gregory's house. Beside the dining table sat Gregory with the priest. In the bed right beside them lay the thinnest woman she had ever seen, skin and bones, her eyes sunken deep in their sockets.

"Welcome, Irena," the priest rose quickly. "Please, meet dear Zosia and her beloved husband, Gregory. Irena is the daughter of a good friend who studied with me," he explained to the sick woman who stared at her with curious eyes.

"Where are you from?" she asked.

"From Ciechanow."

"Ciechanow… I don't know it," as though if she did not know it, the place did not exist.

"Of course, you know the city, Zosinka," Gregory corrected her. "You don't remember when we visited the Grand Fortress?"

"When?"

"Right after our wedding," he stroked her hand. "We went along with your brother and his wife and on the way, our carriage got stuck and..."

"Come on now, enough. You talk and talk, every day, now I have to sleep," Zosia dismissed him irritably. Gregory smiled in embarrassment. That was the cue for Irena and the priest. Father Adam placed his hand on the sick woman's head and then the two went out into the fresh air. Gregory accompanied them.

"You acted the good Christian," the priest told him.

"I will never forget you, your courage and generosity," Irena hugged Gregory, who hurried back inside before his unhappy wife could suspect anything was amiss. It was only when he had returned indoors that he discovered the pair of pearl earrings that Irena had slipped inside his pocket.

"I must get her out of here," said Irena to the priest. "It's too dangerous for her, for you, for Gregory, the whole village... I need you to help me."

The priest looked at the young woman. She looked so decisive and determined, so sure of herself. He liked her. "Think a moment, Irena. It's not so simple. The Jews are being pursued. They have been thrown out of their workplaces, their belongings confiscated, their blood spilled, and worst of all, they are searching for them everywhere. Anyone who hides a Jew is endangering his entire family. What will you do with her, Irena?"

"I will take her to Ciechanow, where she has family."

"Are you sure?"

"Better she should be with us. My husband Andre works with..." She went silent in an instant. She did not want to say that her husband was helping the occupying army. "It's a well-connected family."

They had to carefully plan how to get her out without arousing any interest whatsoever. After all, anyone could peek out of any house, someone might talk, tell, alert the Germans. The priest knew that for a couple of bottles of vodka, someone would hand over entire families.

They planned the rescue mission down to the last detail. They discussed everything over and over until the plan felt perfect.

An hour later, Irena knocked quietly on Gregory's door and he came out, looked around, and signaled that everything was in order. They could go down to the cellar.

"Give her this, she hasn't eaten since morning," he handed her a couple of cooked potatoes and a carrot — a modest supper.

Irena went down to the cellar to explain the plan to Rachelle.

"You aren't afraid," Rachelle asked her.

"I am doing what you would do for me."

"You are amazing," Rachelle placed her hand on Irena's head.

Irena suddenly felt different, as though she had turned into somebody else. No longer was she the little lady from the village, or the woman whose husband decided for her, whose mother dictated her life. She felt strong, determined that nothing would stand in her way. She felt she could do anything, that she was on a crucial mission. Really, a small act, minor in the larger picture, but important. And besides, Rachelle was not just her sister-in-law but the wife of a Polish war hero and carrying his child.

Many years afterward, she likened this awakening to becoming a fearless superhero. In the days to come, when things grew even darker during nights of despair and pain, she would need to return to that moment in order to regain her strength, over and over again, and believe in her own capacity as it had been revealed to her in that cellar. It was a defining moment in her life, a sign from the heavens.

"Is everything clear?"

Rachelle nodded, 'yes.'

Two hours later, as the villagers ate their meal, Irena went over to the seat beside Yuzhik.

"What now, Ms. Irena?"

"Now we go straight home," she said. He called to the horses, brandished his whip, and pulled at the reins. The carriage set off, out of the village on the main road. In the middle of the path, they noticed a man holding a lantern and waving to them, shouting and signaling for them to stop.

"Yuzhik, watch out!" Irena shouted. "It's the priest, Father Adam."

Yuzhik pulled at the reins with all his might, and the horses stopped the carriage.

"Thank you," said the priest and approached them.

"You could have been killed," shouted Yuzhik. "You are lucky that I didn't run you over, Father."

"Bless you, my son."

"What happened? Speak to us, man of God," said Irena.

"Indeed," he said. "I ask of you..."

"Anything you ask, Holy Father."

"Dear friends, Rachelle, my brother's daughter has to get home tonight. She lives not far from Ciechanow, and I thought you might be so kind…"

Irena glanced at Yuzhik. "We will help them, yes?"

"We did not discuss that," said the coachman resentfully. "And it's already very late."

"It's a good deed, a holy act," said the priest.

"Another passenger will further weigh down the tired horses. I will only go as far as Ciechanow," he insisted. "Forgive me, Father, it's a holy act to return home in peace."

"That is fine, she can stay at my home," said Irena. "How can I refuse? His blessings will be upon us. Don't worry, Yuzhik, I will compensate you for the extra trouble."

"Whatever you decide." He relaxed when he understood that his compensation would increase.

"We would be happy to take her along with us," said Irena. "Where is she?"

"She is waiting for us at my home, a few minutes from here."

CHAPTER 12

From Krasne to Ciechanow

A few minutes later the carriage stopped beside the wooden door which led to the church yard. When they opened it, they saw the priest waving to them with a lantern in his hand.

"Here they are," Yuzhik said. "Please hurry."

The priest approached them followed by a woman wrapped in a black scarf holding a suitcase. Behind them stood Gregory.

"Thank you for stopping, my son," said the priest. "I knew your goodness would prevail."

"Whatever you ask, Father," Yuzhik said, who was moved by the closeness to the holy man.

"This is Rachelle Bozhinsky, my brother's daughter," the priest said. "She has to see a doctor as soon as possible. Please take her with you, she could die if she stays here."

The woman began coughing noisily. Yuzhik startled and let out a sound of protest.

"Sick? That… maybe it's not a good idea."

"God will reward you for your goodness, my son," he said and slipped the driver several coins.

"I pray it's not a contagious disease," Yuzhik relented. "Hurry, woman, it's already late," and he tried to take her suitcase from her. But she held it tight and refused to be separated from it.

"All of us will pray for that," said the priest and crossed himself. Yuzhik crossed himself too and spat, perhaps to banish the evil spirits.

Irena got down from the carriage. "Nice to meet you," she shook Rachelle's hand. "I'm Irena, we must hurry. Better you should sit in the back where there are blankets and pillows. I hope you will be comfortable."

Rachelle hugged Gregory, his face wet with tears. "Good luck, I will pray for you," he whispered to her and handed her a bundle with the smell of bread rising from it.

"Thank you," she said to the priest. "I don't know how to thank you…"

"No need. I pray that our God may bring you peacefully to wherever you require," he said and helped her to get up into the carriage.

Rachelle sat in the back of the carriage, her suitcase on her knees. Irena made sure she was comfortable and covered her with blankets. Gregory and the priest pulled a heavy tarpaulin over the carriage to protect them from the snow that was expected to fall.

"Father," said Irena and kissed his hand. "I don't know how…"

"Don't thank me. These days we must be human beings."

"I wish everyone acted as you have," said Gregory.

The priest closed his eyes, praying. The group waited a few moments for him to finish. "Irena," he said, "I pray that these dark days will pass and our Poland be freed from the yoke of foreigners."

"Amen," she said, and Yuzhik shouted that it was enough, that it was late. He could not wait any longer. He had to leave immediately, as the snowstorm was coming.

To her surprise, Gregory approached Irena and hugged her close. When she found the earrings in her pocket the following day, she understood.

Yuzhik cracked his whip and the horses, understanding that now it was their time, pricked up their heads, whinnied, and the carriage set off. Soon Gregory and the priest receded from view. Then the lights of the village disappeared. Only the barking of dogs echoed in their ears until the way grew quiet.

Two hours after setting off, Yuzhik stopped the carriage, apologized, and disappeared into the forest. "Health matters," he explained. That was Irena's chance to move to the back of the carriage and check on Rachelle. When she got up, she heard a slight murmur of fear.

"Hey, it's all right, it's me," she whispered into the darkness. "You're okay."

Rachelle poked her head out from among the bundles of straw which cushioned her spot in the carriage. "Are we there yet?"

"Another two hours or so," said Irena and offered her some cookies that the priest had given her. "Anything else?"

"I'm fine. I'm worried about the meeting."

"It will be okay, my dear sister-in-law," she said and smiled to herself. Sister-in-law. Here is my sister-in-law. My soul sister. Here I am, building our family. Soon we will have a baby in the family and who knows, maybe we will adopt a baby of our own.

Most of the way passed in silence, each of them deep in their thoughts. Now and then, Yuzhik would burst into song, perhaps so as not to fall asleep. What was worse, he took sips from the bottle of wine he had hidden underneath his seat. Sometimes a truck full of soldiers passed them by, or German military motorcycles and Yuzhik would wave to them and mutter in Polish, "Dogs, may they burn. Scoundrels."

The journey lasted four-and-a-half hours. They reached the gates of Ciechanow.

At the entrance to the city, they came to a checkpoint. Two soldiers in German military uniforms instructed them to get out.

"Inspection," said one of them, and the sergeant shone his flashlight on their faces.

Just keep your cool, Irena told herself. Be calm. Be quiet. Don't show them that you are afraid.

"Where to?" The sergeant asked.

"To my parents," said Irena and handed them the address of her uncle Solly.

"At this hour?"

"We left too late, because of the sick woman."

"Identification," said the sergeant in German.

She pulled her papers from her coat pocket. He looked them over, examining the photograph, then Irena, and handed it back to her.

"And yours," he signaled to the driver, looked it over, and returned it.

"And is there someone else in the carriage?" the sergeant asked.

"Yes sir, the priest's niece. She is sleeping in the back," said Irena. "Only be careful, she is very sick."

"Sick with what?"

"Fever and a cough, I only hope that it isn't pneumonia."

The soldiers lifted the tarpaulin and looked at Rachelle lying on the hay.

"Papers."

"Identification please."

Rachelle sat up and instantly suffered a terrible coughing fit. Her whole body contorted and shook and she made a choking sound as if she couldn't breathe.

"What happened to her?" the sergeant asked Irena.

"I told you, she's sick," she whispered. "We put her in the back because we were afraid it might be contagious… I hope that you won't get sick, God forbid."

"Let's go, get out of here at once," the sergeant shouted and let them through.

"Where to?" asked Yuzhik and looked at Irena.

Where indeed?

She had been so concerned with preparations for the trip, planning their exit, that she had not given any thought to where she would bring Rachelle. To surprise Marta and Bronek in the middle of the night seemed like an invitation for hysteria and outrage that might give them away.

She needed a plan. A clever one. The baby with his sweet face, baby smell, and soft skin would open the door to their hearts and their home. But what about right now? To her parents' home in Nuzewo? That was another hour of driving and Yuzhik would not agree to it. The little hotel behind the cinema seemed like a possibility but she knew that the story of two women renting a room so late at night would be too juicy not to be told and people would ask questions.

Uncle Solly – yes, only Uncle Solly. His house seemed like the best option, the most reasonable, most likely to succeed. Her good uncle Solly loved her, after all, and saw her as practically his own daughter. He would not be able to refuse her.

The house was in the center of town and, as was to be expected, the street was blanketed in a heavy darkness. Snow began to fall and cover the street.

As she had expected, the driver decided that he deserved a bonus for the extra passenger. She had seen that the priest had given him special payment but decided not to bicker or make an enemy of him. She softened him with a few more zlotys and promised to use his services again. He was so pleased he even helped Rachelle down from the carriage.

"Goodnight," he said. "Be well, I hope that I don't catch whatever it is you have."

"I only infect Germans," she said and they all laughed.

"If only that were so," said Irena. She was careful not to arouse suspicion.

"Come, let's go in quietly so we don't wake them at this hour…" she whispered and the two of them crept inside the house, trying not to make a sound. In the hall before them stood Uncle Solly.

"Just a minute," I stopped Mom. "Explain —"

"Which part isn't clear?"

"Grandma, why did you leave your pretty house in the village? Didn't you decide to wait for your Polish man?"

"I had to."

"Because…"

"Because I was Jewish."

"But also a Polish officer's wife."

"That did not help me, maybe even made it more dangerous. Intermarriage with Jews was its own evil to them."

"She didn't leave of her own will," said Mom. "Tell her."

"You're right," Granny Tulla hugged me. "I didn't tell you what happened in the village. So, we will leave Irena and Rachelle at the entrance to Uncle Solly's house for now and go back a few weeks in time. Then you will understand… Are you ready? It's not easy," she smiled at me and Mom.

Granny Tulla, once Rachel, then Rachelle, had the smile of a queen.

CHAPTER 13

Krasne, 1940

The winter of 1940 was cold - very cold.

But worse than the cold was that I felt so lonesome. Days and nights, I wandered about in the huge house, alone, asking myself as to what I should do. Should I stay, or go to Pruszkow to find out what had become of my father, or should I search for Johann's regiment?

Should I go on waiting?

Due to the lack of firewood, I was unable to heat the entire house, only part of it, so I turned the kitchen into my living space. I moved the mattress, blankets, and my books and lived in there.

Hannukah, 1940. Christmas, 1940. January. February.

I already felt the baby moving inside me, kicking me with his little feet, and still, I had not heard anything as to the fate of Johann or my father. The loneliness began to gnaw at me.

My worry became despair. Despair became fear.

What was I supposed to do? Who could I trust? Who was a friend and who an enemy?

I could already feel the eyes of the villagers boring into me. I saw the way the butcher shook his head telling me there was nothing left, that the egg seller left me only bad eggs, that the women grew quiet as I approached them. I was afraid.

I went to bed with Johann's medals clasped in my hands, as though doing so kept him safe, and the baby too, and me.

God, I prayed every evening, my God, God of Abraham, Isaac, and Jacob, keep my Johann safe and my good father and the chosen people who live in all of Poland.

To be on the safe side, I gathered the silverware, my jewelry, the medals, and everything that may have attracted burglars to the house and I hid them in a suitcase which I hid in the closet behind the bookshelves.

After Yosef Weiss's family along with most of the Jews in the village had left, I felt alone and exposed. Even though I was on good terms with the neighbors and villagers, I began to feel their gaze boring into my back. I sensed the whispers when I passed by and it was clear that I could not trust them forever, mainly because there were Gestapo already sniffing around the area looking for Jews in hiding.

The arrival of the Gestapo to the area was a bad sign to everyone and certainly for me, a daughter of the Jewish faith. To them, I was lower than a cockroach, and their Fuhrer promised to root us out of Europe entirely.

I saw them when they passed through the village in their black uniforms, their polished boots, racing through on their motorcycles or shiny cars, their eyes flashing about like hungry hyenas. All of us in the village knew that their job was to stop the "enemies of the Reich or the regime" and to act against the "inferior races". The Gestapo flooded Poland, hunting Jews and shooting those they found in the forests or rounding them up and into the ghettos or work camps.

Had I been too complacent? Too naive? Had I really not sensed the hatred for Jews that had been simmering beneath the surface?

How had I not felt the eyes of the wicked following me... lurking, peering, looking for evil?

One evening I heard the gate creak. Someone was standing there.

Johann? I leaped to my feet and peered out the window and saw Father Adam at the entrance.

"Rachelle," he whispered, "Rachelle can you hear me?"

"Father?" I hurried to open the gate for him. His face was pale.

I led him to the kitchen where I lived. He looked around the room quietly.

"I see that you don't have enough firewood?"

"I want for nothing except my husband."

"Listen," he said, then stopped. He turned toward the entrance as though listening for someone at the door.

"You must escape. The situation is bad. I hear that all over Poland they are putting the Jews in ghettos, cramming them in with terrible conditions."

"I know."

"You have to get out of here, and quick. I know my people, and they are harmless but when the bad seeds poke their heads up out of the soil, the village will turn… I worry about you."

I did not answer. Instead, I took out Johann's medal of excellence and placed it on the table. He stared at it and nodded.

"I take it that's your answer."

"What if he is on his way back here right now? Crossing the fields, on horseback, galloping, waiting for the moment I open the gate for him?"

"He knows…" he pointed at my belly.

"Not yet. He will be back and he will protect us. No, dear Father, I'm not ready to leave."

"What will I do with you?" said Father Adam as though speaking to himself.

"Pray for us."

He placed his hand on my head and muttered his prayer, then left.

I was still stuck in my little kitchen, spending my days listening to the radio, reading, knitting a little, cooking, helping the elderly, and praying for the well-being of Johann and my father. I believed in my heart that by doing so I protected them.

One night, a few days later, I woke up to the sound of noises in the yard. The gate creaked.

Was I simply hearing things? Maybe it was the wind in the trees?

I stood up and listened.

No, that was not a fox or a cat rattling the gate. There was someone there. Friends don't creep around like that. Johann? Is that you?

And then I heard the voices. Several voices, talking amongst themselves, planning. "Wait," said one voice, "are you sure… money?"

"Of course, Jews always have money."

"But maybe it's not worth it, and the police…?"

"Police? Police?" Voices laughed in response.

"Tell me, are you afraid of her?"

"And what if they knew it was us?"

"It's a good deed to steal from them."

"And if they catch us?"

"Then what? What will they do to us? She's a Yid, she has a cupboard full of gold and silver, that one."

"What's with you, have you forgotten?"

"Forgotten what?"

"That those Yids of hers killed Jesus the Messiah," said another voice.

"Let's go, death and destruction to the Jews."

"Cleansing Poland of Jews," said another voice.

"See? Look, she lives in this house alone."

I realized they were not coming simply to take my money. They wanted more than that. Me. My life was at risk. My palms were sweating, my legs shook, I felt faint. I was in great danger. I was afraid.

Calm down and try to overcome your fear. You can't let them smell fear, I told myself.

And what will you do? You're alone, all alone.

I won't let them. They won't win that easily.

They are stronger than me, maybe they have knives!

I had my life and that of the baby growing within me. Are you frightened, my baby?

I had to fight for him.

I peered out of the window. I saw three young men. I knew one of them, Lucian Yeruslavsky, the egg seller's son, a neglected boy who helped his father distribute eggs. When I looked closely, I could see another shadow crouching behind the fence as though watching and looking out for the others. There were four of them and only one of me.

The tallest of them was wearing a big black coat. He was holding a club and waving it around. He was not familiar to me. Maybe he came from one of the nearby villages. It seemed that he was the hooligans' leader.

They were very noisy, weaving around, maybe drunk, which was even more frightening. But not one of my neighbors, my friends, those who always thanked me for my services, came out to see what the noise was about or if I needed any help.

In the bedroom closet, I found the gun that Johann had left me. It was a little revolver that he had gotten in England. He wanted to know that I had a weapon. Just in case. We had a fight about it. He made me learn how to use it and I asked him to take it, not to leave it there, but he said, "It's for your own safety. This way I will feel a little more at ease leaving you all alone."

"And let's say," I said to him, "that at some point I should become angry with you and, in a fit of fury, I use it against you." He grew serious and said that if I was angry at him, better he should die.

Johann was an artist in matters of love.

The gun was in its place inside a wooden box, and in another box beside that one, I found the bullets. I hesitated for a moment and then loaded the gun. I immediately regretted it and took the bullets out again. I only wanted to frighten them. I didn't want any bloodshed.

On second thought, I loaded one bullet into the revolver.

I heard them getting closer. They stopped beside the front door. Angrily they tried the handle but it did not budge. Someone smashed a window, tried to get in that way, only it was too high and they began to kick at the door, trying to break it down.

"Push hard," shouted one. I heard a smash and they were inside.

Just don't be afraid, I told myself, the most important thing is to show no fear. A bunch of weaklings, I encouraged myself, a gang of pathetic drinkers, brats.

The gun would do the work.

"What are you doing here?" I stood before them with the gun raised.

They stopped instantly, surprised, stunned, their eyes practically popping out of their sockets.

"Mrs., what are you..."

"This gun... Mrs., what do you... it's just a visit."

"Careful, that's not a toy," shouted the one with the mustache.

"Get out of here at once, or else..." I said, raising my hand and pointing the gun at them, turning it from one to the next, left, right, staring at them as if trying to decide who would be first. Yes, the gun did its job.

"You heard me, get out, now," I tried to keep my voice steady. "Or else I will shoot."

Silence.

"I have four bullets in here, one for each of you, even the guy outside."

"That's not very nice of you," said the tall man holding the stick, weighing whether he should take the chance and attack or wait. "What did we do to you? Is this how you treat your guests?"

"I did not invite you. You are not my guests. Get out, at once." I wondered where my daring came from.

"We… Don't you see, we just came for some amusement."

"It will be nice, Mrs."

"Maybe you have some vodka for some thirsty people."

"We'll have fun," laughed the third, and added, "They say Jewish women are easy."

"I'm not joking with you. Get out of here, now."

"Crazy Jew, give me your gun right now," shouted the tall one with the club but he did not dare move from where he stood.

"You wouldn't dare…" shouted the one I knew, the son of the egg seller.

"Get out yourself, right now," said the third.

"I am counting to three and all of you better be gone or else…. one… two…"

I tightened my fingers around the trigger as if I were about to pull it and aimed it towards the tall one's head, not intending to hurt him, only to scare him.

"Crazy."

"Get out you disgusting…"

"I'm not playing around, you watch it, I'll shoot," I shouted, as though I wasn't shaking, terrified as if I didn't know that they could finish me off in an instant.

"She's aiming at you," someone shouted and I slowly pulled the trigger and then shot.

I was careful not to aim at him but rather above his head. Way over his head.

He froze for a second, staring at me, and then let out a terrible screech, turned and escaped, and the others after him.

God! I did it. Bunch of weaklings.

They ran off like rabbits. I heard the sound of their steps getting farther away. Another moment and silence returned to the house. Only the gate went on creaking into the stillness of the night and the bitter cold came through the broken door.

I kept standing there for a long minute, unable to move. My body was locked in position, my feet to the floor, my hands raised, unable to put down the gun. I was frozen.

Only after I returned the door to its proper place, tied the handle with a rope to keep it shut tight against the wind, and checked that the rest of the house was closed up properly, could I allow myself to sit down on the mattress and cry. I cried and cried, cleansing my body of all the built-up tension. I cried over everything: my father, Johann, and my love that might be lost to me forever.

That was the moment when I realized that my life had changed, that I had to get out of there. But where? I knew that this incident would invite a reaction, but I could not have predicted what happened.

The following day when I went out, the villagers were crowded around my fence. They whispered to one another and pointed at me. Someone held a sign that read "child-killer." Two young men threw stones at me and there were shouts from every direction.

"Out with the Jews," shouted one woman.

Another, whose birth I had attended, spat on me, and cursed, "May you birth a rat, murderer."

Something had changed, as though the ground was shaking beneath me. I hurried back into the house and shut myself inside.

After sunset, the clown who had been made our mayor by the Germans arrived at my home. He was accompanied by two police officers. They claimed that there was a complaint against me.

"You see this?" the mayor waved a stack of papers, "Testimony from four young men that you shot at a defenseless youth."

"I shot over his head, just to frighten him."

"You threatened to shoot them, no?"

"They broke into my house and I… Yes, I told them that if they did not leave, I…"

"Threatening them with a gun? Innocent kids? That's very serious."

"It was self-defense, I was one against four."

"Do you usually threaten your guests with guns? And why didn't you call the police?"

"They were already inside my house, they broke in with force, they had a club… I thought that the gun would scare them a little."

"I have three witnesses who claim quite the opposite. The youth that you shot at is in the hospital. He is in bad condition."

"You must know that is not true."

"Are you calling me a liar?" the mayor reddened. "And anyway, how is it that you have a gun?"

"It belongs to my husband. You know him. Johann is a decorated officer."

"I understand that he is no longer with you, that he's missing."

"This is his home. He is fighting for you, for all of us."

"Jews are not permitted to bear arms," the police took my gun from me as well as the box of bullets.

"You won't need it anymore there," said the police, chuckling.

"There? Where?"

"There, where all the other little Jews are. Tomorrow morning you must come to the council building. Bring one suitcase with you, no more. We are moving you to a camp that was set up for your kind."

"Wait… please, don't let them take me."

"You have nothing to worry about, they will take good care of you," they snickered and left.

I knew that their decision to move me to the forced labor camp in my condition was essentially a death sentence.[8] As soon as it got dark outside, I took all of my belongings to the priest's house. He looked at me and without asking, hid the suitcase under the altar in the church. He said that he had heard what had happened from the villagers and asked to hear my version. I told him everything, without hiding any details. He listened, then bowed his head and sat still, his eyes closed, his lips whispering prayers as if waiting for a sign, a clue that would show him the way. After some time, he sat up, asked me to go and put on several layers of clothing, coats, warm shoes, and come back to the church in two hours.

"Make sure nobody sees you. Come by whatever side roads you can."

"Father," I said, "you are scaring me."

"We both know what a work camp means. So, it has to be tonight."

"Aren't you risking…"

"Me? I'm an old man, what can they do to me? Go, there's no time, we have to work quickly."

I did as he told me, tucking all of the money I had in the house into various pockets. I wore two coats and several woolen layers, socks, and shirts.

---

8 A labor camp is a prison facility designed for the forced exploitation for various purposes, and even mass murder through labor. Work camps served Nazi Germany as part of the Final Solution. They produced weapons, chopped wood, mined in quarries, paved roads, etc. The great majority of prisoners were sent to death camps afterwards. Mortality in the labor camps grew throughout the war as a result of abuse, primitive work conditions, hard labor, malnutrition, and overcrowding. Few women were sent to such camps, but those that were worked in the kitchens or laundries. Any babies brought into the camps or born there were put to death.

I was very careful not to make a sound or turn on any lights.

Two hours later I snuck toward the church. I took side roads and when I was certain that nobody was following me, I entered through the back door.

CHAPTER 14

Gregory was waiting for us at Father Adam's home. That wonderful man was among the very few who actually lived up to his values. He knew what it meant to be a good person during these impossibly difficult times.

Gregory was known in the area for his prosperous dairy farm. Gregory's milk was famous throughout the region. I knew him well. I had been called numerous times to treat his wife, Zosia, who was devoutly religious and suffered various ailments. On account of her poor health, her fasting, and prayers, she rarely left her house.

As a token of thanks for caring for his wife, the good Gregory would leave fresh milk by my doorstep. They had no children. I knew that Gregory spent his days on his farm looking after the cows and sheep and that she was busy with her own concerns.

Gregory? What was he doing here? At times like these nobody could be trusted.

When I entered, Gregory welcomed me with a nod of his head.

"And now?"

"I will take you to my house. I've prepared a hiding place for you."

"Now?"

"The situation is dire, Rachelle, the Germans are hunting Jews, going from village to village and shooting them like dogs, and the Poles… antisemitism is coming out of the woodwork. It doesn't seem like you have a lot of options."

"But I am the wife of a Polish war hero."

"I know people stupid enough that for a bottle of vodka they would happily tell of the Polish officer's wife who never went to church, never bought pork, lights candles on Friday evenings, and prays in a different language."

"And Johann?"

"When he gets back, he'll find out."

"Gregory," I turned to the kind man who was listening to our conversation. "Are you sure… after all, they have no sympathy for anybody who hides Jews…"

"Everyone must contribute what they can. I believe that your God and mine will look after us."

"Go with him," said Father Adam. "Meanwhile I will look for another place for you. Just for a few days…"

Gregory's wagon stood at the entrance to the church. He made room for me between the big jugs, set down a pillow and blanket, and helped me take a seat. I had to take up as little space as possible so that nobody would notice. The trip felt longer than usual; I assumed that he was taking a roundabout route to be sure that nobody was following us. We knew that tomorrow, when I did not show up at the council building as instructed, investigations would begin and it would be best that nobody harbor any suspicions.

In Gregory's case, there was nothing unusual about his behavior. He was always circling about in his wagon, delivering his dairy products.

When we arrived at his house, the sky was clear, a new day had come and I got down and followed him to the hiding place he had prepared for me.

My new home in the house of good Gregory, a man of honor.

The smell of mold and sewage was suffocating and made me dizzy. I saw rats scampering away and heard the shriek of bats and their wings flapping but it was a proper hiding place.At least for a while.

Until Poland was liberated.

Or until someone discovered my whereabouts.

CHAPTER 15

Ciechanow 1940

When we arrived at Solly's house, the city was still in a deep sleep.

Although we tried to enter quietly, on tiptoe so as not to wake anyone, we found Solly standing in the entrance.

As soon as she saw him, Irena hurried to embrace him as though we had not just now been trying to creep into his house unnoticed. As though he knew that we were meant to arrive.

"God, girl," he said. "I could have killed you." Now I saw that he was holding a gun in his hand.

"What is that Uncle Solly, a gun?"

"These days, any unusual sounds make us nervous. Terrible things are happening. What happened to you?"

"What happened?"

"To show up at this hour…"

"Everything is fine," Irena replied, trying to appear lighthearted, as though nothing was out of the ordinary. "Meet Rachelle, my friend, she…"

"Friend? From where?"

"We study together and she just needs… Rachelle, this is Solly, the best uncle in the world."

He nodded coldly and did not shake my outstretched hand but took a step into the house.

It was clear to me that he was suspicious of my identity.

We followed after him into the spacious kitchen. He tried not to make any sounds that would wake his wife, who was asleep upstairs. I remained standing. The ground burned beneath my feet. I knew that I was not wanted here; I could tell that he was worried. Naive, innocent Irena. She believed that the whole world was like her.

The uncle made us tea and offered us butter cookies but still did not say a thing. I knew he was thinking, deliberating, trying to understand.

Irena chattered endlessly, trying to cover over the uneasy feeling in the kitchen with words. When she ran out of stories, she began humming a song to herself about a violet blooming in winter.

"Who are you?" Solly turned to me. I was not ready for the direct question.

"She's my friend from the course and she needs… just one night."

"Why can't she go to her own home?"

"Because she lives far away?"

"Where did you come from? Why not at Andre's house, why at this hour?"

"Where did we come from? We came… from the village, yes… from the village, because…" she was not prepared for the onslaught of questions.

"Where did you come from now, Irena?"

He kept looking at me. Peering into my soul. Trying to uncover the truth.

"There was a party tonight, for…"

"I'm Rachel, Rachelle, Johann's wife," I replied. There was no point in lying.

"She's my sister-in-law, my sister at heart," said Irena.

He nodded. I think he had guessed who I was.

"You need a place to hide? That's why you came?"

"Irena offered to bring me here. She believed you could help me."

"Irena…" He signaled her to come with him to the hallway.

"What?"

"I have to speak to you."

"About what?" He did not answer. "Uncle Solly, we will help her, right?"

He did not answer. He remained standing, holding his cup of tea, his eyes on me. I could not stay there. I got up and began to retreat toward the door.

"Where are you going?" Irena hurried after me.

"I know when I'm not wanted," I told her. "Your uncle is worried about giving a Jew shelter, and I think he's right. It's not worth the risk."

"Give him a moment. He… don't go outside, it's cold out there."

"It's cold inside too. Perhaps there is no place for me in this world."

"He… Uncle Solly, tell her… Tell her not to go."

He did not reply.

I picked up my belongings and went out. I remained beside the door holding my suitcase. It contained everything I owned.

Snowflakes began to fall. Every now and then, a dog barked and was met with a chorus of street dogs barking in response. A cat snarled at me and a cold wind blew through my hair. Here I was, in an unfamiliar city, where my beloved husband had grown up, without knowing where to turn. From afar I saw the walls of the great fortress. Behind it spread the forests. That's where I would go.

"Rachelle, Rachelle, wait, wait for us," I heard them calling my name.

The door opened and Uncle Solly stood at the entrance. Behind him, Irena peeked her head out. He looked at me with a smile and held out his hand.

"Rachelle, I don't understand why you ran off!"

Was he going to hand me over to the police?

I did not answer.

"You gave up so fast?" He approached me. "Jesus, Mary, I thought you might have disappeared already. Come with me."

"Please don't hand me over, I will get out of here tomorrow and I won't…"

"Rachelle, from the depths of my heart I am sorry if I offended you," he said and came close enough that I could see his eyes. Uncle Solly had kind, luminous eyes, that put me at ease. "If I was rude, I apologize. These days make everything complicated."

"I thought… I don't want to put you in danger."

"Come inside," he held out his arm. "We will get through today and think about what to do next."

"I can understand if you don't want…"

"Come," he took my little suitcase from me. "I might have an idea."

He and Irena offered me a bed, put clean, pleasant-smelling sheets on it. All I wanted was to rest. I was exhausted and in need of a few hours of sleep. But sleep was beyond me. Every sound outside terrified me. Maybe he had reported me? Maybe the neighbors had seen us come in in the early morning hours and reported us? Maybe the soldiers from the checkpoint would wake up and report the mysterious passenger? They had seen Irena's papers. They knew how to find me.

That night I tossed and turned, restless. Too many things had happened. The bad news of Johann, Irena finding me, leaving the village, the journey to Ciechenow, the soldiers, the way the uncle had greeted me… More than anything, what was I to do?

At some late hour of the night, I awoke to find Irena asleep on the mattress beside me. She let out the occasional groan, as though she bore a heavy weight on her heart. I observed her. She was gorgeous: her skin fresh as a baby's, her long eyelashes and honey-colored hair forming a halo around her head. She had called me her soul sister. Had I really, amidst these dark times, been so lucky as to be granted a sister, a true friend? Or was she too another Pole within whom that germ of antisemitism might awaken…

When I finally woke up, the sun was high in the sky.

I heard Irena and Solly talking. They were trying to speak quietly so as not to disturb me, or so I wouldn't hear.

I did not dare get up. I kept lying there listening. I had to know what would become of me.

"What will I do with you, my girl?" He was saying to Irena.

"Help us."

"You clearly do not understand the meaning of hiding a Jew. There are clear instructions. You are putting your entire family in danger."

"Which is why I have the smartest uncle in the world."

"Charm won't help. Yesterday they found two Jewish families in the cellar of an acquaintance of mine. He'd hidden them in exchange for diamond rings. The Germans took them outside and shot them, just like that, in front of everyone, and left their bodies on the sidewalk, so people would know the consequences."

"Just until she gives birth, after that…"

"Have you considered your mother-in-law? The moment Marta lays eyes on her she will call for the Gestapo."

"She won't. We will bring her a grandson. The son of her Johann, her hero."

"You are so naive – Irena, what am I going to do with you?"

"Help us, she…" She went quiet. She took a deep breath. "She's my friend, sister, sister-in-law, soulmate. I have to save her."

"And Andre? You know that he…" The voices became whispers. All I could hear was Irena crying.

When Irena returned to the room, I closed my eyes as though I was still asleep. She rearranged the blanket over me, then sank to her knees and prayed to Jesus and Mary, every so often glancing at me to see if I was still asleep. She prayed for me, for Johann, for the baby, asking that Mary show her the way. For a moment she was quiet, then asked that the God of the Jews look over us. I smiled. Soulmate?

Through her vitality and desire to do good in the world, I knew that she was sad, that she was going through hard times. I opened my eyes. She smiled at me.

"Good morning."

"Good morning," I said. "Are you all right?"

"Very much so," she nodded, but I saw that something was bothering her.

"Irena," she sat beside me. I touched her hand. "I feel very fortunate, despite everything – all the danger and fear because I have gained something invaluable: your friendship."

She smiled.

It was a sad smile.

Irena was unhappy.

CHAPTER 16

Ciechanow - Nuzewo

After dinner, as Rachel helped the aunt wash dishes, Irena asked Solly if he had come up with a solution.

"I've thought and thought; I don't know how to solve it. You made a mistake coming here."

"My uncle, you wouldn't have done anything differently," she replied in a voice as sweet as honey. "If you had seen where I found her... she was in a moldy cellar... what would you have wanted, for me to leave her there?"

"You know that I would do anything for you. But right now, when the reality is changing every day..."

"What happened to the values that you were so proud of, of mercy and compassion? Was it all just words? You believe in Jesus, don't you? Would he have just left her there?"

"Irena, I'm worried about you."

"She will have the baby in two months. We will wait a little and then go to Marta. The grandchild will change everything."

"I wouldn't count on that."

"So, what do you suggest? If she were a sick cat, would you throw her out? Uncle Solly..." she whined like a child asking for chocolate. "You're the only person I trust... who else do I have, besides you?"

He smiled. He knew these tricks.

"I thought of something. Let me talk to your father."

"My father? It won't work. He only listens to Mama and she is so suspicious she'll be rid of us before..."

"I know how to convince them. We said four months, right?"

"I knew it!" Irena cried and threw her arms around his neck. "I knew it...

three months, five… just until she's well."

"Wait, my girl, I have not promised anything."

Irena hurried to tell Rachel the good news.

Solly was disturbed by what he had to do the following day. At dinnertime, Solly informed them that they would make the trip tomorrow. He did not say where. The less anyone knew the better. These days one couldn't know who might be listening, who was an enemy, and who a friend.

They planned to set out as quickly as possible before neighbors began asking questions, wanting to know who the stranger was, or, God forbid, run into Marta, who was sure that her daughter-in-law was with her parents…

In the morning, they ate their fill in silence, which was interrupted by shouting coming from the street. Someone yelled, then others joined him. People were pleading, begging, crying… then the sound of gunshots. Again, and again, and again. Then the street grew silent once more.

"What was that?"

"Whatever it was, it's over," said the aunt. "We don't interfere."

Rachel got up and hurried to the closed window to try to open it. Solly caught her by the arm.

"What are you doing?!"

"I'm a doctor, I have to see. There was shooting, maybe I can help…"

"Nobody can know that you're here!"

"But it's my duty."

"They will see that you came from this house and they will arrest all of us. Our fate will be tied up with yours. I ask that…"

"But there… there's a child crying and I…"

"I will go and check. Maybe I can help, but you must promise me that you won't even consider leaving the house. You understand what it means for all of us?!"

She nodded.

"I promise, but help him, he's a child."

Solly returned a few minutes later. His face was white. He looked at Rachel and shook his head. She understood right away. The child would not make it.

"And his parents?" He did not answer. "Nobody?"

He looked pained.

"That's what they will do to us, Solly!" the aunt shouted.

"We are getting out of here," he tried to pacify his wife. "She is going back to her village."

They packed blankets and pillows, warm clothes, something to eat, and were about to leave.

"Just a minute," said Irena. "What will we do at the checkpoint when they ask us for papers?"

"I can hide like…"

"We managed that once, I am afraid to try it again."

"We will have to find you some papers."

"My marriage certificate won't suffice?"

"Certainly not," he answered, looking at Rachel, then Irena, then back at Rachel as though trying to gather strength from them. Then, he disappeared.

"Trust Solly," said Irena. "Here in Ciechanow, he can solve anything."

The aunt gave them a long, angry look, then she too disappeared.

Irena ran after her to appease her, to explain, to find out if she intended to betray her guest.

When the two of them left the room, the aunt's eyes were red, but she smiled and even gave Rachel a jar of homemade marmalade.

A few hours later, Solly returned and handed Rachel a worn leather ID case.

"Nice to meet you, Tulla Svidansky."

"Tulla?"

"Yes, Tulla, and you'd better get used to it fast. Repeat it until you forget your old name. Your maiden name was Tulla Yvgenia Chevnesitz from Oponeo, a little town not far from Lodz. Your father worked in a sawmill, and you moved here when you got married. Now you are Tulla the widow, Tulla Svidansky."

"Solly, who is this Tulla?"

"She… well actually there was such a woman."

"And what happened?"

"Better not to know. Just remember that in dark times like these we have new kinds of heroes: those who do important acts, acts for which silence is safest. Here, you're lucky. Take it and learn it. Got it, Mrs. Tulla Svidansky?"

"Yes."

"You have to know her, know everything about her, construct her character. What does she like to eat, who were her friends, what was she good at, what did she hate… you have to construct her life and stick to her story. Lucky for you,

you have Irena, who is very good at telling stories."

"One thing I know about her," said Rachel who had, this moment, become Tulla. "Her husband was a Polish officer who was captured by the Germans."

"A captured hero? No that's no good, I worry that capture could endanger you. You are pregnant, your husband is dead... not in battle... maybe... of a disease? He wasn't young."

"He fell off his horse."

"Excellent. He fell and died of his injuries. Your husband was a hunter."

"Kolin Svidansky was a hunter, primarily of wild boars."

"After two months of terrible suffering he died and left his pregnant wife behind."

And so, Tulla was born anew in Solly's home.

Even after the war ended, she went on carrying the name given to her by Irena's good uncle. Rachel remained a distant memory.

The route to the village where Irena's parents lived passed quietly. Rain fell throughout the entire journey as though the skies shared the travelers' mood.

Irena and Rachel/Tulla sat in the back wrapped tightly in blankets. Each of them was deep in her thoughts of the days to come, of the dangers and hardships before them. The carriage was covered with a tarpaulin to keep out the rain, and the air inside was thick and heavy.

Irena thought of Andre. She missed the smile that would creep up onto his face when he saw her come in, the touch of his hands, the smell of his cigarettes. Over two months had passed since he left. His last letters were too short, mostly recounting his successes in his role as liaison with the Polish population. She did not like the idea of him working for the Nazis, or how he believed that this was the best way to build his future and that of their family. After all, she thought, the occupation would pass and then beautiful Poland would be liberated and renewed, and then what? Would they accuse him of collaboration? See him as a traitor? Am I trying to save Tulla to atone for his deeds?

Her Andre, she believed, was not a bad person. On the contrary, he was generous and loving. It amazed her that he was so drawn to the evil of the Nazi occupiers and wished to cooperate with them. She was sure he would hear of her doings, of her rescue mission, and hurry to support her. Of course. He would be proud of his brave wife. I have to speak with Andre to tell him the truth. How would he take the news of her infertility? Would he agree to adopt a child? She was worried. She knew that he wanted a child of his own seed to carry on his family line.

Military trucks passed them filled with soldiers sitting facing one another with stern expressions. Passing jeeps flung stones and mud at the carriage, reconnaissance planes circled overhead, and SS soldiers stood at junctions examining them suspiciously.

Uncle Solly who sat beside the driver waved to them in a friendly manner, as though a Jewish woman were not sitting right behind him.

If they were to find out they would shoot Rachel/Tulla without a second thought. And they would shoot him and his wife and niece — for the forged papers there would be heavy punishment, as bad as for hiding Jews.

Irena sat across from Tulla. She would have to get used to calling her that. Tulla was gently stroking her belly as if calming the baby inside. She was happy with the baby, who was lively that morning as if he was participating in the journey, as though he wished to remind them of his existence. Was this any kind of world for a baby, she thought, not for the first time.

Uncle Solly promised to use his many connections to find out where Johann was and make contact, at least to let him know where his wife was. As Tulla had requested, Solly sent a letter to Father Adam whose response told her that the house in the village had been taken over and all of her belongings looted by the villagers. She was amazed at how little this upset her. But she suffered from the worry, God forbid, that they might get to Gregory. A shiver went through her. She knew that the Germans could punish the entire village because of her.

"Do not worry," Irena moved closer to her. "My parents will be happy to help."

Of course, she did not speak the truth entirely. She knew that her uncle had made sure to sweeten the deal in exchange for her parents' kindness. He knew that her father needed a new plow, that the horse was getting old, that he wanted to fix the roof. The sum of money that he tucked into his pocket should help convince her parents to give Tulla a place to stay.

"What wouldn't I do for you?" he whispered to Irena as they left - she was the daughter they had never had.

When they neared the village, Irena was gripped with excitement. All at once. she was awash in memories of her childhood. Here was the church where she and her parents prayed on Sundays, the well-tended flower garden in her schoolyard, the grassy fields where she and her friends would play or jump rope, and the bench on which Locke, the boy she had loved when she was 16, the son of the upholsterer, had kissed her. I wonder what became of him, she thought, and what my life might have looked like had I remained in the village.

She hid her worry from Tulla. Her sister-in-law was soon to give birth... who would help her? Who would be by her side when the baby came into the world?

Peter, the elderly driver whom they had hired instead of Yuzhik, whose curiosity and chatter might arouse suspicion, stopped beside the house and helped the two women get out.

"Wait here," said Solly. "I have to have a quick talk with my brother first," he said and disappeared into the house.

The two women stood for a few moments breathing the fresh air and enjoying the flowering of the oak trees when Irena suddenly noticed her brother Oleg. He lay on a mattress in the yard, his face exposed to the sun, his hands under his head and his eyes closed, sleeping.

He was the last person Irena wanted to see at that moment. She thought that he was living in a different city, as her parents had written her. She knew that he was as chatty as he was curious. That could be dangerous.

"That's my brother," she told Tulla as if calming herself. "He is a good man, not smart, but cheerful."

Oleg did not notice them and went on dozing in the sun. But something disturbed Irena. A pair of polished boots were neatly arranged beside him – quality leather, stretched tautly, and shining. Oleg hated shoes. He ran around barefoot almost all year round claiming that he did not like to imprison his feet. Why did he have such boots, especially now, in the springtime? Was he... like Andre... collaborating?

A few minutes passed and Uncle Solly returned and invited the two inside.

As they entered the house, Puchoy, Irena's dog, burst out of one of the rooms, barking and whining happily. Andre had not allowed her to take him with her to Ciechanow as Max, his dog, was territorial, so Puchoy had had to remain behind.

The happy dog leaped onto Irena, afterwards on Tulla, then back to Irena, and then jumped in the air five times and rolled on the carpet and remained lying there, breathing heavily. He was so funny that even Tulla, who had been as tightly wound as a spring, burst out laughing.

"Please meet Tulla," Irena smiled, "my best friend from bookkeeping school."

"Nice to meet you," said Tulla, and scratched Puchoy's head while he went on rolling on the carpet. From that moment on, she was neither Rachel or Rachelle. She had become Tulla. Only Tulla. Tulla who had been born in a small town and lived in Ciechanow. Tulla who went to church every Sunday and decorated her Christmas tree in December. Tulla, the wife of Kolin Svidansky the hunter who had slipped from his horse and died.

Rachel must be forgotten. She had never existed.

When Irena's parents came into the kitchen, their faces were pale. Her father avoided looking at her, and her mother shook her head warily. They embraced Irena and suggested that Tulla come look at the room in the yard, where she could stay until the birth.

Solly remained smoking in the yard, giving the family a chance to digest the new reality. For a moment everybody stood around looking at one another, trying to understand.

"I wanted... I wanted to say..." said Tulla, "you are so very generous, noble people. I will never forget your kindness."

They did not answer.

"Father..." said Irena when her mother and Tulla left. "Thank you."

"I don't know... maybe this is stupid... a mistake like this... this could cost me dearly. Let's see... I hope not."

They had set up a place for her in the old shed. Solly and her father had cleared out the bricks, aired out the shed, cleaned the windows and brought in a bed, a cupboard, and made it a pleasant room. Compared to Gregory's cellar this was a spacious palace and, best of all, sunlight came in through the windows.

"I am sure it will all go smoothly," Irena embraced her father. "Tulla can help you, she is a quiet and hardworking woman."

"How long have you known her?"

"Two years," she said without hesitation.

They ate lunch in silence and afterwards, Irena and Tulla washed the dishes.

"You could help my mother in the vegetable garden or around the house," Irena suggested. "That will help explain to anybody who wants to know what you are doing here."

"I thought the same."

"It will be fine," she hugged her as they parted. "I will come again in a week."

"Irena," her father stopped her. "Her family…"

"She is afraid of their response. Her father is… you know, he won't want to take in a bastard."

"And the baby's father?" She raised her hands in the air. "Son of a bitch, he did what he did then disappeared."

"Listen to yourself," her father blushed.

Before parting, Solly repeated his warning. "Make sure you stay in your room, don't chat with the neighbors, don't explain or apologize. You can never know who's watching."

She promised.

"We will send you books," Irena promised. Then they left.

They returned some two weeks later. When she got off the train, Oleg was waiting for her.

"You have secrets, and I need money, a few zlotys, I'm parched." She gave him everything she had in her pocket.

"And you'll bring me more?"

"Why?"

"You'd better." She gave him more and to avoid worrying her, did not say a word to Tulla. She knew Oleg - a few zlotys would buy his silence.

Some five weeks later, her father appeared at her house, his face pale. "Quick," he said. "The contractions have begun."

"Where are you going?" asked Bronek when he saw them getting into the carriage.

"My mother is sick."

Listen my baby my little baby to the story about the rabbits that brought evil into the world

Once there was a kindly **rabbit** family who lived right beside a pack of wolves. The wolves always hated how the rabbits lived. They believed their own way was the only correct way.

One night there was an earthquake that killed a few of the wolves. The rabbits were blamed, since after all, everyone knows that rabbits pound the earth with their feet, and doing so causes earthquakes.

Another night, one wolf was struck by lightning and killed, and who did the wolves blame? The rabbits, of course, since, after all, everyone knows that lightning is caused by lettuce-eaters.

That winter the wolves had trouble finding food and who was to blame? Again, of course, the rabbits.

The wolves called an assembly and declared that if the rabbits continued wreaking such havoc, they would have to become educated to learn the wolf ways or be removed from the society of animals.

The rabbits decided to run away to a deserted island, but all of the other animals berated them: "You should be ashamed, you have to stay where you are and be courageous. The world is no place for cowards."

"But the wolves are threatening to kill us."

"Don't worry," said the other animals. "If the wolves attack you, we will come to your aid."

The rabbits were convinced and continued living beside the wolves. One day a terrible flood swept the land and drowned many wolves. And who was believed to be at fault? The rabbits, of course, since as everyone knows, long-eared, carrot-eaters bring floods. That's just science.

So, the wolves raided the rabbit family's home and trapped them in a dark cave. "It's for your own good," they explained to the rabbits, "so we can keep an eye on you."

A few weeks passed and the other animals had not heard a thing from the rabbits. They demanded to know what had become of them. The wolves told them that all the rabbits had been eaten, so it was essentially an internal matter. The animals protested, demanding a clear answer or they would unite against the wolves.

So, the wolves offered their reasoning: "We know they are guilty because they tried to escape... and as you know, there's no place in this world for fleeing cowards."

First moral of the story: Don't go, run, to the nearest deserted island.

Second moral of the story: The rabbits are always at fault.

CHAPTER 17

Nuzewo - Ciechanow, Autumn 1940

My baby girl smelled of hope.

Ilona. My Ilona.

I knew her name from the moment I heard her first cry.

I gave birth to her by the first light of dawn.

Because I was afraid of alerting the neighbors, I kept my pain inside. I did not groan or sigh or cry out but let her make her way quietly through me, then slip into the good hands of Irena, who managed to arrive and be by my side along with the midwife she brought with her.

She was there for the entire birth... embracing, encouraging, wiping away my sweat. Wetting my lips, squeezing my hand.

"Congratulations," she said, and handed me my baby. "She is the most beautiful baby in the world."

"My Ilona." I placed her on my chest, close to my heart, and immediately felt it connecting with hers through invisible threads. That special connection... motherhood. Unconditional love. A lifetime commitment.

"Ilona?"

"Ilona," I said. "Ilona the shining, the resplendent. Look at her, she's radiant. Ilona."

"Wait a moment," I stopped her. "So that's why you called me Noga, like..."

"Good job, Noga! Yes, like Ilona. You are alike, you bring light, you shine."

"And Dad calls you 'Ili' for short..."

"Short for Ilona, he thought that way the Polish name would sound Israeli."

"And as always — I was right," said Dad, who had decided to join us out of nowhere.

"Only Grandmas Tullerina still called Mom Ilona. Any other secrets I should know?"
"Patience," said Dad. "We still have a long way to go."
"Don't tell me that you too..." Dad winked at Mom and she smiled.
"Patience, Noga."
"Where were we?" asked Tulla.
"We were at the moment when you chose Mom's name — Ilona."

"My Ilona," I whispered over and over to myself. A big light. You are mine and I am yours and nobody will separate us, I whispered to the newborn who rested peacefully on me with her huge eyes and tiny, pretty hands.

Hey, my little Ilona, I inhaled her scent, I listened to her small sighs, I kissed her tiny fingers one at a time.

"Our baby, Ilona."

Irena picked Ilona up and held her on her shoulder. Irena's whole body seemed to curl around the precious newborn, which sensed the love around her and made small, contented sounds.

"Ilona," she said and returned her to me. "Our bright light."

That was the moment that determined everything, that set the course for the rest of our lives. There was no other way.

The midwife finished cleaning up the room, changed the sheets and towels, took her payment, and disappeared. Irena swaddled the baby in white cloth, rolled her until she looked like a tiny gosling, and moved her to the basket that we had prepared. She covered her, hummed a Polish song, placed her beside me and left the room to let me rest.

We had to be quiet. Silence was necessary for our safety. Like the lioness who hurries to lick and clean her cubs lest the scent of blood alert predators to their surroundings, we had to be careful of predators.

When I woke up, I saw Irena holding Ilona. She was rocking her gently and then presented her to me.

"Ilona wants her mother." To my surprise she began to nurse right away, hungrily. If only Johann were here, I thought. How happy you would make him. He would wrap you up in all of his great love and guide you through the great journey of life.

Even though we had initially agreed with Irena's parents that I would stay for only a few months, we decided to wait until Ilona was at least one year old

-when she would begin to walk and talk – before we would bring her to meet Johann's parents. Irena was certain that Marta so badly wanted a grandchild. Although she herself could no longer conceive, Marta did not stop hoping and paid a lot of money to the nuns or witches who would bless her daughter-in-law with fertility.

I don't know what Irena promised her parents in exchange for their willingness, but I assumed that their new oven was part of the transaction. When I suggested that she take something from my jewelry for compensation, she laughed and told me not to worry.

I knew that Irena was delaying her inevitable conversation with Andre. When she told me, I asked her to speak with him, not to delay. He deserved to know, I told her. But every time I asked her about it she said, "It's not a good time, not now, everyone is tense, let's wait a little."

But our plans were shattered one evening. As my mother always said, 'Man plans, and God laughs.'

One evening I heard footsteps. Irena, is that you? Maybe sweet Puchoy had come to visit me?

All at once I saw Oleg's grinning face. I knew he was always hanging around, inspecting me, and trailing me. More than once when I lifted my head, I saw him watching me.

When I asked Irena about him, she said that's how he was, nosy, nothing to worry about. But that evening he truly startled me. He stood at the entrance to the shed where I was living and watched me with a strange expression.

"Good evening," I said lightly to him.

"Tell me," he said. "Does your baby have a tail too?"

"Tail? Why only one? Three, maybe five…" I chuckled.

"Where do you hide it, then? In your underwear?" He neared me and tried to touch my backside. I moved away from him lightly and laughed aloud as though he had said something funny. As if I didn't understand. There was a bad smell in the room, the smell of fear.

"Tell me," he said. "You eat pork?"

"Do you?"

"If I bring you some good quality ham, will you eat it?"

"First bring it to me, if you really want to know."

"I know everything; I know you're a *Yid*. Did you think I was stupid?"

"You? Who said that?"

"I am very smart. What will you give me so that I don't tell on you," he threatened explicitly.

"To whom?" I smiled at him. Don't show fear - none - I told myself.

"I have all kinds of friends who might be looking for the likes of you," he said.

I heard Ilona sigh in her sleep and went to her, ignoring him.

"All kinds who might be looking for *Yids* and who would give me a lot if I… do you catch what I'm saying?" He went on, his eyes darting around like a hungry tiger observing his next meal.

Relax, calm down, just don't show fear. Fear will give you away, I told myself.

"You are so funny," I said. Ilona began to cry as if she could sense something and I did not move. I was signaling to him that his time was up. She began crying harder until it became a scream.

"She's hungry," he said and before I understood what he meant, he came close to me and placed both his hands on my breasts. "I'm hungry too. Would you deny me?" He whispered and began to knead my breasts, trying to pull my shirt off while Ilona went on screaming.

"Stop it," I pushed him. "You should be ashamed! Get out of here. If not…" He leaped back all at once, let out a blood-curdling yowl, then turned on his heel, laughed, and disappeared. That same night I put the bread knife under my pillow, as well as a few stones.

A week later he returned. "Hello, *Yid*," he chuckled. "Thought of me lately?"

"You're bothering me. Get out of here."

"I actually thought a lot about you." He grinned. "I have a few ideas… want to hear?"

"All I want is for you to get out of here at once."

"It doesn't work like that. It's not about what you want around here," he said and came close to me. "We have to reach some kind of agreement."

"Not interested."

"My friends are interested."

"You have friends?"

"Lots. But they are sad. They want a woman so… I thought… why not? It doesn't cost anything. They can have what they want." He grinned as if he had made a clever joke.

"Get out, right now!"

"It's a lot of money. You can buy a house for your daughter. You know I can always go and give up the woman with a tail who is hiding..."

"Get out of here. If you stay I..."

"You what?" He danced around me. "You'll call the police? Maybe the Gestapo? They love whores like you."

Any move I made could endanger me.

"What a genius I am," he admired himself. "My friends really want to see your tail and it's a lot of money, get it? I'll be back tomorrow... prepare yourself."

I held Ilona to me, rocking her gently in my arms. She was so helpless.

I locked the door and the window. I pushed the table, the chest of drawers and the bed against the door while Ilona watched me quietly.

I gathered any means of defense in case he decided to follow through with his threat. Big rocks, a tree branch, some shards of glass. I almost never left the shed at night. I stayed inside my little house. I stopped sleeping at night, only dozing off during the day.

To my surprise he did not return. Nor did I see him dozing on the grass. I did not dare ask after him.

Only two weeks later, when Irena came to visit, she told me that he was in prison for having been involved in a violent fight, a drunken brawl. He had hurt someone badly and was arrested by the police.

"Dad is furious with him and Mom weeps for him. Right now, he is awaiting trial."

Ilona was nine months old. She had already taken her first steps and mumbled some words, so Irena and I decided that the time had come. She was a gorgeous baby. She had huge blue eyes, plump skin, and fine, downy red hair just like Johann. How could anyone refuse such a beautiful baby, Johann's daughter?

We got into the carriage and set out for Ciechanow.

Irena sat beside the driver with her lips pursed. I sat in the back with Ilona, who fell asleep as we traveled over the winding path. When we stopped for a break she demanded to eat. We turned to Uncle Solly's house and there I could rest and take care of the baby. I was worried about meeting Johann's mother.

But Ilona needed a home, a warm room, and calm.

Marta was my only hope.

CHAPTER 18

Ciechanow 1941

"Coming," I heard Bronek shout. I knew from Johann that his name was Bronek and that he was a generous, kind-hearted man and, most importantly, decent. Solly hinted that he already knew who I was and that I was coming with Johann's baby.

The door opened.

He stood before me and looked at me, then at Ilona, then back at me. Ilona held out her arms to him and he blushed and gestured for me to come inside.

I entered. We stood there for several minutes and then he approached the baby, held her in his arms, close to his heart, then returned her to me and smiled. That first step was a success.

"Mama," Irena called. "Come, look, we have a guest."

"I'm in the kitchen." Marta responded. Irena motioned for me to follow her.

"Look, Marta, your granddaughter, Johann's gorgeous baby."

Marta stood with her back to me. She froze where she stood.

Then she turned her head very, very slowly, looked at me and Ilona, and turned her head back.

"Here," I said to her. "Meet Ilona, your granddaughter."

She got up slowly and approached me. Her face had turned crimson.

"Your granddaughter," I smiled at her. She folded her arms indignantly and gave Irena a look that oozed with hatred.

"Who's that?"

"This is Tulla, Mama, and this is your granddaughter. Look at her, she looks just like…" Marta responded as though someone had just punched her in the face.

"Get out!" she screeched.

"Look at the baby, Mama Marta."

"Irena, go to your room immediately and don't interfere."

"Marta, Mama," Irena pleaded. "Look at her… that's Ilona, your granddaughter."

Marta turned to her husband Bronek, who stood at the doorway to the kitchen. "Bronek, answer me: did you know about this?"

"Marta," Bronek hurried over to her. "Think how long we dreamed of a grandchild…"

"Go!" Marta screamed.

"Marta stop it! What's happened to you?"

"Get out, right now!" she screeched. "Get out and take that bastard of yours with you…"

"Why must you speak like that?" said Irena. "Look at her, she inherited your hair color."

"That's not the daughter of my Johann. Get her out of here. Cheater! Thief!"

"My dear Marta…" Bronek tried to speak to her but Marta went on screaming, threatening.

I was overcome by dizziness. I had to hold onto the table to keep from falling over. I could not let that happen. I had to stay strong. The little one looked at me, trying to understand the meaning of the shouting, then burst into tears. She held her arms towards the door as if begging to get out of there. Children can feel when they are not wanted…

"Out!" Marta slapped both hands on the table, then took off her apron and with a scowl and hurried up to their bedroom on the second floor.

"Get her out of here before I call the police," she shouted when she had reached the top of the stairs, then added, "Irena! Come up here right this minute!"

Irena came over to me and took Ilona in her arms.

"Papa," she approached Bronek. "Look at her, are you really willing to throw her out of the house?"

He recoiled, "Did you not hear Marta?"

"Papa Bronek, this is Johann's daughter. What will you tell him when he returns, that you threw his daughter out of your home?"

"I… I don't… Marta… I think that she should get out of here, and fast." His face was pale and he trembled.

"Bronek… this is our family," Irena tried again. "They need a home, for safety."

He raised his voice. "Did you not hear what we said? That is her bastard, not ours. Get her out of here immediately!"

They didn't want Jews in their home. Me. We had been mistaken, all of us. Naive, innocent Irena. Maybe I had been wrong all along to believe her and leave my refuge in Gregory's cellar.

"You are willing to throw your granddaughter out in the street?"

"They have to go," he turned to the stairs up to the second floor. "Do exactly what Marta says and fast, before she, before she calls the police… this is bad…" He climbed the stairs haltingly.

The house was silent.

Irena looked at me with great sorrow in her face. She raised her hands in despair as if to say, "I failed, I'm sorry, I tried." Upstairs, Marta went on screaming, demanding that Irena come up and join her.

It was finished. That was clear. I began walking toward the front door.

"Wait," Irena said. "Just give them time."

Ilona reached for Irena, who picked her up. "My darling, sweet girl, what will I do?" she whispered.

Ilona began to wail.

I took the baby from Irena's hands. She did not protest. She remained standing as if she had lost all the power that until now had burned brightly within her.

"I was wrong… forgive me… I believed that they… she's Johann's baby… I will find a solution, don't go." Ilona's cries grew stronger.

"Don't cry," I rocked her. "Enough my baby, it will be okay, everything will be okay."

I covered the two of us with a big scarf and went out of the house. I heard Irena calling to me, asking me to come back.

Outside the world went on as usual, everyone going about their business. Shop owners stood in the entrance of their shops and offered us their wares, children ran after balls, running into one another, two girls stood in the corner singing, a bowl for coins beside them. Heavyset women carried baskets, and two German military motorcycles screeched. A cold wind blew around me, as if it were trying to get me out of there, and an autumn rain began to fall. Ilona was quiet. She looked at me with her intelligent eyes, as if she were trying to anticipate what I was going to do. Where would I go? My poor girl. What would become of us?

Kicked out. Exiled.

I just stood there, considering what I would do next. Everyone who passed stoked my fear. It seemed to me like people were pointing at me, wondering who I was, what I was doing there. Maybe word had already spread. Maybe they were already summoning the police. I had to get out of there quickly, before Marta followed through on her threats against me.

I crossed the street and waited.

Maybe they would call me, ask me to come back. Maybe Irena would come out to find me and tell me that they had changed their minds, that they wanted to see us after all.

"Mrs, are you all right?" asked someone. "Are you ill? Do you need a doctor? Is that your daughter?" People began to gather around me. I had to get out of there.

I kept on walking wherever my legs would take me. I passed gardens, churches, municipal buildings and went down to the big castle. I walked and walked, with no destination, not knowing where I was going. Every now and then I stopped and glanced to see if the Gestapo were already coming after me. Soon it would be dark. The last rays of light, the end of the day, and my hopes were dashed. I walked until I reached the banks of the Lydinia River that divided the city. There I stopped.

Where would I go from here? Was this the end of the road? I was overcome with deep despair. There was nowhere to go from here. Was this the end of the journey for us?

I walked along the lengths of the Lydinia, which flowed fast, angrily slapping at the rocks on the riverbank, pulling mud and stones with it, swallowing everything in its path.

The river!

Yes, the river. The water would take us in. The end of our hardships. It wouldn't hurt... just a few minutes and it would be over. Then other voices from within, shouting no! I was shocked by the terrible thought I had had.

No, my little Ilona, I will take care of you. You have only just begun to get to know the world. What right do I have to take that from you?

My little treasure lay in my lap, unconcerned, feeling safe. I walked along the riverbanks. A wooden bench not far from the riverbank called to me. I sat down. It was wet and cold, but I had to nurse the baby. She would eat then fall asleep, and then she wouldn't have to see that we had reached the end of the road.

All at once the figure of Hagar arose before me. Hagar, the beautiful sorceress who became the consort of Abraham our patriarch and was sent away by Sarah. Hagar, who found herself in the desert without bread or water, with no chance of being saved, and who threw her son Ishmael under a bush so as not to witness his death. Those terrible words rang in my ears over and over, "She put the boy under one of the bushes. Then she went off and sat down about a bowshot away, for she thought, "I cannot watch the boy die." And as she sat there, she began to sob." (Genesis 21:15)

That's what I would do. I would place Ilona on the bench and not watch her death. I'll pray for her. Maybe, as with Hagar in her hour of need, God would answer my prayers, and someone would find her, have mercy, and give her a home and love. That's what a child needs: love and a home. And I have nothing left to give... I'm empty.

Just like Hagar. I too had been sent away, into the desert.

I rocked my baby until she fell asleep. Her pink mouth hung open, her huge eyes and long eyelashes fluttered. Forgive me, little one, forgive me. There is no room in this world for me. But you... I placed her gently on the wooden bench and covered her with a blanket and my big scarf. I am sorry my child, I cannot go on. There's no way out for me. Wait here. We will pray that someone will pass and take you and give you a warm home, plenty of food. I have nothing left to give you...

Don't cry, Ilona, you have a new chance. Hope. Just like it was written in the bible, "God has heard the child crying as he lies there..." Maybe this time, too, God will hear your cries and send you someone who will save you.

Hot tears rolled down my face and burned my cheeks. I kissed her again and again, breathing her in, gently so as not to wake her. Then I began to walk.

I thought, "I will walk into the raging waters, the water that swallows up everything. There I will find rest."

The sound of Ilona's cries reached my ears. Quiet at first, weak, pleading, urging me to come back, and then stronger...begging, demanding, needing me.

I kept going. First step. The water was as cold as ice, rocks that were swept up hit my legs but I did not care. Second step. Third.... Ilona suddenly began screaming at the top of her lungs, as if begging mercy from the heavens. Maybe God would hear her voice...

A few more steps... just a few more steps...

"Tulla, Tulla, Tu-laaaaaa..." I heard voices calling my name. Were those angels calling to me? Drawing me to them? I advanced slowly.

Fourth step, fifth, the water lapped at the hem of my dress. I didn't stop. Take my baby and give me rest. I want to sleep.

"Tulla, Rachelle... stop... please, stop my dear," someone shouted. Irena?

"Look, here's Ilona, she's right here, she's asking you to come back, Tulla..."

I turned.

Irena was holding my Ilona in her arms, crying and laughing, waving with the girl, pointing to me. "Look here's Mama, tell her to come back... and then all of us will walk home together. Home."

Beside her stood Bronek.

I stopped.

"Come, Tulla," Bronek said gently and began walking towards me. When he was close, he held out his hand, "Come with us. We, Marta and I, want to get to know our granddaughter."

I grasped his hand and let him pull me from the water.

Irena handed me the baby.

"Thank you, God," I whispered when she was safely back in my arms.

From that moment on, I stopped feeling afraid.

I felt that nothing could hurt me anymore.

CHAPTER 19

Ciechanow, 1941

Better days came to pass.

There were nights when I was able to fall into a deep sleep and managed not to be awakened by every sound, as I had for so long.

Slowly but surely, I relaxed. Slowly but surely, we all relaxed.

At the start, life in the home of Johann's parents was full of worries and concern about the guests who had come to the house as I tried to ascertain if, God forbid, she would hand me over to the Germans. After a month in which my body remained tense and stressed, she had not turned me in, and I began to settle in. Sometimes I even sang…of the summer sun and the lark looking for seeds.

My baby had a warm house to live in, good food, nice clothes, and a grandmother and grandfather. But it was clear that my presence caused Marta grief. It was hard for her to accept me in her home, despite my trying to diminish myself as much as possible. I would clean and do laundry and whatever tasks she threw at me. I ironed, scrubbed, and polished, but she remained strong in her resolve not to talk to me. She was unwilling to eat in my presence or be near me for so much as a minute. I would eat my meals alone, after the others had finished, and was required to remain in my room after I finished my work. But if she despised me, she adored the little one. Ilonichka, she called her. My darling, she called her. My love. My Johann's little girl, as though she had not come into the world through me.

She would sit for hours and tell her stories, sing songs in Polish and German, show her photographs of her father. She would walk with her along the streets of the city, telling everyone about Johann's daughter. To anyone who asked about me, she answered that I was a village girl whom she had hired as a servant. God forbid she should admit I was the mother. As for the mother, she told everyone something about the sickness and death of poor Johann's wife.

I agreed to all of it, of course.

The room given to Ilona was beautifully decorated and filled with games and toys. Each day, Bronek would return home from his shop bringing some new book or plaything for the baby. I continued to be despised.

Irena told me not to worry, that time would work its magic. Marta would come to terms with it, and everything would change for the better when Johann returned.

I went on breastfeeding. Marta knew how healthy it was for her little Ilon-ichka to keep nursing, even if it was the milk of a *Yid*, so she agreed to the arrangement. And so, I was able to be alone with Ilona five times a day, snuggling her close against my body, telling her stories of her father, the hero, who would soon return, of her wise grandfather, of spring flowers and summer nights…

At first, they meant to keep me in the shed out in the yard. It was a dirty, flea-ridden hovel that had been colonized by rats. When Irena saw it, she argued that it would be better for me to be closer to Ilona who still sometimes needed to be nursed during the night, and suggested that I stay with her in her room… just temporarily, she explained to Marta, until Andre came back. To our surprise they agreed. Seven months passed and it seemed that we had found some kind of balance, a kind of strange togetherness between people forced to live under the same roof; little Ilona brought us together.

When the subject of baptism came up, I did not know what to do. Marta insisted. Bronek sided with her, of course. I refused.

I asserted that my Ilona was Jewish. Marta argued that according to her religion she was a Christian, and once again the hatred peeked out. Little threats were dropped here and there.

Irena tried to reconcile us. She tried to convince me. "What does it matter?" she said. "After all, Ilona will be yours in the end and this arrangement is only temporary. Johann will come back, and everything will be sorted out. He won't care."

The morning that they took my baby to church, dressed in a white lace gown and ribbons and jewelry, I remained in my room. It's nothing, a stupid matter, I tried to convince myself. Ilona is yours, so she is Jewish and will always be Jewish. This ceremony is meaningless in my eyes and in the eyes of God.

They returned joyful from the church. The house filled up with guests, relatives, and friends, and my Ilona was passed from one to another. I was asked to assist Irena. I was the helper, after all, a miserable village girl she had found to help out. Good for you Marta, they all said, you are a generous person.

Gradually, more of Bronek's German friends showed up. Military officers and then some. There were those who arrived in black uniforms, who loved to brag, telling stories about how they captured Jews who were hiding like mice in the gutters, how they shot them mercilessly, and how the cooperative Poles were happy to help the Germans in their mission.

The "friends" would bring good wine and German sausage and enjoyed Marta's cooking. She made a special effort to prepare them foods that would remind them of home: pies, soups, and meat with cabbage.

Sometimes I would be asked to help her set the table or serve the wine. At such moments I could feel the eyes of the Germans on me and pray that the evening would pass peacefully, without questions. I would answer, "The baby is Marta's son's child. The mother died in childbirth." And Marta would hurry me out of the room.

Once, when I served a rabbit stew, I heard one of them asking who I was.

"A poor young woman for whom I am providing a home," came the response. "She nurses my Ilona."

And then someone said, "Pretty like a Jewess."

"Maybe she's actually Jewish?" one of them said. "Have you checked, Marta?"

Marta chuckled, "You think a *Yid* could work in my house?"

"You are Jewish, aren't you?" someone in civilian clothes once asked me.

"Just don't tell Marta," I said and added, "she should not find out that I'm a Jew." And I spat. There was a moment of silence. Then everyone burst out laughing.

I saw Bronek stare at the floor in that moment to hide his concern.

Sometimes they would present Ilona to the guests. They would pass her from hand to hand, kiss her, sing her songs in German, and she would dance, wave her little arms, stamp her feet.

She especially loved the song about little Maier who climbed the Himalayas.

"*Was macht doktor Maier,* little Maier in the big Himalayas."

One evening, something that I had been afraid would happen did.

One of the regular guests brought an officer who was staying in Ciechanow.

He was a Major General, a high rank, above the level of the usual "friends." Everyone treated him with great respect. He drank endlessly until his face turned red and his eyes were little holes in his burning face, but he went on filling his cup, tapping his heels, and shouting, "heil Hitler" with each glass.

When I passed by, he pulled me to him and sat me forcefully on his knees.

"This is the best seat in the house," he said, and the others laughed. I saw Bronek turn pale and Marta grin.

I tried to get up but he held me down.

I had to get away from him and I had to be wise about it and not incite his anger. I removed his hands and tried to stand up.

"Where to, Fraulein?" He asked. "A general's knees are no good for you?" The pungent smell of alcohol rose from his mouth and his eyes darted around quickly.

"Tulla," Irena called me from the kitchen. "Where are you, lazy girl?"

"She's busy," shouted one of the officers.

"If you don't come here immediately, I'll send you back to..."

"Sorry, they need me," I tried to get up again, and again he pulled me back down.

"You will get up when I say so."

"If I keep sitting," I said, "who will heat up the general's soup? It is the best in all of Poland," I tried as best I could not to anger him.

"That's why we have Mrs. Marta," he replied. I pushed him off of me and he teetered, then fell from his chair. There was silence in the room. I knew that this act would not pass quietly. My mind worked quickly. How could I get out of this embarrassing situation without him turning on me? I could not lose my senses now. I pretended I lost my balance, let out a small shriek and fell on top of him.

Everyone laughed, including him.

Bronek helped him to stand up. I did not move. The room was silent.

"Long live the Fraulein," the major general held out his hand to me. "Here's a girl who understands how things work." He waved a glass before me and bowed to me. We smiled congenially at one another before I disappeared into the kitchen.

When they left, Bronek and Marta came into the kitchen. I went on scrubbing the oven as if they weren't frowning at me.

"What was that supposed to be?" Marta began, but Bronek shushed her.

"Crazy woman, do you realize that you put all of us in danger?" Bronek moved toward me.

"Did you see that—"

"The next time one of our guests or friends touches your filthy Jewish bottom, you tell him thank you, understood?"

"Sorry," I replied. "Forgive me."

"They will do what they want with you and you will keep your mouth shut, understood?" He was basically a good man but he feared Marta's tantrums and did everything he could to please her.

"Or maybe you would prefer that the Gestapo explain it to you," said Marta. "You do as I say and only as I say so long as you are here. Not what you think. And tell my honorable wife thank you, every morning, every evening, Scum," Bronek raised his hand and slapped my face once, twice. I remained standing.

"I'm sorry," I said. "I understand, I made a terrible mistake."

"There will be no next time," said Marta.

They left the kitchen, righteous and justified in their own eyes.

From that evening on, Irena did whatever she could to keep me from having to serve those German pigs.

"Why do you flatter them?" I heard Irena ask.

"They're our friends, they help us."

"I don't understand why you are willing to host those pigs."

She asked them to inform us when they would be coming. Bronek and Marta had their own concerns; with the help of the Germans they had a chance of finding out where Johann was. Thanks to them, Andre had become a successful, powerful man, and the household was comfortable... we did not want for anything.

Marta forbade us from listening to the news. In their "cultured" home we listened only to music. But we heard what was happening at Uncle Solly's house. Solly told us that hunters had seen trucks filled with Jews driving into the forests. They heard shots and shouting but did not dare get closer. There were convoys of youths sent to forced labor camps and people disappearing mysteriously. Whole families were being uprooted in the middle of the night.

Solly knew that the Jews in the ghetto were in terrible shape. There was hunger, insufferable crowding. Fear and disease ran rampant. If only I could help. I wanted to give aid to the captive Jews. After all, I was a doctor. I had sworn the Hippocratic oath to help the unwell and always try to save life. I felt helpless.

But I could not endanger Ilona, Irena, or Johann's family. If the Germans were to find me treating sick people in the ghetto, all of us would be in danger. I consulted with Irena. She pleaded with me not to do anything reckless. I should not take any action that would upset Marta, who was already unbalanced.

"Think of Ilona," was the sentence that stopped me from going into the ghetto. But destiny had its own plans.

One morning, I went to the market to buy groceries. I saw a group of youths kicking another boy who lay on the sidewalk, trying in vain to defend himself.

"What's going on?" I asked. People stood around watching. Nobody interfered. Nobody tried to stop them. Without thinking twice, I pushed my way in and stood before them. "Stop it!" I shouted.

"Don't interfere, Miss."

"Three against one? What did he do to you?"

"Hit the Jew," one shouted and began jumping around like a madman.

"Enough, you've done enough, now leave him be."

"Who are you to tell us what to do?"

One of the youths, who was holding a stick, approached me, waving his stick from side to side as if he were considering hitting me with it.

"I suggest you stop here," I said to him.

"Look at her, Jew-lover," he shouted and his friends joined him. "Hit the Jews!"

Fortunately, the noise attracted other passersby who tried to calm the commotion, talk sense into the youths, and send them on their way. They left, still cursing me. They disappeared and I approached the boy lying on the sidewalk. His thin hands covered his head, which was bleeding, and he looked as though the life had been sucked out of him. He had the yellow badge on one arm, so we would make no mistake, we would know he was a Jew, whose blood was fair game.

"Will you let me treat you?" I bent over him and began to wipe his wounds with a cloth that one of the passersby had placed in my hand.

"Just let me go."

"Don't be afraid."

"I'm fine," he pressed his hands to his head and recoiled from me as if I intended to hurt him too.

"I can help you," I whispered. "Let me clean your cuts. Are you able to stand?"

"Who..."

"I'm Jewish, like you. I live in the city."

"You... are a Jew?" He whispered.

"My name is Rachel, and yours?" He opened his eyes and whispered his name, "David."

I helped him up. A stench came off his filthy clothes and he could barely stand on his feet. I led him to a bench not far from the market. I felt the gaze of onlookers. "What happened exactly?"

"I went out to get medicine for my mother. When they saw me leaving the ghetto, they followed me and beat me."

"Beat you? Do you want to file a complaint with the police?"

"Police? Have you forgotten? I am a Jew living in the ghetto, they can do whatever they want."

I wiped his head carefully. I was relieved to see that the blood was starting to dry. "Show me the prescription." He handed me a piece of paper stained with blood. Based on the medicine prescribed by the doctor, Dr. Levy, I understood that his mother was sick with dysentery, an illness that could be fatal if it went untreated. Cholera, dysentery, and typhus break out when there is polluted water and raw sewage in the streets. The ghetto was an ideal environment for these diseases.

"Wait here," I told him. "Please don't move. It's better if I bring you the medicine."

The pharmacist took the prescription from me, looked at me with suspicion and asked who the patient was.

"Why is that important?" I asked him.

He asked why I wanted a medicine that was not for me and I explained to him that it was for a woman who lived in the ghetto and her courageous son had left it to get the medicine for her. He gave me back the prescription. "Impossible. I have instructions."

"I hope that you have not forgotten the doctors' oath." He refused to meet my eye.

"I am sorry. I have instructions, I can't help them. It's too dangerous." I left the pharmacy, furious. When I crossed the street, I heard steps behind me. I turned and saw the pharmacist's young helper. He caught up to me, stood before me and handed me a brown bag.

"He asks that you understand, he's afraid. All of us are afraid these days," he said and disappeared.

I returned to David. I explained to him that his mother must drink a lot of water and that it was important to boil it first. He listened and promised to look after her. He was only 17 years old, a young man who had had to grow up all at once. I accompanied him to the gates of the ghetto. At that time people could still come in and out.

Four soldiers stopped me and asked for my papers.

"You're Tulla?" said one.

"Always," I smiled.

"Go, this is no place for you," I saw David signal to me that everything was okay. That evening, I told Irena what had happened.

"You're crazy, if Marta hears…"

"What will she do to me?"

"I think that you don't fully understand who you're dealing with here."

"I have to help them."

"And endanger everyone? When they break open Ilona's head on the pavement, what will you say?" I did not answer. Maybe she was right.

Since I knew she was following me, I waited a few days before returning to the ghetto gates. I hoped to find David and hear how his mother was doing.

I stationed myself not far from the gate. I asked everyone who came out if they knew how David's mother was doing.

"Why?" a young woman asked me.

"Because… we are old acquaintances and I worry about her."

"You don't have to worry any longer."

"I'm glad she is well; I was very worried."

"She died," said the young woman.

"And David?"

"After the funeral he escaped from the ghetto. He's a brave boy, said he was joining the underground."

I hurried to get back before Marta began asking me questions about where I'd been and whether I had spoken to anyone. She ordered me to behave like a village girl in the big city: quiet and a little stupid. When I walked through an alleyway, I sensed someone following me. I did not turn around. Was it Gestapo?

When you live a lie, faking, denying who you are, any moment could blow up in your face. I started to walk more slowly as if I had nothing to hide. The pursuer continued behind me, walking at my pace, maintaining a consistent distance. I felt his presence like a knife in my back. What did he want? Who was it? Someone who knew? Someone who wanted to harm me? A spy? Had someone caught on?

I took bigger steps, and so did he. I slowed down and he slowed down too. Who are you? At the end of the alleyway, I stopped all at once and turned around.

David. Yes, David, still with a bandage on his head and his eyes burning.

"David," I said, "God, you scared me, I'm sorry... I heard your mother died."

"Yes, she passed out of this world and everything that awaited her in it. Maybe she was lucky to get out of here."

"They told me that you ran away and..."

"It was my sister Sarah who told you that. She did not know your motives so she lied. A lie to protect us. Tulla, we need your help."

"My help? I can barely..."

"We need more medicine."

"I'm so sorry, but my medical license is not valid and there's no way someone will..."

"I'm talking about drugs that can be found in any pharmacy. Here's a list. Please. Children are dying, typhus and cholera are running rampant..."

"I don't know if..." but he disappeared. All that remained was the list of medicines in my hand. What would I do with it?

Should I risk everything? Ilona would not survive the ghetto, I couldn't. I can't...

The next day, I walked to the pharmacy. The pharmacist looked at me and understood at once. I waited patiently in the long line until his helper gestured for me to follow him.

"What do you want now?"

I showed him the list.

"That's going to cost a lot of money. Who's going to pay me...?"

I took a gold ring with a red stone off my finger. "Here, as payment. It's gold." The pharmacist examined it carefully. "It's not enough."

"These are inexpensive medicines... this is more than enough."

"Cheap medicines and great risk, I'm sorry," he handed me back the ring. I noticed him glance at the other ring I wore. My mother had bought me that ring to celebrate my *bat mitzvah*. What should I do, give up the one souvenir that I had from my mother?

I could hear my mother's voice speaking to me: A ring or saving lives, what's more important? You know exactly what to do. You remember me in your heart, not because you have a ring on your finger. That's just decoration.

"Here, take this," I told him. He looked at it. "Another ring with an expensive pearl. Take it, but on condition that you double the amount of medicine." I saw him smile.

Your day will come, I thought, when we will be victorious and we won't forgive your greed. He tucked them into his pocket and placed the bag of medicines on the counter.

"Not enough," I told him and he looked at me.

He added more medicine: anti-diarrhea, medicine to bring down a fever, and everything they needed in the ghetto. What do I do now? How would I get these medicines to them? David must be nearby tracking my whereabouts and waiting for the opportunity to come collect this treasure. I decided to walk the city streets. I was sure that David would follow and find the right moment. As I entered an alleyway, he caught up to me. Without saying a word, he took the bag of medicines from my hand and kept on walking as though we had never met.

At the end of the alley he turned and waved to me. "How will I find you if we need something..."

"I will come to the ghetto a week from today. Wait for me there."

The sun was already high in the sky when I began to head back towards the house. I took a deep breath. I had to prepare for meeting Marta, lest someone tell her. Maybe someone had witnessed what I'd done. Before I opened the door, I stopped.

Eagle-eyed Marta, who was trying to catch me in some blunder, would notice my naked hand and want to know what I had done with the rings, to whom I had given them or what I bought for them, and would threaten to call the police at once. But I had done something important for my people. Something small, but important. Starting tomorrow, I would go to the ghetto every day to care for the sick. Yes. I had the good fortune of a comfortable life so long as I helped others. That's what I thought, not knowing what awaited me at home.

Fate was not finished toying with me.

I opened the door slowly, hoping that Marta was still enjoying her afternoon nap. To my surprise, I found Bronek sitting at the table, holding his head in his hands as if it would fall. Bronek was home in the middle of the day? Was he drunk? Ill?

Something must have happened. Ilona! Thoughts raced through my mind.

"What happened, Bronek?" He let out a heavy groan. I saw that his face was wet. My heart was gripped with fear. "Ilona?"

"Where have you been?"

"I... what happened?"

"You disappeared... we've been looking for you for hours..."

"Who? Why?" I hugged him. "Bronek, what happened?"

Now I heard the wailing, as though someone were being slaughtered. A soft howl that grew louder until it was a blood-curdling scream, then suddenly froze and fell silent.Ilona? Had something happened to my baby?

"Quick, what happened to Ilonichka, Bronek?" I shook him. "What happened to my baby?"

"Here, this is what happened," he handed me a piece of paper. A telegram. I understood at once. I did not need to read the telegram. Johann.

"Fallen... dead... in the line of duty," Bronek read off the telegram.

"But... they said... isn't he being held captive?"

"He was killed on the fourth day of the war."

"And only now..."

"Misidentified. Now they are telling us... we can't even bury him."

"Marta?"

"Bad. You don't understand... the doctor gave her something to calm down. She just wants to die... I suggest you don't go to her now..."

"I have to share my grief..."

"Be careful, Tulla."

I should have taken his advice. But I had to talk to her, to calm the mother of my beloved. I raced up the stairs. Ilona's bed was empty. I peered into Marta's room. She was lying on her back, staring at the ceiling. Her arms were by her sides and she was breathing heavily, as if she had lost the will to live.

I did not dare enter.

Irena? Where had she disappeared to? She'd probably gone for a walk with Ilona, removing her from the terrible grief that had overwhelmed us all.

Johann? My darling, my heart had not lied. That morning he left I knew it was goodbye. I knew he was going to his death. I needed time to myself to grieve. I sank onto my mattress and a river of pain washed over me, flowing through me, blocking my lungs, releasing groans from deep within that tore at my insides. Johann? Where are you now? I can hear your voice, smell the sweet, bitter smell from your body. I can feel your hands on me, pleasuring me, loving me.

Through the shutters, the world was visible, as if my whole world had not just now grown dark. The trees reached their branches to the heavens, hiding the nests of birds among them. Children rolled a creaky wheel around, and the footsteps of Wehrmacht soldiers' boots on the sidewalk echoed in the distance. Only the heart wept.

"Tulla? Tulla are you sleeping?" It was Bronek, his voice heavy and ominous. "Tulla, get out. Get out of there quickly."

In the mirror I saw a woman who had aged a hundred years. New wrinkles dug into my neck and face, my eyes were sunken and my hair faded all at once.

"Tulla, open up right now," he spoke in a tone I had never heard from him before. What had happened? He stood before me, pale. I saw despair in his eyes. From that moment I was afraid.

"You have to get out of here, at once!"

"Where?"

"Quick," he pulled me roughly.

"Why, Bronek?"

"Because… you don't understand? Why, why did you do this to us?"

"Nobody is guilty here, Bronek," I tried to approach him, to place a calming hand on his arm, to hug him. "Your son Johann was a hero; war takes many victims and…"

"Don't you dare say his name." Now I saw that Marta was standing behind him. Now it all made sense. Marta. Her hatred. "You brought this upon us, you vile woman -out!"

"Marta…"

"Get out or I hand you over to the Gestapo."

I moved towards them, my arms out to embrace them, to be together in our pain.

Marta's face twisted and she turned her back to me. Bronek hurried to my room and began throwing my clothes after me, shouting again and again that I had to leave at once.

"Ilona…"

"Get out of here, now!"

"I am not moving from here without my daughter. Where is she?"

"Cheater, she's not yours! You stole her from some poor woman… we know everything, the police will take care of you."

I heard the door slam and Irena humming a children's song. Irena! Finally! I raced to the door like a mad woman. She was here now. She would explain everything. From now on everything would be okay. Marta would calm down, Bronek would smile. This was just a temporary crisis.

Ilona stood at the entrance to the house with a blue silk ribbon on her head.

"My darling," I called her and held out my arms. She pointed to the ribbon in her hair. "New, Mamarina bought it for me."

"Wonderful, come to me, baby," I held out my arms but Irena kept holding her, not letting her go. I tried to take my daughter. Irena lifted the girl to her, beginning to spin her around like she loved, the little girl laughing, ignoring me.

"Come to Mama, we need to go for a walk," I tried to stop her, take her, get out of here, but Irena went on singing and spinning around and around the room until they were beside the stairs leading up to the second floor.

"Irena, my sister…" it was as if she did not hear me. "Please," I begged. "She's hungry, let me nurse her."

"I'm sorry," she whispered.

Marta stood at the top of the stairs, her eyes blazing with hatred.

She gestured to Irena to come up with the girl.

"Wait, Irena," I pleaded, crying, wallowing in pain. "Give me my daughter."

Irena looked at Marta and continued up the stairs.

Ilona began to cry. "Mama! Mama Tulla!"

"Get her out of here."

"Not without Ilona, my daughter."

"She is not your daughter, you thief, you kidnapper of babies."

I heard Ilona somewhere crying, screaming, pleading. Asking for me, her mother. Mama. Her Mama Tulla.

"She needs me," I begged. Marta stood before me, showed me the door. "Please Marta, I will do whatever you ask of me," I went down on my knees, kissed the hem of her skirt, pleading. She did not even look at me, just swatted at my face with her foot.

"Go."

No, I cannot go. I sat down in the middle of the room. "You won't get me out of here without my daughter."

"Like that?" shouted Bronek. "I will call the Gestapo. I will tell them that you are trying to steal our baby." Bronek and Marta, who had gone out of their minds, began to drag me by my hair and pushed me toward the door, hitting and screaming and blaming me for terrible things, as if I were the source of all the evil in the world...

"Irena!" I cried, "Irena..."

She did not answer. I just heard her voice, singing to my Ilona, a song that she loved, of little Maier in the Himalayas.

"What was happening here? Was it all a conspiracy that they had come up with together?

"Get out, bitch."

Marta was hysterical, hitting with all her might, kicking, screaming, as if possessed.

"Not without my daughter," I tried to shout. "Give me my daughter."

"You won't touch her, she's ours. She was born to Irena and our Andre."

"No!!!"

Bronek lifted the big broom he used to clear the paths and pushed me out as if I were trash and hurried to lock the door. I sat down beside the door.

The world became quiet again, and the lights in my soul went out.

Darkness came over everything.

There was no way out.

CHAPTER 20

Ciechanow, January 1942

When the telegram came saying that Johann had been killed, Irena was in Ilona's room. That same day, Marta had asked her to come home early from her work doing bookkeeping for Uncle Solly, as important guests were expected. Tulla was sent to shop for groceries in the market, and Irena put the baby to sleep.

Ilona was restless that morning and, uncharacteristically, would not stop crying, as if she sensed something. Irena tried singing to her, changing her diaper, rocking her, but the little girl would not calm down. She cried, wailed, hit her pillow with her fists. Irena decided to take her for a walk.

"Stop," she said and dressed the resistant girl in her coat. "We will go for a walk. Perhaps we will meet Mama Tulla at the market and eat strawberry ice cream together."

As she was wrestling the girl into her coat, she heard the doorbell.

Ilona went quiet.

The two waited to know who had rung.

The door creaked, then slammed, then she heard Marta screaming, yowling as if someone had hit her.

Irena picked up the girl and hurried downstairs. Marta stood by the door, her face puffed up, her hands holding the telegram. Irena understood at once. "Oh Marta, my dear, this is terrible," she said.

"Johann… is dead… my boy… he…" she tried to snatch Ilona but the child held tight to Irena, refusing to let go.

"I'm so sorry Marta, I'm so, so sorry."

"It's her!" she shrieked suddenly. "It's her! It's all her fault!"

"Should I call Bronek?"

"That Jewish bitch is the one who brought this disaster upon us."

"Marta, stop."

"Yes," she shouted, furious, "She... all of it is because of her, all of it! Why did you bring her here?"

"Marta, stop, war has many victims, it's not..."

"If he hadn't met her, he would still be alive. She is our misfortune, our downfall."

"It's a terrible tragedy, Marta, but there's nobody guilty here, just..."

"Shut up, now!" Marta ordered and nearly hit her.

Irena approached the hysterical woman, trying to embrace her to calm her, but Marta went on screaming.

"If she dares set foot in my house, I will call the police at once... no, the Gestapo, I will stab her myself with a knife! I will ruin her pretty face. Get her out of here."

Irena hesitated. What should she do? Look after Marta? Call the family doctor?

Better to let Bronek take on Marta and then she and Ilona would hurry to the market to tell Tulla, to warn her. Marta trembled like a madwoman, crying and blaming, wailing and threatening. Only Bronek could calm her down. Without asking, Irena placed the little girl in her carriage and hurried to the clock shop to call Bronek home.

Bronek received the news with a stern expression.

"Go to her, quickly," she said to him. "Call the doctor. She must calm down, she... she isn't talking sense." He shook his head heavily and left the shop.

Irena knew that she had to find Tulla before she came home and discovered that everything had been turned upside down in her absence. Not only was Johann dead, but she would have to face Marta's rage.

She knew Tulla's regular route to the market, which had once been the bustling center of life and was now almost silent. Most of the stalls were closed. Here and there were farmers who offered her cabbage or carrots at outrageous prices, men who stood idle, and ragged children who begged for small change. Only the sound of soldiers marching as they passed not far away reminded them of the occupation. The Germans needed food to feed their army. Sometimes they would descend on the bigger farms and confiscate their produce.

Nobody had seen Tulla that morning, but the seller at the vegetable stand said he thought she might have gone to the pharmacy with a boy.

"A boy? Are you sure?!"

He was sure, he had seen her with a boy.

"What boy?" Irena wondered. "And why to the pharmacy?"

There was only one pharmacy in the market area. When she entered, she found several customers standing in line, and the pharmacist was busy explaining to the protesting crowd that he was out, all out. His order had not come. He did not know when it would arrive. What could he do? Of course, he wanted to sell them what they needed...

His wife tried to calm the angry crowd who accused him of inflated prices. If two soldiers had not come and stood in the entrance, a melee would have broken out.

"Yes?" said the pharmacist when Irena's turn came.

"Maybe you saw my sister-in-law, Tulla, here..." but then she noticed Tulla's ring on his wife's finger.

"Nice ring," she said to her, then smiled and waved. The pharmacist repeated his question, "What do you need?"

"Just to know where that ring came from."

"My husband bought it for me," she raised her hand and turned it to show off the ring. There was no mistaking it.

"Are you sure?"

"Why do you ask?"

"Because it belongs to my sister-in-law, Tulla."

"I must ask you to leave," the pharmacist grew impatient. "Or I will call..." he pointed at the soldiers.

"For your information, she paid me for medicine with that ring."

"Medicine... for whom?"

He shrugged. "You should ask her yourself. Who's next?"

Could Tulla be sick and hiding it from her?

"What medicine did she buy?"

"All kinds. For diarrhea, fever, pain, nausea, some bandages, a thermometer, whatever I had," he said and put the ring in his pocket. "This is mine, it's all above board."

"Who did she..." she stopped. She saw the soldiers looking at her with interest and hurried out. Ilona waved goodbye to them. Irena was furious.

She knew exactly who those medicines were for.

Tulla had mentioned more than once that she felt the need to help her Jewish brethren in the ghetto. And each time the subject arose, Irena begged her not to dare to try. Behind my back? How dare she, she's risking everything! We will have to have a difficult conversation about this. We'll give it a couple days. For now, there's bad news waiting for her and first we will have to overcome Marta's fury.

She heard the shouting as she approached the house.

Marta was screaming as if she were being slaughtered. Irena could see neighbors peeking out from behind their blinds, trying to find out what was happening. Everyone needed to calm down and fast, before someone found them out.

All of Marta's hatred, all of her anger exploded at once. She blamed Tulla for everything that had happened to her beloved son and demanded that she leave immediately. Now. To the street. Just like that. Without any of her belongings or she would scream and call her friends, the Gestapo. She heard Tulla's shouts as Bronek and Marta pulled her by the hair and pushed her forcefully out the door as if she were trash.

"Irena!" she heard Tulla shout, "Help me!"

Irena froze on the spot. What can I do? She thought. All is lost, who could stand up to the hysterical Marta and ailing Bronek?

A moment later there was quiet. All she heard was Tulla crying and Ilona wailing. The baby refused to calm down. Maybe she was demanding her mother. When Marta and Bronek went up to bed, Ilona finally fell asleep, her face burning, and Irena took a blanket and warm coat and went out to the street.

Tulla was still lying beside the door. She looked lifeless. Irena bent over her, tried to stroke her hair, but Tulla recoiled. "Bring me my Ilona."

"You know that now…"

"Bring me my baby," she pushed Irena's hand away.

"I want to help. Let me…"

"That's all you wanted from me?" She said. "Now you have your own baby, you and your Andre… you defeated a lowly woman…"

"Tulla, please, believe me…"

"Bring me the girl."

Irena was unable to sleep the whole night. She tossed and turned for hours. The day's events passed before her eyes again and again, from the news of Johann to the terrible exile of Tulla. What should she have done? What would she do tomorrow? The next day? How could she change Marta's mind? She looked for a clue, a sign, some indication that would show her the way.

Towards dawn, Irena knew exactly what she wanted to do.

But to do it, she needed time. She had to get organized.

She went out to the street. Tulla still lay there. Maybe she had fallen asleep. My poor sister, she thought, and left her the note she had written:

My beloved Tulla, my sister, my darling, please, give me a chance. Go to Solly's office this morning. Wait for me there. Don't worry, everything will be okay. I know exactly what we must do. Please have faith in me, trust me. I am your soul-sister forever.

CHAPTER 21

Ciechanow 1942

I woke to daylight spreading between the alleyways and the voices of the neighbors telling one another their stories. I was covered by a thin woolen blanket and a blue jacket.

Who had put them there? Bronek? Or was it Irena? Maybe some miracle had happened and Marta had come back to her senses. Was it possible that she had realized her mistake?

Perhaps they would open the door to me after all. I went back and knocked on the front door, "Open up," I said. "It's me, Tulla. Marta. Irena? Please… open up."

The door remained shut.

"Open up, open up!" Again, and again, I banged on the wooden door. I knocked, banged, rang, pleaded.

After a few long minutes the door opened and Bronek stood before me. He looked older. Shorter. His eyes were red, his face lined, furrowed.

"Bronek, please, let me come back…"

"Go," he said, his voice flat. "Quickly."

"She's my daughter, not yours."

"You idiot, save yourself, get out of here. She reported you."

"She…"

"She already reported to them that there's some Jewish woman trying to steal a baby. It's dangerous, go!"

"At least let me say goodbye to my baby."

"No," he threw a bundle at me. "Get out of here, quickly - save yourself."

"Wait, Bronek," I wedged my foot in the doorway so he couldn't slam it shut.

"I warned you," he pushed me over the threshold and slammed the door. I pressed my ear against the wood. I heard muffled sounds. Somewhere inside I heard Ilona crying and Marta trying to calm her.

"Irena? Irena open up!" I shouted. "Please, Irena…"

She did not respond. Didn't even peek out from the window.

Where would I go? Where could I go? Because of them I had not befriended anybody. There was nowhere I could go or ask for help or refuge.

Irena…

My legs would not budge. My arms were heavy as if they had turned to iron. I was empty; all of my life force had drained away.

There, in that big house, were the papers that Solly had provided me and the jewelry that I had tucked underneath the mattress. Even the photograph of Johann, my beloved, remained there. They had left me empty. Finished.

I dragged myself around the city streets without any destination.

Should I go to the ghetto? Tie my fate to that of my people? And when they ask me who I am, what will I tell them? That I'm Polish? Jewish? That I was faking? Introduce myself as Tulla or Rachel, as Bronek and Marta's daughter-in-law?

I didn't even have papers for Rachel – those were back in the village, and Tulla's documents were in their house. And I was here, between the different worlds. Alone. Cast off.

In the bundle that Bronek had thrown at me there was money in bills and coins. I immediately understood… he pitied me. Later I would go to his shop and ask that he give me back my papers. I went on wandering the city streets, slinking from alley to alley like a street cat, checking that nobody was following me, that nobody had noticed me. I passed by the municipality building, again and again, the cinema that stood closed, the remains of the burnt synagogue, the bridge that sparkled in the sun, the locked-up bakery, Mr. Cohen's ruined hat shop. All at once a big building rose before my eyes: Hotel Centrale.

At least I could try to freshen up, wash up, think. A moment of peace.

And if, God forbid, someone should suspect me?

Let them hunt me, let them catch me, let them do what they will. Take the last thing that remains – my life – what else could they take from me?

No! The voice returned. *Don't give up!* I must act, do something. I had to fight for my life, for the life of my daughter. I had fallen into a bottomless pit, just like Joseph in his day, and he, from the moment he fell, only rose up and up until he became king of Egypt.

Ilona. Her name ripped open the bleeding wound once more. What are you doing now, little one? Crying? Wondering where I am? Angry that I did not come like every other morning to hug you? Did they remember to leave the light on in your room the way you like? Did they wake up in the night to cover you? Did they tell you the story of the rabbit? About the clouds? About the girl who loved to dance?

That was the moment I decided not to give up. To fight back. To defeat them.

I entered the hotel via the main entrance as if I did so every day, greeted the soldier who stood drowsily by the gate, waved in a friendly way to the other guard who was peeing by one of the trees, and made it inside.

I proceeded slowly down the corridor, ignored the two men in grey suits who smiled at me, waved to an older woman in a red coat who pulled a large dog after her. A waiter with an enormous tray in his hands smiled and asked me if I needed anything. Where is the bathroom? I wondered. I stopped beside a shop window and examined the watches on display with feigned interest. What is the green-uniformed man up to? Does he think I'm a prostitute, a hostess looking for clients? Where in God's name is the bathroom? There's always a bathroom for guests on the ground floor.

Why don't I see the sign? I walked slowly as if I were a guest of the hotel, a woman of status. As if... here it is. Women's bathroom.

Another moment, another five, four, two more steps.

"Sorry," a voice stopped me. "Where to, Miss?"

"Here?" I turned and smiled at a black-haired youth in a green uniform with golden epaulettes on his shoulders.

"Are you a guest with us?"

"Of course," I answered. "I'm pleased that you guards make sure that not just anybody can come in off the street." He nodded his head gravely, asking himself if he had seen me before. Just so long as he didn't ask anything further. Onward, I hurried myself along... walk like you just bought the hotel, like you've been living here for months, because any hesitation could alert security, who would hand you over to the Gestapo.

I opened the door slowly. He remained outside.

"Good morning, Miss." Before me was a cleaning lady in an orange smock with the hotel insignia stamped on it, holding a rag dripping water.

I smiled at her.

She did not smile. She blocked my way, her face set.

"May I?" I asked and she nodded. I handed her a coin from my bundle that Bronek had given me and she let me pass.

Wait a moment, this is my chance.

The earrings. The pair of pearl earrings that my parents gave me at the end of my first year of medical school. Oh, they were so proud of me!

Without pause I held them out to her.

"Want these?"

"I didn't take them."

"I asked if you want the earrings." She nodded her head. Of course, she wanted them.

"They're yours if you will do something for me." She waited.

"My earrings for your smock."

"This smock?"

"Yes, I want to buy it from you."

She fingered the edge of the smock with uncertainty.

"Yes," I confirmed.

"But why? Not good you clean, Mrs."

"It's perfect. You understand... his wife... she is nearby and she cannot see me... I..."

A smile lit up her face. Someone working in a hotel has probably seen it all, certainly some act of betrayal or adultery.

"Here," she said, unbuttoning swiftly, as if concerned I would regret it and handed me the stained smock. It gave off a sour smell.

I handed her the earrings. She looked at them quickly and tucked them into her clothes. I put on the smock, and she asked if maybe I had some cash.

"Hungry children, crying, sick mother, the girl needs glasses."

I put a few coins from Bronek in her hand and she smiled.

"The coat..." she pointed at my wool coat. "My Mamushka is very cold."

Before giving it to her, I checked the pockets and found an envelope. I immediately recognized Irena's handwriting.

And so, armed with an orange smock, a rag, and a bucket, I walked slowly through the main lobby. Nobody looked at me, not even the youth in uniform. Cleaning staff belonged to the invisible class.

I began to wipe down the telephone in the lobby, examining the hotel entrance as I did so.

There was no room for error. Two of them – messengers of evil, the Gestapo – were standing there dressed in black uniforms, wearing shiny black boots. They looked everyone over as they came in and out, watching closely.

Would they suspect me and stop me, check if I really worked there? Ask me for papers? And then what?

I could not show any fear. I raised my head and slowly left the hotel. I whistled the song that the Germans had taught the baby to sing. The song about little Maier in the Himalayas.

"...*De kleine Maier...*" I hummed and the Gestapo man smiled pleasantly, letting me pass.

I was free and safe, for now.

On the corner of the main street, I stopped. I checked that I was alone and glanced at the envelope.

"My dear Sister, in the morning go to Solly's shop... I am your soul sister, forever."

I read the note four or five times, trying to read between the lines. Should I believe her? And what if they cast me off again?

Your soul sister forever.

Soul sister. I was not alone. Irena had a plan. She knew what to do. I had to believe in her. Suddenly there was room for optimism. But I never could have imagined how extreme Irena's plan was.

CHAPTER 22

Ciechanow 1942

I walked slowly toward the shop, following the instructions closely.

The cleaner's smock, bucket, and rag made me invisible; people avoided looking at me. After passing by the shop several times, checking that nobody was following me, I entered.

In order to get to Solly's offices I had to pass through the shop, which was empty of customers. Who needed a bathmat or a new iron these days?

The sellers wore blue uniforms and were grouped together waiting. Maybe in better days the shop would have been full. They looked at me suspiciously. What was a cleaning woman from the hotel doing here? I smiled at them and asked where the company offices were.

"You must have made a mistake, Miss," laughed a worker sitting on a ladder. "The place has been cleaned already."

I explained to him that I had come for a job interview with Solly and he pointed me toward the hallway at the end of the shop.

There was no sign of Irena. Solly's office door was closed.

Maybe I had come early, or worse, too late.

Or was it just a ruse to get rid of me?

The last few months had made me suspicious. Every whisper, every footstep reminded me that the Gestapo could be anywhere…

I sat on a bench that was close to the door that led out to the yard. Sometimes when I had come to visit Irena here in the shop, we would sit out there and smoke cigarettes that she had rolled for us. Little sins in anxious times.

I left the door partway open. An escape hatch. Experience is the father of survival – one must always have an escape route to have some control of the situation.

"Tulla," I heard a voice. "Is that you?" It was not Irena.

I stood alert, ready to run if necessary.

"Tulla, it's me... where are you?"

Uncle Solly. A good man. He hurried over and hugged me as if he had found his long-lost daughter.

"You must be hungry." I nodded my head and he handed me half a loaf of bread with a slice of cheese inside. I tried to eat slowly, not devour it and lead him to suspect that it had been more than a day since I had eaten.

"Listen," he said when he saw that I had finished. "We have to act fast. Irena sent me."

"I want my daughter."

"Not now, you will have to wait."

"I am not going anywhere without..."

"It seems you don't understand," he said angrily. "Irena is afraid that Marta and Bronek reported you to their German friends, so we must hide you. Afterwards we will worry about getting Ilona back."

"Where?"

"We have made arrangements."

"Uncle Solly, you know that if they realize that you helped me, they will punish..."

"What can we do, this is who I am, a little stupid, unable to refuse Irena."

"Me neither," I said and the two of us burst out laughing.

"Here, go to this address..." he handed me a yellow note and looked me over. "Your smock... definitely a good idea with the bucket. Let's add a floral headscarf and here, you are a cleaning woman nobody will notice."

"What is this address?"

"Maybe not a fancy hotel, but you can hide there until we are sure and then we will proceed."

"Ilona..."

"Exactly, now you are going underground."

"Solly, thank you, you are a special man..."

"Me? I'm nothing, I'm just a crazy man who does whatever that dear girl asks of me. You have a gift for life with her friendship."

"And I thought that she betrayed me."

"Now, now, all of us think and do stupid things. Remember, even though we are racing against time, do not hurry, don't run. Running will arouse suspicion, and we cannot have that."

I added that to the list of iron rules for my survival. Another moment and I was in the street. I went along slowly as if I'd had a long day of hard work cleaning the hotel and not a refugee who could be recognized at any moment.

With the address in my hand, I arrived to a large brick house with a huge sign on it that read "storage" and the address of the shop. This was Uncle Solly's warehouse, my new hiding place.

I entered through the back door and descended two floors to the basement.

This time I was lucky to have a relatively comfortable refuge. At least I could walk some five, six paces from wall to wall. The mattress had a pleasant smell and they had given me two pillows. Almost perfect, apart from the squeaking of mice running around in panic, unhappy to have their home invaded. Sure, there was a moldy smell, no window or other opening for fresh air, but undoubtedly as good as I could have hoped for. Everything in life is relative.

Irena arrived late at night after putting Ilona to sleep.

"Tulla... Rachel..." She said in her good voice and reached her arms out to me. "Come, my sister, everything is okay." I came out of my hiding place and was enveloped in her arms. My soul sister. My friend. My God is your God, my life, your life. Everything felt possible once more.

She pulled a packet of tobacco out of her pocket, a few cookies that had been crushed on her way over, and a cup of plum wine which she must have snatched from Bronek's cupboard. She laid her plans out before me. Everything sounded wonderful.

"Irena... are you sure?"

"Of course."

"And if..."

"Why would we be caught? Trust me."

"You know that if they catch you helping...»

"I'm not helping, we are doing this, together, like Ruth and Naomi... like in that story you told me? Wherever you go I shall go... Your people are my people."

"It's not the same thing. Ruth had nothing to lose whereas you, you are risking everything, your marriage, your love, your life."

"Your house is my house, no matter what, I walk with you."

CHAPTER 23

Ciechanow 1942 -1943

Tulla had told Irena the story of Ruth and Naomi right after Ilona was born. They had sat in the little yard behind Irena's parents' house, out of sight of the neighbors. The sunlight had caressed their faces, the wind had rustled their hair, and Ilona had dozed off in her arms. A wonderful morning.

Tulla had told Irena the story of Ruth, which is read during the Shavuot holiday and was taking place that month. Tulla told her about Abraham and Sarah, Rebecca and Isaac, of Joseph and his brothers, King Saul and David of the prophets and judges.

The story of Ruth was her favorite. Something about the devotion, the grace, the rare connection between the two women enchanted her. Irena was a romantic.

That night, when Tulla was kicked out of the house and Irena tossed and turned, restless, she remembered the words that Ruth whispered to Naomi, that wherever you go I shall go... Yes, that was what she wanted. To go after her, not to leave her behind. Wherever you go... but where? How?

She knew that Tulla would never agree to leave her baby behind in the hands of those who had cast her into the street, who were willing to hand her over to the Gestapo.

Wherever you go I will go... how could they leave without arousing suspicion?

Irena needed time to calm Marta and Bronek and to assure them that Tulla had disappeared, that she would not come back to claim what was hers. Speed and recklessness could arouse the demons who were better off sleeping.

The great concern was how long could Tulla remain in that hiding place with the rats and smells of sewage and mold.

"Don't worry," Tulla told her. "I'm stronger than all of you know. I have something to live for, so I must survive."

Tulla hid in the warehouse building for over five months. Solly and Irena brought her books and food. In the third month they were able to bring her a radio which connected her to the world.

"How are you?" Irena repeated her question every time she visited the basement. Tulla's face was wan, her hair faded, her skin had lost its glow, and she had grown very thin.

"Don't worry," Tulla would tell her. "Survivors have to be patient. We cannot afford to be reckless."

Only one thing disturbed her peace... the longing. She longed for Ilona with an intensity that drove her mad.

Meanwhile Marta and Bronek held a lavish celebration for the second birthday of their beloved granddaughter. Relatives, neighbors, and their German friends were invited to a celebratory dinner. At the head of the table sat Ilona, with a flower crown on her head, and beside her, the proud grandmother Marta and grandfather Bronek. It would not have occurred to any of the attendees that in the moments when Irena left the party to go out to the yard, it was so that Tulla, in hiding, could see her.

When they went out, the little one waved her hands and Irena turned her around so Tulla could have a good look at her, enjoy her beauty, hear her laugh. And Ilona? Did she hear her mother wordlessly crying out to her?

She held out her hands toward Tulla's hiding place.

Tulla yearned to touch her, to cover her hands with kisses, to take in her scent, to press her head to her heart, but she could not take such a risk. They played, gesturing in the dark, until she heard Marta calling them back.

"Say bye," and Ilona waved towards the place where her mother stood. As if she sensed her.

"You remember Mama Tulla?

"I want Mama, why doesn't she come anymore?"

"Tell her you love her and she will come back."

"I love you, Mama Tulla!"

"Bye, my love," said Tulla but her voice went unheard.

"Come let's get you strawberry ice cream."

"Who are you talking to?" Marta stood in the entrance to the yard, her face pinched with suspicion.

"We are speaking with the moon," she replied. "Irena loves the moon."

The girl waved toward Tulla. "Bye, moon, bye Mama, bye-bye."

Children have some miraculous sense, understanding without being told.

Among the guests who attended the party, one was Andre.

He had come directly from Warsaw and looked different dressed in his new uniform, his black leather boots, his hair combed back, and strange glasses on his nose. He was accompanied by friends: two SS officers of high rank who placed a children's book in German in Ilona's lap along with a bag of candies, then went to celebrate with the bottle of schnapps that Bronek had acquired for them.

At night, Andre and Irena made love.

"Do you miss me?" she asked him when they stood beside the window smoking.

"Of course, you're my wife."

"Just because I'm your wife?"

"I'm busy, Irena. I do many important things. Soon they will promote me to a more senior position, maybe in Krakow."

He kissed her and turned away.

"Andre, if I want to move to another country will you come with me?"

"Come where?" But he was already asleep.

In the morning she accompanied him to the train. Ilona was dozing in her baby carriage.

"When are you thinking of moving to be with me in Warsaw?" he asked her.

"Soon," she said. "Very soon. How is the apartment?"

"Huge. It used to belong to a Jew who was the deputy director of the bank."

"And what happened to him?"

"I don't know. Wasn't interested," he pointed to the carriage. "You'll have to part from her."

"I thought of bringing her."

"Mother won't let you. She's decided to raise her. The child is giving her a reason to live."

"Mother and Father are getting older - why don't we adopt her?"

"What? Me raise a child of Jews?" He was red with anger. "Do you want to ruin my career? Do you understand what that would do to me?"

"Don't be angry, please," she neared him, kissed him, and felt a coolness in his manner.

"Andre?" She put a hand on his cheek. "Is everything all right between us?"

"It's not the time to discuss such things." He pressed against her and kissed her. "Come and we will talk. Call before you come - sometimes I'm busy."

She promised. Promised to call, to come, to help Marta, to go to the doctor. She promised to go to Madame Sheptzinda, the local witch who brewed drinks and knew all kinds of spells that would bring them a son.

"Yes, I promise." The ticket agent whistled and the train began to move. He leaped up and was swallowed by the train car.

Irena's plan was to go to him by train, to bring along the "nanny" that she hired so that the two of them could enjoy the city. She knew that Andre had never before met Tulla, as he had already been in Warsaw when she arrived at his parents' home.

Irena believed that they would have peace in his home and would be safe. She trusted him and his good heart. He knew people and got along everywhere. He would know how to help them.

"What if he doesn't agree to take Ilona?" Tulla asked once day.

"Of course, he will agree," she said. "I will explain to him that the witch he sent me to told me that the presence of a baby in his life will awaken my body, that it's a hormonal thing. Trust me."

"Is that what she told you?"

"Since when do I believe in witches?"

CHAPTER 24

Ciechanow - Warsaw 1942

Autumn had arrived and the nights were freezing. I was still hiding in the basement. Besides me, the abandoned warehouses were home to mice and worms and various roaches - the unpleasant group of neighbors whose kingdom I had invaded. I had to protect myself against them... they were hungry. Every forgotten crumb brought a massive onslaught of new critters.

I once read that hungry mice could bite through human flesh, so at night I would cover myself with anything I could find to protect myself. I heard their squealing and winced... I could feel worms crawling around me. They would chew through anything they could - wood, plaster walls - looking for food remains. Humans can grow accustomed to any situation, and I somehow got used to the horror of living there.

The months in the little storage space, the minimal food, and the lack of air and light left me weak. My skin was grey and my hair grew wild.

Sometimes at night, when there was not much moonlight, I took advantage of the darkness to leave my little cell and go out to the yard to breathe in a little fresh air, move my legs, feel the world outside of my hiding place, hear the rustling of the leaves and let the winds blow around me.

I knew that I could not go on living like this much longer – the loneliness was terrible. My longing and worry for Ilona ate at me ferociously, and I had not even managed to grieve properly for Johann.

Irena made sure to bring bread, eggs, a slice of cheese, or the end of a sausage - whatever she could take from the house without Marta noticing. She also brought books which became my dear friends in those days. I read everything she was able to bring for me without raising suspicion. Sometimes she brought me old newspapers from which I learned what was going on in Ciechanow and in the rest of Poland.

From the newspapers and the radio they had managed to smuggle to me, and from what Irena told me, I learned that two years after establishing the ghetto in Ciechanow, the Germans had decided to eliminate it and, soon enough, they had expelled all of the Jews. After all, the ghettos were just the method for concentrating the Jews and making them easier to control.

Some of the residents were sent to the ghetto of the city Nova Miasto. Life there was impossible. There was terrible crowding and, worst of all, hunger and diseases like typhus broke out. It was only later that I learned of the Zyklon B gas, the gas chambers, and the mass murders. But why get ahead of ourselves? Meanwhile I, like many others, was still living under the illusion that everything would be okay, that we had a plan, that we just had to stay steady and soon Poland and its Jews would be liberated.

One day, Irena surprised me and gave me the best of all possible presents: a photograph of Ilona. Marta had decided that it was time to send photos of her granddaughter to relatives who lived in other parts of the country, as well as in Germany and Hungary. The family wore their holiday best and went to the photographer and smiled at his camera. I held the photograph in my hands. My baby had become a gorgeous little girl. My Ilona. Her red hair hung in pigtails and she had a big dimple in her right cheek. Only - why did her eyes look so sad? Why aren't you happy? I placed the picture under my pillow along with Johann's medal and the last letter from my father.

"Are you all right?" Irena asked me every time she came. I nodded.

"You're too pale; this grey color does not look right to me. And your pretty hair… next time I will bring you scissors and shampoo."

She set down the little bit of food she had managed to sneak out, two books, old newspapers, and a sliver of soap. "Anything else you need?"

"Everything is fine, Irena, believe me, I am here and not in the ghetto, not in some work camp, or on a train to that place… Auschwitz."

The date of departure was set for close to Andre's thirtieth birthday, March of 1942. Irena chose the date, said that this way it would be easy for her to explain her journey to his parents. It would be a surprise party, she explained to Marta, and made her promise not to tell him. Marta even helped her to make his favorite honey cake.

The problem was how to take Ilona. How could she convince the grandparents to be separated from their beloved granddaughter? To her surprise, Bronek took Irena's side. Apparently, from the moment that they kicked me out of their house, Ilona could not bear Marta. She screamed when her grandmother tried to lift her and escaped when she came near. There was no candy or toy that Marta could tempt her with to buy her love - nothing helped. In the mornings, she cried for hours until Irena returned from her work. In the evenings, she demanded Irena. Only Irena. Smart girl – she learned quickly how to distinguish between good and bad, not to believe everyone who tried to tempt her with candy or toys...

I asked how Bronek had convinced Marta.

"He just told her the truth, which she might not have liked, that perhaps it would be best if Andre and I were to adopt the little girl."

"Just like that?"

"Worse, he stood firm, said that they were too old to raise her."

True.

March crawled slowly by. We went over every detail of our plan, again and again, to be coordinated and precise in case, God forbid, something should go wrong along the way. We anticipated potential problems that might arise. All of my hopes were riding on this plan. I went over every detail, every second. I knew at exactly which minute I would board the train, which train car I was to sit in, what point on the way I would join them. According to this plan, I was the girl's nanny. A mute nanny. Irena thought it was better that way, that only one of us would speak.

On the final days leading up to Andre's birthday, I was so excited that I could not sleep. I couldn't eat a crumb of the bread that I had and left it to the mice and the other inhabitants.

It seemed time would not pass. Every second seemed to last a day. When could I embrace my daughter, hold her to my breast, take in the smell of evening, the smell of freedom? The day was soon to come.

It was one of the first days of spring. The sunlight warmed the earth, and the sky was a deep blue. Green leaves and buds were sprouting from the big elm trees, as if all of nature were a part of our happiness.

Solly's car was already waiting for me beside the entrance, as planned. I leaped inside and lay down on the car floor, praying that everything would go smoothly, that we would arrive in Warsaw without difficulty.

Solly did not say a word the whole way. It was quiet, too quiet. I knew how dear to him Irena was and I respected the worry with which he drove me. She was the daughter he and his wife had never had. Anticipating separation from her was torture for him.

When we left the neighborhood, he signaled to me to sit beside him.

"Worried?" I asked, and he nodded.

"And you?"

"Shaking with fear. How could I not be?"

"We'll be fine. Irena decided to save you, and so it shall be."

"Bless her."

"I will pray for you," he whispered and added, "Irena has the factory phone number. Please, call when you reach Andre, and let me know that you arrived so I don't lose my mind from worry."

"I promise."

"He's actually a nice man," he said as if convincing himself. "He loves Irena."

"Of course, how could he not?"

"Just that today... who knows? People change. This cursed war, I see things I wish I did not see."

"You'll see, everything will be all right," I said, partly to myself, partly to him.

Irena was certain that as soon as we arrived in Andre's home, everything would be wonderful. We could rest easy there. We would walk in the big parks, feed the ducks, listen to the street musicians, and in the evening she and Andre would go out to take in the sights. Her optimism was contagious. She was sure that the plan was perfect.

My naive friend. How could she know what was waiting for us in Warsaw?

Just as we had carefully planned, Uncle Solly dropped me off not far from Ciechanow, at Irena's train's first stop. Only twenty minutes between us.

He helped me out of the car and returned to his place at the steering wheel.

"You are a good man."

"I am a crazy man," he said. "Go fast, and good luck."

Finally, I was outside in the sun breathing fresh air. Sun and wind are luxuries people do not appreciate until they do not have them.

The platform of the little station was almost empty. I waited. Another ten minutes. Eight. Two men looked at me, perhaps wondering what a woman was

162 | My Daughter's Keeper

doing alone at a station. God, look out for me, I prayed.

The train approached the station. I was sure that everyone on the platform could hear my heart pounding. Another moment and I would hug my baby. What if, God forbid, she had not gotten on?

Or if Marta had not let them travel alone? Or if...

The train whistled cheerfully, and its wheels whirred, trying to stop.

According to the plan she and Ilona were sitting in train car number four.

I had to find a spot in car five or six, not beside them.

A few more meters and I would be on the train. Another hour and I could hug my daughter.

"Papers," a German soldier blocked my way.

I pulled out the cloth sack that Irena had made me and handed him my papers.

"Tulla," he looked up at me. "Where to?"

I produced a little wooden clipboard with paper on it and wrote, "To Warsaw."

"You... what's wrong with you?"

"I am mute, can only hear," I wrote him in German. Mute. Poor woman. He nodded.

"And what will you do in Warsaw?"

"I have a job there," I wrote and he gave me a suspicious look, as I continued to write quickly, "house cleaning and laundry." He smiled and handed me back my papers. The first encounter had gone smoothly. A good sign.

Just as we had planned, I got onto the fifth train car. Thank God, I looked around the car, the platform I had just left. Had anyone suspected? Why were people running? Had someone reported me? Why wasn't the conductor whistling? What were they waiting for?

On either end of the old building I noticed Germans sitting on the bench. Were they looking for me? Could they smell my fear? Why wasn't the train moving?

God, let's go already! What was the delay? Had someone stopped her, reported the Jew? Someone ran on the platform. A soldier. Was he looking for me? Had he decided there was something suspicious about my papers? He stopped, looked in his pockets and pulled out a metal box from which he drew a cigarette. Panic for nothing. Everything was fine. Breathe. Breathe deeply, just don't panic. It happens. The conductor waved his hand. The long-awaited whistle sounded.

I held the bundle in my hands tightly, then put it up on the overhead shelf. I smiled at the boy sitting across from me. He moved closer to me and his mother pulled him and set him on her knees.

Second whistle. Third.

Slow movement, getting faster. The train left the station.

I knew exactly what to do. After all, we went over the plan for days and nights. Every move was calculated. I counted to one thousand. I added another hundred. Now I got up from my spot, smiled to the mother of the boy and walked toward the fourth train car.

It was supposed to be their car. The passengers looked at me. What did their look say? What did they see? Could they tell I was Jewish?

Irena was not there.

I continued calmly trying to locate her. She wasn't there! There was no sign of her in the fourth car.

What had happened?

A metallic taste in my mouth. Where are you?

Was I mistaken? Had I boarded the wrong train? Maybe this one was going the opposite way? Where had she disappeared to? Where are you, Irena?

I returned to my seat. I must have looked terrible because the mother of the boy gave me a strange glance. What did she know? What could she have ascertained?

"Are you feeling all right?"

"Thank you," I pulled out my clipboard, wrote my response and showed it to her.

"Why is she always writing like that and not talking?" the boy asked his mother who said she would explain it to him later.

"You look a little... I just don't want us to catch anything," she pulled the child to her. Not good. Anything unusual could put me at risk.

I wrote on my little board that there was nothing to worry about, that it was just the day of my women's matters and she smiled. "That's how it is for women, we must suffer," she said and squeezed my hand.

"Where is the bathroom?" I wrote. She pointed to the door at the end of the train car. I got up and went back to car four. She wasn't there. This time I didn't give up and continued on to the third car. When we had made the plan, Irena had reminded me that if there was no space available in carriage four, she would go to the third and if not there, the second.

Here she is. Irena. Thank God. I nearly burst out into cries of joy. Irena! Everything was okay. I could relax. Ilona was curled in her arms, asleep. Across from them sat a German officer who did not stop speaking, waving his hands excitedly and giving the occasional pat to my Ilona. There was no room for error. We had not anticipated this situation.

Should I return to my spot? Sit across from them? Next to them? I had to restrain myself from plucking Ilona from her arms and running the length of the train to find us a spot, some little corner for just the two of us. Was there such a place?

I had to be smart, to restrain myself. God forbid they should notice me. Ilona could recognize me and run to me and then what? Who was he? What was his role and where did he know them from? To my relief I noticed that he was not wearing the Gestapo uniform. Not as bad. An air force officer, not as dangerous. Maybe he was a friend of Bronek and Marta, maybe they had heard of the mute nanny and knew.

What did Irena expect me to do now – wait, go back to the fifth car? What a nightmare. Terrible. Here she was, my daughter, so close but off limits to me. I yearned to hold her beautiful head and whisper, "Mama Tulla is here, I love you."

I passed slowly by my baby, trying to brush past her but did not stop. I continued on, my heart in pieces, my breathing painful. Don't start, don't take her and run to the end of the train and kiss the curl across her forehead, her little hands, her small feet. I moved slowly as if nothing was out of the ordinary.

Irena did not appear to look at me, oblivious.

She moved her hand over her hair and shook her head, hinting that she had seen me, but went on speaking cheerfully with the officer, stroking the head of the sleeping child, indicating in her way that this was not the moment. I had to wait. Wonderful Irena, keeping her cool and not losing her senses.

I told myself to breathe deeply, relax, to think of everything we had been through together. We had considered the possibility that some acquaintance of Marta might sit beside her, recognize her, ask questions. We had constructed the whole story, detail by detail, but a German officer?! We had not thought of that. Not far from them was an open seat. I sat down and waited. The two went on chatting in German. I could not make out the subject of their conversation, or who he was. The little girl's head with her auburn hair rested on Irena's arms.

I kept sitting. I thought about Plan B, our backup plan in case of emergency. If we could not meet on the train for whatever reason, I was to get off in Warsaw and wait. That was what we had agreed upon. Wait a little more. A little more. She will get off after and look for me as though she had lost me, the silent nanny swallowed up by the crowd.

It was only 100 kilometers between Ciechanow and Warsaw but that morning it felt like a million. Suddenly, she got up from her spot, woke Ilona and said something about a diaper while making a face as if to indicate a bad smell. He got up after her, gave her a small bow and turned, walked away somewhere.

I went on sitting. I felt as if I were being tested. He might come back.

I had to wait. Plan B. Ten more kilometers. Eight more. Two.

I could see the houses of the city already, the familiar bell towers, the dome of Warsaw's cathedral.

Get off already. No. She was sitting, staring out. What's the delay, Irena? Finally, she got up, Ilona in her arms. A young man in a grey suit helped her take down her large suitcase. Ilona was smiling. At me? Did she recognize me?

I ignored it. Sorry, baby girl.

I got up and returned to my original seat in the fifth carriage, just as we had agreed. The boy smiled happily at me.

"Where were you?" the boy's mother scowled.

"In the dining carriage," I wrote to her and drew a plate with an egg and hambone on it.

The boy smiled.

"Your things… I thought you had forgotten."

"Thank you and good luck," I wrote. I took my little bundle and got off the train. Someone held out a hand to me. Who was that? Not a soldier. Not a guard. Just a nice man in a hat. I stood on the platform and waited, just as we had agreed.

Where was she? Irena? I kept standing there. Just as we had said.

"Here she is," I heard her voice, "Tulla, Tu-lla!"

Who was calling me? Should I turn around? Wait? Irena? Maybe the officer remembered me from his visits to Marta and Bronek?

"Tulla… Tulla where are you?" I heard Irena behind me. "Here, quick."

She waved to me and I felt my heart beat faster.

I smiled and hurried to her.

"Tulla, I've been looking for you, where did you disappear to?" she shouted. I tilted my head as if accepting my fate. From the corner of my eye I saw the boy's mother looking at us with great interest. Too great. What did she think was happening? I took out my clipboard and wrote, "Careful, someone is watching us." She nodded and handed me the suitcase. "Take this and don't you dare disappear again!

She went on talking as if explaining to the world, "Servants today... insolent!"

"Let's go, I don't want you losing my suitcase," she began to walk with my baby, my Ilona in her arms. I walked after her, struggling with the suitcase.

Ilona turned and gave me a look. Did she recognize me? Did she know who I was?

In the taxi that picked us up, I whispered to her, "Ilona, my Ilona," and she, the smartest girl in the world, smiled, got off of Irena's knees and sat on my lap stroking my face and said, "Mama?"

"Yes, Mama."

"Mama Tulla, why did you go?"

"I'm sorry," I held her close. "Here, I'm back, now we will be together."

She leaned her pretty head on my chest, and I felt joy filling my whole body as I breathed in my baby.

Finally, we were together.

Would life let us be?

And what were those dark clouds hovering overhead?

CHAPTER 25

Warsaw, Spring 1942

We did not go straight to Andre's house. First, we dined, giddily eating to our heart's content in one of the city's restaurants. It was Irena's idea. She wanted to be ready for the reunion. They had not seen each other for more than a month, and it was important to her that her husband see her fresh and beautiful. She slipped into the small women's room and when she returned, I saw that she had put on make-up, tied her hair in a red velvet ribbon, applied red lipstick to her lips and blush to her cheeks, and adorned herself with the gold earrings he had bought her. Her blue eyes sparkled with excitement. Undoubtedly, Irena was a very beautiful woman.

"How do I look?"

"Very pretty, like a woman about to meet her beloved."

She laughed. She was so happy.

We also changed Ilona's dress and put blue ribbons in her hair. I was the caregiver. The transparent woman.

When we arrived at the building where Andre lived, the city was already growing dark. We stood in the small entrance and I, as the would-be nanny, stood several steps behind them.

Irena entered the building first, then came out and signaled to me to approach. She took the honey cake out of her basket, placed three candles on it, one for every decade, and together we ascended to the third floor where Andre lived. Irena held the cake and I pulled the baby carriage with Ilona in it behind me. Irena knocked on his door.

"Who's there?" A hoarse, male voice answered.

"It's me, Irena."

"Irena? Don't know you, who invited you?"

"That's not Andre's voice," she whispered, and immediately said, "Please open up, quick, Andre is waiting for me."

The door opened. We had not anticipated this.

A German officer stood in the doorway, his shirt unbuttoned, barefoot. He held a glass of cognac. "Are you sure this is Andre's apartment?" I whispered to her. "It looks like there may have been some mistake."

She did not answer. I saw her face was pale. She was trembling.

"Well, Miss?"

"Andre … isn't this his apartment?"

"Maybe, maybe not, did he invite you here?" he asked and wavered a little, reeking of alcohol. Behind him we heard music and the sound of women's voices singing.

"I am Irena, his wife."

"I did not know he had such a pretty wife," he said. "Where was he hiding you?" He approached Irena with a malicious smile and held out a hand to touch her. She smacked his hand.

"Don't you dare. Savage! I'm warning you. You'd better not dare touch me. Take me to him at once!"

Wavering slightly, he gestured for her to follow him.

I pushed the carriage and followed them. I wanted to stay with her, not leave her alone.

"Not you," the German stopped me. "Get out of here and take that girl with you - this is no place for babies." I took a step back and stopped. I had to stay.

From somewhere inside I heard peals of laughter, the sound of glass breaking, two men in just their underwear chasing a naked, giggling young woman. Before me, I saw an enormous dining table filled with dirty dishes, half-eaten fruit scattered across the tablecloth, chicken bones, and a large pig's head looking at us with a red rose in its mouth. Shards of glass were scattered on the carpet. A large woman with her breasts exposed looked at us and scurried away. The apartment stank of sin.

I remained standing beside the door to the apartment. Ilona grew impatient, got out of her carriage, and held onto my dress, observing the goings-on. Two beautiful women in sparkling evening gowns approached us.

"What a doll," they tittered. "How old are you, sweetheart?"

I felt Ilona clutching me as if frightened they would snatch her away.

One of them bent down and handed Ilona a chocolate cookie. "I'm Maria," she patted her head. "Like the mother of Christ." The other woman turned back and invited her friends to see the beautiful little girl before them. Three of them came over. They were drunk.

"How old is she?" asked Maria.

I did as we had decided and pulled out my little clipboard. "Two years old," I wrote. "I don't speak. Mute."

She nodded her head gravely and asked if she could pick up Ilona. "No," I wrote quickly. "Forbidden. Her mother won't allow it."

"Who says it's forbidden," the officer who had opened the door to us came into view. "I make the rules around here," and tried to pull her from me.

Ilona burst into heartrending tears.

"Stop crying," a silver-haired man in civilian clothes came over and extended his hand. "He's only joking, right? Maybe you'd like to dance, Fraulein?"

He began to sing in German. Ilona stopped crying and looked at him.

"Look! The child likes songs," said Maria and joined him. All at once the room filled with singing. The Germans swayed and closed their eyes, singing of distant Germany.

Mid-song, we heard a shriek. A terrible shriek that pierced the room and everyone froze.

"Don't touch me, you cheating snake!"

"Wait, my love."

"You... you Nazi shit," Irena screamed. She shrieked and cursed in Polish.

The singing stopped at once, the men froze, spellbound. Ilona began to cry. Maria pulled me into a side room and told me not to move from there. I held Ilona. She was breathing heavily, as if she understood...

Not a few seconds passed before we heard, again, "Scum, human scum, filth!"

"Don't touch me, you shit! Scum!" A door slammed. Shouting. Quick foot-steps and then I heard Irena looking for me. "Tulla," she screamed. "Tulla, Ilona, where are you, quick, let's get out of here!"

"Wait! Irena, what was that?"

From the back room burst my Johann's twin, a little shorter than his brother. He was plumper but redheaded, just like my husband, and wore just underwear and a blue velvet ribbon on his head.

"Irena, please, my love. Irena don't go," he wailed and fell to his knees. "I love you." But she was in a rage. Her eyes bulging from their sockets, her face burning - she looked like an animal about to attack.

"Scum. You Nazi dog."

"Please. It's just a game."

"Then this is a game too," Irena's face was grim. She took a bottle of drink from the table and poured its contents onto Andre's head. He looked defeated.

Then she pulled me after her. "Quick, we must get out of here." She picked up Ilona and marched out. There was silence but for her footsteps descending the stairs.

Andre remained on his knees, liquid dripping from him, his face wet. Suddenly he raised his head and looked at me.

"You..." he pointed at me. I began to retreat. "You... wait... who are you?"

I held up the clipboard, "Just the nanny."

"Please tell her that I love her, she must come back, I ... tell her I..."

"Nanny," I pointed at the board, then left the apartment. Had he guessed who I was? Picked up on something?

When we were out on the street, sure he was not following us, I asked, "Irena? What was that?"

"Son of a bitch," she whispered. "Sick dog. Forget we ever knew him."

"What happened there?"

"Two brothers. One a hero, the other - scum. One faithful to his homeland and his wife and the other, a traitor in every way possible. One killed and remembered forever as a hero, the other sold his soul to Satan."

She refused to speak, just marched furiously. I ran after her, pushing the carriage. We were in front of the municipal building once again, the gates of the garden, and she was walking furiously, her face set.

We looked for a place to rest. To sit. We saw a sign promising luxurious rooms. We went inside. The Polish owner had a huge gut, eyed us for a long moment, trying to understand what we were doing at this hour of the night with a baby sleeping in my arms.

His squat wife heard voices and came out to us wearing a plaid nightgown. She looked at us and said she had no rooms available.

"Perhaps you have some type of solution for us," Irena asked.

"We don't want any trouble with the police."

"There won't be any," Irena promised and handed her a bill.

"Maybe we can find something," said the woman. "But you cannot bring men here, understood? This is a respectable establishment. And what's that?" She pointed at me.

"The nanny."

"A few more zlotys," she added, "and you have to pay for the child, half board."

Her husband took our papers, promising to write down the details and give them back in the morning.

The stench of urine hit us as we entered the little room.

"That one can sleep on the mattress here," she pointed at me. "Tomorrow we can bring the girl a bed but meanwhile, this is what there is, and you're lucky to have it."

"Thank you," said Irena, but the innkeeper did not move from his place.

"She doesn't speak? She's mute?" He asked, pointing at me.

"Yes," said Irena. "Since childhood, poor thing."

He nodded and left.

The decision that I was the mute nanny had been meant to avoid extra questions, any dangerous conversation. Irena would be our voice. One voice. We waited a few minutes until we heard his steps descend the stairs.

"Irena, what happened there?"

"What happened, happened. I don't want to talk about it. He does not exist for me."

"A woman?"

"I wish. You don't understand... they were there together, two men and a few women... naked... entangled with one another, shocking..."

We were silent.

"Andre, the history teacher that I met, has turned into a Nazi pig. As far as I'm concerned, it's all over."

"Irena, my sister," I whispered to her. "Just think, what if he wants revenge after you humiliated him in front of his friends."

"He won't."

"How can you be so sure?"

"Stop, let me be. He isn't our problem anymore."

In light of what had happened, and since Andre's apartment was no longer an option, we had to think of another plan. We agreed that she would try to find work in Warsaw as a bookkeeper and I would look after Ilona, starting the next day. We would look for a place to live instead of the wretched room at the inn.

That night we felt that everything would work out. Nothing would stop us. We felt like two strong women.

After the light breakfast that we ate at the inn, I took Ilona to spend the spring morning in Łazienki Park, Warsaw's royal hunting park.

While Irena was looking for work, Ilona enjoyed a visit to the palace and ran around after the squirrels and peacocks and I enjoyed being with my daughter once again. Children can adapt to anything and she somehow understood that we couldn't speak so she invented movements for me which became our secret language.When Irena returned that evening, I saw failure written on her face. She went on searching, running all over Warsaw for months, to every office, every potential place of work, looking for a job. She offered her services as a bookkeeper to any possible employer and was repeatedly turned away.

We heard nothing from Andre. Had he given up on her? What had he told his parents? They must have called to ask, or written, or even come to visit? Had they realized that Ilona was lost to them, and would they seek revenge?

Every stranger who followed me scared me. Every knock on the door worried me. We had to find another solution; Warsaw seemed like a trap. Besides, we were quickly running out of money.

One day the innkeeper stopped me. "Tell her that you owe me for a week."

I nodded.

"And tell her that the rent went up. There are lots of people who want this room."

I nodded.

"Or," he came close to me, "you can pay some other way."

"You will receive the money," I wrote him.

"Think about it. It's good, easy income." I went on walking and him after me.

"Tell her that someone asked about her. He looks to me like a German."

The inn had become a dangerous place for us.

Irena dismissed my concerns. "Even if Bronek and Marta show up, they are not dangerous."

"How can you be so sure?"

"I told him that we must divorce and I warned him that if he refuses, all of Ciechanow will know what he has been up to here."

"Irena, when did you meet with him?"

"We met, what does it matter? What matters is that everything is fine, and we have a new life here. He might have even been happy to be rid of me."

"And he didn't ask about Ilona?"

"My dear Tulla, they don't worry me. What's important now is that we find another place to live."

Another week passed and she was still looking for work, to no avail. The innkeeper raised the rent. Every week he found new reasons to squeeze money from us: a fine for using water after nine o'clock, a fine for hanging our clothes to dry in the bathroom. In addition, he hinted that the police would require details about us. Although I had identification papers, and although I was a nice, mute widow, any meeting with the police would be a real threat.

One day when I returned from the park, a woman approached me and asked me if I happened to be from Ciechanow. I pulled out my clipboard. "I don't speak, I'm mute."

"I understand," she said. "It's just that the little girl looks like... maybe I saw her before, or else I'm mistaken. Where are you from?"

"From Prachow," I wrote. We had a relative in that village which was not far from Ciechanow.

"Strange," she said, as if to herself. "I could have sworn that your little girl..."

I nodded and went on walking. I hoped that she could not hear my heart pounding in my chest, that she would not ask after us at the inn, where the innkeeper would love the excuse to demand more money.

Of course, we could not stay there much longer. Every day the danger grew. Someone might recognize us. I had an idea, but I did not know how Irena would respond.

When she returned, disappointed from another day of wandering the city and failing to find employment, I told her of my plan.

My plan was to join a kibbutz. The Warsaw kibbutz. During my time as a student, Haim Sarvikovitch, a history student who had been interested in me, had invited me to visit the estate of Mr. Zatwarnitzki, a Polish nobleman who invited young Jews to work on his farm. They had built what they called "the kibbutz."

I had gone with him for two days and stayed a week. The estate was beautiful. There were good people there who had faith in the path they were on. I loved the atmosphere of the place, the excitement of the young people, the dedication to the idea – a community of idealistic youth teaching themselves agricultural work in advance of their immigration to Israel. Perhaps if I had not met my Johann, I would have completed my medical studies and joined them.

Haim, who had decided to join the group of young people and give up his studies, had been disappointed when I left, and even more so when he heard of my marriage. He wrote me an angry letter in which he accused me of betraying our goals, abandoning the idealism, and turning my back on my people. But he finished by assuring me that I would always be welcome among them. I never forgot those words. These days they offered me some hope.

I had to find out the fate of that farm of beautiful ideas. Were the people still there, or had they, God forbid, been sent away to some ghetto? It could be a place of refuge for us.

One day, while Irena was out searching for work, I took Ilona on the train to a suburb of Warsaw, where the estate, as I recalled, should be. We walked up to the heavy iron gate but I did not dare enter. I did not know what exactly was going on there and who was managing the place now. I spoke with several young people who worked outside and told me that, indeed, when the war broke out and Warsaw had become occupied, the members of the farm had dispersed, and the estate had been abandoned. But these days, in spring of 1942, some had recently returned to settle there.

"And what about you?" One of the young men asked me.

"Me?" I was stunned.

"Come, join us," they said after I told them my story. "We need doctors, and this is the safest place in Warsaw. This war has to end sometime and then all of us will emigrate to the land of our forefathers."

I told them of Irena and they said that she would be welcome, too. They needed anyone who could work.

I wanted to suggest to Irena that we move to the estate. Ilona could enjoy the fresh air and the company of young people and Irena and I would have a safe place to live, without threat or risk and, most important, at a distance from Andre and his friends.

Irena refused to even hear of it. She was stubborn, certain that the situation would soon work out. She had even found us another apartment in a quiet suburb.

How would we pay?

"Remember what we said? Women can always work as help around the house."

As my father had always told me, "Man makes plans and God laughs."

One evening, Irena returned later than usual. I was already nearly asleep when the door creaked open. There in the dark doorway I could see Milek, the innkeeper, swaying on his feet and holding a bottle of vodka. He looked around the room and began to curse us.

"Where are you two bitches?" he slurred. I shrank into the corner so he might not see me.

"Come, open your legs, you whores."

I crawled toward Ilona and pulled her to the far edge of the room, away from him and what he wanted.

"You're there, come here," he screeched. "Milek wants you and said come here, whore."

He charged into the room looking for us, his face red and wet with sweat. He smelled of vodka and tried to pour some into the little glass he held in his hand. When he could not manage, he threw the glass at the wall and tried to corner us.

"Here you are, whore," he shouted but I was faster than him and managed to escape. He tripped over one of our suitcases and fell down.

He must have hurt himself because when he stood back up, I saw his head was bleeding, which only made him more dangerous. He chased us, fuming and screaming, trying to corner me, stepping on the mattress, the bed, waving his arms around, trying to catch me, shouting and threatening.

Ilona! Just so long as she was still sleeping… I had to get him out of here. At once I opened the door, looked at him provocatively and went out. I knew that he was following me, he wouldn't give up. I ran downstairs to the entryway and he hurried after me.

The sight of him was terrible, like a charging bull. When I was beside the entrance door, I heard him scream,

"Stop right there, you worthless dog."

I turned to him and waved my hand in his face, provoking him, which drove him mad.

"Wait, I'll catch you…" he put his foot down on a step, missed it, and rolled all the way down over the uneven wood and loose screws. His big body became a helpless mass and his hands fluttered desperately trying to stop the momentum. He hit the floor with a thud and lay there, unmoving, a terrible mass of man.

Was he dead? The thought crossed my mind. God, did I kill a man? Was it my fault? What should I do? They would arrest me! Just like that, everything would go down the drain, all of our plans, our dreams…

That moment, Irena walked in the door. She stopped, looked at Milek who lay on his back like an enormous cockroach. Then she raised her eyes and saw me, looked back at him, and understood what had happened.

"Is he breathing?"

I approached him. Hallelujah! He was breathing. Still alive. Definitely alive. I tried to wake him and wipe the blood which kept dripping from his head. He let out a snort and tried to roll over.

"Stop, leave him be," said Irena.

"But…"

"Better he doesn't wake up and find you here."

She was right, as usual. We hurried to our room. First, I checked on Ilona. Still sleeping. Her curls spread over the mattress, the sweet sleep of children.

I found that I was shaking. Irena brought me water and covered me with a blanket, then waited.

"You were very brave," she said after I told her what had happened.

"And what should we expect tomorrow? Anything could happen."

"Don't worry, when he wakes up, he won't remember what happened and we will carry on as if everything is as usual."

I was not as sure as she was, and even if she was right, what about the next time he got drunk and looked for prey? The next day I suggested my plan to her again.

"Ki-… Ki-bbutz… what is that word, what does it mean?

"'Kibbutz' is a Hebrew word in the ancient language of the Jews."

"The language of your prayers."

"Correct, and it means 'together,' collective, a kind of life that is shared, completely."

"And where is this kibbutz?"

"It's in a Warsaw neighborhood, and not just anywhere, but in a beautiful, enormous estate. It's an agricultural settlement, a big farm that belongs to a rich, generous Pole. Young Jews live there, they work hard, study, and train themselves for their move to the ancient homeland. They are building a future together."

"And what will I do there? You forgot that I'm not Jewish."

"They invited you, too. It's the best place for us in this situation. As it is, every moment we are at risk, anyone could find us out."

She wanted to know more about the place with the strange name and I told her that it was in Cherniakov, a neighborhood of Warsaw, belonging to a Polish nobleman who, out of the goodness of his heart, had given us free rein over his estate. The young people, members of the Dror movement who work there, were Zionists and socialists and together they were building their dream: to resettle the land of Israel with more such likeminded communities.

"He is not your typical Polish man," I told her. "He is a rare friend and brave, like you."

"What will we do there?"

"I will work in the clinic and you will help me there or you can work in the offices. The main thing is that we will live in peace. Just think how good it could be for our Ilona to live in a village."

"It's a Jewish community."

"It's a place for anyone who wants freedom. You'll see, we will be able to rest there, grow vegetables, milk the cows, and give Ilona the peaceful environment that she deserves."

We argued over it for the entire night and by morning it was decided. We would go to the kibbutz.

The next day we paid the innkeeper's wife what we owed. She counted the money three times and then smiled. We packed up our minimal belongings and got into a taxi. Irena told the innkeeper's wife that we were returning to our city, to Ciechanow, as we had just been informed that my husband, that is, the husband of the mute nanny, had been released from captivity, missing a leg, and that she was returning me to him. They were excited by the story and gave us some pieces of sausage and a few beads for Ilona as a kind gesture.

We did not say a word about the previous night, which was only evidenced by a bandage on Milek's head.

To cover our tracks, we asked the coach driver who came to collect our things to pass by the train station which was in exactly the opposite direction. When we were sure that nobody was following us, we asked him to take us to the estate.

"And what will you do there?" he was interested. "That's no place for gentle women such as yourselves."

Irena explained to him that she had gotten a job managing their accounts.

"How? After all, they're all Yids there," he said and spat.

Irena explained to him that in exchange for her work she would be well paid and given a place to live in the master's estate. He shook his head and suggested we not get close to the Jews who lived there.

In mid-May of 1942, we entered the estate. Two young men stopped us at the gate and I, finally, after so many months as Rachelle, Tulla, the mute servant, was able to hug them and shout, "My name is Rachel! Your sister! And this is my daughter and we are Jews like you and we came to be with you, to live here!"

Dozens of young men and women hurried to us, laughing and hugging, asking and listening, happy that we had arrived, as if we had found long-lost relatives. They were thirsty to know what was happening in Ciechanow, or if we had heard any news from the front. Now it was time for me, like the rest, to wear my yellow badge as required. Now I was part of the community.

But Irena was unable to rejoice. She stood off to the side, her face sad, as if looking at a party that she was not invited to. She looked shocked at the sight of the yellow badge, as if I had changed the color of my skin.

"Come with me," I pulled her after me. She looked pale and weak.

"What happened, Irena?"

"I... I don't know... this is not the place for me."

"But you are welcome here."

"I saw how the men looked at me, they don't understand what I'm doing here. God..."

"But remember, where you go, I will go, where you live, I will live. Even Ilona belongs to both of us." She walked after me uneasily. While I felt like I had come home, reached a place, people I could live amongst, she felt like an outsider. I was among my people and she felt superfluous.

I could not find Haim. He had left the estate and nobody knew what had become of him. A curly-haired youth who introduced himself as Moshe helped us carry our belongings and gave us a tour of the farm, then showed us our lodgings. They gave us a pleasant room, which even had a window overlooking the garden. Another young man brought us blankets and pillows and helped us get organized, then led us to the dining room. After the meal, we joined them and listened to one of them play the flute and heard a conversation about the bad news, of those who had been deported from the Warsaw ghetto to a work camp in eastern Poland.

Following a conversation with the leaders of the community, two young men from the Dror movement, it was agreed that I would help them in the clinic and that Ilona could join the children's group. There were five other children of different ages on the kibbutz. I suggested that Irena join me in the clinic as help was always needed. But she refused. I told Moshe that Irena was a bookkeeper and he promised to give her suitable work but that meanwhile, "she could help with the harvest".

Irena remained gloomy. Had I gotten carried away? Was I insensitive to her feelings? When she returned from work in the evenings, her hands were wrecked and her feet swollen. She told me that she could not go on working there; it did not suit her. The others regarded her with suspicion.

"You're imagining it."

"They asked strange questions, spoke between themselves and pointed at me. It doesn't feel right."

"But everyone has to work here. It's a collective, what will you do?" I asked her. She said maybe she would go look for work nearby.

"Reconsider, I think you could help me in the clinic."

"I don't think so," she said. "I'm an outsider here. I will find work in the area so we can keep living together."

At that time there were some 170 people living and working willingly. They worked hard for the owner of the farm in exchange for a place to live, regular meals and, most of all, they were preparing themselves for their dream to leave and settle in Israel.

The next day, Irena left the estate early in the morning. When she returned, she told me that her luck had changed and she had found work as a bookkeeper at the farm next door. But she was not telling me the truth. She had been hired there to cook and clean. Nobody needed a bookkeeper.

"Are you really leaving us?" I asked. She nodded. She had tears in her eyes.

"I don't understand you. You know that you and I…" She covered my mouth with her hand, gesturing for me to stop. I accompanied her part of the way to her new home and we parted only after she promised that she would come to visit us the coming Saturday.

Ilona cried all night, asking for Mamarena. That's what she called Irena, 'Mamarena'.

Tulla stopped talking.

"You really parted ways?" I asked.

Granny Tulla did not answer. She looked out the window. I knew that she was crying, reliving that moment.

"I don't understand, why did she go away?"

"She felt like an outsider," said my father and stroked her hand. "Maybe, like she was not needed. She saw that Tulla had found a place for herself and did not want to interfere."

"Why?"

"Because Tulla wanted to go back to being Rachel Eisler, to belong, to be a part of a community."

"To be a Jew, without having to lie or fake it, and Irena thought that maybe it was time for her to carry on by herself."

"Tulla is tired," said Mom, "I'll continue." Tulla kissed both of us, patted Dad on the back, and disappeared into her bedroom.

"This next part won't be easy," said Mom.

"She's ready," said Dad and sat beside her.

CHAPTER 26

Cherniakov Estate, Summer 1942

By the evening of their first day there, Irena already felt she was not needed, as if her role had come to an end. She saw Tulla join the circle of dancers, her face red with excitement, jumping, singing songs in a language she did not know, and understood that this was not the place for her…

Tulla had found friends. Tulla had found a home, a family. She had found her place among her people.

On Friday, welcoming the Sabbath, Tulla stood with some of the other women of the kibbutz and blessed the candles. Their eyes were closed, their hands cupped around the flame and they whispered the prayer, "asher kidashnu b'mitzvotav ve tzivanu…"

She remained sitting even though Tulla and Ilona begged her to join, to sing Shalom Aleichem with them.

Tulla has found her place and what about me? she thought.

"Your people are my people, your God is my God," Tulla had reminded her. "Stay with us." Irena had promised that this was not goodbye, that she would find work and go on living on the kibbutz, but when she announced that she would be moving to the neighboring farm, Tulla was worried that Irena was trying to put distance between them.

Irena left the kibbutz two weeks after they had arrived there. She moved into the house of the Sovrichek family. They were an older couple. Their son had been killed in the war and they needed help managing the house. Irena did not leave the address or name of her employers. She preferred that Tulla not know she was doing housekeeping work, so she did not let Tulla accompany her there. They parted ways at the gates to the kibbutz.

"When will we meet next?" Tulla asked.

"How can I promise anything? It depends on my employers."

"Promise me we will see you soon," Tulla gripped her arm, refusing to let her go. "Promise me and Ilona."

She promised.

They agreed that she would come visit them on Saturday, the Jewish Shabbat, the day of rest on the kibbutz.

They embraced, waved goodbye, and Irena disappeared.

The first Shabbat, Tulla and Ilona went down to the river where they had agreed to meet Irena. They waited for several hours but Irena did not show up.

The following week she did not come either.

"Where's Mamarena?" asked Ilona.

"She must be very busy with her new job."

"So when?"

"Next week," and again they waited for her. Another week passed and another, and Irena did not come. She had disappeared.

Tulla felt hopeless. On the one hand, she was happy living and working among the people of the kibbutz. Because of the proximity to the Warsaw ghetto, there were those who escaped to the farm, sick people who needed her help. On the other hand, she missed Irena. It seemed strange to her that she would break from them when they had found so rare a friendship. And if not for my sake, she thought, then for our Ilona.

A month after their separation, Tulla took Ilona and the two went to look for Irena.

There were five farms in the area, one next to each other, around the outskirts of the city. They visited each one of them and asked if anyone had seen or heard of Irena. Tulla even showed them an old photograph that she had. But no one had heard or seen the bookkeeper named Irena who had begun working on a nearby farm.

As they left the final property, despairing, the farmer's wife hurried after them.

"Wait," she cried, "maybe I know of her. Are you sure she is a bookkeeper?"

"Why?"

"Because our friends Lulak and Eugenia, our neighbors, recently hired a new housekeeper named Irena. She cleans for them."

"We will check. Thank you." She took down the address.

As they entered the farm, they noticed a figure at the entrance to the house. Tulla stopped. Irena? She saw her dear friend was dressed in a smock with a big apron over it and a flowered kerchief on her head.

She thought, should I go back to keep from embarrassing her? But Ilona broke into a run.

"Mamarena, my Mamarena!" Irena raised her hands to her forehead and turned away, as if hoping they wouldn't see her. But then she dropped the rag she was holding and opened her arms wide, welcoming the girl into them and swinging her around in a warm embrace

"I said I would come to you," she said in embarrassment.

"We couldn't wait any longer," Tulla said simply. "Is there somewhere we can sit? I have so much to tell you."

"I... I didn't want... you to see me like this."

"Have you forgotten? Where you go, I will go. I am your friend, your best friend."

"I was ashamed."

"Everything is all right, my dear, you really thought I would just give up on you?"

From that visit on, they met once a week on Saturdays or Sundays. Irena would come visit Tulla and Ilona at the kibbutz, or occasionally they would come to her at the farm.

Every evening before Irena went to bed, she would pray to Jesus and Maria, mother of God, to whom she had prayed since she was little, and then added a prayer to Tulla's God.

"God of Tulla, God of Abraham, Isaac, and Jacob, look after them, please."

Not far away, in their little room in the Polish kibbutz, Tulla embraced her daughter and prayed that God look after Irena, Ilona, and herself.

Just when it seemed like everything was working out, when life looked rosy again – when Tulla's body was filling out and her skin had regained its glow, and Ilona was singing not only of little Maier but songs of Shabbat and the Hebrew blessings over the meal – troubling rumors began to arrive at the estate.

The evening of Tisha B'Av, the holiday marking the destruction of the temple in Jerusalem, members of the Judenrat were informed that the Germans would be clearing out the ghetto and sending its inhabitants east. They would be sent to the new camps that were bigger with better conditions. The Germans called it the 'Jewish settlement.'

Senior officer Hermann Hoefle announced that the quota was for 6,000 people. But soon enough, the quota grew to tens of thousands of people per day. The Jews, who had been living in the ghetto and were already hungry and ill, worn out by the situation, did not rebel. They believed that they were being transferred to some camp where they would have fresh air, not to their deaths...

German efficiency proved itself once again and, within several months, no fewer than 300,000 Jews had been "resettled" in the new camp which came to be known as Treblinka...more precisely, the Treblinka death camp. The Germans were determined to liquidate the Warsaw ghetto. It was the next step in their plan to exterminate the Jewish people.

Among the youth on the farm, there were those who believed that the Jews really were being moved to live in eastern villages and wanted to join them, while others claimed that it was a ruse and preferred to wait.

In November of 1942, the Germans informed the kibbutz that they must cease production and that the Jews living there would be moved to the ghetto. A special SS force was sent to close the place. By the end of the month, the kibbutz no longer existed.

Nobody remained on the beautiful estate. That dream, too, had been lost.

CHAPTER 27

From the Cherniakov Estate to the Warsaw Ghetto, 1942

Just like every other morning, this morning, too, Irena had her hands full with work. It was early autumn, and she had to make sure to air out the blankets and pillows, to boil the towels and wash the sheets, feed the chickens, and water the plants. There was always something to do.

While she was hanging the laundry, she heard Lulak and Eugenia, who were the farmers and her employers, talking with their neighbors about what sounded to them like good news.

"They finally got rid of the stinking Jews from the estate."

"Finally."

She dropped the sheet she was holding and hurried to the front yard where, under the elm tree, the farmers and their friends were telling one another what had happened the previous night. Each was eager to tell what he knew. All of them praised the deportation.

Finally, the area was free of Yids.

"I prayed that they would get them to go away."

"Now we can breathe clean air."

"The Yids are gone and the fleas with them."

"I always knew that we had to get rid of them."

"They threw them out like dogs, those bloodsuckers."

"Who did they get rid of?" asked Irena. She saw Lulak looking at her, stunned.

"The Jews," they replied.

"When?!" she cried out, and everyone looked at her. What was this impudence? What kind of servant dares to interrupt her masters' conversation?

"What's wrong with you?" Eugenia bellowed. "Get out of here at once and don't bother the guests. You've already finished the laundry, so you'd better get started cleaning the oven."

But Irena was not so easily dissuaded. "Please... just tell me... when did they kick them out? Where were they sent?"

"What's the matter with you?" Eugenia was red with rage.

"Perhaps you've been hiding a Jew here?" said one of the guests. "You know what happens when you hide Yids?"

"Irena is one of us," Eugenia was quick to clarify. "She's a good girl, pure Polish, like us."

"Just impudent," Lulak raised his voice. "Get out of here, Irena, and bring wine for the guests. We have reason to celebrate."

But Irena persisted. "Please," she pleaded. "Where were they sent?"

"How should I know?" Lulak softened. "Yesterday, German soldiers scoured the estate and removed all the Jews."

"You should be glad we're rid of them. Everyone knows that it's their fault the winter is so cold."

"My mother had her foot cut off because of them."

"Gone, thank Christ, who cares where?"

"All of them?"

"They said that a few men managed to escape and were shot, but the rest were sent to the ghetto."

"God," shouted Irena, as she pulled off her apron and began to run.

"Irena, get back here at once!" shouted Lulak. "There's nobody left there."

"I don't understand what's happened to her," Eugenia apologized. "She's usually such a nice girl."

But Irena ran and ran. She raced over to the estate to look for her friend, her soul sister.

When she reached the gates of the farm, she saw at once that it was too late. The place was silent. The gates hung open, as if they had spit out their occupants. She entered the orphaned farm walking among the empty rooms, the dining room still full of dirty dishes, the infirmary deserted, the storage sheds filled with tools.

The estate had been deserted.

"Tulla, Tulla!" she cried over and over, hoping that somehow her friend had managed to hide in some medicine cupboard or under one of the sick beds.

"Ilona, Tulla, Ilonaaaa!" she shouted over and over until her throat was raw. Maybe this was all a bad dream, a nightmare.

She ran over to the living quarters. There were clothes, hats scattered around the corridors leading to the rooms.

In Tulla's room, Irena found some of her belongings remaining: the blue scarf that Tulla loved, her hairbrush, the towel that was still damp, the socks she had knit for Ilona. In the corner of the room she found two wooden squirrels from the box of animals that Bronek had carved for her. She tucked them into her pocket. For better days ahead. But there was no trace of Tulla or Ilona. They had disappeared.

She sat, despairing in the corner of the room and looked around, asking the walls, as witnesses, to tell her what had happened there. Had Tulla tried to fight them? Had the Germans hurt them? Had they left peacefully? What about Ilona? Was she afraid? What had Tulla told her?

Wait a moment, she thought. Maybe Tulla left her a letter, or some clue? She began to look among the blankets, under the mattresses. When she pulled one of the pillows from its place, she found the packet of Tulla's papers and ID that Solly had had made for her.

Had she forgotten them in her haste, or was she afraid that the Germans would see them?

Irena gathered them up and put them in her pocket before going out to the yard. Two soldiers looked at her curiously. She waved to them and went on walking, were not bursting inside, a volcano spitting hot ash everywhere.

Tulla, Ilona! She fell to the ground. Tulla and Ilona had disappeared, as if they had been swallowed up by the earth.

CHAPTER 28
Warsaw Ghetto, 1942

The dream was cut short in one fell swoop. Without any warning, without preparation, we were cast out of our safe nest where we were trying to build our future.

Had we been naive?

Along with the decision to liquidate the ghetto and send the Jews to extermination camps, it had also been decided to finish off this place, the one haven where we Jews had enjoyed some degree of freedom. Sure, we had had to work hard for long hours, but the conditions were reasonable and we had relished a certain degree of autonomy. Most importantly, we had had hope. SS soldiers, known for their cruelty and fanaticism, were sent to expel us.

They broke in, spread out all over the farm, shouting orders through their megaphones while their dogs, who were as cruel as their masters, ran all over the estate, trapping those who tried to escape. Gunshots were heard. Someone screamed. Someone fell. Then silence.

The end of a chapter. The death of a dream.

Two soldiers and a black dog entered my infirmary and instructed us to clear out. "Now," they shouted.

"We can't, we have…" The nurse tried to explain to them that there were patients for whom it would be dangerous to move. One of the soldiers struck her on the head with the end of his rifle.

"Now can you?!" he shouted. Blood began to stream from her wound and she looked unsteady. I quickly bandaged her head and together we urged the patients to obey their orders. Everyone who could got up and went out to the yard where the kibbutz members were gathering.

"I'm sorry but there are patients here who cannot be moved," I said to the officer overseeing our expulsion.

"Who are you?" he approached me threateningly.

"I'm the doctor in charge. If you move them from here there's a chance they will die on the way."

"And why do you think that I care if a few stinking Jews die?" he said and pulled Lieb, who was suffering from severe pneumonia, from his bed. Lieb slipped and fell.

I helped him up and together we left the infirmary.

The Germans shouted and pushed the patients out forcefully, threatening those who limped or had difficulty. There was no doubt, the Germans had come to destroy what we had built.

After helping my patients get onto the trucks, I hurried to look for Ilona.

Where was my daughter? There was chaos in the yard, people running in every direction, trying to escape, to protect themselves. Some were looking for their friends, some passing blankets and warm clothes into the trucks while those who tried to climb the walls were caught by the dogs and shot on the spot.

It was a terrible sight.

The German officers stood to the side with their rifles in their hands, laughing.

Ilona! I shouted. Had anyone seen her? I ran about like a madwoman from one place to another, until it occurred to me to go back to our room. Perhaps she had made it there. And indeed, that was where I found her, my clever girl. She had heard the shouting and done the one sensible thing, return to the room. To our nest. The place where her mother could protect her.

"Why are they angry at us?" she asked.

"They want us to go quickly."

"What did we do to them, Mamatulla?"

What indeed?

I picked her up and whispered to her not to worry. We were moving to a new home once again, and we would have a new, nice place to live.

"And you will get me a dog?"

"Maybe." She closed her eyes. She believed me.

We got into a truck where friends from the Dror movement were already seated. They hurried to make space for us. Wait, I wanted to shout, wait a minute, I don't belong here. I'm Tulla, my daughter Ilona was baptized in a church... what could I do? Betray the others? Abandon my friends? Go and leave them behind?

Yes, I had to get out of here, wait! I'm Tulla, I don't belong... God... Tulla whose husband... here, I have papers... I'm Tulla, not Rachel, not Rachelle... Tulla whose husband was killed at war.

God! Where were they? My papers... where were the certificates? My last hope.

In all the haste and confusion, I had lost the papers that Uncle Solly had made for me. The identification that said I was Tulla had been forgotten. Left behind. At least I still had the bundle of jewelry against my body in a small pocket. We were already moving.

One of the men asked Ilona who was holding me tight if she wanted to help him sing a song. She shook her head no.

"Maybe a song that you know?" he suggested. She looked at me and I smiled at her.

She began to sing. In German. She sang about little Maier in the Himalayas. That stupid song that some Wehrmacht officer had taught her, some friend of Bronek who used to love coming to the house.

"What is Maier doing, little Maier at the top of the Himalayas..."

All of the passengers in the truck listened to the little girl singing to them about little Maier climbing the mountains and smiled. They hummed along with her, trying to sing and it quieted our fear a little, for the moment.

She sang and sang, pleased with her audience, as our convoy of trucks crammed with kibbutz members neared central Warsaw.

"Where are we going?" asked Miriam, who sat beside me. She was shaking. I put my hand on hers and she weakly smiled.

"To the ghetto," said someone beside her.

"At least not to the trains," said someone else.

"Patience, we will get to those too, eventually."

"What's wrong with the trains?" I asked.

"Treblinka is what's wrong. Do whatever you can not to wind up there."

That was how I first heard about the trains to Treblinka, the place from which nobody returned. And of the barbed wire fences covered with tree branches so it looked like an innocent farm.

The ghetto gates opened and the trucks drove in. We were in the Warsaw

Ghetto. It was the biggest ghetto that the Germans had built, right after occupying the city. The truck door opened.

"Out, out, schnell, schnell," the Latvian guards ordered, beating us with the clubs in their hands as the German soldiers aimed their rifles at us. We hurried off the truck. They shouted to scare us, so we would know that our lives depended on them. To shoot or hit a Jew was of little consequence.

Someone helped me down and then passed me Ilona and the bundle of my belongings. Jewish women with big kerchiefs on their heads passed slowly through the street while men with black shtreimel hats and worn clothes looked at us in curiosity. Small children gathered around us, holding their hands out begging.

"I'm hungry," whimpered a little girl beside me. I had a dry slice of bread in my pocket and held it out to her. She snatched it from me and quickly found a place to sit and chew it, so nobody else could take it from her.

Here I am, in the ghetto.

We began to walk. The houses looked abandoned, deserted, dismal.

"Here, this was where we would celebrate the holidays," Miriam pointed as we passed by the synagogue on Okopova Street. "Not far from the cemetery."

I was happy Miriam had joined us. She had been the kibbutz tailor. From the little she had told me, I understood that her husband, who was a known welder in Warsaw, had been sent to a work camp at the beginning of the occupation and was kept paving roads for the German army. At the beginning he would come for short holidays, each time thinner and more desperate, until he stopped coming. She knew that he would not return. Like many others.

Someone told us to hurry to find a place to live. But where?

There was no shortage of options. The ghetto occupants who crowded around us explained that many of the apartments had been evacuated since the Germans had come through in recent months and taken away thousands of Jews.

"Where is our new house?" asked Ilona.

"We'll get there soon," I whispered and picked her up.

"I want a house with a yard and a dog," she said.

Had I made a mistake? Perhaps I should have left her with Marta and gone. Then I would have given her a chance. I hugged her tightly. I could not lose hope. It will be okay. Yes, everything will work out.

And what about Irena? Did she already know what had happened? Had the rumors of the kibbutz evacuation reached her? At the latest, she would come to visit in a week and discover that we were gone.

"Here," someone shouted to me. "Come here."

"We should stay together," suggested one of the kibbutz members. We hurried after one of the ghetto veterans who helped us find a place.

The ghetto was in terrible condition, with evidence of destruction everywhere. Raw sewage flowed through the streets, and filth and long-uncollected trash lay piled high. Two children sat on the corner of the street trying to sell cigarettes, and people peered at us through broken windows with despair in their eyes. The once-pretty houses that I remembered from my student days looked like slums.

The Warsaw Ghetto in November of 1942 looked like hell. Yakov offered me one of the rooms in a big apartment. Each of us got a room of his or her own. I was pleased that Miriam took the room next to mine. Do not despair, I told myself. Here, we have a room with a window. The room contained the furniture of the previous inhabitants. I put Ilona down on a mattress and sat down beside her. I stroked her soft cheek.

"Don't worry, I am here with you and I will protect you from evil," I whispered.

Could I really protect her? Was I reckless to make such promises? Those words I whispered, what else could I give her? What would happen to us now?

Some of the kibbutz members who had settled nearby invited us over and served me a cup of bitter tea.

"How is the little one?" Shmuel Perlmutter, one of the group's leaders, asked me.

"She's sleeping. But what will become of us tomorrow?"

"You will see," said Shmuel. "Here we live from moment to moment. Each slice of bread is a gift."

"I'm Tulla. How long have you been here?"

"Nearly a year."

"An old-timer," said someone and everyone laughed with sad eyes.

"They took my parents away a month ago."

"Where?"

"Treblinka." Everyone was silent.

"What is this Treblinka?" asked Miriam.

"They say it's a farm," replied a youth with a bandage around his head.

"Treblinka is Hell. It has thick smoke covering the sky," cried someone behind me. "Why do you believe the German propaganda?"

"Who believes those animals?"

Silence.

"What will happen tomorrow?" I asked Shmuel again before going to my room. He said that I had already been signed up for work detail and I would have to take instructions from the Judenrat[9] who manage the ghetto on behalf of the Germans.

I don't remember how I fell asleep.

"Get up, up!" shouted someone beside me. "Get up quick!"

What now?

I got up quickly and found myself facing an elderly man, his head covered with a black shtreimel. He looked like he was dressed relatively well for a ghetto dweller. I heard Ilona looking for me.

"Mama, Mama, where are you?" She came over to me. She looked around the room, at me, at our guest, and did not say a word.

"Yehuda," he introduced himself. "Yehuda Weiss. I am from the Judenrat. Welcome to the Warsaw ghetto." He tipped his head as if I had come to attend a gala evening at the Warsaw opera. This was my first meeting with one of the representatives of the council of Jews assembled by the Germans to disseminate their orders.

He looked at Ilona and asked how old she was.

"Two and a half," I answered proudly.

"Big and pretty," he smiled at her and pulled a sweet from his pocket. "You're lucky. We have a nursery for children your age."

"There is no way she will go there. I'm not separating from her."

"You must. You already have work detail," he said.

"Work? What work?"

"In the factory."

"How have I already been given work when we just arrived yesterday?"

---

9   The *Judenrat* was the council of Jews, established by the Nazis, who served as intermediaries between the Nazi regime and the Jewish community. It was a temporary institution meant to carry out the Nazi policy in service of the Final Solution. *Judenrats* were established among Jewish communities in territories under German occupation and took care of public services.

CHAPTER 29

Warsaw Ghetto

"The Germans are organized," said Yehuda Weiss. "We received the list of *kibbutz* members. You should be grateful - working in the factory is good, there are people begging me to let them work there. The conditions are relatively decent..."

"Why me?"

"You seemed suitable to me... strong, quiet, like you'll follow instructions."

"Can we put it off a day?" I pointed at Ilona. "Give me until tomorrow. We've had a hard day."

"Understood. You have a day off. I recommend you tour the ghetto, but tomorrow you have to be at the factory at six in the morning. Ask people where the transport leaves from."

Now I had to explain to Ilona where we were and to introduce her to the terrible place that was the Warsaw Ghetto.

We went out to the street or, more accurately, to what had once been a street and was now in ruins. To my relief, Ilona was happy that morning. She hopped playfully on one foot, smiling at everyone she met.

"Where's Mamarena?" she asked me suddenly. "I want a visit."

I felt a tightness in my throat. What was happening with Irena? Did she know yet?

"She is very busy now, but soon she will come to see us."

"Why don't we go to her today?"

"Because..." How could I answer her? "Because you are going to the nursery school and you will meet new children. It will be nice for you."

"But I'm hungry," she said. "Let's go to Mamarena, she always makes me cookies in the shape of the moon."

I told her that Mamarena was busy and that she couldn't come.

"Ever?"

"We will go to her and she will make cookies shaped like moons and suns, but we have to be patient, my girl - everything will be all right." I promised her again while I howled inside.

"What's that there?" She pointed at the skinny corpse of a child lying on the ground. It was swollen.

"It's an angel that fell from the sky," I told her. "And now you have to turn around so he won't know that you saw him."

"And he won't do anything to me?"

"No. Turn around and whistle and then it will be easier for him to return to the heavens."

She turned and pursed her little lips, trying to whistle.

I bent over the child and closed his eyes which still gazed up at the sky as if he were seeking hope. A final mercy. Ilona went on trying to whistle. I hugged her and we walked on.

"And he will go back to the sky?" she asked.

"Of course. He was an angel who was here for a short time and is going back to where he came from."

So, Ilona learned that she had to turn and whistle every time there were fallen angels on the street. Sometimes we encountered a big angel and then she had to turn and sing at full volume to help him fly...

We found four more angels that morning.

I went to the Judenrat offices to report it to them. A young man sat writing. "We had a lot last night," he said.

"You..."

"Yes, soon the wagon will come."

"And that's how he will get back to the sky?"

"Of course. The wagon will collect the angels?" I winked, and the young man explained to Ilona that yes, everyone would return to the sky.

The ghetto, as I understood, was divided into the big ghetto and the little ghetto. We were living in the little ghetto. In order to get to the big ghetto, where the factory was, we had to cross a bridge over Haludna Street.

That morning we climbed the bridge and looked out on the street below us. It was an unnerving sight. Here in the ghetto, people were dying of hunger, and children with swollen bellies were prying through trash looking for potato peels. The houses were empty and abandoned. There, beneath us on the outside, life was carrying on as usual. People walked along complacently in their fancy suits, smiling to one another. Children with violins hurried to their lessons, and girls with their hair tied back in bright ribbons trotted along in their dance clothes... while right above them, the people of the ghetto passed overhead. We had become shadows that nobody wanted to see.

"What's that there?" asked Ilona.

"That's the tram. It's like a city train, but it only has one carriage."

"When will you take me on the tram?"

"Soon."

"And we'll bring Mamarena."

At night I sang her a song that she loved.

"My two daughters lie sleeping. Do not weep bitterly. Beside you sits a mother who guards against all evil..."

In the evening, we gathered in the apartment where Shaul, one of the kibbutz members, was living. He had taken it upon himself to look out for the group. He handed us slices of bread and jam along with some weak tea. It was the only food we got to eat that day.

People sat staring, downcast, as if there would be no tomorrow.

"You will get two meals at the factory," explained Miriam, who had gathered some information for me. "It's no gourmet restaurant, but you can bring some back to Ilona."

"And you?"

"I will work with the burial society."

After dinner, members of other young Zionist movements[10] joined us, and an argument started up. People wanted to know what would happen to the ghetto's inhabitants. Rumors had been flying that the Germans had decided to liquidate the ghetto and it was only a matter of time before they would follow through on their plan. Most people agreed that we had to resist and not be led like sheep to the slaughter. But how? Where could we get weapons? Who could face the German

---

10 In July 1942, the ZOB (the 'Yiddish camp organization,' in Polish) was established with the aim of rebelling against the Nazis. The leaders of the Jewish fighting organization included representatives of different Zionist movements from the ghetto.

army as they were, armed and well-fed? And their dogs, rifles, tanks... We were a weak group against the strongest army in the world.

The next day Miriam took Irena to the nursery school and I got on the transport that took me to the Schultz weapons factory. It was a new life and different from one day to the next. A new life with no future.

At night, I listened to Ilona as she slept fitfully. She was restless. She groaned and tossed and turned, seeming to have nightmares. She began coughing, and I grew concerned. I could not risk her health.

I saw the beleaguered children, hungry, neglected, with and without their mothers, wearing rags, their eyes pleading, holding out their thin hands. They were starving.

"Please, good people, just a little bread, some mercy for your Jewish brethren."

"I haven't eaten for two days myself."

Fear hovered among the ruined houses. The gates were closed and more Jews were forced to live in this atmosphere of hunger and death. The ghetto inhabitants moved like specters, silent, their eyes filled with fear.

People passed by me, looking to buy a little food. A happy few were holding a packet wrapped in newspaper, hurrying somewhere, moving as fast as they could to avoid running into one of the guards who moved about the ghetto looking for an excuse to shoot. They didn't pay attention to the small hands of the children or to their strangled pleas. The ghetto was no place for youth. I saw them, the miserable survivors, those who risked climbing the walls or trying to squeeze their thin bodies through the cracks to sneak into Warsaw, to maybe find some food in exchange for valuables or money. Sometimes they were caught and punished. There was no law here, nor mercy. Jews, even the youngest, could be shot like sick dogs.

A girl who looked about Ilona's age pulled at my dress, her face withered, her big eyes pleading. I touched her. She was burning, sick. I could see the signs: typhus. There was no hope for her. I put a few coins in her hand and she disappeared out of sight, hurrying to bring the money to her parents. And what about tomorrow?

Tomorrow we would have to whistle to help her get back to the sky as an angel.

Was that to be the fate of my own daughter? If Irena were to come wanting to save her, would I be able to give her up?

CHAPTER 30

Warsaw Ghetto, 1942-1943

On the truck that took us to the work site, those who had been in the ghetto for some time told me about the Schultz factories. Ghetto residents made for cheap, available labor which could be exploited from morning to night. If someone became ill, he was immediately dispensed with and they found someone else to take his place.

Fritz Emil Schultz, a German industrialist with ties to the authorities, had set up textile and shoe factories in the ghetto to supply the Wehrmacht. A job in the Schultz factories was a matter of envy, as those lucky enough to work there were promised food and protection from being rounded up in the aktions - as long as they worked well, of course.

"You're lucky," they told me. "Stay strong. The longer you are there, the more likely you'll survive."

I was sent to the factory that produced socks. Menahem, who managed the workers, showed me my worktable and showed me exactly what to do. "It's important that your work is precise, because they check. You cannot sit, stop working, or take your eyes off the machine without permission," he said and pointed at the Lithuanian guard who was watching us like a snake waiting for an opportunity to strike. In the large, crowded hall, there were some forty machines that made a terrible noise, making socks for the soldiers so they would be warm as they loaded Jews onto the trains or blew up cities. And so, I became part of the production line.

The work was exhausting, primarily because we had to stand beside the machines for over ten hours a day. And God forbid anyone should try to sit or take a break. There were guards in every corner following us, looking for fatigued or idle workers. I saw the pleasure they took in kicking a young woman who worked in front of me when she stopped for a moment. Every now and then they would burst into the hall and drag one of the women out, hitting them until they would bleed.

On the way back, Menahem explained to me, "Be careful, they're like dogs. They're waiting for us to slip up. If they find any mistake, no matter how small in your work, if you dare sit, talk to the person beside you, they will beat you without mercy."

The noise was terrible and the air was dense and smelly with sweat but when we gathered for a lunch break and I managed to tuck a tiny piece of meat and half a potato into my pocket so that I could bring it to Ilona, I understood my good fortune.

Two months after our arrival in the ghetto, as winter approached, I sensed Irena. She was here, nearby, looking for me. It was as if she had suddenly risen and stood before me, smiling her broad smile. All at once I felt a wave of warmth, as if a light had broken through the dark clouds. I felt hope. Irena knew I was here.

I hurried to the bridge that connected the two parts of the ghetto. Maybe I would be able to see her from there. Maybe she was walking somewhere nearby, looking for me, shouting, calling my name. A tiny chance, but worth trying. No such luck.

At night Ilona was coughing again. I put my hand on her forehead. She was burning up. I knew that I could not leave her alone so I decided to take her with me. Maybe they would take pity on me. Maybe they would let me off for the day without taking away my job.

Menahem made a face when he saw us and called me to his office. "Are you crazy?" he shouted.

I explained the situation to him and asked for his help. He was worried he might catch typhus or one of the diseases that ran rampant in the ghetto, or that she might infect the other workers. I promised him that it was just a flu.

"How do you know?"

"I'm a doctor. Can you help me get medicine?"

"A doctor? Since when?"

"I completed medical school in Warsaw."

"Why didn't you tell me at once? They always need doctors here."

He agreed to let me leave early. A few hours into the day, he came to me with a bag of medicine and some vegetables.

"I will let you treat Jewish patients but on condition... that you also treat Germans."

"I can't."

"It's up to you. Just think of it as the cost of saving Jewish lives."

And so, I found myself working at a sock-making machine as usual, but from time to time I was summoned to take care of the better-connected among the Germans, or the Jewish council who enjoyed such privileges as medicine and decent living conditions. It was not long before I was made factory doctor, but only as needed. I was still on the production line.

Although the living conditions of the Judenrat members were more comfortable, they were trapped. On the one hand, they had to make sure to follow orders from the Germans; on the other, they had to serve the needs of the community. Their status gave them certain privileges but came with challenging, if not impossible duties.

Although our situation had improved, I was very worried about Ilona. She had become a shadow of herself. She had lost weight, her face had grown pale, and she was sad, too sad for a three-year-old child. I taught her to sing and dance and count. I told her funny stories about animals, but I saw something in her eyes that I had never seen before in a child. Beyond the deep sadness, something else - fear.

CHAPTER 31

Warsaw 1942

Irena arrived in Warsaw two months after the Jews had been kicked out of the kibbutz on the estate. She told her employers on the farm that she had to leave since her elder sister was ill and in bad condition in the hospital, and she had to move to Warsaw to look after her. As they had come to care for her, they begged her to promise to return when her sister's condition improved and even bring her sister back with her.

Eugenia added with a smile, "After all, the village air will do her good."

They gave her the address of a relative of theirs, a widow who would be happy, they thought, to rent a room in exchange for help cleaning and cooking. They were so good to her that she felt guilty about her lies. White lies, she comforted herself.

Kassia, the widow, was an old woman in her eighties who suffered from edema in her feet. It was hard for her to walk, so she was happy for Irena's help. She had been a high school teacher and lived on a meager pension. In exchange for her help, Irena received a little room and two meals daily. It was a good arrangement for all. Irena explained to Kassia that during the day she would have to look after her sister. Kassia agreed, allowing her time to go to Tulla.

She had to be careful not to run into Andre. To be sure, she made sure to wear her baggy peasant clothes when she left the house and a flowered scarf on her head that covered most of her face. Who would recognize the beauty who had stood by his side reciting vows in church not so very long ago?

A few days after she got settled, Irena began to wander the streets of Warsaw. The long occupation had left its marks on the city.

The proud capital that she remembered from visits with her parents was now grey and sad. The cafes were full of Nazi officers. Soldiers marched the streets, keeping order, ready to stop anyone. Every movement was suspicious. In the center of town, like a bleeding wound, stood the ghetto.

She knew that Tulla must be living somewhere in there.

High walls enclosed the ghetto streets where, as Kassia had told her, hundreds of thousands of Jews were living in terrible conditions. Kassia knew the ghetto well as she had lived nearby when the gates were still open and people were still allowed to move in and out freely. At that time, Kassia would visit her good friend Sarah Greenberg, a piano teacher whose family had been forced to leave their beautiful home and move to the ghetto.

Kassia told her how shocking it had been to visit the ghetto. Many of the buildings had been damaged by bombing and were uninhabitable. Tens of thousands had been forced to leave their homes and had become homeless, and disease had run rampant. Since people had begun succumbing to illness and starvation, entrance to the ghetto had been forbidden, and Kassia no longer knew what had become of the Greenberg family.

Irena found the ghetto easily. It was hard to miss. Its high walls cut it off from the rest of the city. She reached the gates and was stopped by a soldier who asked her if she had permission to enter. Her explanation – that her good friend had been taken there by accident although she was actually a good Christian like herself – fell on deaf ears. She had to see her, she explained, to try to help her to get out. She pleaded, cried, and shouted, but the soldiers insisted that she could only enter with official permission.

Irena was afraid to request such a permit. How could she be sure that it wasn't Andre approving the applications or, God forbid, that one of his Nazi friends wouldn't see her paperwork and show it to him? She was afraid of his wrath.

She decided not to take the risk. She knew that he would not be satisfied and might go looking for Tulla and Ilona to take revenge on them. She had to find another way. She tried a different gate. She walked the entire way around the walls but found no way to enter. She walked this route every day, sending Tulla-Rachel her love. She sent her strength and prayed to the God of the Jews to help them meet again.

She was sure that Tulla could hear her.

One of the days, as she entered Mr. Pushnok's shop to buy bread and potatoes for soup, as she did every day, she heard the store owner, a heavy, good-natured

Polish man, proudly telling of the stupid Jews that would pay him six times the price for an egg or a carrot.

"You're the fool," said one of the neighbors. "They pay for a potato and steal five more."

"They're like roaches, they're everywhere."

"They'll steal anything."

"They should be shot," shouted the neighbor. He was a cruel Hungarian who lived upstairs from Irena.

"Like rats," his wife agreed.

"Where did you see Jews?" Irena wondered aloud. "They're all shut inside the ghetto."

"It's their children. They come through the holes in the ghetto walls and the sewers."

"The ones who manage to get out come to get food for their families."

"That's what I said - they steal. It's good they're getting rid of them."

"They should be shot," the Hungarian proclaimed again and left the shop.

Kassia told her that there were more than 100,000 children in the Warsaw ghetto and that they had become the sole breadwinners for their families who depended on them. They managed to dig passageways underneath the ghetto walls or crawled through the barbed wire. They found cracks and tunnels, any way they could to sneak out and bring back a piece of bread or a potato.

"You realize they're risking their lives coming and going like that. The German guards will shoot at any figure they see on the wall or anyone trying to cross through the sewers."

"These children have to grow up all at once. I saw it in my friend's children. Her three-year-old had to adapt to the new reality, learned to hold out his hand and ask for handouts. It's heartbreaking."

Irena knew exactly what she had to do. She had found a way, a crack in the wall. She would wait for the ghetto children beside the walls. Or she would try to recognize those who came begging and try to speak with them. But she found they always slipped away. So, she waited beside Mr. Pushnok's store until one evening she saw one of them enter the little shop. She went in after him and waited. He held out a thin hand to her. "Alms, Miss?" She looked him in the eyes and saw everything.

"I'm hungry and my mother is sick."

She gave him a green potato. He looked at with suspicion before tucking it quickly into the pocket of his worn-out pants. He immediately held out his other hand.

"I have other brothers, Miss. Please."

"What's your name?"

"Why?" He took a step back.

"Don't be afraid. I'm Irena. You look like a smart boy."

"I'm the smartest in all the ghetto. My name is Nathan."

"And do you want to earn some money, Nathan?"

"Depends what I have to do for it." He looked at her.

"Deliver something."

He stared at her in suspicion.

"How much?"

She handed him two bills. "You will get three times that if you bring me a response."

He handed back the bills. "It's not enough."

She gave him another. And another. He smiled and hurriedly put them in his pocket. "Come back and I will give you four times that okay?"

They agreed.

She handed him a letter she had written and added one of the squirrel toys she had found in the abandoned room back on the estate.

"Her name is Tulla. Or Rachel. She has a young daughter. Ask about the people who arrived recently from the kibbutz."

"I know them," he said. "I know the whole ghetto. Just remember we said four times."

"And I'll add three potatoes for your brothers." He smiled at her and she thought, what a handsome boy. She tried to hug him but he ran off and disappeared. Now she had to wait. It was clear that he would hurry to do as she had asked. After all, she had offered him a generous sum, nearly all of the money she had saved from the last month.

Two days later she saw him at the entrance to Kassia's building.

"How do you know where I live?" she asked.

"I know lots of things, Miss Irena."

"The letter."

"First the money," he said. Still a boy, but he knew about survival. Only when she had paid him did he hand her the letter in response. She recognized the handwriting at once. Tulla! She had to sit down. She went up to her room and he followed her. He was careful not to rouse Kassia, who was dozing in her room.

"Anything else, Miss?" he said suddenly before he left. "Anything you want... anything... I'm here." He handed her a sketch of the ghetto wall. "See?" He pointed at a spot beneath the bridge, marked in pencil. "Walk there, go around once, twice, three times. Carry a newspaper under your arm and I will know that you're looking for me."

"How will you know?"

"I'll know. Trust me."

She felt a sudden affection for the boy. She handed him some sausage and two apples that he hid in his clothes.

"How old are you, Nathan?"

"Actually, Miss Irena, I'm called Noah, but I didn't know if I could trust you."

"Nice to meet you, Noah, how old are you?"

He shook her hand seriously. "I'm nine, nearly ten. Remember, a newspaper. Folded under your arm..." And he disappeared.

She opened the letter, her heart pounding.

My dear Irena, my soul sister,

I knew you were there. I knew you would find me and wouldn't give up on us.

Suddenly everything is cut short. Ruined. We were taken before we could say goodbye. Things are hard here, but we are surviving. It's hard for me to see our beloved Ilona. It looks like the light inside her is going out. Our beautiful girl barely smiles. She doesn't sing. She doesn't even ask after you anymore. As if she's given up. It's terrible, the fate of my people... Don't stay in Warsaw, it's too dangerous. You should go back to your parents' village and live well.

Your letter was like a great light for me - it filled me with happiness. I read it to Ilona and she smiled, yes, smiled.

Get out of here, Irena, this war is not over yet.
We love you forever.
Tulla.

CHAPTER 32

Warsaw Ghetto, 1942

In the second letter delivered by Noah, the boy that Irena had recruited, she asked again how she could help me. Was there any chance of getting us out of the ghetto, what should she do, who should she speak with? Along with the letter, she added a little bag of food: some chicken, potatoes, and carrots. I gave half of it to Miriam.

Get out of Warsaw, I wrote her back. Go to your parents' house. You can't save us.

But she wrote back: Tell me what to do and I'll do it. I am waiting for you, my soul sister.

At night I heard Ilona crying in her sleep and banging her head against the pillow. I knew exactly what was bothering her. David, one of the children from her nursery school, had died that morning. They had simply found him dead. Silent. Like a fallen bird.

I held her tight and stroked her red hair. My little girl... Mama will look after you.

From the moment when we had resumed contact with Irena, from the moment when I knew she was somewhere nearby, wanting to help, the question had plagued me... what would I do with Ilona? The ghetto was no place for children. We encountered numerous angels every day. How could I save her from this hell?

What was I supposed to do, get her out of here and be separated again? Would I be capable of sending her out of the ghetto and splitting from her a second time? \Yes, screamed one voice, you gave her life, now make sure she survives.

On the other hand, cautioned another voice, can you go on without her?

Was it my duty to hand her over to Irena? To give up? Every night I was restless, troubled. What should I do? Then something happened, and there was no longer any question as to the path I should take.

It began when we encountered the devil as we walked home one night.

Since my 12-hour days at the factory ended long after Ilona's nursery school closed, I would pick her up her from the nursery school teacher who had agreed to watch her after hours in her own home. When we left the teacher's house that day, the ghetto streets were completely dark, the streetlights were out, and the stars in the sky were hiding above a blanket of clouds. It was on nights like those that I hurried us home as fast as we could go. We walked, her hand in mine, careful not to slip on the ice or trip over the heaps of trash littered around the streets. She was singing one of her Hannukah songs that she had learned that morning. "Ma-a tzur yashu-a-ti," she sang, bungling the words. It was funny and sweet, walking close, hugging each other to stay warm.

When we turned into the alley that led to the building where we lived, still happy, a black car stopped beside us with a screech of its wheels. It was impossible to miss the SS officer looking at us.

Ignore them, I told myself. Keep on going as if it's nothing.

I held Ilona's hand tighter and we went on walking, her singing.

A young man in a green uniform came out of the car. He went around and got back in on the other side.

There was a siren from somewhere in the ghetto. Something was going on.

"Mezuztzuk mash-u-a-ti..." sang Ilona in her sweet voice.

"Um aufzuhoren,"[11] the car door opened and the two of us were trapped on the sidewalk.

Be smart, don't panic, don't let Ilona see you're scared.

We stopped. We had to. There was no other choice.

I waited. Maybe it was just routine, a surprise check. They would ask for my papers and carry on with their business.

"Does the little girl want chocolate?" The SS officer got slowly out of the car in his impeccably ironed uniform, black boots, and black wool coat. I could

---

11 stop

see he was high ranking, a captain at least. I remembered them from my days back at Bronek and Marta's house. Meeting SS officers like this could be deadly. After all, they were in charge of the Final Solution. I tried not to frighten my child and acted as if it were all a game and not that it could end with the us as two more ghetto angels.

Chocolate? Of course, Ilona wanted some. She desperately wanted chocolate. She hadn't tasted it in months.

"Yes," she nodded and he handed her a piece which she took and then cowered close to me.

I was trapped. Satan did not just go about giving chocolate to children.

"Cigarette?" He pulled a silver packet of cigarettes and held them out to me. Why was he being nice to us? Was he preparing us for the worst?

"Thank you." I took a cigarette, just to keep from angering him. I could see the gun at his side.

What did he want from me? He went on smiling. The smile of this python would not let up until he had sunk his teeth into his prey.

"Shall we take a trip, Miss?" He put his hand on Ilona's hair. She smiled. Yes, of course, how could she not. A ride in the car, how great, Mama. She pulled my hand, trying to pull me into the car. Mama, Mamatulla, come, come for a ride.

I tried to stop her but she evaded me and climbed up onto the black, leather upholstered seat, smiling happily, licking the chocolate.

"I'm not... Ilona, come, you're bothering the gentleman."

The officer indicated with his finger to do as I had been asked. I got into the car, my heart fluttering. What did he want? He lit his cigarette and sat beside me. I felt like a butterfly in a bell jar.

"Pretty girl, look at that hair... suits her perfectly," he said and lifted Ilona onto his lap. Ilona was licking her chocolate. I was quiet. I did not protest. Every cell in my body was sending me warning signals. Be smart. Be smart.

"You're a good girl, right?" She nodded her head.

"Red hair just like my wife wanted," he stroked her hair. She was no longer smiling.

"You're lucky," he turned to me. "Some think that we should send the children out of the ghetto." I did not dare respond. Where was this going?

"But she is like a beautiful flower, she must be taken care of." I tried to calm my shaking hands.

"You know, my wife, she doesn't have any children…"

"I'm sorry," I said.

"We thought… the ghetto is no place for children, why shouldn't she come and live with us?"

Be smart. Smart. No histrionics, nothing that might end badly.

"When?"

"Now, and you should be grateful for your good luck."

Be smart, be careful, be smart, be smart, Tulla. One wrong word and you'll be thrown into the street with a bullet in your head.

"Just like that?" I tried. "In these dirty clothes? Without saying goodbye to her father? Maybe if you come by tomorrow, I'll have time to do some laundry…"

He held up his hand and slapped me, again and again. I heard Ilona screaming.

"Now. I told you, scum."

I didn't cry. I looked at him and did not cry. No, you will not have the pleasure of seeing me break down. Ilona threw the chocolate down and began to scream, "No ride, I want to go home!"

"Tell her to calm down," he said and put his hand around her neck. "You don't want to make me mad…"

"Stop it, little one, everything is okay," I smiled and took her into my lap. She relaxed and I handed her back to him. Be smart, be smart.

"Of course," I said. "I'm sure she will live better with you, better than here." What are you doing, woman, what are you doing?

"It will be good for you, Ilona, you will have toys and dolls." She looked at me, at him, and back at me. He smiled. The predator had caught his prey.

He stopped the car and I got up to get out.

"Wait," I told him calmly, as if we had just returned from a picnic. "You will need to take her medicine."

"Medicine?" There was disappointment on his face.

"But there's nothing to worry about, if she gets good care, she has a good chance of getting well."

"What does she have?" He got out of the car and I followed him. Ilona tried to get out too.

I slammed the door in her face. She stayed sitting, stunned. One day you will understand, Ilona.

"It's typhoid fever."

He lit himself another cigarette. "She got it because she lives in a basement. She got it from the lice or fleas or maybe the rats."

"Rats?" He stubbed out his cigarette angrily and immediately pulled out another.

"If you are careful it will all be fine. She's a wonderful child."

"Careful?" His boots looked less shiny. He was angry.

"Yes, careful. It's a very contagious disease and if it goes untreated one can die from it. When you take her home, first put her in quarantine so she doesn't…"

Then I bent and kissed his hand. Yes, it's true, I kissed the hand of the messenger of Satan. "Thank you, you are saving her. Here she has no chance. She only had maybe two days left. You've been saved, you hear? My dear, you are so lucky," I smiled at Ilona who was screaming from behind the glass window of the car. "Not like the others! You will get better!"

He took a step back from the car then signaled to the driver to come closer and whispered something to him in German. The driver opened the door, picked up Ilona as if she were highly contagious, and threw her onto the street.

I remained standing where I was while my daughter bellowed. The car disappeared. I was unable to move. I was frozen on the spot. Ilona got up and hurried to me. Her eyes were red, and she was screaming and hanging onto me, begging me to hug her, to bandage her where it hurt. "Don't cry, my love," I tried to say but my mouth wouldn't cooperate. I tried to hug her but my arms shook. I couldn't hold her.

I sat down on the sidewalk and she sat beside me, her little hand searching for mine, looking for comfort. Comfort I was unable to give her.

I had managed to save her this time. But next time?

When we entered the apartment, Miriam stared at me intently and asked me what had happened.

"I ran into a wall."

"A wall? Tall with boots?"

"Stop it Miriam."

"Looks to me like a meeting with the SS? What happened, Tulla?"

"I'm fine, everything is fine." She hurried and brought rags and water and washed Ilona's cuts.

"Tulla, what happened?"

"I had a meeting with Satan." She did not need more than that.

That night, Miriam slept in my room, unwilling to leave me alone. She told

Ilona funny stories until she fell asleep and sat beside me, not leaving my side until I fell asleep too. There, I found solace… When I woke up, the room was still dark, Ilona was sleeping. I could hear her sighs and listened to her heavy breathing.

All at once I was possessed by the realization that I could not protect Ilona. It was selfish to keep her with me in the ghetto.

I knew that to send her away would feel like dying, but it was my only option.

That night I wrote:

"Dear Irena, my soul sister.

You asked how you could help us. I thought about it a great deal, and there is a way you can help. I ask that you take Ilona with you, get her out of here, save her from the claws of evil. She won't survive here in the ghetto."

I wrote the letter in agony. Take my only daughter, whom I love, Ilona… just like God had said to Abraham: take your only son, whom you have loved… was God testing me too? Would Ilona survive as Isaac had?

What kind of mother gives up on her child?

"You are very brave to admit the truth - you can't protect her here," said Miriam when I told her of my decision.

The letter was sent and Irena did not respond. Noah assured me that he had delivered it to her immediately. Had something happened to her? Maybe Andre had found her? Or she was worried about taking the child?

Perhaps you are hesitant, I wrote her again. But it's the right choice. There's a moment where we must think of what is best for others, even if it hurts us. Ask Noah to help. He's smart, and brave, and knows how we can get our girl out. Irena, please, at least let's save this one soul.

I went to Noah and asked him to take my letter and this time I told him what I had in mind.

"You want to get Ilona out?"

"We must. She will die here, look at her."

He looked at me for a long moment and said that he had to consider the matter. I told him I would give him a pair of gold earrings and a bracelet that should cover food for his family for a long time. He did not answer. He took the letter and disappeared as if he'd been swallowed up by the earth.

Two days later he turned up and I could tell from his face that he had gotten a response. "Here," he said and handed me a letter. "Then let's speak."

Tulla, my dear, I send you my love. How can I do as you ask? You want me to take Ilona from you? To uproot her from you after everything we've been through? I am afraid for your health, Tulla, that without her you might lose your will to live. But I will do whatever you ask, whatever you think is right for you and for her. I've already spoken with Kassia, the landlord where I am staying and she will allow me to bring the girl. Don't worry, our precious baby will be in good hands until we can meet again.

Noah waited. When I finished reading, he said, "Whatever you want, Tulla, I'm here."

I handed him the pair of earrings and he handed them back to me. What was wrong? He didn't want the earrings or the bracelet or Johann's medallion. "I don't want your money or jewelry," he said.

He had a surprising request.

"The one condition, is that she leave along with my brother, Baruch."

"What do you mean?"

"Baruch is four years old. I have to get him out of here."

"And your mother..."

"We are alone. They took our vineyard and brought us here. I don't know where my father is."

"And your mother?"

"She... it was too much for her. One day, when she was waiting in line to buy bread, they took my baby brother from her as if it were some kind of joke and she screamed, demanded that they give him back. They smashed in his head, a two-month-old baby... Mother went mad, tried to hit them with her fists and they laughed and kicked her, six, seven, eight times until..." He stopped. Noah, the hardened youth, was crying.

"God!"

"Why 'God', Tulla? Don't you understand? God hasn't been listening to us for a long time."

"My poor Noah," I hugged him. "We must save him at once."

"He's in bad shape. He hasn't been growing. His belly is swollen and I can see rats' bite marks on his skin. He won't survive here. I have to get him out."

"But where will he go?"

"To Irena."

"Irena? You mean to bring her another child… Noah!"

"Baruch is a quiet child. And he doesn't eat much."

"Wait a moment, Granny," I stopped her. "You mean, are you saying that Baruch… that Baruch is…"

"Exactly," answered Mom and Dad together.

"So… Uncle Brocky isn't actually my real uncle?"

"Of course, he's your uncle - he was reborn, like all of us, into a new life. He's much more than a brother."

"At Irena's funeral the two of you whistled so that she would be an angel?"

"Precisely," laughed Mom. "Like back then, in the ghetto, when we would whistle so the dead would rise up to the sky and turn into angels."

"And Noah? Who's Noah, then?"

"Patience," Dad smiled. "Let's continue."

"That's impossible," I told him. "I can't ask that of Irena."

"So only your child is important? Only she deserves help?"

"That's not what I said, only…"

"You see Ilona, she has a mother, she has Irena. Who does Baruch have? The train to Treblinka?"

"But it's not my…"

"So, find someone else who will get your child out of here," he took a step back as if about to leave, then shouted angrily, "But I'm the best. It will be the safest with me."

What could I do? He was just nine and a half, still a child, but two years in the ghetto had taught him the rules of survival. He wasn't kidding, he meant what he said.

"It's not up to me, it's up to Irena."

"This way she will have a child of her own too," he said.

"What am I going to do with you?"

"Nothing, you can figure this out on your own." He left and I followed him.

"But if she doesn't… agree."

"She will take what we give her." I stood there embarrassed, hesitating.

How could I send her another child?

"Do what you want, that's my condition. But I know that look… of despair," he said, this child who was old before his time. "Your daughter, I've seen her. Like a fire that's run out of kindling. She doesn't smile, her hair is dry, her arms are as thin as matchsticks. I know it... sores all over the body, lice, a swollen belly and then..."

"Enough!" I shouted.

"She has you, to hug her and love her and look after her. What about my Baruch? Who does he have? He needs someone too and I can't look after him anymore. The situation here is tense, like before the war."

"What do you mean like before the war?"

"There are rumors... the SS is planning another aktion. People are at their limit. So, what is your decision?"

He had won. He held out his thin hand and we shook on our deal. We moved on to the planning stage. He suggested we hand over Ilona on Friday because the ghetto would be especially quiet. I would dress her in layers of clothing so she wouldn't have to carry anything. He would determine the meeting place with Irena.

In the letter he brought Irena, I didn't mention Baruch. That was his suggestion. We decided that we would simply bring him to her.

Now was the hardest moment, explaining to Ilona that she was moving again, to a new place, without me.

"Why?"

"Because Irena really misses you."

"So why doesn't she come with us?" I saw tears gathering in her big eyes.

"Now it's Mamarena's turn."

"But why can't you come too?" She clasped my neck, trying to hold on to me.

"Don't worry, I will come soon." Lies again.

"When?"

"Let's say in two months. That's not so long."

What could I tell her? That there would be more aktions? That I was getting weaker? That there was no place for weak people here?

"Will you really come?"

"You don't believe me?"

"Why are you sending me away?"

"Enough!" I shouted. "Do as you're told!" It was terrible.

She broke away from me and sat down some distance away. I knew she was crying. I held out my arms to her. Forgive me.

"Sometimes it's hard for you, too," said my little girl. She already knew so much.

"Don't forget the little squirrel that Irena brought you and your teddy bear."

"He doesn't want to come."

"Here, take this," I held out one of Johann's two medals. "This was your father's. He was a hero."

"He never even saw me."

"But he knows how wonderful you are."

She took the medal from me and put it in her pocket. Then she laid her head down on the mattress. Her sadness was too hard for me to bear. I wish she would cry, shout, rebel, kick me, swear, do something, but she was so dejected, helpless in the face of my decision. Children don't rebel; they take the world as it is. Only afterwards do they understand and crack with sorrow.

Friday came.

I accompanied them to the spot we had agreed on. Noah walked ahead, holding Baruch's hand. He was small for his age, wearing pants too big for him and a shirt so white it was remarkable. Noah must have gotten his brother a clean shirt so he would look his best. Ilona walked beside me, her hands at her sides. She did not take the hand I held out to her and would not look at me. She just looked straight ahead.

"Here," said Noah. "From here the guards can see us, so it's best we part here."

I stopped. I tried to hold Ilona to me, hug her for one more moment but she moved away and closer to Baruch.

"One more moment."

"There isn't time," Noah urged.

I ran after her and picked her up in my arms, hugged her, inhaled her. I stroked her wet nose and kissed her little hands. She looked at me with an expression that I carried with me for months afterwards. As the days grew harder and harder, Ilona's sad face remained etched in my mind. The disappointment, the silence, the tears streaming down her cheeks.

"See you soon," I whispered and set her down. "Tell Mamarena that I love her and not to forget to keep a light on for you at night."

Instead of a response she dropped the squirrel I had placed in her hands and left.

They left. And I stayed behind, crushed, holding the squirrel.

They got farther away, then she turned, her face wet. Suddenly, she dropped Noah's hand and ran to me. "Come quick, Mamatulla!"

Of course. I gave her the squirrel. "Tell him how you are doing every evening, so I will know."

"Every evening." She hugged the squirrel.

"I love you, Ilona." She hugged me.

A few more seconds and they were swallowed up by the darkness. They followed Noah to one of his secret ways out of the ghetto. They would crawl underneath the wall and come out onto the street where Irena would be waiting for them.

Don't cry, don't feel sorry for yourself, I commanded. You did the right thing. She will be somewhere safe, a better world. She got a chance that you might never get.

Better for her to forget, for her to keep on moving forward.

Miriam was waiting for me back in my room. She handed me a cup of tea and sat beside me. There was no need to talk.

That night the pain was too much to bear. My body went dark, the light had left me. Sorrow stabbed me like a stake, like a thorn in my side, as I lay alone in the empty room without my daughter. And then, relief …comfort, knowing she was saved.

CHAPTER 33

Warsaw Ghetto - Winter 1942

A week after the two children [the ghetto – seven days that lasted an eternity – Noah left a message for me with my good friend Miriam.

"Your friend asked me to tell you to meet him tomorrow at six o'clock on the bridge," she said.

"When was he here?"

"When you were at work. Do you know what he is planning?"

I told her I did not. I had no idea. Miriam looked at me and went on her way. She had been busy lately with something she did not want to share with me, something secret.

I had a feeling that something was going on, some scheme being planned in the rooms of the group she was active in. She did not ask and I did not explain. That was another rule of survival. The less people know the better. Fewer loose lips were less likely to endanger anyone. Information is power, but in our circumstances it could be corrupted.

I got to the bridge by five to make sure I would not be late. I tried to guess what might be going on. Something would happen, beside or underneath the bridge. But even if Ilona walked past, the chances of seeing her were slim.

The minutes passed so slowly. Underneath me, on Haludna Street, people hurried home. They wore fur hats and their warmest woolen coats, protecting themselves against the terrible cold. A hot meal awaited them in their heated homes - a cabbage soup or sweet roast. Just the thought of steaming krupnik soup or meat pie made me suddenly dizzy. I held onto the railing to keep from collapsing and then I heard a small rustling sound like a mouse. A moment later, the little guy stood beside me.

What? What was going on? He gestured to me not to speak, just to listen.

I had no idea what to expect but my heart beat wildly. What? Noah smiled and cupped his hand around his ear. Then I heard. Yes. That voice made me grip the bridge railing hard to keep from falling over. The sweetest sound of all, the sweet voice of my little Ilona, floating up from the street, over the sounds of the rushing people, rising as if to hold out a hand and stroke my heart. I had no doubt it was my Ilona singing beneath us. In the city where people were free to choose, to be themselves, to do as they liked, there she was, singing. Her song. The song she always loved, that had already opened doors for us. The song about little Maier in the Himalayas.

Was macht der Maier...

Only this time Ilona was singing for me, only for me. That stupid song that she learned from some German in Ciechanow to impress Marta and Bronek's Nazi guests... now she was singing it for me.

And I was laughing.

I remembered and laughed, cried, and laughed.

What was little Maier doing in the big Himalayas? She sang.

I couldn't see her, but I heard her sweet voice clearly and then another voice joined hers. The clear, strong voice of a boy. Baruch? Brocky. The second verse and the third.

The children were singing. I took Noah's hand. It was shaking. He was happy too, his face shining as the song finished and we heard clapping and cries of 'Bravo.' As if the whole street were listening to them.

"Noch einmal, Noch einmal," someone shouted in German. "Again!" And the children sang it again. They were singing for us, hoping the words would reach our hearts directly. The song of Little Maier was their way of saying, we are here, everything is all right, don't worry about us. We've found a peaceful, safe home and we will not forget you.

Bless Irena. A great light in my life.

From that evening on, I would make my way back from the factory via the bridge where I would listen for those sweet voices singing.

Sometimes they were there. But only sometimes, as the letter that she sent me explained, because "We must be careful. We cannot tempt fate."

On those lucky days, I would stand on the bridge with them below me, singing in their sweet voices, the whole street listening to them... what is Little Maier doing in the big Himalayas?

And my heart danced with joy as if everything really were all right. Although I could not see them, I knew that they were standing in the busy street, surrounded by a big crowd of people, their eyes huge, sending the song to me and to Noah. And that the words to that silly song were bringing happiness to the street.

Bravo!

"Noch einmal! Again!" cried those in uniform, enjoying the stupid song in their native language. How smart of Irena, to give us this pleasure over the heads of the SS soldiers.

Again, please! It made the hunger and the cold easier to bear. It made me hopeful that I could live another day. Sometimes they would change a line in the song just for me. It lit up the darkness that had descended upon me.

Hi Mamatulla, how are you tonight? We don't know where and we don't know when, but we are sure we'll meet again!

Not more than that and not every evening. Sometimes. They could not afford to take chances, to arouse suspicion or too much attention. They didn't want anyone asking questions or taking an interest - who were these sweet children? Where had they come from? How old were they? And was Irena really their mother?

And if they asked, did she have papers to prove it? She had Ilona's baptism certificate, but they might look into it and find that she had "stolen" the child. And what about Baruch?

One evening as I returned home, happy, I found Miriam beside the door to the ruin that was my home.

"Tulla, follow me."

"What happened?"

"They want to speak with you. Come."

"Who? Who wants to?"

"They will answer all of your questions, come with me."

I didn't ask where or why. Sometimes I was called to look after someone sick or wounded that had been hidden out of sight of the Germans. They relied on my silence. A rule of the ghetto: the less you know, the better. Any information in the wrong hands could be harmful.

To be safe, we moved through the little alleyways around the periphery of the ghetto for nearly an hour. Her face was fixed, grim, and she did not say a word to me. I stepped through sewage water which flowed freely. Here and there we had to step over some body that had not yet been removed.

It was evening but even the beggars and sellers of cigarettes were out of sight, only shadows popping up and then disappearing back to wherever they had come from.

When she no longer feared that we were being followed, she stopped beside a building on Mila Street. She bent down as if to tie her shoe, looked around and whistled. She waited. She whistled again and then disappeared into the building and I followed her. I felt my way in the dark. There were steps. I tried not to slip or fall. We went down farther and farther until she stopped. Slowly my eyes grew accustomed to the darkness and I understood where I was.

I had arrived in the bunkers, the place where the rebellion was being planned. I had heard about the organizations of fighters who had been planning for months to escape and fight the Nazis, and I knew some of them from the Dror movement. The decision to escape and fight had come after the mass exportation in July 1942. There remained some tens of thousands of people in the ghetto and we realized that we would be next. Plus, we had heard about the Chelmno and Auschwitz extermination camps. It was clear to all of us that we were doomed. The trains would take all of us to the place from which nobody returned. I knew, as did the others, but we went on hoping for a miracle.

Here in the bunkers, out of sight of our enemies, the ghetto fighters had begun to organize. In a few months, when spring returned, the Warsaw Ghetto Uprising as it would later come to be known, would break out. Courageous and desperate heroes dared to rise up against the strongest army in the world. The uprising that surprised the Germans and ultimately ended the ghetto was planned in the bunkers.

Miriam gestured to me to keep going. There was improvised electrical wiring travelling the length of the walls and here and there were vents for air. I noticed more than one coal oven with a stove and chimney, mattresses, metal cabinets, or a pile of sacks whose contents I could only guess.

"Soon," she said, without my asking.

We passed by a number of youths, some of whom were armed with rifles or guns, nodding to us, and continuing on their way.

"Here," she said. "Sit here, someone will come for you."

I remained standing. Someone held out her hand and led me inside a small room. I stood, awaiting instructions. I noticed two young men sitting on bunks with pistols in their belts.

"Do you know where you are?" asked one of them. He looked very young to me, hardly more than a boy. I nodded. I had guessed. Like many others, I too had heard of the bunkers being built and the plans to escape.

"Welcome to the Eyal Organization's Bunker," said the second man who looked a little older. A big bandage was wrapped around his head.

"All I know is that Eyal is an underground organization within the ghetto."

"A military organization," he corrected me. "Tulla, or Rachel, we called you here because we need your help."

"My help? Look at me, I can barely stand on my feet. The walk here was hard for me."

"You're a doctor."

Only then did I notice another youth standing, leaning against the wall. He had an authoritative voice. Probably the commander.

"Do you really think you can…"

"Let us think!" he said and approached me. "Nice to meet you, I'm Jacob."

"… you think you can face the most powerful army in the world with a few guns and a starving army? What chances do you have?" I went on.

"Listen!" Jacob cut me off. "We called you here to help, not for advice."

"A hundred men? Two hundred? How many of you are there?"

"Our organization has expanded. Political party activists have joined us - the Bund is with us along with the Leftist Zionist activists and soon other groups will come. We are building our base."

"And you need me? There must be some mistake."

"Have you heard of the Ghetto Cat?"

"Cat?"

"The Cat," he gave me a long look. "He seems to know you and suggested we ask you."

"Strange, what is it you expect from me?"

"We are acquiring weapons, fighting materials, gathering food, drink, and among other things we are building up our infirmary here. We will need doctors, equipment, medicine. I am asking you to train medics, teach people to tend to the wounded. You understand?"

"You think that I…"

"Are you willing to help us?"

I nodded.

"Excellent," said Jacob. "I'm your contact person."

He gestured for us to follow him. There was a lot of activity going on then. There were people learning Morse code, others organizing food on shelves, cleaning weapons, teaching fighting techniques. In one corner there was a sign for the infirmary. He stopped there and pointed at two young men in white robes. "Here is the head of our medical corps."

The older of the two shook my hand. I was sure I had seen him before. He did not show any sign of knowing me and I did not ask. That very day I gave my first class to volunteer medics. I became a part of the Eyal Organization, the ghetto underground. I was not afraid. I had nothing left to lose.

Besides teaching, my main task at that stage was to obtain medicine and medical equipment. They knew, through Miriam, that I was asked to look after army officers and members of their families once in a while, which gave me the chance to acquire some of the needed supplies. They gave me a long list of medicines that they lacked.

"I understand that you have a good friend living in the city," said Jacob as he accompanied me out of the bunker. "Do you think she could help you?"

"No," I answered at once. How did he know?

"Why not?"

"It's too dangerous. Any link to her could bring the Gestapo."

"I heard that she is a brave woman."

"I ask that you not include her. Please be careful with her, her ex-husband is a collaborator," I ended the conversation.

Apart from that, I did whatever they asked. Every evening I taught young people to bandage and treat the wounded. I started stealing. Just a little at first, carefully. Then eventually, hungrily.

The first time I stole something the task felt impossible to me. I was treating one of the workers at the factory who had hurt his hand on the job. The Lithuanian who guarded me went out to smoke and left us alone. This was my chance - with a shaking hand I slipped bandages, sheets of plaster, painkillers, and two bottles of iodine into my pockets. It was my first theft, which would be the first in a long line of them. From that moment on, I lost all shame. I brought the booty I had plundered to Miriam who took it with a serious expression.

I became an expert at stealing medicine. Every chance I got, I would slip something carefully into my pocket. I didn't overdo it. I didn't want anyone to notice. Did Menahem, the Jewish factory manager on behalf of the Judenrat, notice anything? I thought he might suspect something but preferred to stay quiet.

With the stolen goods in my pockets I hurried to my home, gave them to Miriam, and ran to the bridge. Maybe they were there, singing to me of Maier in the Himalayas. It had been a week since I had last heard them. I complained to Noah.

"They waited for you yesterday. Where were you?"

"I'm sorry, I worked until late."

"Be careful Tulla," he whispered. "Don't let them notice anything missing."

"What are you talking about?"

"Nothing, I worry for you."

"Tell me," I wanted to confirm my suspicions, "Do you happen to know who the Ghetto 'Cat' is?"

"Cat? In the ghetto? I only know mice," he said, then disappeared.

We had no doubt that soon the rebellion would break out. We knew we didn't have a chance, but it was the last battle for our honor as human beings.[12]

---

12 Preparation for the uprising included constructing and smuggling weapons into the ghetto, building bunkers - underground hiding places which took months to build. In the final stages, the underground city in the central part of the Warsaw ghetto absorbed great numbers of Jews.

CHAPTER 34

Warsaw Ghetto - January 1943

For many in the ghetto, this was their third winter. Conditions only worsened from one day to the next. My factory, along with the others, was closed. Like many, I was dependent on the small portion of food given to us: a thin soup and dry bread. The school and daycares closed and cholera and typhus were widespread. The ghetto was faltering.

The comforting news of the German failure to conquer the city of Stalingrad gave us hope that vanished as soon as we heard rumors of further aktions.

They will kill us all, people whispered. The Germans were determined to liquidate the ghetto as part of their plan to wipe out all of European Jewry. The Final Solution.

Stubborn rumors kept coming that the work camps were not as promised, that they were extermination camps with poisonous showers and unthinkable ovens. There were those who preferred not to know, not to hear, not to believe any of it. But it was clear to me that those who had been taken in previous aktions would never return.

Just stay strong, I told myself.

Something good has to happen. It was a foolish belief, the kind held by those condemned to die.

It was the coldest winter I had ever experienced. The frigid cold was penetrating, like a blow to the face, when we went outside. Painful. Paralyzing. There was nothing with which we could heat our homes. My coat was in tatters. It had holes that I tried to patch with newspaper. I would search, along with others, among the ruins of houses in hopes of finding some forgotten blanket or coat - yes, the belongings of those who were no longer with us. The dead still had something to give to the living.

Miriam was fading away. She barely got out of bed. Noah, who would come in and out of the ghetto, passing through the walls as if they weren't even there, brought us the occasional egg or bit of sausage and I would make us a hot soup from potato and cabbage.

All of us looked like we were fading, each day moving closer to death.

At the end of February came Purim, the holiday in which Jews rejoice because the God of Israel overturned the evil decree by the wicked Haman and saved our people. Here in the ghetto, Purim had a special significance. Hitler was the evil Haman of our times and we prayed for his end.

We went to great effort to celebrate the holiday. We gathered and read the Purim story, the ghetto orchestra marched in the streets trying to bring cheer with holiday songs and – to my happy surprise – I even received a holiday gift of a small cookie, one of the customs of Purim. The meager gift delivery passed among the Jews of the ghetto with a little note that read, "From the Warsaw Jewish Quarter Supply Company." It was a special moment for me to be a part of this culture whose traditions would be kept at any cost. But I was not happy. Happiness was an emotion we could scarcely recall. We thought of what we had lost.

"On this day, the Jews must rejoice!" someone shouted.

"Rejoice about what?"

"Wait and see, welfare and salvation will come."

"Where is it? Where is God who sees all? Why doesn't he care that the chosen people are dying in the streets?"

"Wait and see. May all our enemies perish!"

"Wait? Children are dying of hunger and he does nothing?"

"Only yesterday I buried my son and he's telling me to rejoice?"

"You must believe," cried others. "Only the believers will be rewarded."

"God is dead," a chilling cry pierced the ghetto streets. "Our God is dead."

The ghetto children sang a song about the fall of Haman, the song of Shoshanat Yaakov, and the song by Yitzhak Katznelson[*13] who wrote a poem for Purim and added several verses that spoke of hope for eliminating the evil enemies of Israel.

---

13 Yitzhak Katznelson was a poet and playwright who lived in the Warsaw Ghetto. One of the poem's verses was written in the ghetto.

Life got harder from one day to the next. There was incredible tension in the ghetto. The SS soldiers sensed something and increased their forces. The sound of their marching gave me chills. Were they coming for me? Or Miriam? For all of us?

We decided that in this situation, Noah would go out to visit the children only rarely. Each meeting could bring disaster upon us all. The Germans encouraged spies. Just tell us what you see or know, and it will be worth your while. Indeed, there were still those among the Poles who, for a sausage or bottle of vodka, would be willing to hand over an entire family.

CHAPTER 35

Warsaw Ghetto - Winter 1943

We were eating frozen potatoes, rotting turnips, and stinking greens. The lucky among us would occasionally get hold of an egg or sometimes a piece of sausage. Doors, windows, and roofs from abandoned houses were used for firewood.

More than anything, we had lost faith. Where was our God who had performed miracles for our forefathers? But this time…had we been forgotten?

Who could save our people from Antiochus or Haman?

"Did you know that it's Passover soon?" Noah mentioned one day.

I noted the irony in this, "What, and we'll celebrate the holiday of freedom in the ghetto?"

"A holiday is a holiday. I'll get us wine and nuts and maybe some flour to bake matzah."

"Please promise me you'll be careful, Noah," I begged, and he laughed.

"Are you worrying about me? Noah? You know that no wall in the world will stop me."

"There's a lot of tension in the ghetto. Since the incident in January, they have brought in another SS unit. We can do without wine or matzah."

"You know what they say. Jews survived the Pharaoh; we'll survive this too."

"They are waiting in the ditches beside the walls."

"Don't worry. Nobody catches Noah."

"Wait, Noah!" But he had already disappeared.

Soon it was Passover. At my parents' home it had always been the most beautiful holiday of the year. We would invite anyone who was alone or without family. Sometimes there were as many as forty people crowded around our seder table.

Winter. Rain hit the walls and leaked inside. Every so often we heard the whistle of the trains. These trains were not bringing greetings from loved ones from far-away places. These trains were coming from places of murder. Slaughterhouses.

One day I was called to the home of one the officers, Muir Efrstadt. Odelle, his wife, had fallen and hurt herself and needed medical attention. This was my chance. I gave Muir's driver a list of creams and medicines twice as long as she needed.

When he brought me the bag, he looked me over suspiciously. I told him to stay in the front room while I treated Muir Efrstadt's wife. I bandaged her and instructed her to rest and take the medicine.

"You bought way too much. What will you do with it?" asked the driver when I came out.

"Stuffed cabbage," I told him.

Odelle laughed. He looked at me as if trying to understand my meaning.

"I will come again tomorrow to bandage you," I said.

The next day I went to visit again. She asked me to come near her and whispered in my ear that the driver had reported me to her husband, saying that I was stealing medicine from them.

"I'm not," I told her.

"As far as I'm concerned, take what you want. I assume there is a shortage where you are living."

I could not know if she was checking me or warning me. Another of my rules of survival was not to believe anybody. I would not reveal secrets, even to those who appeared to be dear friends. And certainly not to fall into this sort of trap.

"You are a generous woman," I told her. "But I can't take anything that isn't mine. I hope that your husband did not believe that stupid man."

"He only believes me." She thrust a bag into my hands. "Take it. Here. He won't know, and we have everything we need." I thanked her for her generosity and left without the medicine. When I was in the hallway, the driver stopped me and asked to see my bag. When he saw that it was empty, he let me leave.

Had someone been spying on me? Was the German woman testing me? Did she mean to betray me to the Gestapo? Or toy with me?

This incident stayed with me, and I worried that they might know what I was doing and follow me. I asked Miriam to take me to the bunker where I told Jacob what had happened. He told me that it would be best for me to wait a few days before resuming my activities. But I also brought him important information.

"They said that the Germans have decided to liquidate the ghetto. I overheard Muir's wife talking on the telephone."

"Not now, Tulla."

"Listen, hundreds of thousands to Treblinka, and you know what happens there."

"Stop, Tulla."

"They surrounded the place with green trees and leafy plants as if it's some sort of farm. But inside they're poisoning and murdering people."

"We know everything Tulla, that's why... You understand that we must do something." He pointed to the bunker.

"All of us are going to be sent to the death camps."

"Stop!" he turned red. "We know. But they'll be surprised to discover that..."

"Surprised about what?"

"I'm asking you to wait a week and then return to your role," he said. "We have a real shortage of medicine."

I promised him.

"This year we will celebrate the Passover seder together inside the bunker."

"Some celebration of freedom," I said bitterly.

"Indeed, it will be a celebration of our freedom, a holiday that the whole world will hear of."

I didn't ask what he was referring to. I didn't ask if he meant starting the uprising. The next day, when I was nearly asleep, I heard a faint rustling sound. What was that? Noah stood by the entrance to my room. He looked terrible, bleeding all over. I quickly brought him inside and began to clean his wounds.

"What happened?"

"I'm fine, just a little..."

"You promised to look after yourself," I hugged the boy who held his secrets close.

"Will you tell me what happened?"

"Don't ask. All you need to know is - it's not easy to kill me."

"Because you have nine lives?" I asked. He didn't answer.

"And what about whoever did this to you?"

"Are you worried about him?" He rolled his eyes and laughed. "You can be sure that he is in worse shape. Enough questions, Tulla."

I knew that he was looking for revenge for what had been done to his family. He would never tell me how; he followed the same rule as me - the less that is known, the better.

His body was covered in cuts and bruises. Although he did not hurry to depart, I didn't want him to even leave the room. I wanted him to fall asleep there so that I could watch over him. I brought him a pill for his pain and a sleeping pill and he fell asleep at once. A man already, at just short of ten years old. In the outside world, children his age were kicking a ball around or playing marbles.

I covered him with a blanket and sat beside him to make sure he made it through the night in peace. How could I know that that would be my last night in the ghetto? Who knew that when morning came, my world would be turned upside down once again?

I woke up to the sounds of shouting and banging on my door.

"Open up!" I hurried to the door of my room. Two armed soldiers stood waiting for me.

"You, quick, to the street."

"What happened?"

"Out," they shouted. "Take only what you need for a week and come out to the street." I still did not understand.

"Hurry," they shouted and banged their rifles on the door. "Schnell."

Noah! I looked over at him, curled up in the fetal position. Despite the noise he was still asleep. Better he stays asleep. I had to look after him!

"Where are you taking me?" I went out into the hallway and asked them.

"Let's go, Jewish whore!" they pushed me into the room and ordered me to take my things.

"Now!"

"Where are you taking me?"

"On a trip, on the train," said one of them.

"You'll see cows that go 'moo,'" they laughed and I felt chills. Every train whistle was a reminder of death at the end of the journey.

"Dress nice," said his friend. "You will meet lots of nice people." They laughed again.

The train. My fate was sealed. I guessed this was the end. I had known about this for so long and here it was. Something inside me went quiet, as if I had been waiting for this moment. I checked on Noah. He went on sleeping and had not heard a thing. Poor child. I kissed him. He will wake up and find out that his last friend is gone. I left him a note. "You are my family, remember that. I will return when I can. Take care of everyone. Love, Tulla."

I went out to the street, holding my little bundle. I wore several layers of shirts and underwear, just in case. In the bag that I tucked against my body, I put the papers that Solly had made for me and that Irena had sent to me via Noah. They were pressed against my belly along with the few items of jewelry that remained. Who could know, maybe I would still need them.

In the street there were a few hundred Jews already waiting. They stood close to one another, each with his or her own little bundle, ashamed to look at anyone else. Children stood with their parents. Men held tight to their wives. All around them stood soldiers in metal helmets holding onto dogs who bared their teeth. Satan's messengers.

A few weeks earlier, we had been given an instruction to report to the plaza. That was where families were loaded onto trains and never heard from again. But this time, unlike the aktions or previous deportations, the heads of the rebel organizations decided to rise up. Fighters from the Eyal and Etzi organizations[14] stood among the gathered Jews. With the agreed-upon signal, the fighters pulled out their weapons and opened fire on the guards. With extraordinary courage, they had a shootout with the German police. The transports were stopped. "Only" 5,000 Jews were deported.

It was clear to all of us that the Germans, who had taken an unexpected blow, would neither give in easily nor fail to deliver on the orders from higher up to clear out the ghetto. All of us who had been ordered out that morning was part

---

14 At the beginning of the uprising, two Jewish resistance forces were formed in the ghetto: The Jewish Fighters' Organization (Eyal) under the command of Mordechai Anielewicz, which was established as part of the anti-fascist bloc headed by the communist Pinchas Kartin, and included youths who belonged to a variety of factions and left-wing organizations from the Bundists to the Zionist workers' parties. The Jewish Fighters' Organization (Etzi), under Pavel Frenkel, which was established by the Revisionist movement.

of a greater revenge. They kept on sending us to the final station.

We proceeded to the transport area. Nobody dared to speak or ask anything. We were silent and obedient. The guards awaiting us there were Nazi collaborators, Lithuanian and Ukrainian guards known for their cruelty and hatred of Jews. To keep us from thinking of fleeing or rebelling, they would occasionally take someone out of the line who made a wrong move and beat him, pull his beard, or hit him in the head with whatever they were holding.

The train stood ready to take the Jews to the camps. There were more Polish and German guards than usual. There was great tension in the air. I knew that any movement could bring disaster.

Together, we marched toward our death... others would say like sheep to the slaughter. No. We marched, ashamed of our God who had promised and forgotten us, ashamed of what we had become... subhuman. Small children, women, elderly people, helpless people, all of us hungry and abused.

On January 18th, 1943, the second wave of transports that led to the uprising began. Groups of Jews who were headed for a transport and gathered in the square before the train opened fire on the guards and fled before boarding the train. The ghetto transports slowed down. Only 5,000 Jews were sent to the camps instead of the 8,000 as planned.

CHAPTER 36

Leaving Warsaw - 1943

Irena couldn't believe her eyes when, on the night she was waiting for Ilona, two children emerged from the darkness holding hands.

"What's this?" she asked Noah, who walked after them.

"This is my brother, Baruch," said Noah. "He's a good boy, very smart, right Baruch? You won't give Auntie Irena any trouble?"

The boy fixed his gaze on her. His big black eyes looked full of sadness. Before Irena could manage to say anything, Noah had vanished. That was one of Noah's talents - to appear and disappear in the blink of an eye.

Irena remained standing, facing the two children who were still holding hands.

What should she do? Ilona's pretty eyes looked sad. Where was the smiling little girl she remembered?

"Come, Ilona, I missed you," she said and spread her arms wide. Instead of one child, both ran to her. They were like Siamese twins: inseparable.

The boy looked at her with his wise eyes as if examining her, then approaching and clinging to her, too. As if to say, I belong. Take me, too.

They stood there in a long embrace until slowly she felt the sad boy, whose name was hard for her to pronounce, extend his arms toward her and she hugged them tighter.

"Brock?" she said. "I'm Irena."

He tried to smile but grimaced instead. Her heart went out to him. I will make you smile, she thought and suddenly felt happy. Here is what she wanted, a sense of purpose.

"We must hurry," she said to them finally. "It's dangerous to walk around at night with small children."

Kassia was waiting for her and when she saw the two children, she brought them both a bowl of hot soup and some honey cookies. She watched as they held the cookies, afraid to chew them.

"I thought we said one girl," she whispered.

"And then there were two. Here, this is Ilona and that's Brocky. Say hi to Auntie Kassia."

Ilona did not reply. She stood closer to Baruch.

"I'm a quiet child," said Baruch, just as Noah had taught him. "And I don't eat much."

Kassia hugged him. "Nobody in Warsaw eats much anymore..."

"So, you won't get rid of me?"

"No," said Kassia, barely hiding her tears. "Welcome, quiet child, Brocky," and so he came to be renamed.

Irena had a thousand questions to ask Ilona. She so wanted to know what was going on with Tulla... where she was living, what she was eating, who her friends were, what was this factory that she had mentioned in her letters, what was the bunker, and all the details of life in the ghetto. But the girl didn't speak. She refused to answer questions and would not let go of Baruch's hand. A week later, Noah returned to the house.

He wanted to check on the children. Ilona and Brocky went over to him and didn't want him to leave. They begged him to stay, not to leave them alone and he calmed them and gave them hope. Before leaving, he gave Irena a bundle of jewelry. She looked at the surprising treasure. "Where did this come from?"

"Tulla sent it," he said. "She said it's better you should have them anyway."

"Give them back to her," she replied. "She will need them more than me." He put them back in his pocket.

"Wait a moment, Noah. Give her this."

"What is this?" He looked at the tattered wallet.

"It's more important than any jewels in the world," she replied and handed him the forgotten papers for Tulla the widow.

"I will give them to her."

"Don't you dare lose those. She will need them."

She hugged him and asked him to look after Tulla. He gave her a salute. The children laughed. Laughed! He would report this to Tulla when he got back.

"Noah," Irena whispered as she accompanied him to the door. "Tell me the truth. Is there any chance of her getting out of there?"

He shook his head. "Who knows? The situation is getting worse. The Germans have increased the security presence. They've sealed gaps and openings in the wall. Only very small children can come in and out through them. The sewers too, which we used to be able to escape through, have turned into traps. The soldiers wait for people there and shoot them on the spot.

"Listen, I have to get out of Warsaw," she told him.

"Why?"

"It's not safe here anymore," she whispered. "I feel like I'm being followed. People look strangely at the children, ask about them, where they came from. Yesterday, a soldier stopped me and asked to see their birth certificates. Luckily Ilona started singing Little Maier and he was so delighted he let us go. But who knows how it will go the next time. We need to move somewhere else."

"Where?"

"I don't know yet. I'll tell you."

Irena considered where. Her parents' house was a possibility but she was afraid that they would send her away at once or worse, that her brother Oleg would give them up. The house in Tulla's village was too dangerous and Ciechanow was out of the question: Marta wouldn't hesitate to report them and take Ilona for herself.

Kassia came up with the solution. Three weeks later, Irena and the two children set off for Eugenia and Lulak Sovrichek's farm, where she had worked while Tulla and Ilona were still living on the kibbutz.

She would bring her sister's daughter, Kassia wrote to them.

They replied that that was impossible. A child would be another mouth to feed.

"A nice, quiet child."

"It's hard enough as it is."

But she took the train and went to convince them.

"You will have the best worker you will ever have here to help you around the farm... what's a small child...?"

Lulak was quiet. He would be happy to hear the sound of children's laughter.

"It would be an act of Christian charity. The girl needs a home and Irena will work for free," he said. They gave in.

They agreed on the terms and shook hands. But God forbid they should find out that the children were Jews.

On their last evening, before they left Warsaw, when everything was already ready and packed up, Irena and the children went to the street under the bridge one last time. Kassia joined them. They sang, hoping Tulla was there listening. How could they know that at that very hour she was bandaging Noah's wounds? She did not make it to the bridge that night and missed the sweetness of the children's singing.

"What is little Maier doing in the Himalayas?" they sang and, as always, the passersby crowded around them. The Germans who knew the song well joined in, clapped, and asked them to sing it again and again. They threw them coins, candies, and apples. Irena hoped that somewhere out there Tulla was listening and able to understand from the song where they were going. For their final performance, Irena had added some words in Polish for Tulla.

Hello from Ilona, hi from Brocky.
Hello Mamatulla, we will meet soon,
We're off to the farm
All of us to the farm
Come join us there Mamatulla
Auf Wiedersehen, geliebte Mutter,
wir sehen uns bald wieder[15]

***

The Germans in the crowd were surprised by the new additions to the song. Maybe they missed their mother...

The next day they left Warsaw, sure that Tulla had heard and understood their song. She must know that they were going to the farm, and as soon as everything was over, she would come and join them. But at the very same time that Irena was taking the two children to the train station, on the other side of the ghetto wall, the Nazi-collaborating guards were dragging Tulla and her friends to the street and from there to the train.

Luckily for Irena, the owners of the farm, who had been notified by Kassia of her return, were happy to have her back and told her so. "Along with the poor

---

15   Goodbye, beloved Mama, see you soon (in German)

orphan," they wrote. After all, Irena had been an excellent worker.

"We thought you said one girl," said Lulak with a concerned expression on his face when they got into the carriage that awaited them at the train station.

"This is Brocky," she said. "He's a sweet child, you won't even notice him."

Lulak sighed. When they arrived at the house, Eugenia looked the children over, gave them pea soup, and asked Irena to join her outside in the yard.

"Why are there two?"

"My sister didn't manage to make proper arrangements and I thought… it's just for a month."

"Who will pay me for their food? Children cost money."

"I'll pay," she said. "My work in lieu of payment."

"Times are hard. Electricity is expensive, water is expensive."

"Hard indeed," said Irena and handed Eugenia her engagement ring that Andre had given her, then added two bracelets. Eugenia inspected the ring, tested the bracelets with her teeth, considered the deal, then held out her hand to Irena who shook it. They had an agreement.

Had Eugenia understood?

She stuck to the story that both of these children belonged to her sister Tulla who had died after a deadly disease, and the good Eugenia agreed to give them a home. The two children knew what to answer if anyone came to interrogate them.

Another day, another week, and Ilona, who until then had refused to speak, her face frozen and grim, was transformed… going out of the house, playing with the puppy, running after butterflies, and laughing when the cat tried to catch one and fell over.

Brocky would run after her, as if he understood that his job was to watch out for her. Irena would get up before dawn to bake the bread, then hurry to gather eggs, feed the chickens in the yard, take out the two cows for their walk and prepare the fragrant coffee to be ready when Lulak and Eugenia woke up. Her hands were full all day but every evening she would sit with the two children, telling them stories, singing them songs of ducks and chickens and teaching them reading, writing, and arithmetic.

Brocky turned out to be an excellent student who easily took up reading. Ilona, who was a year younger than he was, loved to solve math problems using seeds as a counting tool.

Ilona refused to speak of Tulla or about life in the ghetto, as if she had decided to close the book on that chapter and forget. Whenever Irena mentioned Tulla, the girl would disappear into herself. Brocky, meanwhile, was happy to talk.

But Ilona's ongoing silence troubled Irena. She was only willing to talk to Brocky. Was she angry at Tulla? Did she feel betrayed? Was she deeply wounded?

"Do you miss her?" she regularly asked Ilona, who would cover her face and refuse to answer.

A few days after they moved to the village, Fania, the village gossip, came into the kitchen. She saw everything and spoke harshly about it all. She had to know what was going on with all of her neighbors and the sudden appearance of the two children had aroused her curiosity. She was dangerous.

"What a nice girl," she said and touched Ilona. "But too thin."

"But healthy as an ox," said Lulak. "She runs faster than I do."

"What's your name, little girl?"

"Ilona," said Brocky.

"What a pretty name, the same as my sister. And where are you from?"

"They came from Lublin," replied Eugenia, and hugged the two children.

"Poor little orphans," Irena whispered.

"Both of them?"

"My sister's children. She died and their father was killed in battle over the occupation of Warsaw," Irena explained.

"Show them Daddy's medallion," said Lulak, and Brocky pulled it out of his pocket, displaying it with pride.

"My Dad's," he said. He knew his role.

Fania took Johann's medallion and turned it over, examining it.

"He received that from his military commander," said Irena.

"Do you love Jesus?" Fania suddenly asked Ilona.

"I love Jesus," Brocky said. "He makes miracles; we pray to him every day."

"And I love his mother Mary," declared Ilona.

Irena sighed with relief.

That evening, Lulak hung a big cross in the room shared by Irena and the children.

"What for?" she asked him.

"It's important," he replied. "He will watch over you. I hope that the children really do pray every night."

"Of course," she replied. She then taught them both to pray to Jesus, the son of God. They did whatever they could to avoid arousing suspicion.

Soon spring would come to the little village where they lived. Buds had already begun to emerge on the trees and the chicks began to chirp in the storks' nests. But with spring came the bitter news of the ghetto deportation.

On May 16th, General Jürgen Stroop, who was brought to Warsaw to liquidate the ghetto, declared, "There remains no Jewish Quarter in Warsaw" Not a Jew remained in the Warsaw Ghetto. "We cleansed the city and the air is already cleaner."

They had destroyed the ghetto and burned all that remained of it.

What about Tulla? Irena tried to communicate with her at night. What happened, Tulla? Where are you? Where were you when they threw grenades into the bunkers? Where is Noah? She kept her pain to herself to keep from frightening the children. It was easier if they didn't know.

CHAPTER 37

The train to Treblinka, 1943

They organized us into groups of six and instructed us to march to a fenced-off square, where we were grouped together. A pathetic march of people whose star was fading.

Where to now?

We stayed there all night. In the morning they gave us a little bit of bread and thin, salty soup. One dry slice per person. Half a slice for a child.

A boy, maybe five years old, stood near me. He was staring at my piece of bread. He did not say a word, just looked with his sad eyes. Here, poor thing, do you know where you're going? Where they're taking us? That these might be your final hours? I offered him the bread which he snatched from my hand and ran to share it with his brother. They gnawed on it until it was soon gone, as if they were afraid that I would try to take it back.

The soldiers were accompanied by dogs that barked like mad, threatening to attack us. The guards walked around us with their clubs, looking for victims, enjoying their special status. We did not dare protest. One word and they would hit us mercilessly. Like the others, I lowered my head. I gave in, I was broken. Yes, they had broken my spirit.

I was tired.

What was my strength next to the soldier who looked at me with the expression of a hunter examining his prey, his hand on the trigger of his rifle, waiting for the chance to press and shoot and kill? Who was I against an enormous guard who was just waiting for me to make some suspicious move, against a dog who was baring its teeth at me and could easily tear my flesh?

People were restless, huddled, wondering as to their fate, trying to understand. Many of them were wounded, hurt. Poor, little children walked about without parents. Elderly people tried to lie on the ground. Many of them would never get up again.

It was a clear night and nobody slept. We quenched our thirst with dirty rainwater from a drainage barrel. A few more drops of life. Dawn broke and all of us were hungry and felt like beasts being led to the slaughter.

"Onward!" the guards and Nazi soldiers shouted, dragging us again.

We moved like automatons, out of habit, unthinking. The head switched off, the heart empty, dogs running all around us. I looked at a dog beside me and waved a hand in peace. He looked at me, was silent for a moment, then resumed barking and baring his teeth.

Evil dogs.

A command came to leave the platform. And again, there was shouting and dogs barking. We walked slowly along the tracks. A convoy of people whose light had been put out, who had been stripped of their honor. It was daybreak but the light was hesitant to arrive. Even the sun was hiding, examining us. Following their orders, we were walking from the big station – to where? Better not to ask.

"Onward!" the guards prodded us.

"Onward!" barked the dogs.

"Look here," said someone, "they are taking us to a remote station, so we won't be seen. So no one will know." The last stop.

Now I could see it. There at the end. A cargo train was waiting for us. A train designed for transporting cattle.

Schnell.

Schnell, they pushed us. Schnell, move it, get up, don't stop. Schnell, no talking. Onward, Jewish pig.

Here and there I heard the sounds of explosions, screams, shots, crying all around and dogs barking like crazy. Schnell, schnell.

Had anyone seen Miriam? I had lost her in the commotion.

Train car number 17.

On the side of the carriage was written: 6 cows. They crammed more than one hundred people inside. Schnell. Get on the train that we prepared especially, the last train of your life. The final train.

I was pushed along with everyone but felt a hand pulling me in.

"Miriam!" I shouted, and the German soldier turned his rifle on me. I went quiet.

There was no room to sit. The air was dense and hard to breathe. Children were crying, hungry, thirsty. Mothers tried to quiet them, to promise them that soon everything would be okay. Someone was passing out water, hardly a sip each.

The train began to move. Slowly. Heavily. Too great a load. Too many Jews.

"Where are they taking us?" someone shouted.

"Heaven!" someone else replied.

They said a new life was waiting for us. But I knew that all that awaited us were the ovens of Treblinka and the poison that would spill from the showers and kill us. I'd heard it worked fast. I was silent. No talking.

"Keep quiet, Jews!"

"Mama I'm scared," a girl was crying.

All of us were scared. Afraid of the next moment, the last stop. Hunger gnawed at my stomach. Someone pulled out a piece of bread and looked at it.

"Mama I'm hungry."

In the corner was one bucket for a toilet. One bucket for one hundred passengers. By then nobody was shy anymore. Men, women, children. There was a terrible stench in the train car.

Slowly we were losing our humanity. Just as they wanted. Just as those sick Nazis had planned it.

The distance from Warsaw to Treblinka was just eighty-five kilometers. Under normal circumstances it would have taken two hours. Two hours for normal people who had dressed well, bought tickets, put their suitcases in the upper compartment, and sat down, perhaps to doze off, chat with their neighbors, or eat in the dining car.

But the train to Treblinka was in no hurry. It was crawling, heavy, too heavy. It was carrying a great load. It was a cargo train carrying too many Jews. They needed to take as many as they could. The killing machine worked quickly. The ovens were hungry.

The train inched towards that new hell. An hour passed and the train stopped again. Why? Because a military train needed to pass. Headed east. Where the Russians were beating them back, a small shred of hope for us.

The train stood for many hours. We were hungry, thirsty, packed tightly against one another, looking to rest against whoever was in front of us. The train was stuck. The hours passed and it was night. Darkness descended. I could hear the dogs barking like crazy. Every so often a ray of light came through. We could not look one another in the eye. We were ashamed of what we had become.

I was trapped between a tall young man and an elderly man in a black coat with a shtreimel on his head. He sweat and prayed the entire way, for himself, for his family, for all of us, for the world. He rocked back and forth until he stopped suddenly. Mid-prayer, standing pressed between passengers, his soul returned to its maker.

As a final act of mercy, I closed his eyes, which had remained open as if refusing to forget. Some said he was redeemed, others said it was a shame, and some said soon things would be better. Others said soon we would arrive at our new home in the green farmland of Treblinka. I did not correct them. I did not tell them what Treblinka was, what that monstrous place really was. I couldn't.

Some of the young people began to think how they might escape the train. The windows were barred and some were covered with barbed wire but they pulled at the bars, hit them in despair, used sweaters and coats to improvise ropes to pull the barbed wire aside. The train began to move again. I was almost pleased. What a nightmare. I was pleased that the train, whose last stop would bring my death, was moving along. A light breeze filled the train car, but not for long. The train stopped again. People were crying, pleading. They were so thirsty and it was hard to breathe.

"Mama is dead!" a child shouted suddenly. "Help!"

I was unable to move or help. We went on standing there, as if stuck to one another.

"Mama!" cried the boy.

I prayed for the soul of the poor woman who had left this world. I prayed for my own soul and the soul of each of us on the train. It was quiet but for the sobbing of the boy.

"My Mama!" He did not know that soon they would be reunited as angels.

Stop, child, don't you see? We're all dying, we're all lost.

"When will we get there?" asked a woman who was reciting the prayer for the traveler over and over.

"We should jump," someone cried.

Young men were climbing on one another to reach the barred windows. They tried to open them, pulling with their remaining strength. They tired quickly but then resumed pulling. Here it was opening, a space large enough to push through into freedom.

"No! They will shoot you!"

"It's dangerous, don't do it."

"It's dangerous to stay, we have no choice."

"What will they do to us if they find out that you escaped?"

"We must!"

"And what about us?"

"I can't jump."

"I have to, I have to, this is the moment."

Silence.

One of the youths poked his head out of the window, pulled it back in and said, "Jews, whoever can, it's time."

People began screaming and crying, praying and jostling. No, please no, it's dangerous! Two youths climbed up and disappeared through the small window.

First, I heard the thump, then the gunshots. Then silence. They didn't shout. Did they make it?

Someone tried to push his head through the window and failed. Mothers were pushing their children through. Go, run to the forests. Save the children.

"Go," a bearded man pushed me. "I can't, but you're thin, you're lucky."

I couldn't breathe.

"Yes, you could, someone else said." I hesitated. "Try, what do you have to lose?"

Truly what did I have to lose?

I climbed onto the bearded man's shoulders and he gave me his soft hand. "God is with you," he whispered to me. I reached the small window and put my head through. The wind hit my face; I could smell freedom.

"Careful," people behind me shouted. "They'll shoot you like a dog."

"Jump!" someone shouted.

"You don't have a chance!"

"You must! You're dead anyway."

"Jump, it's your only chance!"

I put my head out the window.

"Wait a moment until the train turns," someone shouted. A split second of a half chance.

"Jump! You won't have another chance!"

"Don't do it!"

I put my head back inside. Hundreds of eyes were looking at me. They would shoot me. Just as well. What was waiting for me at the end of this trip anyway?

Ahead of me was the deadly Treblinka, its ovens and smell of death.

No!

I had to get out. Better to try, to die trying to get free than there in the killing machine.

"Hurry," said the young man beside me.

Jump! Said the voice in my head.

I pulled myself up and out. Barbed wire cut my hand. The wind hit my face. I closed my eyes, spread my arms, and jumped.

CHAPTER 38

… And I jumped.

I hit the ground and rolled down, down, down. Fast. Before any of the guards from the train could see me.

My whole body cried out. The pain in my right leg hit me like a red-hot iron but I kept on rolling, down, down, down. I had to find some cover for myself, to disappear before they started shooting.

A big, thorny bush stopped my fall, its cruel thorns piercing my body, but hiding me.

Silence. Nobody shot. Nobody shouted. No dogs barking. I dared to raise my head and look around. The thorns hurt; I had to get up from that bush. I crawled toward a big rock which stood like a defensive wall and huddled behind it.

I saw the train. Why was it so slow? Hurry up! Go, go, go. Train cars #30, 45, 47, 52, and I was still there. In pain. In agony. But there, breathing.

Car 60 passed and a sweet quiet prevailed. The train kept chugging slowly, sagging under the weight of that tragic human load. Heading east, crossing Poland on its way to that unthinkable hell.

Quiet. What glorious quiet.

No more dogs, no rifles, nobody shouting.

Wait, I whispered to myself. Don't move. Maybe they will come searching for the people who jumped. They might count and find that some are missing. They won't give up, they have to find us, all of us, the bastard Jews who dare seek freedom.

And if they find us? Let them. And if they shoot? Let them shoot. Anything to keep from going there, to the poisonous showers of Treblinka.

I waited. Patience. Don't move. Wait. Wait.

The world around me grew dark. I felt protected by the darkness. I listened to the twittering of birds arranging their nests for the night.

Another spring day... How long had it been since I had heard birds chirping?

I smiled at a procession of ants passing me. How are you doing? They stopped to look at me, then saw I had nothing to offer them and hurried on. Two worms tried to climb on me but slipped off. I heard the whistling of the wind, the leaves swaying in the trees above, and the trees themselves joining in the dance, and I was still free. The clouds hurried over me and I was still free. Free!

I waited a while longer to be sure and began to walk, despite the excruciating pain in my leg. I must have broken it when I hit the ground.

I found a branch from an elm tree that looked strong enough and tied it to my leg using one of the shirts I had worn before leaving the ghetto. Now my leg had support.

But where was I going? Where was I?

I knew the direction the train had come from, but it was hard to know how far we had travelled. Over twenty-four hours had passed since we had left the first station, much of which was spent waiting in remote stations. We had started and stopped. I guessed we might have travelled only thirty kilometers.

Was there a chance of getting back there with my broken leg? And what was waiting for me in Warsaw? The ghetto? Irena? I didn't even know where she was living.

The ghetto was not an option. I couldn't go back to living cramped between those walls. Warsaw was too dangerous. There were German soldiers on every corner. It would be better to stay where I was, find some refuge in one of the nearby villages.

Darkness fell. I made myself a bed of leaves, covered myself with branches and sank into a deep sleep.

The chiming of bells and the sweet smell of milk woke me. I opened my eyes. It was a bright morning. Where was I? Had I arrived in the Garden of Eden?

I looked around. The expansive valley stretched out before me, green and peaceful, as if there were no war in the world and everything was perfect. As if the trains weren't racing to the crematoria in Treblinka, Chelmno, Auschwitz.

I could hear sheep in the distance and the sounds of a flock approaching. Careful, I told myself. Who knows what might happen if the shepherds were to find me? A Jew has no place in a world run by Nazis.

I had to find refuge and wait, once more, for evening and darkness. What does one do when she must stay put without moving for fifteen hours? Just wait. The will to live triumphed over every discomfort. Hunger gnawed at me, took over my mind. When was the last time I had had a proper meal? Even just a piece of bread? A bit of cheese? I was dazed with hunger. I had to find something to eat. The only way would be to pilfer something. Not to ask but to take. Another rule of survival.

Steal? Me? The daughter of Rabbi Eisler? Previously I had stolen for an important goal, for others, but now I had no other choice. Nobody would give me food of their own free will. Forgive me Papa, I said. Living is also a mitzvah, a good deed.

Finally, darkness began to fall again. I retied the branch tight against my leg and somehow managed to limp, despite great pain, to the nearest village. I had to find some source of water to wash my face, clean my clothes, try to improve my appearance. It was already dark in the village. A row of gloomy houses gave off tiny lights from their windows. I heard occasional sounds - the rustling of leaves in the wind, voices, children whining. Somewhere I heard a woman singing, perhaps to her husband or putting her children to sleep. Voices arguing. Two cats fighting. The whinny of a horse. A life of peace, routine.

God, please. Let me live a life like this. A dull life. Routine. God, give me a little of this good boredom. Life the way people live. A family. Mom, dad, dinner on the table. A trip in the spring. A hot bath. Rest - just to rest. I was so tired. I had lost the fighting spirit.

For a moment I felt an urge to fall to the ground, to return to it, to ask the earth for mercy, to receive me, to let me rest.

That very same moment, out of nowhere, Ilona's sweet voice returned to me. She was singing to me, What are you doing Mama? What are you doing Mamatulla?

I miss you so, Ilona.

I turned the handle of the gate to the yard of one of the houses and dragged myself inside. At once, two huge dogs, baring their teeth, came at me, snarling and angry.

I hurried away as best I could, in fear, hopping on my good leg.

The two houses next door were surrounded by a high stone wall. From the third house, I heard the screams and cries of a baby and in the fourth, tapping and singing. I made it to the last house in the village.

It was a tiny little house, painted green with a red door and white window frames. There were no stone walls and no dogs coming for me. A strange house, like something out of a fairy tale. Beside it were pear and plum trees whose branches were bursting with fruit, as if they were handing me their treasures. They were inviting me: come take some, come. Come, take, you're welcome to what I have to offer.

I waited for a few minutes. God forbid someone come along and catch me - it would mean a quick trip to the Gestapo.

I got nearer. Around the trees, fruit was scattered on the ground. They had ripened and fallen off. I gathered a few of them, making sure to collect the ones in the worst shape. There was a vegetable garden, too, and I took a few carrots and a green onion. With this loot I hurried back to the forest at the edge of the yard. Another moment. Just another moment and I would be out of sight.

The wind whistled in my ears. I was so close to freedom.

"Stop... stop... yes, you there..." I turned around.

Before me was a short man holding a rifle.

I ran as fast as I could, into the forest, between the trees, hoping to be swallowed up by the foliage. I ran fast, fast, faster. There were shooting pains in my leg, which cried out to me to stop but I had to escape from whoever that was. I couldn't let him catch me.

"Stop, please," the farmer – or whoever it was – was behind me.

"Stop, I ask of you..."

I didn't stop. I couldn't give up on my bit of freedom. A few more steps and I would be in the forest. My forest. My one remaining friend. There, I believed, I could hide from him. Two broad tree trunks sprung up suddenly before me, their big branches moving in the wind, inviting me to them, offering me cover. I dove behind them and hid, trying to disappear. Maybe I had succeeded. Maybe he would give up and go away. Get out of here, leave me be. Was this the end? Without thinking, I had begun to pray, asking God, hoping he might hear, might reach out to me.

Out of the depths have I called Thee, O LORD.

Lord, hearken unto my voice;

Let Thine ears be attentive to the voice of my supplications.

If Thou, LORD, shouldest mark iniquities, Lord, who could stand?

I was afraid to breathe. Or move. I heard his steps moving farther away. Only when I was certain that he had left, that there was nobody nearby, did I take the fruit out of my pockets. I blessed my good luck and bit into a plum and afterwards a pear. Slowly, slowly. The fruit's juice ran over my fingers and face. It dripped on the layers I was wearing. This pear was the most delicious fruit I had eaten in my entire life. There never was, and never will be a better pear. The pear of my freedom. My survival.

I chewed carefully. I knew that I had to be careful not to eat ravenously. My body was too weak. I closed my eyes and chewed slowly. First the pear, then the plum.

The next morning, I found another pear and beside it a piece of bread.

I had been caught! They knew about me? Another moment and dogs might pounce? What now?

I didn't dare move. I didn't dare touch the fruit in case it was a trap. Or poisoned.

I lay silent and still. My leg hurt terribly. It was agony to get up.

Only when night fell and darkness descended once more on the forest did I dare move. I picked up the piece of bread and ate it gingerly, crumb by crumb.

In the morning I woke up in a panic. I could sense that someone was standing over me. I remained still and did not open my eyes. If he had come to shoot me, let him do it now, immediately.

My hands felt around, looking for a big stone. I had to protect myself. This might be my chance.

"I brought you more, here... here... you should get up..."

I somehow leaped up and tried to run away but the pain in my leg was too intense and I fell back down to the ground.

"Don't move! Your leg... it needs to be checked."

Who was he? What did he want? Why hadn't he shot me?

"Calm down and let me check you. You're shaking... I'm sorry that I scared you. Shh... It will be okay. Give me your hand and we will go to my house. We can have a look at your leg there."

His voice was soft. He seemed to be a peaceful person. He was a slight man of very short stature, wearing a little coat and little shoes. His eyes were good and bright. He held a plate in his hands and on it were two slices of bread and beside them a piece of cheese. Yes, cheese.

"Don't be shy," he said. "Eat, you must be hungry."

I went on looking at him. Who are you? An angel? Was this the Garden of Eden after all?

"Please, Mrs." He pushed the bread closer to me. I took the slice from his hand. It was soft and fresh-baked. I brought it to my nose, took in the good smell and returned it to him. He looked surprised.

"I'm sorry, I stole a plum and some pears from you... don't be angry, they were..."

"God forbid, I'm glad you took them. Otherwise they just rot."

"I will pay you back for everything."

"It will be fine. First, eat, then we will take care of your leg."

"But you aren't..."

"Shh.... Don't speak. I'm Etush." He held out his little hand.

"Tulla. And I ask for your forgiveness that..." He put a finger over my lips asking me not to go on.

And so, I met one of the most amazing people that had ever been born on the face of the earth. Etush Slovitsky, to whom my good fortune had brought me.

Slowly, I learned where I had arrived and about this angel sent to help me. The village, Poreba Srednia, was on the way between Warsaw and Treblinka, not far from the railroad tracks. Here, Etush my savior, was considered the village idiot, most likely due to his small stature. An idiot to push around. He had the eternal smile of a baby, but he was a lonely peasant. He had no friends or family. Etush was the constant target of abuse by the village children who ran after him, calling him insulting names, throwing stones at him, or ruining his garden, pulling up the onions and potatoes he had planted, and even once hanging his cat.

And he? Etush devotedly looked after his two cows who gave an abundance of milk, his chickens who laid the best-tasting eggs, and his little garden which yielded generous bounty. Weeding, picking, smiling, always smiling at children, at people from the village, as if they didn't call him an idiot or throw stones, offering the children apples and sharing his miraculous eggs.

He was the perfect idiot.

Such an idiot that out of mercy, he brought me to his home. So stupid that he helped me live. He gave me back the will to live. He dressed my wounds, bound my broken bone. He was a special person, optimistic even in this terrible world.

With his patience and love, he gave me the most important thing that I badly needed – hope.

He was special, not stupid. A great love for the entire world and its creatures burned within his heart. His house was full of injured chicks, sick dogs, limping cats, you name it. He took care of them, then returned them to the forest.

When we first arrived at his home, I let myself go right to sleep. When I awoke, I found myself in a comfortable bed, covered with a warm blanket, and Etush devotedly and patiently treating the breaks in my leg, cleaning my bleeding wounds, and even preparing a tea for me that dulled the pain and sent me back to nourishing sleep.

I remained in Etush's home for about a year.

He asked me to stay until I healed and got stronger. Until the situation improved and the war ended. Until the Germans that he despised returned to their country. He was boundlessly optimistic.

In the newspapers he would bring me, hopeful news began to arrive about what was happening on the eastern front and of General Winter, which had already subdued Napoleon's army and was now doing heavy damage to the Germans.

A few weeks after I arrived in his home, when I was still bedridden, he told me the bitter news of the ghetto evacuation after the uprising.

He handed me an old newspaper that he had found at the train station and sat beside me as I read it. Did he realize that I was Jewish? Why would he take the risk of giving me refuge? I didn't dare tell him. What if he were surprised?

The news was bad. Shocking pictures from the paper showed harsh scenes of the ghetto burning. They had wiped out all the rebel fighters, it was written, and sent everyone to the extermination camps.

What about Noah? What had happened to him? Where are you, child?

Had he, as was his way, managed to get out this time too…like a smart, swift street cat that always landed on his feet? Or had he too been among the fighters, throwing grenades and rocks and taking revenge on the murder of his people. Had he fought until the bitter end, until ultimately, even his ninth life was used up? He had always said not to worry about him, that he always survived, that he was immune to them. I had a bitter thought. What if I had been there? At least I could have treated the wounded, bandaged them, and helped them get through the inferno.

Etush looked at me and squeezed my hand, as if he understood. I didn't dare confirm. Not yet. I am Tulla. Tulla Sabdinsky, the widow of a Polish drunk who fell from his horse. I'm Polish Tulla. God forbid anyone find out he was hiding a Jew in his home. Better to stay quiet.

Only later did he reveal to me that he had recognized me as a Jew. Even though I showed him my papers and told him about my husband dying in a hunting accident, he knew who I was. He saw the marks on my body, the sores, and understood why I had been fleeing.

To the nosy villagers who wanted to know who his guest was, he explained that I was Tulla, his niece, the daughter of his brother who had died. What was she doing here, asked the town mayor, wearing the black boots and armband of the Nazis?

"She came looking for work."

"With her broken leg?"

"She is strong as a tree and agile as the wind."

"What is she able to do?"

"Cook and clean, everything," I replied. "I am hard working and I don't steal."

"What happened to you?" she pointed at my bandaged hand

"It's funny," Etush hurried to respond.

"What's funny?"

"When she saw that she had missed the station, she panicked and jumped from the train."

"Sure, an idiot like you," said the mayor and burst out laughing.

"I'm afraid you're right," said the village idiot. "We are that kind of family. Idiots."

"So, you're looking for work?" he asked me. I nodded.

"My wife needs someone to do her ironing," he said "but..." he looked at my leg again. "Don't worry " Etush smiled. "She does great work at my house."

"Happily," I replied. "I can start tomorrow."

And so, I became their ironer. Sometimes I was also asked to clean or polish their silver. Very soon I had plenty of work. As my physical condition improved, my limp less pronounced, I took on more and more work. I ironed, did laundry, milked cows, helped with the harvest, looked after babies, all for negligible pay, as they all saw fitting for a relative of the village fool. His brother's hardworking daughter who could be trusted because she was so stupid, and she did not even steal or drink.

Etush refused to take any payment from me. He kept my wages in his safe which was a large pit he had dug in the yard and whose location only he knew.

"Safer than all the banks in the world," he would say and add coin, after coin. He called it, "Tulla's future."

Did I have such a thing as a future?

After we had become friends and the walls of suspicion had fallen away, Etush told me that before the war, some two hundred Jews had lived in the little village. It was a respected community that dealt primarily in textiles and fabrics that the locals produced. They had a little synagogue and even a school where the children studied until they grew up and moved on to the yeshiva in Bialystok,[16] the nearest city. Menahem the butcher had been his closest friend. They would play chess every Thursday evening, and on Fridays, Etush would join their evening meal with Menahem's wife and children.

"They were like my family."

"What happened to them?"

"They were taken."

"Where?"

"Nobody knows. One day they loaded them onto trucks and they disappeared. They have not been seen since. Hunters said that they heard shots, others said they were moved someplace else. When we saw that they weren't coming back, the other villagers took over their houses and looted their belongings."

"That's what happened in my village," I told him. And suddenly I started to cry. My village. My home. It seemed like a million years since I had sat on the little balcony in the shade of the elm trees.

"Hitler released the Polish hatred of the Jews."

"I noticed," I said to him. "But I also encountered others - thanks to them I am still alive."

"Menahem was my only friend. His family was my family and I did not take care of them."

"How could you have done anything?"

"I could have hidden them in my house. I offered them my attic."

---

16   Bialystok is a city in Northeast Poland, not far from the death camp Treblinka. The Germans wiped out the city's Jewish community of some fifty thousand Jews. In July of 1944, the city was liberated by the Red Army.

"Don't blame yourself," I told him.

"You're not guilty either for what happened to your friends in the Warsaw Ghetto, but you still cry out at night."

I did not answer. I was not yet ready to talk about it. I felt guilty. I felt like a traitor. I had jumped and left the others to their death.

But if I had stayed?

CHAPTER 39

Autumn 1943

In time, I came to love the village. People no longer wondered what I was doing there but rather invited Etush and I to their celebrations.

"The children no longer throw stones at me, thanks to you," he said. "They don't know they're up against a tough Jewish woman."

"Best they never find out."

After a few months, when I had regained my strength, I felt ready to set off again. But where? Where would I find Irena and the children? Where could they have gone? I decided to write to Irena's family, to find out her whereabouts from them. I had no idea what had become of them but they were the only contacts I had who might know where she was.

One evening, I turned to Etush and asked him how he thought I might find her. A look of sorrow passed over his face. I didn't want him to be sad.

"I'm sorry but I must…"

"I know. No, don't apologize," It had been clear to him that one day I would leave and look for my daughter.

"Let's plan what is to be done. We must be careful and smart," he said.

We composed a letter to Irena's parents in Nuzewo with a job offer for Irena. I printed the paper with the offer at the mayor's office. The letter explained that a large company which imported agricultural equipment needed accountants and that had received her name from the Ciechanow school director, who had recommended her.

Hand-written by Etush, the letter noted it was a well-paying job at a serious company located not far from Bialystok. As the company's representative, Etush wanted to know if this was Ms. Irena's present address or had she moved.

He went to Bialystok and mailed the letter. Then we waited for their response. One week passed, then another.

After about a month of not hearing back, I suggested that we send another letter to Uncle Solly in Ciechanow. If Irena was in touch with anyone besides her parents, it would be him.

Then we waited for his response. Two weeks later, her uncle replied in a letter printed on his company's stationary. I suspected he understood what was at stake, as his letter was very cautious, yet full of clues. He noted that Irena was living on a farm not far from Warsaw and that everyone was fine but he did not know her address.

Everyone was fine. Everyone was fine. Hallelujah!

Another letter arrived a few days later, this time in his handwriting, addressed to the company manager, Dear Mr. Etush. Solly wrote that he was sorry that Irena's parents had not replied as her mother had died and her father was deep in his grief. He added that her brother Oleg was working as a guard at a German arms factory and that Irena had written that despite the distance from her family and friends, she was happy with her work and it seemed to him that she was unlikely to move to the big city and leave the farm where she and her children had found peace. Just to be sure, he sent Mr. Etush her address, suggesting that maybe he should write to her directly.

I looked at the letter in disbelief. Irena had returned to the same place she had been when we parted! Waiting for me to find her.

And the children? He had said, explicitly, 'she and her children'... That is, Ilona and Baruch. Both of them were there with her. Bless Uncle Solly! It was all there, with great caution, and intelligence, to keep from endangering anybody.

No word of Tulla, and no word to Tulla. Not to give anyone away or invite questions.

In the Spring of 1944, when I was feeling strong, I parted from Etush and went to find Irena and the children. He accompanied me to the train station, gave me a basket with fruits and eggs, made me promise that I would let him know what happened and that I had arrived safely, and left quickly so I wouldn't see him crying. He did not want to be a burden and let me go on my way, because that was who he was, my beloved village fool.

When we went to visit him after the war, his house stood empty. The pear tree had dried up. Neighbors said he was ill. We found him at the hospital in Bialystok. He lay on his deathbed, holding on until he had the chance to say goodbye to me. Evidently, for all of the months I had stayed in his home, he had been ill but had not wanted to bother or burden me, so he bore his illness in silence. I remained at his side for several days until we parted forever. He smiled at me when I put my hand under his head to ease his suffering, and then passed away.

May you rest in peace, dear prince. "Go up to the sky where they will know what kind of wonderful idiot you were," I whispered and closed his eyes.

CHAPTER 40

1944

Irena stood on the platform holding the two children.

Every cell in her body was alive with excitement. She tried to keep her calm, at least externally, but inside she was all stirred up. Who knew what the Tulla who was coming back would be like? Had the suffering changed her? Would their friendship stand this next test? Would she be disappointed in Irena? Or take Ilona and Brocky and go her own way?

Are we still soul sisters as we once were?

Ilona was quiet and stood close to Irena as if afraid she might disappear. Brocky ran about, excited.

"Well, when is she coming?" He pulled Irena's hand as if it was within her power to make the train arrive sooner.

"Just another thirteen minutes, and stop jumping."

"Is that a lot, thirteen minutes?"

"Not at all, it's very little," Ilona answered him.

"It's a long, long time," he said and resumed jumping.

"Careful you don't fall," Irena pleaded, worried he might get dirty or hurt and make Tulla sad.

She had been restless since receiving Tulla's letter. She told her landlords and employers that her sister Tulla was coming for a visit.

"But you told us that your sister had died," said the landlady.

Irena was prepared for this. "The truth is," she said, "we all thought she really was dead but then a month ago I received a letter from her. She was lucky."

"How did she know where to find you?" The suspicious landlady persisted.

"My aunt Marisha gave her the address. You know how it is, these days everything is a mess. It is hard to find family or to know what is really happening to people."

Lulak said at once that he would be glad to host her in his home. He was happy with the little family that Irena had brought into their life. Eugenia, on the other hand, was satisfied with the gold necklace with a sapphire pendant she had been given in exchange for their safety.

"Well, how long now?" Brocky shouted from the wooden bench where he was standing.

"Seven minutes," said Ilona.

How long since they had seen each other? Nearly two years. The last time was by the river which ran past the estate where the kibbutz had been. They had parted from the estate just like on any other Saturday with no idea that everything was about to change so drastically. The war would pull them apart and put them to the test many times over. Everything had seemed so simple and possible during their time at the estate. Irena had found herself work and a home, and Tulla had loved working at the kibbutz infirmary. Ilona had happily run around after butterflies in the fields.

"Lali, Lali, the train is coming!" shouted Brocky, who had climbed onto a railing. "Lali" was his pet name for Ilona.

"I'm tired," said Ilona. "I'm going back to the carriage."

"Wait, please Ilona," Irena pleaded and she burst into tears.

"I see it, here it is!" Brocky shouted and leaped from the railing to the platform.

Irena's breath caught in her throat. Just don't let the children do anything stupid. "Please, behave yourselves quietly. Stand here beside us," and Brocky took two jumps toward Ilona.

"You're sad, Lali."

She nodded. Two tears began to form in her eyes.

"Don't worry, I'm here," he put his hand on her head.

She whispered something to him and he hugged her. Irena was always thrilled by the special bond between the two children who understood one another even without words. They were able to comfort, support, and be there for one another.

All at once, the platform came to life. The horn sounded, again and again, the ticket agent whistled, and white smoke rose above the train car, which finally came to a stop.

Ilona held Irena's skirt, unwilling to let go. Brocky stood and watched the passengers get off the train and come toward them.

"Is that her?" asked Brocky and pointed at a woman getting slowly off the train, pulling a tattered suitcase, and limping toward them.

Tulla is that you?

The woman looked like some other version of the beautiful Tulla they all remembered. She was thinner, grimmer, her hair had gone grey and deep wrinkles lined her face. The events of the past two years had left their mark on her.

"Tulla?"

"Irena? Irena, my angel!"

At once they were in each other's arms, embracing, laughing, and crying. Brocky hovered around them.

"Ilona?" Tulla held out her hand to the girl but she clung tighter to Irena's skirt.

"I missed you," she tried to hug her, to kiss her, to breathe her in.

"Give her a little time," Irena whispered. "Let her see that she can let herself love you."

Tulla looked forsaken. She had longed for this moment, dreamed of their reunion.

"It's because she missed you too much," Brocky explained, and Ilona let him take her hand from Irena's skirt.

They got into Lulak's carriage and travelled silently to the farm.

"Remember?" Tulla asked Ilona as they were nearing the farm, holding up the squirrel that had remained in her hand when they had parted. She nodded.

"We had one squirrel and he was sad."

"Why?" asked Ilona.

"Because he was alone. But now we have a big family. Want to see?" She knew that Ilona was listening and went on. "Look, my best friend Etush sent you all of this."

Slowly she pulled out a package wrapped in newspaper. Inside were toys that Etush had carved for them. There was a princess, a king, dogs and cats, angels and ducks and frogs. He had given her the box the evening before she left.

"I want the frog and the king," said Brocky and hugged Ilona, trying to encourage her. Tulla waited.

"Ilona, decide! Which do you want?" Brocky said.

"I want the princess and the dog and… can I also have the cat?"

Ilona dropped Brocky's hand.

"Great choice," laughed Tulla. "I have a wonderful story about a princess and a cat. Who wants to hear it?"

Everyone wanted to hear it. Even Lulak, who laughed from the driver's seat.

CHAPTER 41

Spring 1945

Tulla and Irena and the children lived together on the farm for a year and a half. Irena managed the household and as Lulak grew older, Tulla helped him more and more with the chores. She milked the cows, took them out to graze, and harvested the grain. In the evenings, the women would teach the children math, reading, and history. When they went to school, they would be ready to be excellent students.

Every now and then, Tulla wrote to Father Adam and told him about her life. From his letters, she gathered that his health was deteriorating and that he needed a wheelchair. He had done as she had asked and sold the house, giving half of the sum to the good Gregory who was widowed and had married a young girl from a nearby village. When he stopped writing, she understood that he was no longer among the living. One day a little package arrived for her. Inside were two crosses and a letter asking Tulla to send them to Irena, "your soul sister."

Irena kept the crosses under her mattress until the day she died.

By January, the rumors had spread from village to village: Warsaw had been liberated. A convoy of refugees began to return from the east. The women carried on with their lives and kept their secret. Who knew what the farmers or their neighbors would say if they knew that they had hidden two Jewish children?

Another month passed and good news kept arriving. The radio announcer declared that the Germans were withdrawing. The Germans were withdrawing! Large parts of Poland had already been liberated, but Tulla and Irena went on with their lives. They were afraid of revealing their identities, in case, God forbid, some xenophobia should break out, as had been reported in the news.

In May of 1945, it was clear. Germany surrendered, and the war was over.

The fighting stopped entirely. The most powerful army in the world had laid down its arms.

Peace came to the world.

Still, they kept their secret. They even went on going to church every Sunday, just to avoid raising any suspicions.

A few months after the war ended and life had returned to normal, Irena decided to visit her father, who remained alone in Nuzewo, her hometown. Her mother had died. Her brother Oleg, suspected by the other villagers of informing and collaborating with the Nazis, had disappeared without a trace.

Tulla remained on the farm to look after the children and help take care of business. When they parted ways at the train station, Tulla asked Irena, "And will you return?"

"Of course, what are you worried about?"

"So, you will come back?"

"Did you forget what we agreed on? Forever. Where you go, I will go. Your home is my home." She hugged her.

"And your God?"

"My God? You know that I believe that there is one God for all of us, all the religions," said Irena and looked deep into Tulla's eyes.

"Promise me you will come back."

"I promise."

Irena found her father sick and weak. He had a severe lung ailment and was bedridden. The house had been neglected and the surrounding land that her parents had always carefully cultivated had been abandoned. The trees stood there, ashamed. Nobody gathered their fruit. The vegetable garden was dug up and the flowers had withered.

Irena looked after her father, making sure to get him out into the fresh air every day. She painted and cleaned the house until it looked as good as new and she hired workers to work the garden and the fruit trees. Not two months had passed before the little farm looked lovely once again.

Chickens sat on their eggs, the fruit trees blossomed with the promise of new offerings to come, and in the vegetable garden, carrot and onion leaves were sprouting. Even the storks returned to their nests at the top of a tall tree.

"When are you coming back?" Tulla asked in her letters.

"I need time."

"How much time? The children miss you, and so do I."

"Soon. My father fell down again. We were at the hospital all week." And another two weeks passed.

"Irena, are you going to come back?"

"My father died," she wrote. "I have to organize his affairs."

"The children fear that you've left us forever."

"I have to fix the roof."

"Ilona thinks that I sent you away. Come back."

"We are planting this week, give me more time."

When she finally returned, Tulla and the children waited for her on the platform, excited. But Tulla was afraid it would be just a visit and that Irena would return to her hometown eventually.

"I came to take you with me," she said and embraced the three of them.

"Where?"

"Home. We have a comfortable and pleasant home. Each one of us will have our own room. Finally, we can live as a family."

Tulla hesitated. She was tired of moving around.

"A house of our own, Tulla. We won't have to lie anymore."

Two months later, Tulla and the children joined Irena. Everything looked so nice. Good days had come again, seemingly for good.

The cow gave plenty of milk, the trees gave plenty of fruit, and on Fridays, their neighbors would come and buy eggs, vegetables, flowers, or the jams that Tulla made. Brocky would manage the sales. Tulla called him their little banker. Meanwhile, Irena prepared bouquets of flowers.

In the evenings, after dinner, they would hold hands and say a blessing for their good fortune and for the God of everyone, of all people, and of the love and abundance he had given them.

Before they parted, each to their own room for the night, they would express their gratitude that they had met one another. They finally had a family. And they believed that easier days were upon them.

They missed Noah, that special boy who had connected them all, who had disappeared. They asked whomever they could for information about him, read testimonies, met with acquaintances from the ghetto, and called up Jewish organizations. Nobody had heard from him or knew what had become of their brave young friend.

Sometimes Brocky would ask if they had heard anything.

"Not yet."

"Do you think…" he said, trailing off, with tears in his eyes.

"Brocky, do you remember what we said?"

"Yes," he replied. "That we don't lose hope."

Tulla knew that Noah was lost. After the uprising, the SS soldiers avenged the insult they had suffered by eliminating the rebels with exceptional cruelty. They destroyed the ghetto and burned the fighters' hiding places.

"We will keep asking and searching," she promised him. "Noah has nine lives, don't forget."

"Like a cat!" They all laughed.

Spring came, and the cow birthed a calf. The plum trees' branches sagged with the weight of their riches. Everything seemed hopeful. But as it is said, "Man plans, and God laughs." Something had sprung up and refused to go away, like a thorn that had gotten stuck and couldn't be pulled out: antisemitism in Poland.[17] That old hatred of Jews raised its head once again.

The Jews, Holocaust survivors, and refugees who had come back, hoped that they were returning to their homeland, but found themselves dogged by anti-Semitism. Up until the end of 1945, well after the war was officially over, hundreds of Jews were killed by Poles.

If, for a short time, it seemed that the glorious Jewish community would return and flourish as it had before the war, the new wave of antisemitism proved that hatred and racism were there to stay. One of the things that the Poles had learned throughout the war was that Jews could be killed with impunity. They did not actually have rights. In hundreds of testimonies from the postwar period, returning Jews who were searching for their families and homes reported being received by Poles with curses, threats, and hurtful cries such as, "Too bad Hitler did not get rid of you, too".

---

17 It is estimated that only one hundred thousand Jews survived the Holocaust within Poland. Some hundred and fifty thousand refugees later joined them when they returned from Soviet territory, as well as survivors from Germany and other nations. In total, after the war, only 250,000 Jews remained in Poland.

***

Meanwhile, Tulla and Irena were in their peaceful village home. But they listened to the radio and read the newspapers. The news was troubling.

"Look how bad the fate of the Jews..." Tulla said one night after the children had gone to bed.

"It's just temporary," said Irena. "The whole world is in a state of uncertainty."

But Tulla read and listened and was uneasy.

"People survived that inferno and now how are they received here? With sticks and stones! I read that the Jews are building the old homeland for my people. Why don't we join them?"

"Now? When we have a home of our own? Look at the pear and plum trees full of fruit, look at the chickens laying eggs, the flower garden... what else do you need?"

"I want security, I feel uneasy. They're chasing us again just because we're Jewish."

But Irena insisted. She was happy in her home, happy with her little family.

"Yesterday, they killed Leon Feldhendler, who was a leader of the uprising in the Sobibor camp." Tulla showed Irena the article in the newspaper. "Look, Polish anti-Semites shot him through a window of his house in Lublin, just because he was Jewish."

"We survived the war and the Holocaust, and we will survive this too. I'm not worried," replied Irena, holding strong to her position. "Anyway, in Israel everyone is Jewish. What will become of me?"

"Where you go, I will go. Come with me, let's get out of here."

"Why the hurry?"

"You saw yourself that even here in our village someone painted on our wall, 'Jews get out.'"

"That was just a few stupid village children."

"I'm not so sure as you. I heard about a Jewish family that returned to their old home where thugs were waiting for them and beat them to death just because they were sure the Jews were hiding gold."

"There are thieves everywhere."

"It's anti-Semitism, Irena. Come with me. They're establishing a home for my people. It is hopeful."

But Irena was hesitant. She was afraid of being the foreign woman in a country where everyone was Jewish.

"But Ilona is so happy here, you are happy here. Why make such a big change?"

Tulla sighed. She knew they would not leave without Irena, her sister.

CHAPTER 42

Summer 1946

On July 4, 1946, there was a raid on the Jews. The pogrom took place in Kielce and was carried out on the basis of a malicious rumor that the Jews had kidnapped a Christian child for the purpose of some religious ceremony and were keeping him in the basement of a house. Hordes broke into the building where the boy was rumored to be held. With sticks, stones, and iron bars they broke everything in their path and beat the Jews, then threw them to the street from great heights. Forty-two Jews were killed in the pogrom and many more were injured.

Kielce was a warning to the Jews of Poland. Anti-Semitism ran deep and would not be defeated forever. They needed to get out of there.

That was not the only pogrom following the war, but the number of fatalities was particularly shocking. Tens of thousands of Holocaust survivors began to leave for Palestine/Israel, where they believed they could build their future.

Following news of the pogrom, Tulla sank into depression. The smile disappeared from her lips. It seemed that all of the horrors of the war had returned to her. She felt she did not have the strength for another struggle. The Kielce pogrom was the last straw - she did not want to go on living in Poland.

"You must understand, this pogrom might have just been the beginning."

"The Polish government promised..."

"They invited Jews to return and made promises that they are not keeping. I can't stay here. This is no place for Jews. Let's get out, let's go somewhere else."

Irena listened and nodded. She was still worried about moving to a new land, a country that was not for her. A country for the Jews. She suggested, once again, that Tulla travel there herself to get a sense of it, and then they could decide."

But Tulla was firm. "I am not going anywhere without you."

Two rocks made the decision for them. Brocky returned hurt from school one day without his backpack and with his clothes torn.

"What happened, Brocky? Irena was shocked.

"They... the children..." and he burst into tears.

"What did the children do?"

"They... they beat me!"

"Why, what happened?"

"They wanted to see... if... if... I was... down there... like they do to the children of Jews..."

"Circumcised."

"They pulled down my underpants and then screamed like crazy and threw my notebooks everywhere and peed on them and... when I ran away, they threw rocks at me and said I was a dirty Jew."

"Why didn't you call the teacher?"

"Because... the teacher wouldn't do anything about it. He just watched and then walked away."

Irena was shocked. Was this her country? Were these her people?

"I am ashamed of my people," Irena told Tulla. "It seems like Poles will be anti-Semitic forever. Tell me about the dream of the Jews."

Tulla smiled. "Here is a map of the new settlements and some photos."

Irena's eyes lit up.

"Look at them, they are building up the old homeland."

"The homeland?"

"Remember what you always said? Where you go, I go. Your home is my home. Like Ruth and Naomi."

"Tulla – will your people accept me?"

Tulla hesitated for a moment. Would they accept her? Would she really be able to live in such a different land with a different language and religion, far from her roots?

She looked at Irena and said, "I'm sure."

"Sure? Me? Catholic Irena?"

"Yes, yes," she hugged her friend. "After everything you have done... you are a part of me, and my people. Besides, it's the land of all our forefathers and the land of the man from Nazareth. Jesus was born and lived there."

"And they will let me in?"

"Ilona and Brocky are your entrance visa. My sister, where you go, I will go. If they do not let you in, we will stay here. One fate for all of us. I won't go without you."

"Fate," said Irena sadly. "If only we knew what has become of Noah."

"He always said I shouldn't worry about him. He has nine lives."

Tulla silently wiped away a tear.

CHAPTER 43

1946

Irena was willing to let me immigrate to Palestine without her to check it out and then decide. But I told her we had pledged that we would stay together and that's how it should be. After realizing that her own homeland had disappointed her, that she did not feel at home in Poland anymore, I began to investigate the possibility of Israel in earnest.

In those days, getting permission to immigrate to Israel was very complicated. The authorities made it difficult to issue exit and entry permits. There were negotiations held to increase the number of immigrants. In many cases, the authorities demanded that people pay them for every Jew that left. The immigrants themselves were forced to leave most of their belongings and take only minimal personal baggage...to leave without drawing much attention, practically on the sly.

Irena agreed to everything.

A short while later, we traveled to nearby Warsaw to request permission to emigrate to Israel. At the entrance to the office building pieces of paper had been posted by survivors looking for lost family and friends - pages of pain with details, photographs, requests, pleas ... "Anyone who has any information regarding the person in question is asked..."

The few who returned from the camps, who had come out from hiding in the forests or moldy basements, that minority who had survived the inferno were frantically looking for their family members. Those who lived wanted only to find the loved ones from whom they had been ripped away. People desperately searched for children, parents, relatives, friends who had been lost.

They were looking for hope.

"Lieb Boznanski from Lodz was taken to Auschwitz... Hershel and Sarah Alboim and their children Moshe and Yitzhak from Lublin... Tzipora and Moshe and their son Simcha from Ciechanow... any information regarding those in question...

Josef, Golda, Shmuel, Abraham, Rivka, Shimon, Leah, Tova, Chaya... Three years old, ten years old, seventy years old... My father, my son, my mother, my sister..." Pages and pages - glimmers of hope and deep despair.

People searched for those who had been lost, to put the pieces of their lives back together. Some of the pages had turned yellow with time, some were torn and faded. Some had been ripped by the wind or crumpled and fallen to the ground. Lost.

"What do you think, maybe..." Irena said, pointing to the pages.

"You're right," I answered her, although I knew. He could not be here. In any case, maybe somewhere among the pages was some sign of Noah. Looking for Brocky, Ilona, us.

We went over the row of notes, went through the old ones, again and again, lest we miss an important one, but we found no sign of our Noah. Irena believed he would return but I was pessimistic. But then, Irena was a known romantic and optimist.

At the desk, the guard passed us forms that we had to fill out with our personal details: first name, family name, names of our parents, birthplace, etc. Without hesitation, I wrote that we were both Jewish. Irena paused.

"But that's a lie," she said.

"Your people are my people; your God is my God..."

"It's hard for me to sign that if it's an outright lie."

"You are hard on yourself," I hugged her. "I had to steal, lie, and..."

"That was war."

"I pretended I was Christian, baptized in Church."

"Thanks to which you survived. I think life itself is sacred, but to declare that I'm Jewish... I can't cross that line."

"Do you think that some God out there really cares?"

"Listen to yourself!"

"I'm saying, listen, Irena: it's the same God who forgot His creation, who let that madman carry out the Final Solution and murdered millions, who maybe isn't even in the skies anymore and so does not see... You think that God cares if you lie?"

She was convinced and wrote her name. Irena Zwiegniev. Jewish.

"May I see your papers?" asked a messenger who introduced himself as Yossi. Just Yossi, no last name. He looked a little strange to me, wearing short pants and sandals with no socks.

"The papers..." Irena muttered and looked at me.

"They were burned along with the ghetto," I replied. "All of our belongings were there."

"We can't give you permits without the forms."

"Maybe instead of papers, we can tell you about life in the ghetto? About months in cellars, hunger, and disease, or do you want to hear how I jumped out of a transport train - would that be enough?"

"I am sorry," said Yossi. "We have to check. We can only send Jews. That is also a demand from the Polish authorities."

"She and I are Jews like you. We have rights to the old homeland."

"We wish to build our home there," said Irena, who then blushed.

"Leave your details, in particular parents' names and place of residence and we will check. Come back in a month," said Yossi and signaled to the next in line to approach.

A month later we returned to the offices, this time with the children. Irena was the one who thought of bringing them with us.

"This isn't an outing for pleasure," I told them and saw that they were smiling at one another. I didn't ask them anything. For the trip into town, Irena sewed them holiday clothes as if she were about to present them to the king of Poland.

Ilona looked beautiful in her blue lace dress and her red hair tied back with a velvet ribbon. Brocky had grown tall and strong for a child of seven. When our turn came, they stood aside and waited.

"This is the situation," said Yossi. "We found papers for you, Rachel Eisler, but Irena... I'm sorry, as I understand it, you are not Jewish."

"She's more Jewish than you are. She is Jewish in her heart and her beliefs."

"But her papers..."

"Papers? Don't talk to me about papers. The children and I owe our lives to her. She took great risks to save us."

He raised his hand to indicate that shouting would not help.

"Look at me. Look at us. We are a family. We are a Holocaust family and these are our children. Jewish children who just want the chance to start over in the land of their forefathers."

"I'm sorry but I have instructions."

"Instructions? You know who else was just following instructions? One instruction and they put me on a train but she... she did not listen to any of them and saved these two children from the ghetto..."

Even though I thought I was immune, that nothing else could get to me, I burst into tears. He looked at me helplessly. "I'm sorry, but you must understand..."

"Let's go, children," Irena said suddenly. "Come, show them."

I had no idea what was coming.

In that big hall, filled with tables laden with papers and forms, among the filing cabinets and people, our two children stood and sang the song of little Maier climbing the big Himalayas and nobody knew how he got back down.

"Was macht Maier... die kleine Maier..."

What was he doing in the Himalayas? I was speechless. This song again!

Now I understood. It had never occurred to me that the children would come ready with their funny song, which was stupid but gave us hope in those hard times.

"Was macht Maier... die kleine Maier..." They went on singing in their sweet voices.

"Stop it! What are you trying to do here? Stop that, right now!" Yossi tried to hush them. "Here! In German - you cannot. You should be ashamed. Take them away!"

And suddenly, like a breath of fresh air, like a refreshing breeze, they stopped, smiled, raised their hands and this time sang in Polish, my beloved children:

Baruch, Ilona,
Tulla, Irena
How did they get from here to Palestine?
How did they travel, when did they sail,
Tulla and Irena want to live in Palestine...

The audience laughed and clapped, "Bravo, bravo! Again, again!"

"Enough. You do not have my permission..." Yossi tried to stop them, but they sang, their arms interlocked, their eyes shining, their heads held high, singing and singing of Tulla and Irena and of Baruch and Ilona who just wanted to get to Palestine.

"Come on, enough, stop, this is ridiculous!"

"You will never understand," Irena moved closer to him, her face ablaze. "You came with instructions and without a heart to really listen."

"How is that relevant?"

"This song was our little bit of light during the darkest days."

"This song? This stupid German song? I don't understand."

"To survive, and to save themselves, in order to live, these little Jewish children had to learn this song," Irena told him.

"Yes, Mr. Yossi, it's stupid and ridiculous and in the language of the oppressors, but they sang, and here we are," I said, now that I understood Irena's intentions.

"Each of us," I turned to the crowd that had gathered around us, "in order to survive, all of us had to do things, much worse than this, - lie, pretend, even steal, but here we are, living!"

"This song was a moment of light and hope, but you wouldn't understand. You have instructions," Irena signaled to the two children to resume singing.

Mama Tulla
Mama Irena
Please Mama take me to Palestine
Just let us go to Palestine

"How sweet," said someone.

"Let's hear it again."

"Again."

"I wish my child had had a moment of light."

Ilona and Baruch sang louder. They sang with their whole being, that song which gave us life and comfort in a world that had been dark and evil. A sign of hope.

And then the whole audience, everyone standing in the hall, moved towards the children, surrounded them in a circle, hugged one another and smiled, laughed, murmured to one another. At that moment, it felt as if the song was blanketing the room, covering the walls, climbing up and up, breaking through the ceiling and spreading through the streets of Warsaw, filling the fields and the forests of Poland and every place that it touched. People were smiling and laughing as it rose up to where the angels reside and they, the angels, laughed too and sang along with them, the song of little Maier filling the world with happiness.

And the world smiled.

Two guards came closer to the children who fell silent, fearful.

"Sing!" I shouted. "Sing, sing!"

They sang, close to one another, laughing, crying, singing. Together. The four of us.

Mama Tulla
Mama Irena
Please Mama take me to Palestine
Let us go to Palestine.

The guards looked at us puzzled.

"Who is that?" suddenly a cry was heard. "Who is that singing? Who's singing?"

The crowd was silent.

"Keep singing!" I shouted to the children who had gone quiet too.

What is Maier doing in the Himalayas?

"Was macht-" a voice answered from somewhere. That voice... that voice! A voice filled with yearning.

"What is he doing in the Himalayas?" The voice echoed.

The two children were quiet and looked at Irena. The great hall fell silent. Everyone waited, somehow realized something important was about to happen.

"Baruch!" A voice was suddenly heard. "Baruch!"

Who was that? Could it be...?

"It's you! My Baruch!" A young man came through the crowd. The young, magnificent man whom I thought I had lost forever.

"Baruch, my brother!" A moment later and Brocky was wrapped in the arms of the young man, who waved him in the air, crying and laughing at once, singing, laughing, looking for me, Ilona, and Irena. And soon the five of us were standing together, a confused, happy group, so happy our hearts could barely believe it. Was it an illusion? A dream? Would we wake up tomorrow and would he be gone? I pinched myself and counted my fingers. Yes, this was really happening, and all of us were linking arms and dancing in a big circle. Noah waved at Ilona, Baruch laughed and laughed. Here, little Maier had brought us big Noah.

Suddenly it was easy to get the necessary permits. Without hesitation, Noah swore that Irena was his legal mother, gave all the necessary information, places and dates and they believed him... how was that possible? We could not believe that this hero had reemerged out of nowhere.

"That's how it goes with war," he winked at me when he finished giving his testimony and signed on it. "You hear all kinds of stories - Rachel became Tulla, and now Irena is Rina."

Irena was so touched she could only respond with an embrace.

"And besides," he whispered to her, "You really think any of us would leave here without you? So, what... a little white lie, clean as snow... the last lie, Irena."

After we calmed down a little and everything was in order, after a smiling Yossi gave us the necessary permits, Noah told us that this incident was no coincidence. He had never given up hope of finding us, so he had kept looking, asking, insisting.

"You know me, Tulla, when I want something..."

"It's impossible to refuse you."

"There was no other option, Tulla. I told you that there is no wall that can stop me."

He told us that for nearly a year he had sat at the offices of the Jewish Agency waiting for some sign, for someone to come along who might know what had become of me or Irena or the children. He had even gone to Ciechanow and there he had met Bronek, who had become a sick, irritable man. His shop had been ordered closed by the Polish government. Noah reported that he had not encountered Marta. He'd heard that when she went to the market, people spat on her, called her a traitor, a German-lover, and since then she had been shut up inside her home. When Warsaw was liberated, Andre tried to escape and was shot by the Russians.

On the other hand, Noah had heard that they were planning to erect a monument to Johann, the Polish hero, which would stand in the Ciechanow cemetery. I would already be far away in a hot country when it was to be dedicated. I would be planting pear trees and flowers in the new, old homeland together with Irena and our little family.

CHAPTER 44

Moshav Pa'amonei Shir

Here we come to the end of the story. The happy ending. From that moment on, everything moved fast. We knew we had to hurry; we had no time to waste. The Communists had already taken over and we could not know how long they would let the Jews leave Poland. Life taught us not to trust anyone but ourselves.

We sold the farm in Poland and one month later, all of us emigrated to the Old-New Homeland: Israel, where we settled here on the moshav…

"Wait," I said to Mom. "If you are Ilona and Uncle Baruch is Brocky, where is Noah?"

"Noah was called up and he was a fighter pilot in the air force… Nogi, maybe you missed it?"

"Enough with the secrets already," said Tulla and gave Dad a happy smack. "Tell her."

"You know Noah but by a different name. Who do you think it is?" asked Dad. My father. They looked at me and the two of them laughed, together, in that special, way of theirs.

"Wait… are you telling me that Shimshon… that Noah is Shimshon? My dad?"

"Precisely," said Dad. "Shimshon Ben Ari. Irena and Tulla were our match-makers. They made me propose to her."

"Of course," laughed Mom. "Brave in the face of Nazis, shy in the face of love."

"We waited two years for him to say those simple words, 'I love you,' Ilona. It's a good thing Baruch pushed him," Tulla explained.

"Tell me."

"That's another story…"

"Your heart, my heart; your home is my home; your life is my life," Mom wiped away a tear.

"You see, Nogi?" Dad laughed. "I was lucky enough to meet those two beautiful women and find the greatest love of all."

My father, Shimshon Ben Ari, the ghetto cat, hugged Mom, Tulla, and me.

THE END

ReadMore Press

DISCOVERING THE NEXT BESTSELLER

Would you like a FREE WWII historical fiction audiobook?

This audiobook is valued at 14.99$ on Amazon and is exclusively free for Readmore Press' readers!

To get your free audiobook, and to sign up for our newsletter where we send you more exclusive bonus content every month,

Scan the QR code

Beneath
The Winds
of War

POLA WAWER

Readmore Press is a publisher that focuses on high-end, quality historical fiction. We love giving the world moving stories, emotional accounts, and tear-filled happy endings.

We hope to see you again in our next book!

Never stop reading, Readmore Press

THE END OF THE BEGINNING

It all began one evening when a guest arrived at our home in Haifa.

I was the one who opened the door to/for her. I was only eight years old.

In the stairwell near the door stood a bright-faced woman that I had never seen before, dressed in a wide skirt with a flowered kerchief on her head, holding a bag of cookies.

"Is your mother home?" She had a strange accent.

"Mom!" I shouted. "Come, someone's here looking for you."

"Ask her who she is."

"Who are you?" I asked. She shook her head.

"Tell me, child, where is your mother?"

"She doesn't want to say."

"Ask her what she wants."

My mother sighed, grumbled, then washed the excess dough off her hands. She removed her apron and approached the door, then froze where she stood. A heavy sigh erupted from her and her hands waved as if to banish the hallucination before her. I had never seen her like that.

"No," she said, "it can't be." Then she said, "I must be dreaming? It can't be... is that you? Irena? Irena!"

The woman came closer and touched Mom's shoulder, then said something in a language I did not understand.

Then the two of them began to cry. Then they burst out laughing, then crying and laughing and all the while talking and talking, telling one another everything for three days straight.

That was how I met Irena, one of the heroines of the book you have just finished.

"What did you talk about for three days and three nights?" I asked my mother after the guest had left and she, my mother, told me exactly what was said to Noga: "I'll tell you when you're older."

Later on, I learned that Irena had been her best friend from school in Ciechanow and since then it had never occurred to her that Irena, who came from a Polish Catholic family, might come to Israel one day and sit down at her table. That is where this all began.

This is the story that my mother told me of her friend Irena who, just like Ruth of the Moabites, followed her sister-in-law, the Jewish Rachel-Tulla, and made our cause her cause, our lives her life.

***

I wish to thank my best friend in the world, Aharon Meidan, who accompanied me throughout this book's process and believed that this story must be told.

To Arlyn Roffman, my dear friend, a unique woman who has been a part of my life and my books for many years now: your talents as an editor and your ability to decipher texts are a blessed contribution to my book. You are attentive to the story, the characters, and the plot, polishing every sentence word by word like gemstones. You are my best reader, and your belief in the book gave me a lot of courage

To Zoe Jordan, my translator who has come along for another literary journey, giving my story and my protagonists further expression in language, ushering them into new spaces so they may touch the hearts of readers everywhere. Thank you for your patient and faithful work.

And most of all, to Benny, Tali, Nave, and Rimon, the Carmi family who believed in the book and in their modest and incommensurably talented way, gave it not just a helping hand but wings to fly.

WONDER
WOMEN *of the*
BIBLE